A STEVE CANNON NOVEL

A SONG FOR DESMOND

B. R. LAUE

Other Steve Cannon Titles

Vegas Wash
Lost and Found
The Knights of Nauvoo

For Sandy,
my beautiful muse

Author's Foreword

In early 1965, there was estimated to be over 5,000 working musicians in Las Vegas, a town of 110,000 residents. From the Hacienda Hotel on the southern edge of the Strip to the Showboat Hotel, the last big casino on Fremont Street before Boulder Highway, music was as much a part of the Las Vegas soundtrack as the crash of slot machines and the rattle of dice on the crap tables. Some played three shows a night with three different groups at three different hotels. Others split their time between Las Vegas and the L.A. recording studios 320 miles away. Until Las Vegas went to canned music behind the splashy floor shows and big name entertainers in the early 80's, the journeymen musicians were a part of Sin City royalty. The eventual return of large ensembles behind mega-stars in the early 2000's completed the rise and fall and the resurrection of real people creating the musical groove of the 24 hour city.

January 4, 1965

A cold cutting wind swept across his face as Steve Cannon opened the door of the red 63' Jeep Waggoner and stepped out onto the hard dirt. He was forty-three years old as he stood at the southeast intersection of Flamingo Road and the Las Vegas Strip. His dark brown eyes stared across the vacant lot to the shuttered Three Coins Motel. The wind ruffled the brown hair revealing more gray than that which was normally visible just above his temples. His right leg ached from the cold and he walked with a slight limp as he moved away from the car.

The sound of large machinery drew his attention northward and across the strip to where the early stages of work on the Caesars Palace resort were underway. The brown dust clouds that rose from under the tires of the large vehicles were gathered up and swept away toward the nine stories of the Riviera Hotel in the distance. The private detective watched as a black Pontiac pulled into the parking lot of the deserted motel fifty yards away. Two men emerged, both bundled against the cold. One was older, tall and tanned. The other was short, stockier and had been a friend of Steve's for fifteen years. Bernie Gold waved in Steve's direction as he retrieved a large white roll of paper from the trunk of the car and handed it to his companion. Together they left the black tarmac of the parking lot and stepping into the desert, began to walk toward Steve.

A twenty-one year old Bernie Gold had arrived penniless in Chicago from Cologne, Germany in 1938. By the time he had saved enough money to open a fruit stand on the Southside, most of his family was already dead in Theresienstadt concentration camp. By the time the victory parades marched along the streets of New York, he owned two delicatessens. Steve watched as the pale blue eyes in the round cheery face came closer.

"Geez, Steve, could I have picked a colder morning than this?" Bernie laughed and pulled off a dark blue mitten to shake Steve's hand. He turned as his companion stepped forward.

"Milton, this is my good friend Steve Cannon. Steve, meet Milton Swanson, the best builder in Chicago." Steve could feel the strength in the calloused hand even though the shake was gentle. The man's smile was warm, as were his dark eyes.

"I don't lay claim to that, Mr. Cannon, but it is good to meet another old friend of Bernie's." Steve smiled back.

"No, it's my pleasure Mr. Swanson."

"Milton." Steve smiled and nodded. Bernie gently grasped the older man's arm.

"Milton's dad gave me my first job in Chicago as a hod carrier, and he and I worked side by side for two years and have known each other for nearly twenty-seven." Bernie turned sideways and they all ducked behind the Jeep as a large gust of wind and sand stung them. When it had cleared off, Steve opened the back of the Jeep and pulled down the tailgate. He found four rocks and placed them on each corner of the blueprints after Bernie had removed the long elastic band and unfurled the thick sheaf. Steve stepped back and looked over Bernie's shoulder as the two men bent over the plans.

"Whadd'ya think, Steve, beautiful aren't they?" Bernie and Milton looked up in unison and out toward the motel and then down at the plans once more.

"Well, Bernie, if you say so, but I am not sure what I am looking at." Both Bernie and Milton turned and Milton took a step to his right and motioned Steve to step under the slight protection of the raised back window. Steve ducked his six foot two inch frame under the glass as the older man pointed to the bottom of the large page where there was a side view of a building displayed in an insert.

"See this bell tower, Steve? Well if you look at the motel there, just where the roof begins the upward slope to the peak, that is where it will be situated, and the whole building will lay out through here." He moved his arm across the horizon to the far side of the property. Steve looked back down at the plans as Bernie swept the first page aside. The second page was an artist's rendering of the front of the hotel, complete with a large neon sign against the building, the word: 'Casablanca', lay across the front of the resort at an upward angle in an elegant cursive script. Steve smiled.

"Of course, Bernie, what other possible name would you come up with." He laughed and shook his head at his friend. Bernie smiled back and turned toward Milton.

"Steve doesn't get Humphrey Bogart. Wouldn't even attend my private screening of 'Casablanca', 'Key Largo', and the 'Maltese Falcon'." He grinned back at his friend. Steve shook his head again.

"It must just be me, I guess, but I never got what was supposed to be going on with that bird." They all laughed as another gust sprang up and threatened to blow the plans farther into the Jeep. Steve put both hands down on them and held them down until the wind died.

Steve stepped back as the two men turned page after page, squinted into the distance and pointed out landmarks on the barren lot before them. It had only been five months since Bernie had wrestled the lease option on the twelve acre plot away from Jay Sarno, the man behind Caesars Palace, the luxury resort which would go up in sight of Bernie's hotel. With the help of just a few wealthy investors, and in two short months, Bernie had pulled together all the money he would need to open the two hundred room hotel and casino. The 'payoff' was the fact that it was all clean money and for the first time in seventeen years, the mob would own no part of a major new Las Vegas casino. Bernie had breezed past the gaming commission interviews, largely on his reputation as a deli and small casino owner, and the governor had even testified on his behalf. All that was left was to negotiate the unions into agreement and rustle up enough labor and materials to keep the project moving forward. Steve knew his friend well and had no doubts that soon the Las Vegas Strip would have a new, well run resort.

His thoughts were interrupted by two short beeps of a car horn. He turned and looked back toward the Strip where a black and white police car had pulled up to the curb. Bernie and Milton had both turned and all three of them now gazed at the car.

"Who is that and what do you suppose they want?" Bernie looked over at Steve.

"I don't know, Bern, but I'll go check." Steve left the shelter of the big Jeep and bending slightly forward against the wind, walked the fifty yards to the sidewalk. From ten yards away, he saw the red faced countenance of Tam Polhaus, the Irish-German detective that Steve had worked with on several cases. Steve reached for the handle of the sedan just as Tam leaned over and opened the door for him. The wind pushed the door against Steve's body as he clamored into the police car.

Tam looked thinner than the last time Steve had seen him. That was two months ago, when Steve was still recovering from the last case they had worked on together, a case that had been disastrous for both of them and had ended inconclusively. Steve pulled the door shut and put both of his cold hands into his coat pockets and watched as the detective looked pensively past him toward the Jeep where Bernie and Milton had turned back to their plans.

"Why are you here, Tam?"

"Something in particular, but let me ask you first, is our meeting still on for tonight?"

"Yeah, we meet at the diner in North Las Vegas at eleven o'clock." Tam nodded and looked down the Strip where a long curtain of dust obscured all the hotels past the Desert Inn. Tam sighed.

"Desmond Rooney was found stabbed to death early this morning." The detective did not look at Steve after he spoke but continued to watch the brown dust stream past the windshield.

Steve let out a long slow breath and looked out across the cold dirt to where Bernie was standing.

"I thought you might want to tell him. I'm sorry, Steve." Tam turned and looked at the private eye.

"Thanks, Tam, I appreciate it, and I know Bernie will too." Steve sighed and pulled a notebook and pencil from his inside pocket.

"Any particulars you can share?"

"Not much, still early on, but it looked like robbery, or at least made to look that way. In any event, that is the way Samuels is laying it out." At the mention of Samuel's name, Steve furrowed his brow.

"Any chance of you taking over the investigation?" Tam sat quietly for a minute before answering.

"I doubt it. Samuels is in a hurry to get this year off to a fast start. He's pushing the junkie theory hard."

"Desmond has been clean for over a year." Steve spoke quietly and evenly as he knew from past experience that Tam could get prickly fast when Steve pushed too hard. Tam shrugged.

"Maybe, maybe not. We'll see what the coroner says. Meanwhile, we sit tight." Steve started to say something, thought better of it and looked down at his notebook. He jotted down a few more particulars and then put the notebook away. He opened the door and immediately a wave of cold air filled the squad car.

"Thanks for coming out Tam, I appreciate it. See you tonight." Tam nodded in reply and started up the car and moved slowly away from the curb and down the Strip, disappearing behind the curtain of blowing sand and dust. Steve stood alone in the wind for several seconds and then slowly walked toward Bernie.

A half hour later, Steve sat alone in the Jeep and wrote carefully in his notebook. When he was done, he counted the names. Five. That was most of Desmond's friends he could remember, he would check with Bernie tomorrow and get some more. He sat back in the seat and looked out at the bare lot and the peeling paint on the doors of the shuttered motel. Desmond Rooney had been a skinny fifty-two year old Irishman with flame red hair. He had also been one of the purest trumpet players that Steve or most anybody had ever heard.

The first name on the list was Joe Nichols. Steve turned off Karen Avenue and into the Palms apartment complex. It was just past noon, and it took several loud knocks before Joe opened the dark green door several inches and peered out at his visitor through heavy eyelids.

"What do you want?" The stocky well-built man kept the door barely open.

"We need to talk about Desmond." The expression behind the door didn't change.

"Desmond's dead. Go away."

"That is why we have to talk. If you think the cops are going find the guy who did it, then close this door and go back to bed." Steve waited as the bloodshot eyes gazed balefully back at him. After several seconds the door opened and Joe Nichols stood to one side as Steve entered the apartment. He strode over to a black leather couch and sat down. He pointed to an identical sofa across from him.

"Sit down, Joe." Joe flopped down and glared at Steve. Steve took out his notebook and pencil and then looked over at Joe.

"Let's make this as easy as we can on both of us. My guess is the cops are likely to show up soon and ask most of the same questions

I am going to ask you, so look at this as a rehearsal." He waited until Joe nodded.

"When was the last time you saw Desmond?"

"Two days ago at the Jungle club."

"Had he been using?"

"No." Joe glared at Steve. Steve sighed and sat back in the sofa.

"Look, Joe, the cop running this investigation is all set to put this down to two junkies falling out over a fix, so I need your help. We don't need to like each other and you don't have to like my questions, but for Desmond's sake you better answer them truthfully." Steve did not wait for a response, but flipped over a new page and continued.

"How did you hear about his death so soon? The call came into the police at one this morning."

"His girlfriend called at the end of our last set, about three, three thirty, told us he was gone."

"She call you?"

"No. She called Stuart."

"Who is Stuart?"

"Stuart Samoza, our bass player." Steve entered the name on his list.

"Why did she call him?" Joe shifted a little on the sofa and looked away.

"I don't know, ask him."

"We're talking about Rowena Vega, right?" Joe nodded, a mild look of surprise on his face.

"She said she found him." Steve stopped and looked back several pages at an earlier notation.

"You sure that was what she said?"

"Yeah, that was what she said."

"So what was your relationship with Desmond like?" Joe stared at the detective blankly. Steve moved his pencil in a forward circular motion and continued.

"Did you play often together, were you working on any projects that sort of thing?" Joe snorted.

"Are you kidding, man? You didn't work on anything with Redness. He might show up once in a while and sit in with you for one or two numbers, man, that was the limit. Louis and Miles and some of the other top cats used to fly him to wherever for a one night cameo, but that was many years ago. He was just too unreliable. Too much trouble." Joe looked over at a trumpet resting in a black case on a table under the window. Steve stood up and placed his notebook and the pencil in his pocket and looked down at the now silent man.

"Who do you think did this?"

"Nobody who ever heard that cat blow, that's for sure." Joe didn't take his eyes from the trumpet. Steve walked across the room and paused at the door.

"Thanks for your time, Joe." When there was no response from the other side of the room, Steve let himself out.

Steve drove two blocks to the Commercial Center complex. On a corner opposite a dress store he entered a phone booth and flipped open the directory. He drove back toward the Strip and fifteen minutes later pulled into a parking space next to the Patrician Arms apartments. He slid a pack of cigarettes from his pocket and slowly lit the Pall Mall. After several minutes he was forced to hunker down in his overcoat as the temperature in the Jeep began to drop. He thought about starting the engine and turning the heat up, but decided that it might cause too much unwanted attention. He had just pulled out his second cigarette and was preparing to light it when he saw a tall woman in a long winter white coat push through a wrought iron gate and approach a blue Chevrolet Corvair that was parked two cars down from Steve. Her long shiny black hair was pulled back in a loose pony tail that reached almost to her waist. As she sat down in the driver's seat she turned her face briefly in Steve's direction. Though he had only met her once, Steve was sure that the fine oriental features belonged to Rowena Vega. She danced in the chorus line in the Samoa Room of the Castaways Hotel. Her brother was in the house band who also performed at the hotel and she had another brother in the Echos, a Filipino band that covered a lot of Little Anthony and the Imperials material and usually played one of the lounges at the Thunderbird.

Deciding that Stuart Samoza was probably awake now, Steve waited until Rowena drove back towards the Strip before locking the Jeep and making his way through the same gate that Rowena had just come through. Steve knocked on the second story apartment door and looked over the railing down at the cloudy green water of the swimming pool, a dark carpet of leaves littering the bottom. Stuart Samoza parted the curtains and looked out at Steve with a blank expression. Steve pointed towards the door. Ten seconds later, Stuart opened the door and quickly looking up and down the deserted landing, waved Steve inside.

Steve stepped into the living room that was full of musical equipment. Amplifiers lined one long wall, some buzzing with their red power lights glowing. There were several electric basses and one acoustic one propped in the corner. There were no couches or side chairs, just a long wooden bench and a metal folding chair. Steve chose the chair and sat down. Stuart Samoza stepped over several instrument cables and sat on the end of the bench, rubbing his bare chest with the hand that was not holding a cigarette. He looked sleepily at Steve and then yawned.

"Mr. Samoza, I am.." Stuart interrupted.

"Yeah, I know who you are, Joe called me ten minutes ago. Said you were going to ask me about Desmond, right?" Steve pulled out his notebook and nodded.

"That's right. Joe says you got the call from Rowena this morning. Is that correct?" He looked at Stuart who was inhaling deeply on the cigarette and squinting at Steve with one eye shut against the smoke.

"Yeah, she did."

"Why did she call you, specifically?" Steve casually flipped back several pages and pretended to be reading something else in his notebook.

"I don't know, I just picked up the phone 'cause I was nearest, I guess. Why don't you ask her?" Steve smiled.

"I would, but she ran out of here so fast, I couldn't. I figure I will catch up with her later." Steve stared through the smoke at the bassist's suddenly widened eyes and chuckled.

"Well, Stuart, here is the deal. The one and only time I met Rowena Vega, she was introduced as Desmond's girlfriend, and I have also heard her referred to as that by other people. Now, if that is incorrect, this is the time to set the record straight." He flipped the notebook to a new page and looked up at Stuart expectantly. The brown skinned young man slumped over with his elbows on his knees.

"More like his caretaker, but yeah, she was his girlfriend. We have known each other since we were kids back in Olongapo City. She needs a friend sometimes and she comes to me, that's all." Steve wrote several lines in his notebook and stood to go.

"One more thing, Stuart. How many times would you say you have been in Desmond's apartment?" Stuart craned his neck back and looked up at the large detective.

"I don't know, five or six, maybe. I would visit Rowena once in a while."

"Was Desmond there all those times?" Steve put his hands in his coat pockets and shifted his weight off his bad leg.

"Yeah, every time, I remember." Steve nodded and looked casually around the room.

"Don't the neighbors complain about the noise?" Steve indicated the amplifiers along the wall. Stuart shrugged.

"Not really, the manager puts all the musicians down on this end and all the day sleeping dealers and cocktail waitresses on the other." Steve snorted and shook his head.

"Well, Mr. Samoza, that is all I have for now, but I may come back and pay you another visit. Thanks for your time."

Outside, Steve pulled his coat collar up to his chin and descended the concrete steps quickly to get out of the wind.

Steve drove toward Sunrise Mountain which dominated the eastern side of the valley and was today obscured behind a haze of dust and low clouds. He turned off Nellis Boulevard onto Ringe Lane and four blocks later descended a small incline onto a gravel driveway that led to his house. The structure had burned to the stone foundation and had been rebuilt in the twenties and was the headquarters of one of the many ranches that had dotted this side of the valley since shortly after the Mormons settled the area in the late 1800's. A one story ranch style, a newer garage added to the south side was the only outside improvement in forty years. Steve smiled as he pulled in behind a white Jaguar XK120 parked near the front door and turned off the engine. He could hear the wind howling even with the windows up. He slid across the slick vinyl of the bench seat and climbed out the passenger door.

He was reaching for the front door handle with his keys when the door opened and he looked up to see the bright smile and soft dark eyes of the most beautiful woman he had ever seen. Remy DeMarche stepped forward and throwing her arms around his neck, pulled him to her and kissed his lips. Steve dropped his keys and running his fingers through her dark blond hair, kissed her back. Remy unbuttoned his thick blue pea coat and slid her arms around his waist, hugging his body to hers.

"Hi ya' Gem, it is so good to see you." He nuzzled the top of her head with his chin. She answered with a pleased moaning sound before she took a half step back and looked up at his dark smiling eyes.

"Come in out of the cold and give me another kiss." Steve lifted her off her feet with one arm and closing the door behind him with the other, carried her across the floor and set her down gently on the sofa that sat across from the stone fireplace and divided the small living room. They kissed passionately as the windows rattled in their frames from the powerful gusts of wind. After several minutes, Steve sat up slightly and looked down at the beautiful high cheekbones and the soft pink lips.

"When did you get in, Gem?" She laughed softly and reaching up, gently removed a small smear of lipstick from his cheek.

"Late last night. I caught the last flight out of L.A. at midnight." He caressed her cheek and she playfully bit the end of his thumb.

"How long can you stay?" She smiled and kissed his fingertips.

"You might be surprised. Bernie called me a week ago and he wants me to put together a chorus line revue for his new hotel. So,.." She shrugged and laughed softly at the large smile that widened on Steve's face.

"That's great news, Gem. Leave it to Bernie to bring you back to me." She rose slightly from the couch and kissed him quickly.

"I was always coming back, Steve, this just all happened more quickly than I thought possible." Her light French accent caught her up slightly on the 'q' of the adverb. Steve gathered her up and carried her down the short hall, through the kitchen and into the bedroom. A few minutes later, on top of the four poster bed, they made love slowly and smoothly.

Two hours later, when they were again aware of their surroundings, Steve retrieved a pack of cigarettes from the top of the bureau and lit one for both of them. He settled back into the bed and propped up the pillows behind their heads. He took a deep drag on the Pall Mall and passed a green glass ashtray to Remy.

"It seems like a lot longer than three weeks since I last saw you, Gem."

"It seems that way for me too, Steve. I was looking so forward to you coming next week, but now, all that doesn't matter anymore."

"Are you going to stay in your old house on the Desert Inn golf course?"

"Yes, for now. They have been very kind and I can stay there until August, rent free." For a few seconds, there was silence as Steve thought back to that bad time last summer and the events that had led to the death of Remy's husband. Steve mentally shook off the still fresh images and looked down at Remy.

"Tell me about the revue." He slid an arm around her shoulders and pulled her up slightly onto his chest. She smiled and took a short inhalation on her cigarette.

"It is going to be called: 'Casino de Casablanca', and Donn Arden has agreed to co-produce it with me. I have convinced my sister to move here for a year and design the costumes. She is working on a movie right now, but she should be here by March at the latest. Bernie has given me carte blanche to start hiring girls and he will pay them even for rehearsals so, I should be able to take my pick from those I know here already as well as some new ones from France."

"That sounds like Bernie. It will be top drawer all the way or not at all for him." Steve chuckled. Remy reached behind her head and stroked the side of his face.

"Bernie wants so badly for you to be part of this too, Steve." He stopped her hand and kissed it gently.

"I know, Gem, and I told him that I would help in any way I could. He is going to need a lot of help getting the casino squared away and the security protocols established. I want someone else to be head of security and work the twelve hour days, but I promised him that I would be close by and he even got me to agree to keep an office there." Remy laughed.

"How many times have I told you that you need somewhere that has a telephone and someone to answer it for you. Just make sure she is not too pretty." Steve laughed and kissed the top of her head.

"No, the switchboard can take messages as well as anyone.

Tommy Carmino has been after me for ages to take an office in the Desert Inn, but that would be just another step in a direction I don't want to go, so this should work out fine."

"Tommy was kind enough to call after Nash died, and told me if I needed any help dealing with the brass at the Dunes to let him know." Steve snorted.

"Yeah, Tommy's saving grace is that under the mobster exterior, he does have his human moments." They both laughed and rolled over, Steve caressing the smooth skin of her body. The wind howled outside the warm room.

It was twenty minutes to eleven when Steve parked his car under the lone light pole in the deserted parking lot. Thirty yards away, and parked in front of the door, Steve noticed Tam's white Chevy Impala. He turned off the engine and lit a cigarette. Five minutes later he entered the small, all night diner which sat just off the Boulder Highway four blocks north of Fremont Street. Tam Polhaus was sitting at a round table set for six against the far wall between two large windows. He was the only customer. In one of the corners a small Christmas tree illuminated the dimly lit dining room with blinking colored lights. Steve removed his coat as he moved to the chair directly across from Tam. He threw his coat, woolen watch cap and gloves on the chair beside the one he sat down in. Tam regarded him impassively as he sipped coffee from a white cup.

"You're early for once, what's the occasion?" Steve watched as a waitress poured coffee in the cup he held out to her. After thanking her, he took a small sip and looked at Tam.

"We need to talk about Desmond Rooney." He looked Tam directly in the eyes and held his gaze. Tam looked down at the saucer in front of him as he replaced his coffee cup.

"OK, talk." Steve retrieved his notebook and pencil from his overcoat and flipped through the first three pages.

"I am pretty sure Desmond was clean when he died, and I need you to help me with my investigation. This is personal for me and it is even more personal for Bernie, and I will get to the bottom of this one way or the other. With your help, it will be sooner rather than later. I have to face Bernie tomorrow and I want to be able to tell him that we have your support." Steve sat back and sipped his coffee, gazing blankly at Tam. Tam sighed and looked out the window at the headlights of a car that had pulled in and parked next to Steve's Jeep.

"I am getting too old for this." Tam muttered under his breath as he looked back at Steve.

"OK, here are the rules. I will give you any information that I can about Samuels' investigation. If at any point he or any one above me expressly forbids it, then the deal is off. Do not show your face down at headquarters unless it concerns something unrelated, and even then, forget you know where my office is. Do not call me at the office. You have my home phone number, call me there after eight at night. If I have anything to impart, I will call you on the same basis. Do we understand each other?" Steve nodded and followed Tam's gaze to the front door where the driver of the recently arrived car had just entered and was heading toward their table. Steve made an exaggerated show of standing up and greeting the new arrival.

"Jack, how you been?" Steve reached down and grasped the man's hand that was held stiffly by his side and pumped it vigorously.

"Hi yourself, wise guy." Jack Cathay rasped in his guttural wheeze as he pulled his hand away. His blue eyes were even more watery than usual from the cold. Though he and Steve were the same height, Jack outweighed the younger man by forty pounds. Jack draped his coat over a chair and sat down across from Steve and Tam. He looked over at Tam.

"Hi ya copper." Tam nodded in reply and sipped his coffee. Steve folded his arms and leaned on the table.

"So, who is chairing this meeting?" He looked from one to

the other and back again. No one spoke for several seconds. Tam cleared his throat.

"If I recall, this meeting was your idea. I doubt I would ever think about socializing with the mob." He cast a small smile in Jack's direction. Jack ignored the remark. Steve shrugged.

"Fine by me. Let's get clear what our purpose is. We all believe that Angelo Sorelli is alive out there somewhere, and if that is truly the case, we also know that he will not let loose ends dangle forever. As long as we are alive we are a threat to him, so I propose we get organized and take the offensive." Jack squirmed in his seat.

'I'm in." He growled. Steve looked across at Tam. Tam shrugged and looked out the window, then back at Steve.

"Officially, I am not allowed to participate in a case that has been closed. Having said that, there are many unofficial inquiries I can make and maybe piggy-back them onto other open cases. So, yeah, I'm in too."

Steve sat back and watched while the waitress filled Jack's coffee cup and refilled the other two at the table. Steve had a feeling that it was going to take everything that the three of them had to run Angelo Sorelli to ground. He had cost all of them dearly and fled with nearly three million in cash. Tam had paid the highest price, but Jack was convinced that Sorelli had killed his little brother several years before. Steve rubbed his aching leg and recalled his near death experience in the desert. If justice was to be done, it would have to start with this meeting.

"So, what's the plan?" Jack's raspy voice escaped from his cup as he drained the tepid coffee in one gulp and held it up for the waitress to see. Steve pulled out a fresh notebook and looked across the table at his companions.

"Let's start with an assumption. Does everyone agree that it is highly unlikely that Sorelli escaped from that desert uninjured?" He waited until both men nodded assent. He turned to Jack.

"You have any ideas about where a guy like Sorelli could get medical treatment without the cops being called?" Jack nodded.

"Yeah, I have some things I can check out in that direction. Yeah, sure." Steve looked at Tam. "You have any ideas?" Tam nodded.

"I saw a copy of Sorelli's parole report and one of the addresses listed is in a small settlement near Sedona, Arizona. He stayed there right after he got out of prison. Might be worth checking out." Tam pulled out his notebook and showed Steve the entry. Steve copied it down in his notebook.

"I will take the responsibility of following that lead. Meanwhile there is someone else I may consult on this." He grinned in Tam's direction. Tam groaned and shook his head. Jack looked at both of them in turn.

"What?" Tam looked at Jack and snorted.

"Cannon, here, talks to an old Indian in the desert that thinks he can see things." Tam rolled his eyes back and shook his head in mock frustration. Steve was not smiling.

"Marcus saw them dump the body and he was dead on with the car situation, so I wouldn't scoff were I you." Tam shook his head again and sipping his coffee stared out the window. Jack's coffee cup clattered into the saucer.

"I don't care if I gotta crawl ten miles on my hands and knees and kiss the ring of the pope, if he knows where this creep is, then I do it." Jack was not smiling but looking hard at Tam who was ignoring him. Steve was about to say something when he saw the reflection of headlights flash through the window and a startled look cross Tam's face. He turned to see a red '63 Cadillac with a white top, pull in and park next to Tam's car. When Jack turned and looked, his ruddy complexion lost three shades.

"Oh, Christ, this is all I need."

The three of them waited for the new arrival to come through the door. The interloper was Tommy Carmino, number two man to the most notorious and powerful mobster in Las Vegas. Tommy presided over the Desert Inn Hotel, but there were strong rumors that his group held interests in the Dunes and the Stardust as well.

He was also Jack Cathay's boss. The figure that came through the small door of the café wore a long dark gray merino wool greatcoat. His neck was swathed in a shantung silk scarf a half shade lighter than the coat. Black leather gloves and a coal black suede fedora completed the outfit. Tommy made a big show of taking off each item of clothing and handing it to the waitress and waiting until she had hung each one up before presenting her with another. When he had finished disrobing down to his dark blue silk suit, he rubbed his hands together and smiled at the small group in the corner He walked into the middle of the room.

"If it gets any colder, we're all gonna have to move to Palm Springs." He laughed heartily at his joke and moved to the table between Jack and Steve. He looked down at both of them.

"You two leave a trail like a couple of snails." He shook his head and moved over to the far side of the table and sat with his back to the window, but where he was facing Jack. He smiled at Tam.

"Happy New Year, officer." He sat back as the waitress poured his coffee and he instructed her on how much cream and sugar she needed to stir into the black liquid. When she had moved away from the table he looked across at the three of them and shook his head.

"So. What is so important that we all have to meet out here in this dog's breath side of town, huh? I thought that is why I have all those beautiful offices out on the Strip. Am I missing something?" He looked at each face in turn. Steve cleared his throat and pretended to cough.

"Excuse me, Tommy, but I called this little pow-wow and I distinctly remember including you out." He smiled at the gangster.

"Well, Slick, since one of my guys is part of this little soiree and you didn't feel the need to inform me about it, I guess that means I don't need an engraved invitation." Steve shrugged.

"Suit yourself, Tommy, nothing I got to say can't be said in front of you." Tommy scoffed.

"Only one thing you three little Indians got in common and

that particular piece of low-life don't interest me, so why don't I just step outside and freeze my lungs until this pajama party is over. I need to talk to Cannon here." Tommy got up to leave. Steve stood up with him.

"You're right, Tommy, I should have come to you with Jack and told you our plans, let me make it up to you." Tommy laughed.

"Oh, you will, Slick, you will. But I'm just twisting your tail. Jack cleared it with me last week after you called him." Steve sat down and looked across at Tam. "Unless either of you have any more to add, I think we can adjourn for now." Tommy smiled and sat back down as well.

"Great. Now for agenda item number two." He looked over at Jack but was not smiling.

"Check in with Myron in the counting room before you turn in. He was whining about something this evening, says you know all about it. Get it handled, I don't want to hear about it again tomorrow." He looked hard at Jack and nodded his head toward the door. Jack stood up, grabbed his coat and quickly strode from the small restaurant. Tam stood up and looked down at Steve. "Remember what I said. There is no wiggle room on this deal." Steve nodded and watched the detective as he reached for his wallet. Tommy held up his hand.

"Hold on officer, I'll pick up the tab for this little party." He held out his hand as if to shake and chuckled as Tam ignored him and turned from the table. "See ya, Tam." Steve called out as the detective opened the door and turned up the collar of his coat. Tam made a small waving motion as he let the door swing shut behind him. Steve turned back to the table and Tommy Carmino. Tommy sighed, held up his hands and shrugged.

"Too bad about his wife. I have always wondered what possessed someone to become a cop? Do you think they just get stuck on it as a kid and eventually can't think up anything better to say when someone asks them what they are going to do with their life?" Tommy shrugged again and chuckled. Steve gazed evenly at Tommy.

"So, I don't think you came all the way out to here to give a vocational lecture, so what can I do for you?" Steve smiled, but any warmth the other man may have detected was overruled by the cold stare that accompanied it. Tommy picked up his cup and sat back in the wooden chair before sipping it.

"One of the things I have always appreciated about our little talks, Slick, is the way the point of it all comes out quickly and is laid on the table, so here it is: I need you to set up a meeting between me and Bernie Gold, and at said meeting, I need you to back me up on my proposal." Tommy put his cup down carefully on the saucer and shooting his left cuff over his gold wristwatch returned the cold smile.

"No problem with setting up the meeting, even though you have known Bernie longer than I have. What is your proposal?" Tommy smiled and leaned forward until his tanned face was less than a foot from Steve's.

"I want to run his new casino." Tommy sat back and again retrieved his cup and sipping slowly from it, smiled over the rim at Steve. Steve laughed and shook his head slowly.

"That is the worst idea I have ever heard. But since you drove all the way out here, let me pay you the respect of asking you some questions about how you came up with this fantasy." Steve smiled at Tommy, whose face held a surprisingly mild expression.

"Sure, Slick, ask away."

"I don't know quite how to put this Tommy, but don't you have a boss? A rather powerful boss. How does he feel about this?" Tommy shrugged.

"Things are changing in this town. The person you have so delicately referred to as my boss is now more interested in putting up shopping malls, hospitals and golf courses with his new part-ners than in the grief that comes with running casinos. You know. All that civic minded crap. So sooner or later, the gaming parts of his interest are going to be sold to someone else. A someone else, whoever it is, that I will not be happy to work for. Capice?" Steve shrugged and looked at the Christmas tree where one of the strings of lights had just burned out. He looked back over at Tommy.

"Ok, I got your side of the deal, what's in it for Bernie?" Tommy smiled widely and pulled a fat envelope out of his pocket. He placed it on the table in front of Steve, who made a point of not looking at it.

"There's fifty big ones in there for starters, and I think that this would be an appropriate time to mention that there is one for you too, if you help me swing this deal. But that isn't what you asked, is it? I can protect Bernie from those that may want to take advantage of him and skim some of his profits off the top for themselves." Tommy sat back with a self satisfied smile. Steve furrowed his brow and looked across the table at the gangster.

"So let me see if I got this right, Tommy. You, a guy that runs a casino that feeds several mouths from Cleveland to Miami with what you can skim off the top of the take from the Desert Inn, is offering to protect Bernie's operation from those who might want to steal from him." Steve slowly shook his head in an exaggerated fashion. "I don't know Tommy, I don't think I would lead with that when we meet with Bernie." Tommy leaned forward.

"That is the past, Cannon, the future is about going legit. My problem, that you are going to help me solve, is that I need to get rid of the reputation that keeps me from getting past the Gaming Commission. I sign on with Bernie, and 'Bingo!' Three years later I got carte blanche to do what I want. In the meantime, Bernie gets his casino run tighter than a witches' knot." Steve chuckled.

"So Bernie would be doing you the favor, not the other way round?" Steve could tell from the expression coming from the other side of the table that he had reached the end of Tommy's famously short patience.

"Are you going to set up this meeting, Slick or not? I got better things to do back in the real world than talking to a dimwit like you. Just set up the meeting and tell me where and when." Tommy stood up, stuffed the envelope back into his breast pocket and threw a hundred dollar bill on the table. Steve could see the startled expression on the face of the waitress from across the room.

"Gee, Tommy, I think coffee is only fifteen cents." Tommy put his hands flat on the table and lowered his face to Steve's level.

"Set up the meeting." He stood up and strode to the front of the dining room where the waitress was already holding out his coat, hat and gloves. Steve waited until Tommy had readorned himself.

"One thing, Tommy."

"Yeah, what's that?"

"Keep your envelope. I won't be taking it whichever way this thing goes." Tommy said nothing but swirled the end of the scarf around his neck and walked out the door.

January 5

STEVE CAME TO a stop right in front of Bernie's deli. He looked up at the large sign. Foxy's. He had always associated his best friend with the comfortable New York style delicatessen, and found it hard to imagine him spending most of his time in a hotel on the strip. He waited a few minutes until he saw the lights go on in the bar area. He looked at his watch. 6:15. Bernie would have just come in the back way fifteen minutes before and was now enjoying his first cup of coffee in the backroom. Steve stepped from the Jeep into the cold crisp air. Though the wind from yesterday had died down to a slight breeze, the temperature was several degrees lower. It had gone well below freezing during the night and was barely above that now.

When Steve swung open the glass door, it was already warm and inviting inside. The only person in the dining portion of the restaurant, smiled and waved.

"Hello, Walter, how you been?" Steve smiled and waved back at the tall thin waiter and pulled the blue woolen watch cap from his head, and stuffed it into the front pocket of his brown leather bomber jacket.

"Bernie here yet?"

"Yeah, he's in the back, told me to keep an eye out for you. Tough about Desmond, huh?" Steve nodded and stopped at the counter.

"Bernie took it pretty hard when I told him yesterday. How is he this morning?" Walter shook his head.

"Pretty quiet. And you know Bernie, that ain't usual." Steve nodded and pointed towards the large double wooden door that lead to a big room that was easily as large as the rest of the deli. Walter nodded toward the door and Steve knocked softly and then went inside.

Bernie stood with his back to Steve. He was looking at the far wall that held over a hundred pictures of various entertainers that had played the strip since the war. Steve had studied all of them several times before. Most were inscribed to Bernie, and as Steve watched him move slowly from one grouping to another, he realized how many dear friends of Bernie's were arrayed on that long wall. He decided to wait until Bernie was done and was surprised when Bernie spoke to him without turning around.

"You know they say that on the day that Sidney Bechet died a few years ago, his big regret was that he never found that one note, that one tone that made all the millions of others that came before it fit together like a puzzle. Never found it." Bernie turned around and looked at his friend. His eyes were bloodshot and his face looked weary.

"I think Desmond found it, and I think he shared it with the rest of us many times over." Bernie shook his head and slowly walked toward one of the round green felt covered tables that held two coffee cups and two saucers. Before he got there, he lifted a silver carafe from the end of the long bar and set it on the table. Steve walked over and sat down across from Bernie. He waited until Bernie had poured them both a cup, took a long sip from his and then replaced the cup back into the saucer.

"We can do this another time, Bern." He watched as Bernie's eyes looked directly into his.

"Naw, we have to get to work for Desmond's sake. Just give me a minute, I'll be right back." Bernie got up and walked several feet down two steps into an open office area where he picked up a sheet of paper from the large oaken desk. When he returned, he placed it on the green felt in front of Steve.

"I made a list last night of the people I think you should talk to. There may be more, and if there are, I think some of the people on this list will lead you to them." Steve looked down at the list. There were only two names that were on the list he had hastily put together yesterday. Bernie's list had seven names along with telephone numbers and addresses. Bernie waited until Steve had finished perusing the list and had folded it neatly and put into the pocket of his jacket.

"What does Tam have to say?" Steve took another sip of his coffee and looked up at Bernie after he put it down.

"Samuels is running the investigation. Tam is going to feed me as much information as he can. Tam says that Samuels is convinced it was a disagreement between junkies. The coroner's report will be out in a few days and it will tell the tale on that score. But Tam made it pretty clear we should not expect a lot from the police on this. With your help, Bernie, I think this is one that we are going to have to solve ourselves." Bernie shrugged.

"Yeah I figured it was that way. You got any ideas?"

"Well, I have interviewed two of the people we met at that party you took me too several months ago. I will interview Rowena Vega today if I can track her down, then move on to the others on the list. I don't have a feel for anything right now, but I am having a hard time seeing what possible motivation there would be to kill a recluse trumpet player. Just don't see it. But I am sure I will know more in a few days. In the meantime, what can I do for you?" Bernie looked up and smiled.

"You can tell me our girl is back in town and doing OK." Steve shook his head.

"You kept that under your hat pretty well. I was plenty surprised to see her."

"Yeah, we have been talking on the phone for the last week and it just came together beautifully. She wanted it to be a surprise for you." Steve laughed.

"That it was, my friend, that it was. When does Milton think we can throw the big opening shebang?"

"Twelve months, if all goes right."

"I think I will get my tux out and see if it still fits." Bernie laughed and then stopped and looked at Steve.

"I got Desmond's brother coming in tonight from Pittsburgh. Gonna stay at my place until he can take Desmond back east for burial. When do you think they will release him to his family?" Steve sighed.

"Could be two days or longer, Bern. My advice is to call one of your connections in the sheriff's office and see what they can tell you. If I talk to Tam I will ask him."

"Yeah, that is a good idea, I'll do that. I called Jack Entratter over at the Sands and he offered the showroom for a memorial. I am getting calls from a lot of people that want to be there and a lot of them want to perform too. Everybody from Frank and Louis Armstrong to Miles and Chet Baker. So I guess I am in charge of this, like it or not."

"You'll do great, let me know if I can do anything." Bernie nodded and snapped his fingers.

"I wonder if Tommy Carmino would kick in some free rooms at the D.I. for some of the musicians? Wadda ya think?" Steve laughed.

"I think your timing couldn't be better in that direction." Bernie started to speak, but stopped and looked at Steve.

"What do you mean?"

"Tommy dropped into a meeting I was having last night and after he shooed everyone out, he threw fifty grand on the table for you and told me he wants to run your new casino. Wanted me to set up a meeting where the three of us can talk it over." Steve drank the last of the coffee in his cup and waited for Bernie's reaction. Bernie refilled the cup from the silver carafe, his face expressionless.

"Call him and set it up." Bernie shrugged. "The rule in this town is that you always talk. I have known Tommy since he was eighteen years old and had just become a made man. He can be a little misguided sometimes, but he wants to go legit and I feel for him on that."

"You wouldn't seriously consider bringing him onboard to run the casino, would you?" Bernie laughed at Steve's astonished expression.

"No, the Gaming Commission would never let me open under any kind of deal like that. But I owe him the respect to listen to his proposal and I may have a suggestion or two for him." Steve shook his head and smiled.

"You never cease to surprise me. I will get hold of him today if possible, set up the date and get you some comped rooms. When do you want to meet?" Bernie crossed over to his desk, pulled a small calendar out of the top drawer, and after studying it for a minute came back and sat down.

"Let's have a couple of drinks here around five on Thursday night. Tommy might be a little more relaxed then." Steve nodded.

"Fine. I will set it up with Tommy. Let me ask you a question before I get out of your hair. How close were Rowena and Desmond?" Bernie shrugged.

"I know that Desmond thought he couldn't live without her, and I personally know that she did a lot to protect him and keep him practicing so that he could guest spot now and then."

"So you don't think there is anything between Rowena and this Stuart character?"

"I'm not saying there is or there isn't. I've never seen it." Steve nodded and got up to go.

"Thanks, Bernie, I will be around quite a bit asking your opinion like I did just now, so if anything occurs to you, anything at all, jot it down real quick and tell me about it when you see me, OK?"

Bernie nodded and followed Steve to the door. Just as Steve began to swing it open, Bernie tugged on his sleeve.

"Don't say no to Head of Security, Steve, not just yet at least. Think it over. It would mean a lot to me if you took the job." Steve looked down at the round expectant face and the pale blue eyes.

"I promise I will think it over and we can talk about it again as the opening gets closer." He squeezed the older man's arm, smiled and turned to open the door. Bernie held it so that Steve could not open it. Bernie's face had a sheepish look that Steve had seen many times.

"What have you done now?" The grin that Bernie was trying to suppress turned into a large smile.

"Don't kill me, but when Jack Entratter called, I couldn't resist asking him to comp you and Remy at Frank's show tonight." Steve shook his head.

"And why did you need to do that?" Bernie's expression grew serious.

"You two deserve it. Look at it as a coming out party. As far as I know, you have never been able to enjoy a night on the town as a couple, so I thought..." Steve laughed.

"Yes, you thought. Someday all that thinking is going to get you in a whole lot of trouble, my friend, but this is a very generous thing you have done. Let me call Remy, so she can get used to the idea and decide what to wear."

"Oh, and Frank knows you're coming, and it is the dinner show, not the midnight one." Bernie shrugged. "How often do you get to see Frank?" Steve smiled.

"Well, the only time was three years ago, when you put on that benefit for the hospital. But he only sang two songs if I remember, and the band was sub-par, this is Count Basie. You should have made it a table for three." Bernie shook his head.

"Naw, this one is for the two of you. Have fun."

"Thanks again, Bernie, I will come in and see you tomorrow." Steve closed the door behind him and was still shaking his head as he waved goodbye to Walter and stepped out onto the sidewalk.

Two miles from Foxy's deli, Steve parked next to the Westchester Garden apartments on Pershing, three blocks behind the Strip. Before he left the deli, he had used the phone and Bernie's list to call Rowena Vega. He had roused her from her sleep and though she agreed to see him, she had been none too pleased and had asked for an hour before he came. Steve sat in the Jeep and decided to pass the next twenty minutes smoking a cigarette or two and placing the names on the list in the order that he would contact them. When the hour was up, he entered the grounds of the apartment complex and knocked on number 10, a bottom floor unit facing the deserted pool area.

Rowena Vega opened the door and stared at the visitor for several seconds even as cold air swirled through the apartment and moved her long black hair away from her shoulders. She was five foot nine, the average height for showgirls in Las Vegas, her slim body and the way that she held herself also testifying to her profession.

"May I come in, Miss Vega?" Steve stood with his hands thrust deep into the pockets of his leather jacket. She didn't respond but stepped to one side of the door, closing it harder than Steve thought necessary after he had stepped across the threshold and made his way to the middle of the living room. He turned and with his hands still in his pockets looked steadily at the young woman who stood in front of the door with her arms folded.

"I think it is important that you talk to me, Miss Vega."

"I have already told the police everything I know, Mr. Cannon." Steve took out his notebook and pencil and sat down in one of the two chairs that along with a table were the only pieces of furniture that Steve could see in the apartment.

"Well, Miss Vega, unless I am able to obtain more information, they are going to close this case in a few days and put it all down to a dispute between two junkies over a fix. If that is what you want, then don't talk to me. But we both know that isn't how Desmond died, and even if that is all you know about it, information you give me, no matter how small or inconsequential it may seem at the time, might be the difference in whether Desmond's killer is brought to justice or not." He flipped over several pages of the notebook and got ready to take down more notes. Rowena stood stock still for several seconds before she slowly crossed the room and sat in the other chair. Steve looked at her brown bare feet and the long brightly patterned print dress that came nearly to her ankles.

"What time did you find Desmond?"

"One thirty in the morning."

"Where were you before that?"

"I was on stage at the Castaways doing the midnight show." She rubbed her eyes and the several bracelets she wore on both wrists clattered.

"Isn't there a three o'clock show most nights?"

"Yes, but I usually come home and spend an hour or so here before I go back."

Steve took a few seconds to flip back several pages and read the entries on a previous page. He looked up at Rowena with a blank expression.

"The cops say that the call came in at one o'clock and that the caller was a man." He waited.

"When I got here, the neighbor from upstairs was pounding

on the door. He told me that he had heard loud voices and things crashing, so he called the police. I came in here and found Desmond in the back room." She motioned toward an open doorway behind Steve. "By the time I came back into the living room, there were two city cops at the front door."

"Did you see anyone leaving the apartment complex on your way in?"

"No. I didn't." Steve nodded.

"What's the guy's name upstairs?"

"Hank or Harry, something, I don't remember."

"Did Desmond know him?"

"No, he didn't. I didn't even know who he was when I saw him that night."

"What is your relationship with Stuart Samoza?" Steve was looking at her when he asked the question, but didn't see any change in expression.

"We are friends. We have been friends for over twenty-five years." Steve nodded.

"Is that why you called him at work, two hours after you found Desmond?" He noted that her dark eyebrows arched slightly at the question.

"The cops had left and they had taken Desy away, and I had to talk to someone I knew."

"You have two brothers in town, where do they live?"

"In the Karen Court apartments, off of Karen, the last complex before the Sahara hotel."

"Did they get along with Desmond?" Steve saw a faint flush of color in the brown cheeks.

"What do you mean by that, Mr. Cannon?" Her dark brown eyes had flashed as she spoke.

"I mean, Miss Vega, that Desmond was over fifty, and you are by my guess not yet thirty. That is at least twenty years' difference. I spent some time in the Phillipines during the war, and while I am no expert on your culture, I can imagine that one of the reasons that your family feels comfortable with you over here is that your older brothers are here to watch out for you. So, again, Miss Vega, what did your brothers think of your living arrangement with Desmond?" Rowena looked down at her lap and turned the bracelets slowly around her left wrist.

"They didn't like it at first, but they saw how well Desmond treated me, and eventually they agreed not to tell the rest of the family." Steve tore the last page from his notebook and handed it to her.

"I will need to talk with both of them, Miss Vega. Write their names and apartment numbers down and phone numbers if they have them." She took the page and Steve's pencil, her long hair falling across her face as she leaned forward on the small table and wrote out several lines before handing it back to Steve. Steve looked at it briefly and then put it in the front pocket of his coat. He sat back in the chair and looked evenly at the young woman.

"How long had Desmond been clean?" He didn't drop his gaze.

"Almost two years. Not that it did him much good."

"Why do you say that, Miss Vega?" The tense expression on her face had hardened.

"Desy always thought that once everyone knew he was off the stuff, that he would get booked for gigs again. Never happened. Nobody would take the chance."

"Well he must have gotten some work, you didn't support him did you?" Steve kept his voice as gentle as he could.

"No, he always had some money coming in from royalties, though not much lately. One of his friends would drive him to LA a couple times each month to record jingles for the radio. Some months he made good money doing that." Steve retrieved the notebook page from his pocket and again handed it across to her.

"Write his name down here, please." Rowena did as she was asked. Steve looked down at the result.

'Buck Monari.' He looked over at her. "No address?" She shook her head.

"No, I don't know where he lives. He would call a couple of

days before the recording sessions and pick Desy up and they would go." Steve stuffed the page back into his pocket.

"Miss Vega, I would like to see the back room if you don't mind." He waited for her to stand up before he uncrossed his legs and followed suit. She led him through the doorway and to the right. They entered a medium sized bedroom that had been turned into a musicians' practice room. There were numerous photographs on the wall, most of them of Desmond with other musical luminaries or groups of luminaries. Steve studied each of the twenty or so photographs one by one. He turned to Rowena.

"Who is this man?" He indicated three different photographs. "I don't recognize him." Rowena moved closer to the wall for a better look and then stepped back.

"That's Stan Gilman. He had a big band in the late thirties, the first big break Desy ever had. Stan was barely older than Desmond and younger than many of the band members."

"He still alive?" Steve got out his notebook again.

"Yes, he was here just a week ago. I thought he lived in LA, but I think Desy told me he had moved here." Steve scribbled a few lines in his notebook and looked at the floor. A rug of some kind had obviously been removed recently, leaving a patch of fresh carpet. Steve decided to see what Tam could come up with in the way of a crime scene report before he pressed Rowena for details.

"Was everything like it is now, when you found him?"

"No, there was a chair that Desy used to practice in that was broken and that table was turned over and all the records that were on it, were scattered everywhere." She pointed to the corner where a card table sat crookedly with a bent metal leg. Steve turned and indicated the door and followed her back to the living room. He remained standing.

"Was anything missing from the apartment, even anything small that you may have noticed is not here anymore?" Rowena shook her head.

"Nothing I know of was taken."

"I am sure the police asked you this, Miss Vega, but did Desmond have any enemies you know about, or do you suspect anyone that might have done this?" She moved to the front door and grasped the door knob, then stopped.

"No, I have no idea who might have done this, Mr. Cannon." She opened the door and stood behind it out of the breeze that had stiffened considerably since Steve had arrived. Steve watched her for a few seconds before he stepped onto the cement walkway turning back to her as he came to a stop.

"I appreciate your time, Miss Vega, and I am sorry I cut into your sleep. I will probably need to talk you again after I have talked to the police and several of the people on my list. If you think of anything that might be helpful, please call me after nine at night or early in the morning." He opened his wallet as he spoke and handed her one of his cards. She took it without looking at it.

"I hope that won't be necessary, Mr. Cannon, goodbye." She closed the door. Steve retreated to the relative warmth of the Jeep and went over his notes, adding comments in the margins of the pages. After ten minutes, he retraced his steps into the complex and walked up the outside staircase next to Rowena's apartment.

The aluminum foil on the windows of number 20, was a silver testament to a day sleeper. Most likely a dealer who got off at two or six. Steve decided to pass for this morning and let the resident sleep. He wrote the apartment number next to his notes on Rowena's encounter with the man. Steve returned to the Jeep and made the reverse journey back to Foxy's. He found Bernie seated with two of his regular customers and took a small table by the door. Before a waiter appeared to take his order, Bernie stood up and saying a few words to his companions came over to Steve's table and sat down.

"You're back quick. No luck with Rowena?" Walter appeared behind Bernie with the cup he had left at his previous table and asked through motions if Steve wanted some coffee. Steve nodded, and Walter placed the cup in front of Bernie and returned to the bar.

"She wasn't happy I woke her up and she was not real excited about some of my questions, but for the first round, I got some information I can work up." Steve held up his notebook. "You know a band leader by the name of Stan Gilman and another musician by the name of Buck Monari?" Bernie nodded.

"Yeah, Stan's name I haven't heard for a while. I heard he was doing personal management in LA. Buck's a very good trumpet player who usually plays behind the Mary Kay Trio at the Tropicana, but I think he's backing Billy Eckstine at the moment. Good golfer. Do these guys figure in?" Steve shrugged.

"Just new names, mostly. Monari was taking Desmond to LA a couple times a month to work sessions on radio jingles and Gilman was, according to Rowena, Desmond's first big gig back in the thirties. You know anyone over at the musicians' union that could give me addresses on these guys? I checked the book and came up with zilch."

"I'll call Carl Fontana, I think he might still be the secretary over there, and if not, he should have an up-to-date directory, if he hasn't left for his tour of Scandinavia yet." Bernie got up from the table, picking up his coffee cup in the process. As he turned away, he almost collided with Walter bringing a cup and a full carafe to Steve.

Steve sipped his coffee and waited for Bernie to return from the backroom. When he did, he held a piece of paper which he handed to Steve as he sat down. Steve looked at the handwritten lines.

"Thanks, Bernie, this is what I need." Bernie reached over and pointed to one of the lines.

"You're in luck, Carl is tight with Monari and says he just moved to a new place. No address for Gilman, but Carl pulled this telephone number out of his personal address book. Doesn't know how old it is, he hasn't seen Stan for over five years, but he figures it might still be good." Steve nodded and folded the paper carefully and slipped it into his front jacket pocket. He smiled at Bernie.

"It is too early to interview these musicians, but thanks to you I have something else to do. I need to see if I can get one of my suits cleaned toots sweet."

"Take it over to the cleaners by Lucky Pierre's in that little plaza on Maryland Parkway across from the church. I bet he will do it, two, three hours tops." Steve slid his chair back and looked down at Bernie.

"I also need to talk to Tam, and word gets around quick down there when my name goes through the switchboard. Do me another favor and call Tam and tell him to call me at home right at five. OK?" Bernie was removing both cups from the table and handing them to a young busboy.

"Sure, I'll do it right now."

"See ya, Bern. Thanks." Steve waved as he crossed the few feet to the front door. He sat inside his Jeep for a few minutes and smoked a cigarette before he drove toward the east.

Thirty minutes after he had dropped off his best blue suit at the cleaners, Steve stood in front of the Blair House Apartments on Desert Inn Road. He looked at his watch. It was 12:30. He walked down a short open hallway and turned a corner and looked down at the long row of apartments. He was reaching for the paper that Bernie had given him to check the door number, when he paused at the sound of long drawn out notes being played on a trumpet and coming from somewhere behind him. He listened for a few minutes and then unfolding the paper he saw what he guessed he would find, the number on the paper corresponded to the number on the door he had just been drawn to. Steve waited until there was a pause in the sweet string of notes and then he rapped quickly on the door. The notes which had resumed again, stopped, and a few seconds later the beige door opened.

Buck Monari was as tall as Steve was. But what Steve noticed first was the smile in the eyes, and the large Italian nose that was the centerpiece of the handsome face. Before Steve could say anything, the man extended his hand.

"Hey man, who are you?" Steve smiled and grasped the big hand.

"Mr. Monari, my name is Steve Cannon." Buck laughed.

"No, man call me Buck. Come in and sit down." Steve followed him into the living room of the apartment. In front of a long couch against the wall, there was a reel-to-reel tape deck on a table, a chair that had a trumpet resting on a towel and a trombone sitting upright on a stand. Buck motioned for him to sit on the couch as he quickly picked up the trumpet, inspected the mouthpiece and placed it on the table beside the tape deck, arranging the towel carefully underneath the instrument. He turned the chair around to face Steve.

"Buck, I know this is not a good time, but I don't see a better one coming around soon. I am investigating the death of Desmond Rooney. I am not a cop, just a friend of Desmond's and a friend of a very good friend of his. If I could have a little of your time to ask some questions, it would be very helpful." The man in front of him sighed and looked at the trumpet that glowed dully in the afternoon sun that slanted through the blinds.

"Redness." Buck looked over at Steve. His eyes were not smiling and his expression suggested he was somewhere else. He looked down at his hands.

"What do you want to know?"

"How long did you know Desmond?" Steve slipped his notebook and pencil quietly from his pocket.

"I met him just before the war. I had just left home in Tupleo, Mississippi and taken the bus to New Orleans. I was walking through Jackson Square carrying my trumpet case and Desmond called out to me from one of the cafes. He wanted to know if I could play. I stayed with him for three weeks and he got me my first professional gig. He left for LA a month after I met him and I didn't see him again until after the war, but we have played together many times since then." He stopped and the faraway look came over him again.

"Have you played with him in recent years? Buck shook his head.

"Professionally, in bands? No, Redness was out of my league. He was the best there was, man."

"Rowena says that you were the main source of Desmond's income lately. Is that correct?"

"Well I don't know about that, but, yes, I did make sure that he was included whenever I could in the projects I was involved with in LA." Buck stood up and went over to the small bar attached to the kitchen. He picked up two short glasses and a bottle of Chianti wine and returned to the chair.

"How were you able to deal with him? The picture I'm getting was that he was too erratic and difficult to work with." Buck smiled as he poured each glass half full and handed one to Steve.

"He was. The only way it worked was because I had control of the projects. The sponsors and the ad agencies don't give a damn who is blowing on their silly jingles. If Desy didn't like the material or was changing things too much, I just came back in and re-recorded it. Made sure he got union scale and he was usually none the wiser. But the last time we went which was just before Christmas, he told me he didn't want to go anymore. He said he was coming into some money and that he didn't need to travel so far from Las Vegas." Steve furrowed his brow as he wrote in the notebook.

"Did he say where the money was coming from?" Buck shook his head.

"No. Didn't say and I didn't ask."

"He have any enemies?"

'No, none that I know of. Everybody loved the way Redness could blow. Everybody. But most people liked him better when he was a user. He was pretty direct and prickly after he got clean. But no, I have no idea why anybody would kill him." Steve got up to leave.

"Steve, if you got a minute, there is something I want you to hear." Buck disappeared into a back room and returned a few minutes later with a flat box that Steve recognized as a reel to reel tape. Buck rewound the practice tape and replaced it with the one from the box.

"This is a tape I recorded in 1953. It is just Des sitting on a couch in Miles Davis's house in LA. He is playing one of Miles's trumpets and improvising melodies." He hit the play switch and sat back in the chair.

Steve listened as intricate trills and soft notes that were followed by quick hard edged runs filled the room. The melodies were fresh and some were developed beyond the bridge and moved along into several variations. All the time, the tones were smooth and controlled and the transitions between the notes were seamless and had a clean light quality. Both men sat mesmerized as the twenty minute session came to an end. Steve sat still for several seconds, the man in the chair studying his face and smiling.

"If you like jazz, Steve, you could not move a muscle while that man played." He laughed softly and stopped the machine as the end of the tape fell from the drive and whipped around noisily in the air.

"I got several more just like that and every album he ever played a note on. Must be near fifty of them. I'm kind of known for making tapes of Desy, so if you want one sometime, I can make one for you. One of my favorites is all the pieces he composed himself." Steve smiled and stood up.

"Thanks, Buck, that is very generous of you. You know Bernie Gold, don't you?" Buck nodded.

"Sure, most all the musicians in town know Bernie. He has always been a great supporter of the music." Steve pulled his wallet from his back pocket and retrieved one of his business cards.

"Buck, do me a favor. Make a tape of Desy for Bernie. He has several of his albums, but I bet you have some stuff he would love to have. Think you could do that for me?" Buck took the card from Steve and laughed.

"Sure for Bernie, I would be glad to." He reached out to shake the hand that Steve had just offered. Steve held on to the hand for a few seconds and placed his other over it.

"Bernie is putting on a memorial at the Sands for Desmond, probably Friday night or Saturday. I'll check it with Bernie first, but would you like to be a part of it?" Buck stepped back in surprise.

"You kidding, man? I would consider it a huge honor." Steve nodded as he stepped to the door.

"I will have Bernie give you a call. See ya, thanks for your time." Buck waved from the middle of the room as Steve shut the door behind him.

Steve drove back over to the Westchester apartments. After he parked near where he had earlier, he noticed that the blue Corvair that Rowena drove was gone. He walked into the complex and made a circuit around the pool until he saw a small sign on one of the downstairs doors. 'Manager'. Steve knocked twice and hearing no reply he turned the knob and opened the door. He was in the front room of an apartment that was laid out exactly as Rowena and Desmond's except it had a large counter a few steps inside the door. Behind the counter a middle-aged woman sat at a small dinette table reading a magazine. The woman looked up from her reading with a puzzled expression.

"Can I help you?" Her hand went reflexively to the curlers in her black hair as she smoothed her blue cotton dress with her other hand.

"Hopefully, you can." Steve leaned on the counter and averted his eyes toward the wallet he had just pulled from his back pocket, giving the woman time to wrap a nearby sweater over the revealing top of her dress. He handed her a card when she approached the other side of the counter. Steve straightened up and smiled.

"I need some information on the tenant in number 20. He is probably a day sleeper and I don't want to bother him if I don't have to." The woman looked at the card.

"This have to do with the murder of that musician?" She looked at the card again and then up and down at Steve. Steve's smile was fainter now.

"Are you related to any of the Cannons?" The woman put heavy emphasis on 'the'. Steve shook his head and sighed. He was no relation to the large and influential clan, but it seemed like he answered the same question several times a week. Today, he chose to ignore it.

"Yes. The murder of Desmond Rooney." She nodded.

"Yeah, that was his name." She nodded again as she turned and dropped the card on the table behind her. "You're not here to turn this place upside down again, are you? The cops did that for five hours yesterday morning. The excitement has just died down." Steve shrugged.

"No, I like to do things quietly and behind the scenes. I don't like to create excitement unless I have to." He looked at the woman with a blank expression. She hesitated for a few seconds.

"Guy's name is Harris McCord. He isn't really the tenant. The guy on the lease left town two months ago, and I am stuck with him. I have been after him to sign a lease for the last five weeks, or the owner says he has to go. He paid the rent the first month, but none this month. The cops spent quite a bit of time with him yesterday morning. They even took him in, though he was back here by eleven." She leaned forward toward Steve and continued in a stage whisper.

"That little cop in the gray hat told me that he had several arrests in LA for drugs and was picked up here for soliciting and procuring." She nodded and returned to the table, Steve waited until she sat down.

"Well that is all helpful information. If I need more I will stop by again." He turned and opened the door, stepped through and closed it behind him in nearly one motion. As it closed behind him, he heard her reply.

"Anytime, honey, anytime."

Steve crossed the complex and skirting the pool area, once again ascended the steps over Desmond's apartment. As he expected, there was no reply after he knocked repeatedly on the door of apartment 20. In his peripheral vision, he saw the curtain move in the window of the unit next door. He waited for several seconds and then walked casually over to the door and knocked on number 21. The door opened a few inches, its travel impeded by a gold door chain. Half of a young female face looked back at Steve. From her posture, he could tell she was holding something. Steve took two steps back from the door and smiled.

"My name is Steve Cannon, I was just wondering if you had seen the guy next door lately?" He shifted his weight to his good leg and leaned back on the black iron railing. The girl pulled back the chain and opened the door, revealing a young infant cradled in her left arm. Steve folded his arms in front of him but stayed with his back against the railing.

"I haven't seen him since the police took him away." Her voice was small and Steve thought he detected a slight southern accent. He nodded.

"Did you know him well?" The young girl bounced the baby gently up and down a few times as she shook her head.

"No. He tried to come over here and bother me a few times when I first started babysitting Nathaniel here, but I haven't spoken to him for over a month."

"Ever hear anything go on over there?" The girl hesitated briefly, and then nodded.

"Sometimes when I was here at night, I would hear people coming and going and sometimes there was a commotion, but like I said, mostly at night."

"Hear anything the other night when the man downstairs was killed?" She shook her head. Steve stepped forward from the rail.

"Well, thanks for talking, I appreciate it." The young girl nodded her head and closed the door. As Steve turned toward the steps, he heard the chain slide into place.

O range flames licked at the three logs that Steve had placed in the ancient fireplace on top of some old newspapers. He sat back on the brown leather sofa, the warm air that flowed through the room had a soft hint of smoke. He set down a fresh tumbler of scotch next to his notebook as he rewrote some of the pages and worked in the newer information. He was almost done when the phone rang in the small office just off the living room. He picked up the notebook and the glass and carried them with him as he entered the room and settled into the couch before he picked up the receiver.

"This is Tam." Steve chuckled to himself as the husky baritone with a slight brogue echoed in his ear.

"Thanks for calling, you got a few minutes?" Tam sighed. "Yeah, I do. I took off early today and so I am home."

"That's good. A little more private this way. I need as much information as you have on the crime scene and the coroner's report if it is in." He heard Tam rustling papers.

"Yeah, the coroner's report came in late this morning. I have it here. Cause of death: loss of blood from three knife wounds to the abdomen. Toxocology report negative for everything but trace amounts of alcohol. The coroner estimates that Desmond had a glass of wine two hours before he died."

"What, if anything, did he say about the weapon?" Tam turned over several pages.

"He says the wounds were consistent with a large knife with an eight inch drop point blade and a serrated edge on top. He figures it was a hunting knife of some kind."

"Samuels got any lead on the knife at all?" Tam grunted.

"Nope. They have had two teams inside that apartment as well as the grounds, and they didn't come up with anything." Steve scribbled quickly in his notebook.

"I am more interested in your take on the crime scene."

"No forced entry. Probably knew the guy. The perp must have locked the door behind him. Definitely a struggle. There was a rather large bump and contusion on the back of his head which suggests he was hit from behind, they struggled, then he was stabbed."

"Samuels still pushing the junkie/robbery angle?"

"Yeah, he is, but he is having a hard time coming up with suspects."

"What about Harris McCord, the guy that was banging on the door when Rowena got home." Tam chuckled.

"Sounds like you been busy. You talk to everybody?"

"I've just been working off a list that Bernie and I came up with. Friends, people he worked with, trying to get an idea of what went on the last few weeks."

"Well, Samuels has pretty much ruled out McCord, even though he is the scum of the earth and should go away a long time for something."

"I was over at his apartment today, no answer, maybe he skipped."

"Maybe. Samuels is now convinced that Desmond was dealing drugs even if he wasn't taking them himself. He thinks that all he has to do is lean on the local hopheads and someone will give him the right name." Steve scoffed.

"I am not surprised. After what I saw last summer, I am sure that Samuels will come up with a way to fill in whatever holes he needs to. Meanwhile an innocent man gets smeared for something he didn't do. Who else has Samuels been talking to?"

"I don't know. The little group around him has clammed up. Somehow he got word that you were working this case and now I am frozen out. But I will keep my eyes open. I should be able to hear pretty quickly if they are looking at someone."

"Don't stick your head up if you don't have to, Tam. Whatever you get is a big help. If I could get a picture of this McCord guy, I would be grateful. On another subject, I think you and Jack and I may need another meeting soon. As soon as things calm down a bit, I will check your lead in Sedona. Maybe by then, Jack will have something to report."

"Yeah maybe. I gotta go. I will call you if I get any more out of Samuels' crew. I will see about the picture."

"Sure, thanks Tam, see ya." Steve held the buttons down on the base unit and dialed a new number. After three rings a female voice came on the line.

"Mr. Carmino's office, this is Miss Horvath, how can I help you?" Steve smiled.

"This is Steve Cannon. Put me through to Tommy, please." Steve heard the exasperated sigh on the other end of the line.

"Mr. Carmino is in a meeting and cannot be disturbed." The words were clipped with little inflection.

"Just put me through, Miss Horvath. If Tommy misses an important meeting just because you don't like the brand of after-shave I wear, I don't think he will be too happy. So let's quit beating around the bush here and let me talk to him." The irritation in Steve's voice grew more obvious with every word. There were several moments of silence on the other end, until Steve heard two clicks and Tommy's loud voice boomed through the receiver.

"Cannon. What do you want?" Steve snorted loudly in Tommy's ear.

"I want that you should get a new secretary. That's what. Hard to believe you get anything done at all around there." Tommy laughed.

"Well she is out there precisely to keep creeps like you away from my door." Tommy laughed again, this time at his joke. "What did you say you wanted?"

"Just a small favor, Tommy. I need thirty-five rooms comped for Friday or Saturday night. I'll have to call you back on the exact date." Steve had to bury his face in his sleeve to keep from laughing out loud.

"Are you drunk? What kind of joke is this?" Tommy's voice was louder now, but he wasn't laughing.

"Oh, yeah, Tommy, the rooms are for about forty musicians that are flying in this weekend. Thirty-five rooms should do it. We'll have a couple of them double up."

"You'll what? I'm getting off now, Slick. I think you better sober up."

"You're putting me in a bad spot here, Tommy. Now I have go back to Bernie and tell him you said no." There was a four beat silence.

"What does Bernie have to do with this?" Tommy's voice was calmer, but Steve could imagine the color of his complexion.

"He has been asked to put on a memorial for Desmond Rooney, you know who that is, right?"

"Yeah, yeah, Cannon, I heard about that, but why my hotel?"

"Because they are putting it on at the Sands and they don't have the rooms." Steve waited for the new explosion. Instead there was the same four beat silence, but this time there was a definite hiss in Tommy's voice.

"You telling me that you and Bernie got the nerve to ask me to help put on an event for the Sands? Don't you know anything about this town?" Steve snapped his fingers loudly into the phone.

"Oh yeah, Tommy, I almost forgot. I was supposed to tell you that Bernie wants the meeting this Thursday at five at Foxy's. Can you make it?" Tommy snorted.

"Yeah, Slick, I can make it. And I'm guessing the price of admission is two floors of rooms for a bunch of deadbeat musicians who don't gamble, make a lot of noise, use room service like it's McDonalds and tip like crap. Is that the picture you're painting here?" Steve laughed.

"Well, you might be right, Tommy, I should have led with the part about the meeting, but yeah, I guess if you put a frame around it, you could hang it in a museum." He heard Tommy muttering under his breath.

"OK, Slick you win. Tell Bernie to call John Bonine in reservations when he knows which night. And, Slick, I better like what I hear at this meeting, got it?"

"Don't worry, Tommy it will be fun. Just three old pals sitting around shooting the bull. See ya." Steve hung up the phone quickly, even though he could hear Tommy's voice still talking as he put the receiver down.

Steve looked at the clock. He had promised Remy he would pick her up at seven and he had less than an hour to dress and drive across town. The blue suit still fit well and looked good with the pale ecru shirt and the blue and green tie. He stood in front of the mirror. After a few seconds thought, he strode back into the bedroom and pulled his black tux from the closet. He checked that he had remembered to dry clean it as well as the shirt. He quickly fastened the stud buttons into the shirt and tied the small black bow.

It was five to seven when he pulled into the semi-circular driveway that fronted Remy's house on the Desert Inn golf course. Steve walked to the front door and was just about to ring the bell when he saw Remy through the side glass panel. She was in the foyer putting the finishing touches to her hair. She wore a long black sleeveless gown that came to the floor but still revealed the delicate black beading on the toe of her three inch heels. Her hair was swept up and secured in the back by a small diamond comb that matched the diamond chandelier earrings that swung gently above her small pearl necklace. On the hall table in front of her lay a white ermine stole and a rhinestone covered evening bag. Steve watched appreciatively from his vantage point and smiled when she caught sight of him in the mirror and turned around. She opened the heavy black wooden door and they embraced in the cold air.

"You look beautiful, Gem." He twirled her gently around, her long dress following her graceful moves as they did a quick foxtrot around the large round foyer. Remy held the back of his neck and kissed him as she fell into his arms laughing.

"We better get going, Gem, if we're late Bernie will never let me hear the end of it." Steve wrapped the soft white stole around Remy's shoulders and held out her purse as he opened the door.

"Can we take the Jag, Steve?" Steve locked the door behind them.

"Sure, Gem, that would be great.

After letting the engine warm for several minutes, Steve steered the sports car smoothly onto the street and accelerated to the corner and turned left on to the Strip, just a long city block from the Sands Hotel.

Steve eased the white Jaguar into the long line of limos, taxis and other cars that were moving slowly toward the entrance to the Sands Hotel. Under the huge portico, hundreds of golden yellow lights reflected off every surface and lit the whole area as bright as mid-day. While Steve was waiting behind a yellow cab disgorging passengers, he spied a bell captain he had known for many years just outside the front doors. The man spotted Steve a few seconds later and caught a bell hop by the sleeve, said something in his ear and then pointed into the casino. When his turn came, Steve pulled the Jag up even with the front doors and handed the keys to the parking attendant, while another helped Remy from the passenger's seat. Steve pocketed the ticket he was handed and retrieved Remy's stole from behind the front seat and had just draped it around her shoulders when he saw a large man with thinning hair come through the front door and head straight for them. Steve was wondering why Jack Entratter was out in front of his hotel in all the traffic when Jack smiled and greeted Remy by name and threw an arm around Steve while simultaneously shaking his hand.

"Steve, how you been?" Steve smiled up at the six foot five figure and shrugged.

"Pretty good now, Jack, though I don't think you and I have ever met formally." Jack patted Steve's shoulder and smiled at Remy.

"I don't know if you know this, Miss DeMarche, but your friend here is a pretty fair poker player." He turned to Steve. "I don't suppose you remember the ten grand you walked away with from Franks' table a few years ago at one of Bernie's get togethers?" Steve's brow furrowed.

"I do, but I'm surprised you do." Jack patted his shoulder again. "Are you kidding me, Frank brings it up all the time." Jack put his free hand gently on the back of Remy's stole and steered them through the front door and into the casino. They walked three abreast through the crowded casino, patrons and employees alike moving to the side quickly when they saw Jack's imposing figure bearing down upon them. When they reached the end of the long line waiting to get into the showroom, Jack steered them around the crowd and just as they reached the maître 'd station, another tuxedo clad figure opened a black curtain and Steve followed Remy and Jack through the dark opening.

Steve and Remy found themselves in a small room that looked out over the showroom. Jack handed each of them a glass of champagne from a small table and took one himself, hoisting it into the air.

"Welcome to the Copa Room." The three glasses tinkled together and Jack motioned for the other tuxedo to step forward.

"This is Mr. Alata. He will personally serve you tonight, at my table." The dark complexioned Armenian stepped forward, bowed to Remy and nodding slightly to Steve, shook his hand.

"My pleasure, may I show you to your table?" Steve looked at Remy, who smiled as she replaced her glass on the table. Steve took her arm, and motioned to Mr. Alata.

"Lead on." He turned and shook Jack's hand.

"Thanks Jack, you didn't have to go to all this trouble." Jack waved his hand dismissively.

"Don't think anything of it. Glad to have you here. I will join you after dinner, when the show starts." He waved again and stepped back out through the curtain.

With the bell captain leading the way, Steve and Remy walked down a white marble stairway that led to the floor of the showroom which was already two thirds full. There was a small gate at the bottom and every head in the room turned as the trio descended. When they reached their destination, Steve could see why it was called Frank's table. It was directly in front of the stage and was slightly elevated compared to those that were immediately adjacent. It was also larger and could accommodate ten people with more elbow space than the regular tables. There was already an ice bucket and a bottle of Champagne in the center with a huge spray of roses offset from the center just enough to allow an unobstructed view of the stage. The usual dinner show staple was prime rib, but Steve and Remy found printed menus beside their plates that listed several entrees as well as appetizers. A waiter appeared with a glass of scotch. Steve took a sip and leaned toward Remy.

"Someone knows what scotch I drink." Later, they toasted and shared portions of their entrees, New York steak and Lobster Thermidor, with each other. The Count Basie Orchestra played big band and Broadway show tune music throughout the dinner. As soon as the waiters had cleared most of the tables, the lights dimmed, and Jack Entratter stepped into the bright spotlight at center stage to a smattering of applause. After he delivered a short history of Frank's appearances at the Sands, Count Basie swung the band into the introduction to 'Fly Me to the Moon.' Frank strode into view from just behind the bandstand and broke into the first verse before he reached the front of the stage. Jack slipped quietly into the seat across from Remy and smiled at Steve. When Frank had finished the first song and was introducing the band Jack leaned in toward Remy and Steve.

"There are a couple of surprises tonight I think you will enjoy."
By now Frank had moved into the main part of the show, the part
that kept the crowds coming back night after night. He introduced
the Rat Pack one after the other and began the familiar banter and
back and forth that was the trademark of the group of friends.
Frank would signal the band and launch into one of his well known
tunes, only to be interrupted by Dean Martin or Joey Bishop or
Sammy Davis, Jr. or all three and one of their semi-rehearsed skits
would commence, with Frank waiting for the hubbub to die down,
start another song, only to have the whole process repeat itself.
When it was Dean Martin or Sammy Davis' turn to sing, Frank
would return the favor. Midway through, Frank slowed the pace
down, introduced Angie Dickinson and they sang a ballad together.
After that, he and Sammy Davis Jr. soft shoed their way through
'Me and My Shadow'. Frank then moved to the center of the stage
and with the darkened room lit only by the blue spotlight, waited
while Count Basie brought the band way down and the first few
notes of 'One for My Baby, and One More for the Road' tinkled
from the piano. When the song finished and the applause had died
down, Frank stood silently for a few seconds, holding the microphone and looking down at the floor. When he spoke, his voice was
barely above a stage whisper.

"You know I come out here every night and I stand here, and at
least once each night, I look out at all of you and I think how truly
fortunate I am as a performer to be in this wonderful room and sing
with this great band." Frank turned slightly and held out his hand
toward the band and waited while applause swelled for the Count
who stood up from the piano and took a quick bow. "I also know
there are other performers who have paved the way for me to do
what I do, and they deserve to perform for you much more than I
do." Frank smiled at the howls of protest and applause that swept
the room. "No, I mean it. I'm just your local humble saloon singer."
He stepped back, looked at the floor, then turned and waved toward
a small group of patrons that were still objecting. "And I would like

to bring out one of those people to sing for you right now. A man that for most of us in this room defined not only an era, but what a singer was supposed to sound like." He paused for a few seconds. "Mr. Bing Crosby." The band swung into, 'White Christmas' as a smiling Bing Crosby came from behind the bandstand and waving in the direction of the Rat Pack strolled over to Frank. Frank said something in Bing's ear as the applause rose and fell several times. Bing looked over at the band and then nodded back at Frank who handed him the microphone and retreated to the back of the stage.

Bing Crosby turned halfway toward the band as the guitarist played the first four barre chords of the song that was a hit for Bing just as the war ended in Europe and the troops began to stream home. He turned back to the audience as the smooth bass baritone voice took over.

"Kiss me once and kiss me twice, it's been a long, long time."

Almost on cue the round crystal chandelier above the stage began revolving, the small silver reflections falling across the mesmerized faces of the crowd held silent and captive by the memories of fathers, brothers, sons and others who had disappeared from their lives, but whose faces lived in those memories as fresh as yesterday. Steve thought of his brother lost in the Pacific, and all the good friends who were not with him when he left Guadalcanal. He squeezed Remy's hand and looked over at her beautiful face and wondered what life was like for a young girl in 1940's France.

Bing finished the song and stood quietly in the blue spotlight for several seconds. When the loud applause finally erupted and rolled across the darkened room, his face still held the same sad expression as he gave a slight bow. Frank came to the front of the stage, hugged Bing, they bowed to the crowd together and the show was over.

As the showroom lights came up, Steve was pulling back Remy's chair when he spotted the bemused smile of Frank's friend and bodyguard, Jilly Rizzo weaving through the departing patrons toward him. Jilly stopped next to Jack and whispered something in his ear, Jack nodded and looked over at Steve. Jilly held out his hand across the table and Steve moved closer to his side and shook it.

"Mr. Cannon, Mr. Sinatra would like to speak with you. Follow me please." Steve turned and looked at Remy. Jack put his hand on Steve's shoulder.

"Don't worry, I will sit with Miss DeMarche until you get back." Steve squeezed Remy's hand.

"Will you be OK for a few minutes?" Remy nodded.

"Of course, I will have time to finish my champagne." She leaned over quickly and kissed Steve on the cheek.

The bodyguard lead Steve around the side of the large stage and through a black curtain. After descending a short set of concrete steps, Jilly stopped before a dark green door and knocked softly.

"It's Jilly." He spoke in response to someone inside. Jilly nodded at Steve and opened the door. Steve stepped through and the big bodyguard pulled the door shut behind him.

Frank Sinatra sat on a leather couch with one foot up on the cushions. He had traded his tux jacket for a light blue V necked sweater. He held a glass of whiskey in his hand as a black and white TV in the corner played a basketball game. Frank pulled his foot down off the couch but didn't stand up. He indicated one of the chairs around a small table that held a deck of cards and a rack of poker chips.

"How you been, Cannon?" Frank reached behind the couch to an unseen table as he spoke and produced another glass and a bottle of Jack Daniels. He poured the glass half full and handed it to Steve.

"I've been good, Frank, how you feeling?" Frank laughed.

"You enjoy the show?"

"Yeah, it was great. Don't know what all the fuss was about, any seat out there is a good one." Frank reached over and switched off the TV.

"Well I hadn't seen you or played cards with you in a while, and since you're looking into Desmond's death, I thought it was the least I could do."

"Thanks, Frank, I appreciate that." The singer picked up an envelope that had been lying next to the TV. He tossed it on the table in front of Steve.

"Here, that's for you." Steve picked up the bundle and quickly fanned through the bills inside.

"Ten grand in there. Ask if you need more." Steve put the envelope on the edge of the table.

"What is this for Frank?" The singer's drink stopped in midair just short of his mouth. His eyes narrowed as he looked across the table at Steve.

"Your expenses, what the hell else would it be for?" Steve chuckled and shook his head.

"I don't know, just a coincidental number, don't you think?" Frank screwed up his face as he took a large sip of the whiskey.

"I forgot about your wise attitude, Cannon, but now that you brought it up, when am I going to get the chance to get even?" Steve shrugged.

"Call Bernie and set it up. Just the two of us. I'll make sure that if the cards are running right for you it will be worth your while." Frank's face held a small smile.

"Sure, Cannon, let's do it that way. But why do you think you can turn down ten grand for expenses? That beautiful broad I saw you sitting with tonight don't look like the cheap date kind. Do I know her?" Steve shrugged again.

"Don't know. If so, she has never mentioned it. I am investigating Desmond's murder because I knew him and he always meant a lot to Bernie. So it's more personal than business." Frank interrupted him.

"He meant a lot to all of us. He was Dorsey's favorite trumpet player, and Tommy was not easy to impress on a good day. I would consider it a personal favor if you take the money, and I am also offering to help you with anything else you need." Steve picked up the envelope.

"Sure, Frank, thanks for everything. I got a beautiful lady waiting. Good luck with the midnight show." Frank snorted and waved dismissively. Steve put the envelope into his inside breast pocket and opened the door. He looked back at Frank who had turned the TV back on.

"I look forward to throwing down the pasteboards with you Frank." Frank raised his glass in reply but didn't look away from the basketball game.

Steve retraced the steps that he and Jilly had taken and entered the showroom that was nearly deserted except for waiters setting up the tables for the midnight show. Before he reached the table he saw Jack introducing Count Basie to Remy. Jack repeated the introductions when Steve appeared and after several pleasantries the Count left to get ready for the midnight show. Steve shook Jack's hand again.

"Thanks for everything, Jack, if I can ever be of help, please give me a call." Jack laughed.

"Maybe you can get Tommy Carmino to back off the name-calling and make peace around here." Steve patted the large arm.

"Unfortunately, Jack, I have no control over forces of nature." He looked over at Remy.

"Say, Jack, the Starlight Room at the D.I. still in business?" Jack nodded. "They are going to close it next week for remodeling, but yeah, it is still open."

Steve swept up the white stole and placed it around Remy's shoulders.

"Would you come dancing with me, Gem? I'm not the best hoofer around, but I promise you will be able to walk tomorrow." Remy laughed.

"Of course, that sounds lovely." She held out her hand to Jack.

"Thank you very much, Mr. Entratter, for a very special night." Jack smiled and leaned over and kissed her on lightly on both cheeks.

"It's Jack, but you can call me anything you like, Miss DeMarche. The pleasure was all mine. You want to come back anytime, it's on me, even if you insist on dragging Cannon here with you."

January 6

Steve flipped the visor down on the Jeep as he turned onto Nellis Boulevard and into the early morning sun. He glanced across the yellow desert to Sunrise Mountain and made a promise to himself that he would make time soon to spend a few days alone in the great expanse. As he neared East Sahara Boulevard, he spotted a black and white police car parked a hundred yards ahead. He quickly checked his speedometer and satisfied he was traveling eight miles below the speed limit he passed the cruiser, stopped at the stop sign, put on his right indicator and turned onto Sahara. He had only gone half a block when he saw the red lights in his rear view mirror a second before he heard the siren. He eased to the curb and shut off the engine. A large city cop he did not recognize got out of the car, his image filling the side view mirror as he approached. He stopped just behind the Jeep and with his hand resting on his pistol grip, he shouted for Steve to exit the vehicle.

Steve pushed the door open and stood in the street his back leaning against the door.

"Put your hands on your head. Slowly." Steve shook his head and did as he was told.

"What can I do for you this morning, officer?" Steve looked directly into the cop's eyes. The cop grunted and took two steps toward Steve.

"Just keep your hands right there nice and easy while I pat you down." The large man moved quickly in front of Steve and in a few seconds had expertly frisked him. He pulled Steve forward by the collar of his windbreaker and then stepped behind him, guiding him forward with the back of his jacket wrapped tightly up in his big fist. As they neared the police car, Steve saw the silhouette of a fedora in the backseat. The cop led him around to the front passenger side, opened the door and shoved him toward the opening. Steve took his hands off his head and slid onto the rough cloth of the bench seat. As the cop crossed in front of the car on his way back to the driver's side, Steve reached up and turned the mirror so that Head Detective Samuels' face came into view from the backseat. Steve snorted.

"Is this really necessary, Samuels? I have a phone." The small sharp face in the mirror turned and looked out the side window.

"Shut up, Cannon, we're just going for some coffee." The big cop closed the driver's door and shooting a disgusted look at Steve, returned the mirror to its former position. Steve watched the strip malls on the outer edge of town slip by as they cruised slowly down the boulevard.

"I get a hundred dollars an hour for consultations, Samuels." The cop who was driving snorted derisively. Samuels didn't say anything. After six blocks, they pulled into a mom and pop diner that was next to a western wear store. They parked under a huge plastic cowboy boot. Samuels opened his door.

"Get out, Cannon." Steve climbed out of the front seat and waited on the sidewalk. Samuels had a brief conversation with the uniformed cop who went back and sat inside the car. Samuels swept past Steve and held the door to the diner open, indicating with a nod that Steve should enter. Steve walked into the half full restaurant and slid into an empty booth just inside the door. Samuels entered and took off his long gray raincoat, hanging it on a three ponged coat rack behind him. Steve stared at the narrow yellow-brown eyes when Samuels sat down.

"I got things to do, Samuels, so what gives? Do you think this is an appropriate use of taxpayer dollars?" Samuels pulled out a pack of cigarettes from his inside suit pocket, selected one, lit it with one quick flick of a silver lighter and frowned at Steve through the gray smoke.

"How come every time I turn around, Cannon, you are dogging my investigations? Wasn't last summer enough to convince you to find another profession?" Steve snorted and held up his coffee cup to a waitress that had just passed by the table. She returned with a full pot and filled both of their cups. Steve watched as the detective poured sugar into the dark liquid.

"It's still a free country the last I heard Samuels. You don't like it, maybe you should try doing a better job." Samuels ignored the remark and casually surveyed the other patrons.

"So who are you liking for this deal, Cannon? Or are you stumped?" Steve sipped his coffee.

"Early days, Samuels, but I know for sure it had nothing to do with drugs and junkies. But if you want to waste your time chasing that pipe dream, I can't stop you."

"See, that's your problem, Cannon. You always take on the personal cases and it clouds your judgement. Everyone in town knows that trumpet player's been a junkie since the forties."

"No, Samuels, he had been clean for almost two years. If you think he was still using, maybe you better read the toxicology report again." Steve reached inside the windbreaker and fished his own pack of smokes from his shirt pocket.

"Well, it doesn't take much imagination to figure out where you got that information, but if you were a trained investigator like myself, you would know that those reports only ever tell half the story."

"Are we about done here Samuels? Because I got better things to do than listen to glowing testimonials about your prowess as a cop. Spare me." Steve lit his cigarette with a book of paper matches someone had left on the table and threw the still smoking taper into a glass ashtray at Samuels's elbow.

"I don't want you interfering in this case, Cannon. In case you forgot, I can make the trouble I gave you last summer look like a day at camp." Steve snorted.

"You certainly tried, but if I remember correctly I never spent even one night in your cells. But I tell you what. In the spirit of friendly competition, let me give you a little clue to help you on your way." Samuels sputtered into his coffee cup, spilling the brown liquid on his white collar.

"What?" Samuels grabbed a napkin and began dabbing furiously at the stain. Steve stood up from the booth.

"Did you ever know a perp to lock the door behind him after running a knife through somebody? Think about that while you gaze up at the 'atta boys' you have all over your wall. Now take me back to my car or arrest me." Steve swung open the glass door and strode to the car. When the uniformed cop unlocked the doors from the inside, Steve climbed in, stared straight ahead and took a deep drag on the Pall Mall.

Twenty minutes later he was seated in the back room of Foxy's, watching as Bernie worked through the previous day's receipts with a ten key and a thick ledger book. Steve enjoyed his second cup of coffee of the morning. His legs stretched out before him, he waited until Bernie had entered the last few numbers and added up the columns. He snapped the book shut, placed it in a side drawer and joined Steve at the green felt covered table.

"I can get Walter in here with breakfast pronto, no problem, Steve." Steve shook his head.

"Naw, don't feel hungry. Besides, we both have a lot to do today. Have you decided what night the memorial is going to be?" Bernie nodded and went back to his desk, returning with a flier that was being distributed up and down the strip.

"Friday seemed to work the best for everyone. We start at seven. Frank has offered to skip the dinner show so that we don't have to be out of there until ten." Steve reached over to the pocket of his windbreaker he had hung onto the chair next to him. He placed the envelope that Frank had given him on the table. The flap was open and Bernie saw the thick stack of bills.

"What's that for, Steve?"

"Frank wants to make a contribution to the memorial fund." He pushed the envelope over toward Bernie. Bernie frowned.

"Franks' already made a donation. I think that Frank meant you to have this." He picked up the packet, quickly riffed through the crisp bills and then put it on the table next to Steve.

"Look, Bern, I know you paid for Desmond's brother and other members of his family to fly out here for the memorial. I also know he has a couple of ex-wives, at least two kids and who knows how many grand kids out there. The fund could use all the juice it can get." Bernie shook his head.

"The fund will have over fifty grand after Friday night. Almost all the tickets are spoken for already, so I think you should have it."

"I only have it now, because I didn't want Frank to go off on me, you know how he gets, so do what you want, but I'm not leaving here with it." Steve took a big sip of coffee and pulled his notebook out of his back pocket. Bernie sipped his cup of coffee and decided to let the subject drop.

"So, who is on the docket for today?" Bernie refilled their cups from the sliver carafe on the far side of the table.

"Well, I still have several names from the list, but I need to talk to some people not on the list. Know anybody that didn't like Desmond much?" Bernie sat back and thought for a minute.

"You know that guitar player, Sammy Sanderson?" Steve shook his head.

"He's played all over the Strip for years. Well he and Des had some kind of falling out about ten years ago over something or other and I don't think they ever patched it up." Steve wrote the name in his notebook.

"Other than him, I can't think of anyone. So Samuels still think this was about drugs?"

"Yeah, at the moment. He doesn't care very much what it was about, all he wants is to collar and convict somebody for it. I need to use your phone. I want to call the number you gave me for Stan Gilman." Bernie walked over to his desk and sweeping the phone cord around toward Steve's side, brought the phone back to the table. Steve placed his index finger in the first hole of the rotary wheel and dialed the number. After five rings a woman answered the phone.

"Good morning, my name is Steve Cannon. I am calling from Las Vegas and I wonder if I could speak with Stan Gilman." There was a short response.

"When was that?"

"Do you know where he is staying?" Steve wrote down an address.

"Thanks. You have been very helpful. Goodbye." Steve hung up the phone and returned it to Bernie's desk. He sat back down in front of Bernie.

"That was his sister. Said he moved here six weeks ago and is living with a friend in North Las Vegas." Bernie scowled.

"That is a little strange. I've never heard of a musician moving here and not checking in with the union. Carl Fontana would have said so if he had." Steve nodded.

"Rowena said he had visited Desmond last week sometime." Steve retrieved the phone book from the desk and flipped through the 'S' section.

"Yeah, Sanderson lives in North town as well. Well there is my morning. I will call you or drop by around noon. Tam may call here with some information on the guy who was banging on the door when Rowena came home that night." Steve got up to go, but paused.

"Hey Bern, Tommy's coming tomorrow at five and I got him to fork over the free rooms. Thirty-five of them. He said for you to call

John Bonine at the hotel and give him the night you want them."
Bernie laughed.

"He kick about it?"

"He tried, but I shut him up when I mentioned your name,
though he was not happy that the Sands is involved." Bernie got up
and followed Steve to the door of the game room.

"I want to thank you again for what you did for two of us last
night. It was a beautiful evening. Jack invited us back anytime, so
Remy is going to insist that you come too." Bernie opened the door
for Steve and leaned against it.

"That's a date. Maybe when this is all behind us and we have
something to celebrate, we'll make a night of it." Steve laughed in
agreement and waving at Walter who was standing behind the register, he made his way through the tables and out of the restaurant.

Steve drove slowly down the poplar studded street. It was one of the
wider streets in North Las Vegas and the lots were large with ram-
bling ranch style houses on both sides of the block. He pulled up
next to the mailbox that held the number he was looking for. The
low slung green and white house had a large concrete driveway in
front that took up most of the front yard except for a small strip of
grass just inside a split rail fence. The driveway was crowded with
at least eight cars. After parking the Jeep in the street, Steve let his
fingers slide lightly over several of the hoods as he walked by. All
of them were warm to the touch. He stepped up onto a small concrete stoop that had been painted red but was faded and cracked.
He knocked on the door and after several minutes of waiting he
knocked again and rang the doorbell as well. He stepped back
on the porch and was just about to leave, when the door opened
quickly and a gray haired man in his sixties held onto the doorknob
from his side and glared at Steve.

"Who the hell are you and what do you want?" The shorter

man wore a red flannel shirt and a frown. Steve turned back to the door but stood three feet away from his inquisitor.

"My name is Steve Cannon, and I would like to ask you a few questions."

"You a reporter? Cause if you are, I got the right to run you off of here any way I care to." Steve relaxed his posture and looked back evenly at the agitated man. In the room behind him, Steve could see ten or twelve men gathered around the table with several newspapers spread out before them.

"I don't think there will be any need for that, Mr. Sanderson, I am not a reporter, I just have a few questions and then I will be on my way."

"Questions about what?" He left the door half closed as he folded his arms across his chest.

"Questions about Desmond Rooney." Sanderson scoffed.

"Why would anyone waste their time asking questions about him? Good riddance if you ask me. And why do you care so much?" Sammy's eyes were squinted and his upper lip curled over his teeth.

"He was my friend and a good friend to several people I know, and I just need to know why he had to die. Perhaps you have a theory?" Sanderson snorted.

"Probably because he was sleeping with another's man wife." He dropped his arms and edged back halfway through the door. Steve stepped forward.

"That your problem with him, Sanderson?" Steve's voice was not as even now and had an edge to it. Sammy Sanderson stopped and drew himself up to his full five foot nine height.

"That's none of your damn business. Get out of here." He pointed toward the street. Steve smiled.

"I'm going. But maybe you heard of Stan Gilman?" Steve watched as Sammy turned and looked at him from behind the partially closed door.

"Another S.O.B. if you ask me."

"More sleeping in the wrong bed trouble?" Steve put his hand in his pockets and looked down the street. When he looked back, Sammy was shaking his head.

"No, he was more into putting his name on other people's music. Stole several good tunes from me, that's for sure."

"Steal any from Desmond?" Sammy shook his head.

"Why don't you ask him yourself?" Sammy swung the door shut. Steve stood and smiled at the front door. He pulled the notebook from his back pocket and wrote for a few minutes. He had the feeling he was being watched from the large picture window just to the right of the door. When he was done, he carefully put the notebook away and stepped casually down off the porch and walked across the gravel driveway. When he got to the Jeep, he pulled out a map of the city and spread it over the hood. He took his time tracing the route to his next destination. When he was done, he carefully folded the map, put it away in the glovebox and slowly pulled out to the center of the street and drove away.

The next address was a mile away off of Lamb Boulevard. The house, a two story, was in an older section than the one that he had just left. There were no cars in the brick driveway, but Steve parked on the street anyway. A concrete sidewalk led to a porch that extended halfway around the Victorian style house. Seeing no doorbell, Steve rapped on the oval shaped, leaded glass pane of the front door, and swept his gaze across the spacious porch. A white curtain behind the glass prevented visitors from seeing inside the home. After a few seconds, a short balding man pulled the curtain aside and peered at Cannon. He then opened the door and stood blinking at his visitor. He was wearing a sleeveless undershirt and gray slacks. He held the morning's paper in his right hand. Steve held out his hand, hoping he would receive a warmer welcome this time around. The man glanced down at the hand, but instead of grasping it, he jerked his head backwards toward the large open front room. Steve stepped into the hallway and waited until the man lead him to a large round table that sat in the middle of the living room. Steve halted just before entering the room.

"Are you Stan Gilman?" The man stopped and laid the paper on the table next to several others, one of which Steve noted, was 'Variety'. He smiled and held out his hand indicating that Steve should sit down at the table.

"Yeah, that's me, alright. And who might you be?" Stan sat down behind a cup, saucer and a percolator that was plugged into the far wall by way of a black extension cord.

"My name is Steve Cannon, Mr. Gilman, I am a private investigator and I am looking into the death of Desmond Rooney, who if I am not mistaken, you knew well." Steve pulled out a heavy oak chair from the table and sat directly across from Stan. Steve folded his hands in front of him and looked blankly at his host. The round pleasant face had a three day beard.

"How about some coffee, Mr. Cannon?" Stan stood up halfway.

"No thanks, Mr. Gilman, I won't be here long." He pulled the notebook and pencil from his back pocket and smoothed out the pages on the top of the table.

"So you knew Desmond since the late thirties, right?" Stan Gilman shrugged.

"No, way before that, I discovered the kid. He was playing in a ragtime outfit in a dancehall in Memphis when my band hit town. I caught the show, liked what I heard, and the rest, as they say is history." Stan raised his cup to Steve and took a sip before placing it back in the saucer. Steve grunted.

"You part company on good terms?"

"Yeah, several times. We last worked together two years ago on a jazz documentary, you know, recreating the old big band era. How did you think to look me up? No cops have been around asking questions." Steve shrugged.

"Your name came up in a couple of conversations I have had recently. Thought I would come out and see what you had to say."

He scribbled a sentence into the notebook and then looked up. Stan shrugged.

"What do you want me to say? He blew a great horn, I am sad that he is gone and I wish we had a chance to do more things together."

"You with him during his addiction years?" Stan chuckled softly.

"I didn't know Des had any other kind." Steve nodded.

"What did the two of you talk about a week ago?" Steve sat back in the chair and crossed one leg over the other. When he glanced up, Stan was looking at him inquisitively.

"How do you know about that?" Stan poured more coffee from the percolator.

"His girlfriend Rowena said…." Steve flipped back several pages in the notebook and then read a line out loud.

"Yes, he was here just a week ago, he lived in LA but Des thought he had moved here recently." Steve held up the notebook.

"Yeah, I met with him. I heard he was off the junk and I went around to see if he needed my services. That is why I am here. I have good contacts in Hollywood, and I can hook guys up with recording sessions."

"So, you were going to manage, Desmond?" Stan shook his head vigorously.

"No, no, no, nothing like that. Desmond didn't believe in managers. I was just trying to set him up with some recording work. He said he already had an 'in' at the studios, and he didn't like going there anyway. So I let it drop. That was the last time I saw him." Steve flipped the notebook shut and stood to go. Stan stood up as well and led the way to the front door. Steve stopped and waited until Stan had turned around.

"Carl Fontana down at the union is curious why you didn't

stop in and put your name on the roles when you got into town."
Stan shrugged.

"I am in the personal management side of things, now. Don't
need a union card."

"Any idea why Sammy Sanderson would tell me you steal other
people's compositions?" Stan scowled and opened the front door.

"Because he is a nut case. If you talked to him, then you went
to his house, because he doesn't go anywhere else any more. Did
you see all those guys in the front room?" Steve nodded.

"Yeah, what about it?"

"They are the Southern Nevada Chapter of the John Birch
Society. So, I would say consider the source. He was a good picker,
but strictly derivative. I never heard an original melody come out of
that big jazz box he plays. You ask anyone else you run into, they
will tell you the same." Stan moved behind the door to let Steve
pass. Steve walked out onto the porch, hitched up his pants and
turned around.

"Thanks for the information. I may need to talk with you again,
you still going to be in town awhile?"

"Yeah, sure, I'm not going anywhere soon." Steve stepped off
the porch and returned the small wave from Stan as he closed
the door.

The steakhouse restaurant just inside the Mint Hotel was crowded
just after noon when Steve stood blinking at the entrance as his
eyes slowly adjusted to the dark interior. He looked up and down
the long rows of tables until he found what he was looking for. He
nodded at the hostess and took a menu from her hand as he made
his way to the very back of the restaurant. He stood in front of the
white linen covered table until Tam looked up from perusing the
menu. When he saw Steve, he snorted.

"If you came all the way downtown on the off chance I would

be here, I hope you at least have the decency to buy." Steve pulled a chair from an adjoining table and sat down.

"Sure, Tam, the least I can do. Especially since I know you have been working hard and have loads of information to share." Tam screwed up his face and took a sip of ice water. He put the glass down, reached into his suit pocket and pulled out a photo and dropped it in front of Steve. Steve picked it up and turned it right side up.

"Who is this ugly mug?"

"One Harris McCord, on the occasion of him being booked for selling heroin." Steve stared at the unshaven face and the dark eyebrows over the vacant eyes.

"Can I keep this?" Tam nodded and looked up as the waitress came to the table. She wore a cheery smile and a black western bolo tie at the collar of her white blouse.

"The usual, Mr. Polhaus?" Tam shook his finger.

"No, Gladys, I think that the New York would be the way to go today. Rare." He smiled at Steve who shrugged and handed the menu to Gladys.

"Make it two, ma'am, and two Coors beers, please." Gladys smiled again and left the table. Tam sat back in his chair and put his hands behind his head.

"I heard that you and Samuels had a date this morning. How did that go?" Steve could see that Tam was trying not to smile.

"The usual. Stay away from my case. Leave it to the professionals. Etc.,etc.,etc. You must have caught some flak today about it, yourself." Tam shook his head.

"Naw. After our meeting the other night, I figured most everything I said went in one ear and out the other with you, so I finally wised up and went to the chief. Told him what I thought about Samuels' take on the Rooney case. He agreed with me, and gave permission to provide you with anything we come up with. Your being right a few times recently has earned you a short stay of execution."

Tam grinned and popped several peanuts into his mouth from a small bowl that sat on the table between them. Steve sighed.

"I figured something was behind that little hijacking I had to endure this morning. How long you guys going to put up with this guy?" Steve shook his head and sat back in his chair as Gladys returned with two large platters which she set down heavily in front of them. Steve thanked her as she left and looked down at the large steak.

"This should last us awhile, Tam. So what else you got on the case." Tam had just forked a piece of the rare beef into his mouth. "Plenty." He chewed quickly and swallowed.

"After lunch, you can give me a ride back to the station and I will give you all the notes on the case up until now. Most of it is just routine interviews with the residents of the complex, but there was one I thought was interesting." Steve looked up from his steak.

"Yeah, what?" Tam balanced his knife on the edge of his plate.

"There was a guy across the complex from Desmond's apartment who claims he was out on his balcony that night and heard someone running along the sidewalk beneath his apartment about 12:30. He just caught a glimpse of the guy going around the corner and down the hall that leads to the south parking lot." Steve cut off another bit of the steak.

"Any other description?" Tam shook his head and resumed eating.

"No, just that it was definitely a guy and he was running pretty fast. It's all in the reports and the file." Steve nodded.

"You know anything about a guy named Sammy Sanderson, lives out in North Las Vegas?" Tam nodded as he finished chewing.

"When I was a patrol officer back in the late fifties, used to get calls to that house several times a year. Usually some sort of altercation between Sammy and his group and either communist agitators or reporters. You want to hear a little known fact? Most people think the FBI set up a field office here to keep tabs on the mob. In point of fact they first came here to monitor Sammy and his group.

Now there are fifteen agents plus a couple of undercover tax guys and they couldn't care less what Sammy and his merry men are up to. It's a strange world, sometimes. What has Sammy got to do with anything?" Tam ate the last bit of his steak and sat back in his chair.

"I don't know about all that, but when I stopped by to chat this morning, he was rather grumpy. He had a run-in with Desmond years ago. From what he told me and it wasn't much, he thinks Desmond had a thing going on with his wife." Tam scoffed.

"I never knew he had a wife. But I tried not to get to know him on a personal level. You think he was grumpy today, you should have dealt with him back then."

"Well, be that as it may, I don't really see him sticking Desmond. I will do a little more checking, but I am having trouble coming up with people that have some kind of viable motive in this deal." Tam chuckled.

"That's why you get the big money." They both laughed sardonically as Gladys returned to the table with the check and put it next to Steve's plate when Tam pointed in his direction.

"I'll meet you at the car, Tam, I saw someone on the way in that I need to say hello to." Steve walked to the cashier and paid the bill. He walked down the long row of tables and stopped at one where a couple was deep in conversation. He waited until the dark skinned woman glanced up at him and smiled. Steve stepped forward.

"I am sorry to disturb you, Miss Malone, I just wanted to say hello." He took the hand she offered and shook it briefly.

"I am glad you did. And I thought we decided last time we met it was Rita and Steve." Steve laughed. Rita gestured toward her companion.

"Steve, this is Special Agent Jacob Hurley. Mr. Hurley this is Steve Cannon, he is a private investigator." Steve reached down and offered his hand. The young agent shook it and smiled up at Steve.

"I am glad to meet you, Mr. Cannon, but your reputation has proceeded you. I think I heard Agent Brady speak of you, in connection with the Sorelli case, if I am not mistaken." Steve nodded and took a step back from the table.

"Yes, that would be me. You tell him I remember him well when you see him." He looked over at Rita.

"Good to see you again, Rita, give me a call sometime, I am working on something that might make a good story. Nice to meet you, Mr. Hurley." Rita smiled as Steve backed away from the table and gave a small parting wave before he turned and exited the restaurant onto the street. Tam was standing on the sidewalk, his hands in his pockets.

"You forgot to tell me where you parked, so I waited for you here." He looked back into the restaurant. "Who is the black woman you were talking to?"

"Her name is Rita Malone, we met last summer during the Sorelli mess, she works for Hank Greenspun at the Sun and wrote a couple stories and she would check her facts with me now and then." Tam nodded and fell in behind Steve as he led the way down the sidewalk to where he had parked the Jeep.

"Know the guy she was with?" Steve turned and looked back over his shoulder at Tam.

"No, just met him. FBI agent."

"Yeah, and he was brought in to investigate somebody we both know, whose initials are T.C." Steve stopped and looked at Tam.

"How do you know this?" Tam smirked and spotting the Jeep three cars down the block, walked past Steve and waited at the Jeep for him to catch up.

"Because I was part of all that unpleasantness last summer, I had to submit to several interviews when he came on board in October. I put two and two together from the angle that the questions were coming at me. He circled around to every answer that even remotely involved Tommy and recast the question in a different way. They also got a tail on Tommy, which is why I had to report that he showed up at the same diner I did the other night before they called me on the carpet for it. You might have just met him, but he already knew you on sight, I would bet on it." Steve unlocked the car for Tam and walked around to the driver's side. When he climbed in, he looked over at Tam.

"That might explain a few things."

"Like what?" Steve shrugged.

"Maybe why Tommy is all of a sudden so gung ho to go legit." Tam snorted derisively.

"He doesn't even know what the word means. To guys like Tommy, legit means coming up with a scheme so tight there is no chance of getting caught." Steve shook his head.

"Someone or something has spooked him. I think he sees the changes coming to this town and wants to get out while the getting is good." Tam looked at the end of the casinos passing by as Steve turned off of Fremont Street and headed for the police center and was silent for the last two blocks before Steve pulled the Jeep into a parking space near the entrance to the building. Tam looked over as Steve turned off the engine. Steve saw the serious look on Tam's face and settled back into the seat and waited.

"You better watch yourself, Steve. There are a lot of ugly cross-currents going on in this town right now and it can be too easy to get caught up in them. Between the Feds and the Gaming Commission, the screws are getting turned tighter on the wise guys. There are already rumors of trouble between Tommy's organization and two of the other groups on the strip. Pretty soon they are going to be like a big school of sharks swimming around in the same pool with not enough to eat. You get my drift?" Steve nodded thoughtfully and looked out the windshield at two cops walking out of the front entrance. One was the cop who had driven Samuels around earlier.

"I know what you mean, Tam." He glanced over at the detective. He looked much older to Steve than he did several months ago. "I will be more careful, I promise you." Tam shrugged, nodded and opened the car door.

"Come on. Let's get you those files, so you can save the world."

They grinned at each other as they made their way to the front of the building.

*

As he drove west on East Sahara Boulevard, Steve could see the Sahara Hotel disappearing in his rear view mirror. After two miles he turned into a large parking lot and stopped the Jeep underneath the huge purple sign: 'Fantastic Fair'. He strolled across the lot and entered the warm store and headed past the checkout stands to the very back and into the sporting goods section. He was looking at a glass case filled with knives when a young clerk offered to help him.

"Can I show you one of the knives, sir?" Steve nodded and pointed to one in the corner.

"That big Buck knife there. Do you know how long that blade is?" The clerk slid open the case from behind, pulled out the knife and looked at the tag attached to the sheath.

"Eight inches, sir." He handed the knife to Steve who slipped it out from the sheath and held the silver blade up to the light. He ran his finger over the serrated edge on the top just in front of the tang and then looked at the price tag.

"You sell many of these?" He replaced the knife in the sheath but didn't hand it back to the clerk. The clerk shrugged.

"I don't know, I haven't sold any and that particular one has been here as long as I have worked in this department."

"How long's that been?"

"Five months." Steve nodded.

"I'll take this one."

After purchasing the knife, Steve stopped in the model department and bought a can of fluorescent orange paint. He threw the knife and the paint on the front seat of the Jeep and headed back to the Westchester apartments.

He drove around the apartment complex twice before he settled on a parking place near the trash dumpsters, out of sight of most of the cars parked against the perimeter of the building. He opened the back of the Jeep and dropped the lift gate. He pulled a long piece of cardboard from the back seat and returned to the rear of the car holding it along with the knife and the can of paint. He took the knife from the sheath and laid it on the cardboard. After shaking the can for a few seconds, he coated the knife with the paint sweeping smoothly back and forth over the blade and the handle. He carefully turned the knife over and repeated the process on the other side. He closed the back and took the paint can back with him to the front seat. He pulled out a pack of cigarettes and lit one with a zippo lighter he carried in the glove compartment.

Twenty minutes later the knife was dry to the touch. Steve slipped it inside the paper bag that had held the paint can and locked the Jeep. He placed the bag under his coat and entered the complex. He stood on the far side of the pool and looked at Desmond's apartment. There were two hallways leading to the parking area near unit number 10. One was twenty feet away on the right if you were coming out of the door, the other was fifty feet away on the left. Steve walked down the first one and stood in the alley between the apartment building and an eight foot cinderblock fence. He looked down the alley toward where the second hallway connected to the parking lot and noticed that directly across from where it came out of the complex was a large trash dumpster tucked in behind a U shaped section of the eight foot wall. He strolled casually over to the alcove and standing just behind the wall he looked back at the apartment building. From where he stood he was only visible to three windows on the second floor and they all appeared to be frosted bathroom windows. Steve placed one foot on the side of the dumpster and reaching up to hold on to the top of the wall, he hoisted himself up until he could see over the barrier. A quarter mile in the distance he saw another apartment complex, in between there was only desert. He climbed down and stood beside the dumpster with his back against the wall. He slipped the knife from the bag, held it by the tip and taking three quick steps to the far wall he threw the knife as far out over the wall as he could.

It arched out over the desert falling end over end until it disappeared from sight. He stuffed the bag in his coat pocket and quickly scaled the eight foot fence and dropped down softly on the other side. The desert was not flat but full of dirt mounds and debris left from the construction of the apartment building. There was a large pile of empty beer bottles and colored streamers up against the wall from someone's New Year's Eve party. Steve started walking slowly around the mounds of dirt in the general direction he had seen the knife fall. After fifty yards he saw it laying near a patch of weeds, it was covered in dirt where the paint was still tacky. Steve stabbed the blade into the dirt and took a long yellow streamer he had taken from the trash pile out of his pocket. He tied it to the handle and let it tail out in the cold breeze. Steve gazed back at the apartment building and using landmarks on the building as his guide he divided the area fifty yards to either side of the knife into ten yard wide corridors. Figuring that the probabilities were better there, he started with the two sections closest to the spot where the knife had come down. He walked each section twice. Once to the wall and once more back to the knife. When he came to a mound or clump of bushes, he made a thorough search of the whole area. He was making his second pass on the third section north of the knife and the streamer when he saw something to his left under a yellow bush that momentarily caught the pale sun and glinted for a brief second. Steve knelt down and probed the ground beneath the dead plant. His fingers touched the cold steel of the blade. Steve stood up and tied another streamer, this time a red one, to the dead bush. He covered the thirty yards to the bright orange knife and the yellow streamer quickly. He wrapped both up in the paper bag and secured them in a zippered pocket inside his jacket. He climbed over the wall and walked to the red Jeep fifty yards away. He stashed the knife and the can of paint under the front seat and threw the cardboard into one of the dumpsters on his way back into the apartment complex.

Steve knocked on unit number 10 for several minutes before Rowena opened the door a few inches and looked out.

"Rowena, I need to use your phone for a few minutes." He stood with his hands in his pockets only a foot away from the door. Rowena cinched the belt tighter on her blue terry cloth bathrobe and opened the door, standing behind it as Steve walked inside. She pointed to the table between the two chairs.

"Right over there, what is this about?" Steve turned to her as he picked up the receiver.

"I may have found the knife that was used to kill Desmond." He studied her face as she walked over to the chair. Slumping down into it, she covered he mouth with her hand and shook her head. She looked up at Steve.

"Where?" Steve swiftly dialed a number and looked down at the young woman.

"I'll show you later." He straightened up.

"Yes. Let me speak to Detective Samuels please." As he waited, he looked out through the picture window. From the far side of the pool, the manager was standing with her hands on her hips staring in the direction of the apartment. After a few seconds she turned and went back inside.

"Samuels? Cannon here. What are you doing right now?" Steve snorted. "That can wait. I think I have your murder weapon. Yeah, it was here all the time." Steve looked back out the window for a few seconds.

"No, you are going to have to come over here to see it yourself." Samuels' reedy voice squawked through the ear piece.

"If you want, I can just leave it where it is and the guys you had here who couldn't come up with squat the first time can look until Easter and still not find it. What's it going to be?" There was a short pause.

"Fine, I'll be here. Meet me in the parking area back of Desmond's apartment. Yeah. Twenty minutes." Steve hung up the phone. He sat down in the other chair facing Rowena. Her dark eyes studied his face.

"How did you know where to find it?" Steve glanced quickly out the window but there was no one to be seen.

"I didn't exactly. I just tried to think like someone who had done something very bad and had to get rid of the evidence in a hurry. But let's talk about something else. The police report says that Desmond's wallet was empty. Did he have some cash in there?"

"Yes, he always had some, and he also had a fifty dollar bill folded and hidden in one of the compartments for emergencies. When they gave me the wallet back it was still there." She shook her head vigorously and her black hair which had been piled on top of her head, cascaded down onto her shoulders. She pushed the fingers of both hands back through her hair and crossed to the small counter that separated the living room and the kitchen. She tested a silver percolator with her palm to see if it was still warm and then poured some dark tea into a cup.

"Have you noticed anything else missing since then?" Rowena shook her head. Steve stood up and looked over at her.

"The report also said that there was $150 in cash in a drawer in the room where Desmond was found. Is that right?" Rowena nodded and took a sip of the tea.

"Desmond always put some there so that if I needed money for something I wouldn't have to ask." Steve nodded his head as he walked to the door.

"If I were you I would get dressed. I have a feeling that the cops are going to have more questions for you soon. Thanks for the use of the phone." He let himself out and stood in front of the apartment for a few minutes smoking a cigarette. He walked across the complex, retrieved the Jeep and parked it by the dumpster he had used to climb over the wall.

Twenty minutes later, two black and white police cars turned the corner and came toward Steve who was leaning up against his car. One passed him, pulled into a parking space, backed out and parked directly behind the Jeep. The other with Samuels in the front passenger seat stopped directly in front of the Jeep blocking him in. Steve shook his head and watched as Samuels and six uniformed cops surrounded him. Samuels walked over to Steve with his hands thrust deep into his raincoat. He stood several feet away so that he would not have to tip his head back at such a severe angle to look up at Steve.

"So let's have it Cannon." He was trying to keep his voice low in front of the men. Steve laughed and shook his head. Samuels took a quick step forward, but then thought better of it and took two steps back instead.

"Do you think I would pick up a suspected murder weapon? Do you always judge everyone else's level of competency by your own shortcomings?" Steve placed a slight emphasis on the word 'short'. Samuels ignored the remark.

"Then where is it, Cannon? Or is this another one of your deflections?"

"It's out there Samuels, but you are going to have to get someone to give you a big boost over that wall there if you want to see it in situ." Steve moved his head in the direction of the wall. Samuels looked over at the wall and then turned to the cop who had stopped Steve that morning.

"Move that dumpster over against the wall." The cop indicated the wall to another one standing nearby and together they wheeled the large metal container up to the wall. Samuels walked over as one of the cops bent over and made a cradle out of his hands for Samuels to step into. Samuels put his left foot into the cop's hands and reaching up, pulled himself up onto the top of the dumpster. When he had steadied himself and was looking out over the desert, Steve spoke again.

"If you look straight out you will see a yellow bush with a red streamer tied to it. The knife is almost completely buried under that bush." Samuels indicated for one of the cops to climb up onto the dumpster. He also turned and waved to the car he had come in.

A pudgy civilian emerged from the front seat. He was carrying a large leather bag and was dressed in yellow coveralls. He moved to the wall and was helped up onto the garbage bin and then over the wall. Steve heard him slide down the other side and plop in a heap in the middle of the beer bottles. Samuels stayed on the dumpster, one foot on the wall and gestured for the other cop to accompany the forensic expert out to where the knife lay.

Steve opened his car door, climbed inside and lit a cigarette. Several minutes later, he watched as the cop standing with Samuels helped both of the men back over the wall. Samuels's forensic expert had torn his coveralls and one of his knees was bleeding. When they had all reconvened at the squad car parked in front of Steve's Jeep, Samuels placed the plastic bag holding the knife on the hood of the car. Steve could see but not hear the discussion that ensued. Samuels packed the knife inside the leather bag and the forensic expert and most of the other cops climbed into the car in front of Steve and backed up the thirty yards down the alleyway and disappeared around the corner. Samuels stepped to the side of Steve's car and bending over, peered in..

"You got until tomorrow morning to come up with a good story to explain how you just happened to know that knife was there. We'll know by then if it is the murder weapon in question. Be in my office by nine tomorrow or I will get a warrant issued. And if you know a good attorney, I would put him on retainer today." Samuels straightened up and without waiting for a reply strode to the car blocking Steve from behind. He climbed into the front seat and stared at Steve through the windshield. Steve adjusted the rear view mirror so he could see the silhouette of Samuels's gray fedora. He pulled out a fresh pack of Pall Malls and took his time lighting up. When it was clear to Samuels that Steve was not leaving anytime soon, he directed the driver to back up and go around. Steve snorted to himself as the big black and white Ford swerved around him and with the brake lights flashing, slowed briefly at the corner of the building and was gone.

JANUARY 7

The gray light that reflected through the white curtains woke Steve from another nightmare. He lay on his back and watched the green jungle fade before his eyes on the ceiling above him. He felt the sweat trickle off his chin and pool onto his chest. The nightmares were always different but they all came from the same night in 1943, from the ridge on Guadalcanal where he and his marine platoon fought off three successive waves of desperate Japanese infantry. Four friends of his died that night and several others including Steve were wounded.

Several minutes later he had controlled his breathing. He rose and took a shower. When he came back into the bedroom to dress he noticed that it was already 7:30. He was preparing coffee in the kitchen when the phone rang. Steve reached over to the wall beside the stove and lifted the receiver.

"Steve Cannon? This is Jim Larson. I am sorry I was unable to return your call from last evening, I hope it wasn't something urgent." Steve smiled into the receiver when he heard the calm voice of the Assistant District Attorney.

"No. No problem, Mr. Larson. There was just a small personal matter I wanted to get your advice on."

"Shoot"

"I have been summoned down to Detective Samuels' office this morning to answer some questions concerning a case he and I are both investigating. I wonder if you have a few minutes to stop by and sit in?" He heard the District Attorney chuckle softly.

"Is Samuels being his thorough self again?" Steve smiled at the sarcastic tone.

"Yes, he seems to like me for every unsolved crime that comes across his desk. In this case I figured out where the murder weapon had to be, I found it and he is not happy."

"Well, I can put a call in to the chief if you want and you can avoid the trip."

"No, I'd rather show up whichever way it goes. Perhaps I should retain counsel." Jim Larson laughed softly.

"No. Don't go to all that expense and trouble. I will meet you at his office just before nine. It shouldn't take too long to get this sorted out."

"Thanks, Jim, I will owe you one." Steve hung up the phone, stretched and yawned. Shaking his head, he put the coffee away and called Bernie to see if he wanted a breakfast companion.

Steve looked down at his plate of bacon and eggs as Bernie sat across from him and spoke on the phone. Since Steve had arrived, Bernie had taken at least six calls, all concerning the details of the upcoming memorial. Bernie wrote down yet another airplane arrival time and hung up the phone.

"Geez, I oughta be in the travel business. I know all the plane schedules by heart. Eat. Don't wait for me, your eggs are getting cold." Steve smiled and dug into the plate of food as Bernie refilled their coffee cups. He sat back and looked at Steve for several seconds.

"How come this cop Samuels always gets away with giving you a hard time? Doesn't he answer to anybody?" Bernie shook his head.

"No, Bernie, he is the star down there. Got everyone thinking that he is the best criminal mind since Sherlock Holmes. Got a lot of other cops covering for him and turning a blind eye. As my father used to say: 'Fair is just two weeks in the summertime.' " Bernie snorted a reply.

"About time some justice was done around here. When the wise guys are more trustworthy than the cops, you know we are all doomed." They looked at each other for a brief second and then both broke out laughing. Steve finished his breakfast and accepted another cup of coffee from Bernie. While Bernie poured it, Steve glanced through the notes Bernie had been scribbling when he was on the phone.

"Bernie, it looks like most of these guys are arriving between two and three thirty. Why don't I drop by here before that and I can make several trips for you, help you schlep these schmos." Bernie laughed so hard the coffee almost sloshed from the carafe in his hand.

"What are you now? Jewish? But, yeah, that would be a big help. We should be done by four and the stragglers I will leave to Walter and Rocco." Steve looked at his watch.

"Thanks for breakfast, Bern, I have to leave now or I'll be late for the inquisition. I will see later this afternoon." Bernie walked with him to the door.

"Make sure you and Remy show on Friday night. You are sitting with me at my table, OK?"

"Sure, Bernie, that sounds great."

Steve left the deli and swung the big Jeep onto Las Vegas Boulevard and headed downtown.

Tam was sitting in his office surrounded by several stacks of paperwork when Steve rapped on his open door a few minutes before nine. Tam looked up but didn't smile.

"Well, if it isn't the number one suspect. Why didn't you come to me with your little scavenger hunt? I could've vouched for you." Steve slipped into the green vinyl chair in front of Tam's desk.

"No, that wouldn't have accomplished anything except get you in hot water too. I thought through the consequences, believe me, but there was no way I was leaving that knife out in the desert. Maybe this is too personal with me, but I can't help that." Tam sat back and swiveled his chair sideways and gazed at Steve over the piles of paperwork.

"So, how did you figure out where the knife was?"

"It was just basic deduction after looking at the layout and making a few assumptions. The key was the guy on his balcony seeing someone running through the complex on the opposite side of where you would expect it. So, I ask myself, why would the murderer, if that was who this was, be running on that side? Wouldn't he have taken the quickest route out of the complex? The answer seemed to be that he would be going that way, because once he had concealed himself in the dumpster area and ditched the knife, that way was the quickest route out to where I assume he parked his car. I have been to those apartments at least four times now and it is obvious there are not enough parking spaces for the number of residents, so it is a normal occurrence that the only open spaces might be on the far side of the complex from your apartment. If his car was parked over there, the shortest way out would have been cutting straight across the grounds around the pool. So…" Steve looked at his watch.

"Well, wish me luck." He stood and saluted Tam before he went out the door and turned right toward Samuels' office. Tam grunted and returned to his paperwork.

When he rapped on the closed door to Samuels' office, he could hear raised voices inside that stopped a few seconds later. The door swung open and a red faced Samuels glared out of the opening at Steve. Steve brushed by him.

"Good morning to you too." He said sarcastically to the man behind him as he smiled at DA Larsen who was sitting behind Samuels' desk. Jim Larsen smiled at Steve and gestured to one of the two chairs in front of the desk. Samuels' office was nearly twice as big as Tam's and much better furnished with chairs that had fabric cushions. Steve sat down and reached across the desk and took the ashtray that Jim was holding out to him. Steve looked up at Samuels who was still standing by the open door.

"You don't mind if I smoke, right?" Samuels didn't reply but closed the door and leaned against the wall next to it. His complexion and demeanor suggested he was not happy. Larsen sighed and looked over at Samuels.

"Sit down, Detective, this is a meeting, not a playground donnybrook." Samuels shot a disgusted look at Steve and unfolding his arms he slid off the wall and sat in the other chair. Steve lit the cigarette he had been holding in his hand while Samuels was seating himself. He used his own zippo lighter, the one he had carried in the war, to light his Pall Mall. He carefully slid the battered case into his front pants pocket, exhaled and looked coolly across at Samuels. Larsen sat forward and addressed Steve.

"I came in early, I hope you don't mind, Steve, to get this meeting started out on the right foot. So suppose we began this phase by you telling us exactly what your thinking was and how you came to find the knife in the desert." Steve nodded, took a package from the pocket of his jacket and laid it on the desk in front of Jim Larsen. As the DA unwrapped the package and revealed the fluorescent orange painted knife, Steve recounted his thoughts and actions much as he had minutes before to the detective down the hall.

When he was finished he sat back in his chair and carefully ignoring the glare from the chair beside him, lit his second cigarette of the day. Larsen, who had been taking notes as Steve spoke, now looked over at Samuels.

"Well, Detective, you have just heard the other side of the story. Are you prepared to concede that everything that Mr. Cannon has done in this case is above board?" Samuels snorted and glared at Steve.

"No, Mr. Attorney, I'm not. All we know for sure is that the knife in question has been found to be the murder weapon, and even though it has been wiped clean of fingerprints, I still stand by my earlier statements." The DA leaned across the table and his eyes narrowed as he stared Samuels down. The detective opened his mouth to protest, but Larsen got there first.

"I am about to take a step that in all my thirteen years in this job I have never taken. And you, Detective Samuels have no one to blame but yourself. From this moment on, I am taking control of the file on this case. You will report to me, and I will decide how our resources are to be deployed. I am also hiring Mr. Cannon here as a special investigator assigned to my office on this case, and he will be paid appropriately. Did I make myself clear, Mr. Samuels, or do you need me to repeat myself?" The attorney leaned forward out of his chair for emphasis. Samuels' eyes became slits and a vein in his reddened temple throbbed, as he glared at the man behind his desk, but he did not reply.

"I need an answer, mister." Larsen's voice raised several decibels.

"Yes, Sir!" Samuels sputtered as he stood up from the chair, his fists clenched. Larsen leaned back in his chair and smiled.

"Very well, Detective, you need to take a walk around the block and cool down, and don't come back until you do." Larsen pointed to the door. Samuels spun on his heels and opened the door, turned and started to say something, then stepped into the hallway instead.

"Shut the door please, Detective." Jim Larson's voice boomed down the hall. When Samuels had shut the door and left, Larsen sat back down again behind the desk and handed Steve a thick file.

"I came in early and pulled these for you. I checked it myself to make sure it is all legible. Hopefully there is some information in there that you can use. What other resources do you need at this point?" Steve hefted the file and flipped through the first few pages.

"I probably won't know until I can put some time in on this, but I do have a request. Can Detective Polhaus be temporarily assigned to this case as a liaison officer?" Larsen leaned back and placed both hands behind his head.

"I don't see why not, provided Mr. Polhaus is of the same mind and agrees. I will speak to the chief, it shouldn't be a problem." Steve smiled.

"Leave that to me, Mr. Larsen." Jim nodded and then grew serious again.

"I have heard some rumors that Samuels is a cop who....let me use the right phrase here...cuts corners. If that is so, I intend to stop him. What if anything, do you know about this?" Steve opened his palms.

"Just rumors, much like yourself."

"Well suppose you tell me what those rumors are. Unofficially and off the record, of course." Steve stubbed out his cigarette in Samuels ashtray and exhaled.

"Unofficially I will say this: If you want to get the lowdown on Samuels, get in touch with his old department in LA. Also, if you have any good contacts in the FBI, he is an ex agent and the word is that there is no love lost, if you know what I mean."

"I know what you mean, Steve. My brother-in-law is an FBI agent and has just been assigned to the Las Vegas field office. Perhaps I will ask his opinion. His name is Jacob Hurley." Steve nodded absent-mindedly and didn't react visibly to the name.

"Thanks again, Jim, I appreciate the effort you expended to save my skin again. Let's hope this is the last time."

Jim Larsen stood up behind the desk and extended his hand. Steve looked him in the eye and nodded. "Let's hope the rest of your day is a little more peaceful." The DA laughed.

"Yours too, Mr. Cannon. I will clear some time on my schedule Monday morning. Please drop by with Detective Polhaus and give me an update. Would that be OK with you?"

"Sure. We'll be there." Steve opened the door.

"See ya, Jim." Steve stepped into the hallway and closed the door behind him. He swung the thick file into his right hand and five steps later he knocked on Detective Polhaus' door.

"Come in." Steve opened the door in response to the muffled reply. He stood in the doorway and smiled broadly. Tam looked up and shoved his reading glasses to the top of his forehead.

"That was quick. You aren't in cuffs, so I assume you can close that door behind you and leave the building of your own free will." Steve took two steps into the office and held up the file. Tam's brow furrowed.

"What is that? Is that Samuels' case file?" Steve shook his head slowly from side to side.

"No, my friend, it is our file now. Or more precisely, it is District Attorney Larsen's file and he has granted you one of your life long wishes." The frown on Detective Polhaus' face deepened.

"And what would that be, I am almost afraid to ask?" Steve's face broke into an oversized grin.

"That you and I get to work together on a case officially." Tam sat back and tossed his glasses on the desk in disgust.

"And whose bright idea was this?"

"Partly mine and partly Larsen's. He will get the official OK from the Chief this afternoon, unless of course you have an objection." Tam sighed and slumped in the chair.

"No, of course not, why would I?"

"Don't be so glum, chum, it will only be half as bad as you think." Steve walked to the door.

"I am going to review the file tonight. I suggest you do the same. We meet tomorrow morning at Bob's Big Boy for breakfast and to compare notes."

"Aye, aye, sir." Tam's tone dripped with sarcasm.

"That's the spirit Tammy boy. See you tomorrow." Steve spun on his heels and closed the door quickly. Ten seconds later he was outside the building and heading for his car.

Steve drove the four blocks to the Golden Nugget. He pulled into the back parking lot and waited while a large linen van finished loading and left. He wheeled the Jeep into the only vacant employee parking spot and shut off the engine. He left the driver's seat and went to the passenger side and retrieved the heavy file. With the file tucked securely under his arm he entered the back door and walked down a long carpeted hallway, descended a short flight of stairs, skirted the edge of the casino and entered the coffee shop.

He found a table in the back near a partition that offered a small bit of privacy even though the coffee shop had very few customers. He shed his jacket and draped it over the chair next to the one he sat down in. He caught the eye of a waitress he knew and held up a cup from the place setting in front of him. When she returned with a carafe he had already separated the file into several stacks.

"Hi Hazel, how have you been? Daryl treating you right?" The short round waitress smiled as she poured coffee into Steve's cup.

"Yep. You bet. And the two of you both know what will happen if he doesn't." They both laughed.

"Is Nick here yet?" Hazel shook her head.

"If he is, he hasn't been in here. He's been coming in at eleven or twelve and staying later." Steve nodded his thanks and took a long sip of the coffee. Hazel set the carafe on the other side of the table that wasn't covered with papers.

"I'll just leave this here, Steve. Let me know if you need anything else."

"I will, Hazel, thanks." A few minutes later, Steve got up and walked to a side buffet and unplugged a white phone. He brought it back over to the table and found a receptacle in the wall next to his seat. He dialed Remy's number.

Steve heard her low voice after the third ring.

"Hi Gem, how is your morning going?"

"I am doing OK, Steve. I'm trying to get a handle on the production side of things. The first step is the hardest. Just trying to figure out what I need. How are things with you?"

"Swell. Mostly the usual. I called to see if you were free tonight and if I could take you to the House of Lords for dinner?"

"Of course I am free. That sounds lovely. What time should I be ready?"

"I will pick you up at seven-thirty. Is that Ok?"

"Perfect. I will be ready."

After Steve hung up the phone, he began to spread the contents of the files out on the large table. The file that DA Larsen had given him was almost an inch thicker than the one Tam had provided, but Tam's was organized and the most important sections were together. He first read all the interviews that had been conducted in the early morning hours just after the discovery of the body. He put Rowena's questioning to one side. He would cross check it later with his own notes for consistency. He sifted carefully through all of the notes and the interviews on Harris McCord. Samuels had taken his finger prints, but had neglected to check his hands and clothing for blood. The search of his apartment had taken place while they were taking him into custody and securing him in the police car. It had been cursory at best, and Steve could find nothing in the notes to suggest that the apartment had been reentered. Samuels had questioned Harris for three hours, the last two with a public defender present. Steve wrote the name of the attorney into his notebook. Samuels had insisted that Harris tell his version of the events three times verbally, the last one was a written statement. All four were almost identical. Steve frowned as he read the written statement, comparing it word for word with the previous ones. In most cases, a suspect in custody for that long, and under stress would show more variance in their versions, the longer the duration of the interviews, the more pronounced the differences became, if only because more details come back to the person answering the questions. Harris McCord's interviews showed definite signs of memorization, and that might also explain the locked door. Anyone truly concerned would not pound on an unlocked door for ten minutes, and someone who had committed the murder would not want to be the one to discover the body. But if Harris was the killer, why run all the way to the other side of the complex before returning to act the part of the concerned neighbor? Steve was mulling over the possibilities when the white courtesy phone beside him rang. He looked at it for a few seconds before he picked it up.

"Steve, this is Nick. I heard you were in the house, got some time to share a cup of coffee?"

"Sure, Nick. I wanted a quiet place to look over some files, but

I also wanted to see you as well. Come on down." Steve hung up the phone and smiled.

Nick Montero was a fixture on the downtown casino scene. If there was a job he hadn't worked in a casino, it was either a new one or one that was non-essential or both. Since he was a young teenager, the Basque had been part of Fremont Street. He now owned a fair percentage of the Golden Nugget, but much like Wilbur Clark at the Desert Inn, he didn't get a commensurate share of the profits. That honor belonged to the group of mobsters who had swung the loan from the Central States Pension Fund that had renovated the casino and built the new tower of rooms. Still, it all ran like clockwork because of him, and unlike a lot of front man owners, Nick had a free hand to run his floor and his games as he saw fit, as long as the house percentage supported the large amount of money that was shipped back east. Steve looked up when the muscular older man appeared at the edge of his table.

"Steve, you need an office. I got plenty of space here, but I hear that you and Bernie Gold have worked a deal on his new casino out in the sticks and you are going to be the Head of Security." Nick plopped down in a chair across from Steve and looked at the small stacks of paper that covered the table. Steve chuckled at Nick's swipe at the Strip, there was always an attitude in the downtown casinos that they had invented Las Vegas and that the Strip 'carpet joints' were interlopers.

"Information travels fast, Nick and the more inaccurate it is, the faster it goes. Bernie and I are great friends and I will help him in any way I can to get his shop up and running, but I haven't agreed to anything permanent and I wouldn't agree to anything like that before I came to you." Nicks' mouth turned down as he nodded.

"I appreciate that, Steve, but what is more important to me is that my friends and the people I work with are healthy and happy in what they do. Sometimes that means the short end for me, but it is always give and take, and it all evens out in the end." He reached over and playfully cuffed Steve on the shoulder. Steve smiled at the gesture.

"You haven't called me to help you out recently. I know I was out of action most of the end of last year, but I am ready anytime you see the need." Nick smiled and nodded.

"I know you are, Steve, but the 'quiet' partners hired some talent away from the Tropicana and the Sands and the cheaters and card counters have gone elsewhere for now." Steve poured some coffee from the carafe that Hazel had left into a fresh cup that sat at the edge of the table and passed it over to Nick.

"You heard about any rumbling out on the Strip? Specifically between Carmino's group and the Sands?" Nick poured a small stream of milk into his coffee and slowly stirred the mixture.

"No, haven't heard about that, but the guys here stay strictly to themselves and the boss back east rotates them out of here regularly, which I wholeheartedly support, that way nobody is around long enough to start figuring angles, know what I mean?" Steve nodded over his coffee cup as Nick continued. "But I did hear through the grapevine that there is a high level investigation of Tommy and some of his activities that got started last summer because of the Sorelli thing, and based on what they found then, there are several new avenues they are pursuing. Probably not news to him, but if you see him, you might give him the word."

"I might just do that, Nick." Nick lowered his voice.

"So what is the story with Angelo Sorelli, you just going to let him get away with all the crap he pulled?" Nick's face had changed color and his lower jaw was set. Steve looked back into Nick's eyes with a blank expression.

"I'm working on it, Nick. I doubt that he has moved back here and taken up residence, so I have to fit that in with all the other irons I have in the fire. He also has three million and change that he can do a lot of hiding with, so it isn't going to happen overnight." Nick was not mollified.

"I can put you in touch with some guys that can help you out if you want." Steve shook his head.

"I got Jack and Tam. I would rather have guys that were directly involved and lost the most in that mess, so, yeah, like I said, Nick, I am working on it." Nick sat back in the chair and changed the subject.

"So how is Skipper? I haven't seen him since he went to get dried out last summer." Steve was pleased that Nick remembered. If there was one good thing that came out of the whole sorry Angelo Sorelli mess, it was that Skipper had decided to stop the downward spiral his life had taken since the war and had voluntarily gone into treatment for his alcoholism. Steve was looking forward to reuniting with his boyhood friend.

"He's doing good, Nick. He completed the program and hasn't had a drink since August, so that is good. The counselors where he was convinced him that coming back to Las Vegas too soon was dangerous, so he is living in a halfway house for recovered alcoholics at least until summer. After that, we'll see. Bernie and I are putting our heads together and will come up with a plan that we hope will keep him moving in a straight line." Nick smiled and nodded.

"Good. I am glad to hear that, Steve, I know how much he means to you. I gotta run, but I want you to come out to the house on Sunday the 24th. Margaret is throwing my sixtieth birthday bash. I want you to be there, and I want you to bring Remy. Margaret is dying to meet her." Steve stood up with Nick and clasped his hand over the table.

"Sure, Nick, I look forward to it. I don't think I have been out to the new house. Rancho Circle is a little out of my orbit." Nick laughed as he turned from the table.

"It's just a house payment, Steve, nothing more, nothing less." He chuckled as he swept past Hazel and patted her on the arm before he disappeared around the corner.

As Steve started to sit down, the coffee in his half-filled cup began to slosh gently against the sides. He felt a small tremor along the floor that grew slightly in intensity and then died away. Steve sat down and looked around at the other patrons that been seated in his section over the last half hour. The tourists carried on with their normal conversations. He smiled at Hazel who had stopped in her tracks with two glasses of iced tea in her hands. Unless you were a native and aware of them, the underground nuclear tests at the Nevada Test Site, just north of Las Vegas and the Sheep Range Mountains usually went unnoticed.

It was just after one o'clock when Bernie and Steve made their first run to the airport. Bernie's plan was that Steve would drop him off at the terminal, and Bernie would corral the first group of musicians, get them their luggage and send them out to Steve who would make the thirty minute round trip run to the Desert Inn, arriving back in time to ferry the next group. In the event that too many arrived at once, Bernie had another guy that worked for him, Rocco, waiting to pick up the slack. On the way to the airport, Steve had turned into the D.I. and was glad to see that his old friend, Shelly Cointreu, was on shift as a doorman. He briefed him on the operation and Shelly had enlisted a front desk crew to meet each musician as they were dropped off, check them in and get them to their rooms with as little fanfare as possible. On his second trip from the airport, Steve had Chet Baker, Coleman Hawkins and Stan Getz, all in the car at the same time. Steve smiled to himself as the good natured banter flowed back and forth between the jazz greats. Steve made sure that he personally carried all their instruments up to the rooms and made sure everyone was comfortable with the accommodations before heading back to the airport. As usual, Bernie had planned the operation perfectly, and Steve was able to make five trips in total with Rocco only required to make the last one with Bernie and Miles Davis.

It was nearly four when Steve pulled up in front of his house. The gray skies and the lowering sun cast a pale light on the mountains to the east. He quickly showered and put on a blue suit with a light blue shirt and dark burgundy tie. As he drove quickly back toward the strip, he pulled down the visor to block out the orange glare from the setting sun.

*

It was growing dark as Steve pulled into the parking lot in front of Bernie's deli for the fourth time that day. The dinner crowd did not usually began arriving until six and the deli only had five or six customers when Steve walked through the door. There was still plenty of action going on in the adjacent casino, and the gambling noise seemed louder than usual in the quiet restaurant. Steve waited at the counter until Walter came through the large swinging doors that lead to the kitchen. He was carrying a pan of roasted chickens and he chuckled when he saw Steve.

"You should get a Sheriffs' card from downtown and punch in on the clock." Steve laughed and nodded.

"You are right, Walter. I think it is part of Bernie's plan to keep the two of us working for him forever."

"Go on in, he got back twenty minutes ago." Steve knocked quickly on the large double doors and then entered. Bernie was tucking in a large white sheet he had draped over a big object on the bar. Steve joined him there and pointed at the large silhouette that covered most of the surface of the bar.

"What is that?"

"Something for later. If we get that far. It's a surprise." Steve laughed, shook his head and sat down at the large green felt covered table that held three glasses and two bottles of Johnny Walker Red scotch. Bernie joined him.

"Thanks for all your help this afternoon. Getting your friend, Shelly involved was a big help. He got everybody set up in no time flat." Bernie took a few steps back and looked at his friend. "I don't think I have seen you in a suit for years. You should buy more and wear them more often. You look like a perfect Head of Security to me." Steve waved him off and sat down at the table.

"Yeah, Shelly being there was a stroke of luck. What can I do to help you tomorrow night?" Bernie shook his head.

"Nothing. That is all being worked out as we speak. Quincy Jones is setting up the program and they will rehearse a little tonight and then for a few hours tomorrow. Just come and be a part of it."

"Sure, that will be easy." The phone on the far end of bar lit up and buzzed. Bernie walked over and picked up the receiver.

"Sure, send him in." He hung up the phone and turned to Steve.

"Tommy is here." The door opened before Steve could reply and Tommy stood in the open doorway and looked around. He was wearing a moss green suit with a black shirt and a pale green tie. Through the open door, Steve could see Walter hanging up Tommy's overcoat and hat. Tommy smiled and spread out his arms.

"Well, gentlemen, here we all are." Steve stood and pulled out a chair as Tommy walked toward the table but stopped halfway.

"Whoa. Are you wearing a suit, Cannon? This must be some occasion. And Johnny Walker Red? You boys went all out." Bernie laughed and gestured for Tommy to sit down across from him.

"Unless your tastes have changed, I always remember you drinking this stuff whenever you could get your hands on it." Bernie poured two fingers of the blended scotch in each glass and set one in front of both of his guests. He leaned back and watched while Tommy took a large sip and held the glass up to the light, admiring the color of the golden brown liquid.

"Its' been a lotta years, Tommy, that you and I have known each other. When did we meet? '45, 46?" Tommy took another sip and smacked his lips.

"1946. And you were the first Jew I ever met in my life. God's honest truth. Those were good days, less complicated, don't you think?" Tommy peered over his glass at Bernie. Bernie smiled and poured more scotch in Tommy's glass and motioned toward Steve who shook his head. Tommy looked over at Steve.

"So, Slick, I assume you have made my friend and yours, here, aware of my proposal?" Steve took his first sip of the scotch and let it roll around softly in his mouth before he answered.

"Sure, Tommy, he knows the score." Tommy shot both of his cuffs and turned slightly in his chair toward Bernie.

"So, Bernie, what do you think? Ready to be partners?" Bernie's brow furrowed as he spoke.

"Well, Tommy, I put a lot of thought into it after Steve told me what you are proposing. I went to see Clifford Jones and ran it by him, and he made a few unofficial inquiries to a couple of guys he knows on the Gaming Commission. Bottom line is: no go. At least not now. You are too connected to all the wrong people where you are now and that is not likely to change any time soon. I am sorry my friend, I wish it was a different story. But I think I have a better idea and one that will get us where we want to go, but I figure it will take us three years to get there." Bernie stopped talking and looked at Tommy. Steve glanced at the mobster out of the corner of his eye, waiting for the explosion. Tommy put his glass down on the green felt and slowly rotated it for several seconds. When he spoke his voice was low and quiet and he didn't look up from his glass.

"I have known you a long time, Bernie, and if you say it can't be done, then it can't be done. I appreciate you considering it in the first place, and now I would like to hear what you have to say." Steve's head jerked back a little as he looked at Bernie who sat across from him with a small smile on his round face. He sensed a connection between the two men that he had not been aware of before. After a few seconds of silence, Bernie spoke again.

"I appreciate that, Tommy, and if you stick with me on what I am about to tell you, you will see that we are going to skin this cat another way." Tommy looked up from his drink.

"I am all ears." His voice was as husky as usual, though his face still held a wistful expression that Steve would have never thought him capable of. Bernie got up from the table, retrieved something from his desk and then sat down with his hand that was holding the object out of sight. When he was sure that he had the attention of both Steve and Tommy, he laid the object in the middle of the table. Tommy was the first to speak.

"It's a lightbulb, Bernie, what am I supposed to do with that?" Tommy snorted and looked at Steve, there was no trace of a vulnerable expression now. Bernie sat back in his chair, took a sip of his scotch and looked at both men.

"How many lights do you think there are in this town, just in the frontage signs alone?" Steve shrugged when Bernie looked in his direction, Tommy snorted.

"I have no idea and my question is, why should I care?" Bernie laughed.

"Maybe you should, or maybe you shouldn't. There are four million, three hundred thousand, give or take a few thousand. So bear with me for a few minutes while I take you through this." Tommy groaned audibly and settled back in his chair as Bernie continued. "Milton, my builder and I spent the better part of an afternoon last week doing this." Bernie had risen as he spoke and walked over to the bar. He pulled off the sheet and revealed a long row of boards with several lights of different colors in each. He stood in front of the display and looked back at Steve and Tommy.

"I didn't realize how important lighting is in creating just the right image, especially in the front of a hotel. Milton introduced me to Andre Malick and his father who are wizards at this lighting stuff. Real artists. After our session, I sat down with them at dinner and after what they told me I started to think." Now it was Steve's turn to groan, but he did so silently.

"All the lights in all the signs in this town are installed and replaced when they burn out by four companies. Two in LA, one in Salt Lake City and Andre and his dad who work out of Henderson. The outside guys rotate crews out of here every three or four weeks and rent their equipment from a guy out on Boulder Highway. They buy these:" Bernie switched on one of the boards and several bulbs of different shades of yellow lit up and reflected off the mirror behind the bar. "And then they mark them up three hundred percent and sell them to you." Bernie pointed in Tommy's direction as he flipped the switches on the other boards and filled the room with the multicolored display. He returned to the table and poured a little more of the scotch into each glass. Tommy Carmino stared at Bernie as Bernie took a small sip.

"That's great, Bernie, and I am sure you have a lot more wonderful, fascinating things to share, but I have to ask you again, why should I care?" Bernie smiled.

"You care, Tommy, because this is how we are going to get you into the casino business." Tommy leaned back in his chair and stretched his arms over his head, rotating his left wrist and checking his watch. Bernie waited until he had Tommy's attention again and then continued.

"The elder Malick wants to retire and Andre wants to go deeper into the artistic side of things. So, Tommy, let me show you something." Tommy threw up his hands.

"Oh, by all means. This is better than the floor show at the D.I." Bernie had left the table briefly and now returned with a long roll of white paper. Still standing, he looked down at the two of them and unrolled the sheet and turned it around facing Tommy. Steve craned his neck and shifted in his chair to view it. The sheet had two drawings on it. One was a Chevrolet work van and the other was a piece of heavy equipment that was used to work in high places and was commonly called a 'cherry picker'. Both featured a three color logo; 'Carmino Lighting,". Bernie placed his glass and Steve's glass on opposite corners of the sheet to hold it down, and grinned down at Tommy. Tommy looked down at the images for a few seconds.

"I don't get it Bernie, what the hell am I looking at here?" Bernie pulled a small piece of paper from his inside jacket pocket and laid it on the sheet in front of Tommy.

"What you are looking at is a check for one hundred thousand. Here is the deal, Tommy: You match my hundred thou and we buy all the vans and cherry pickers we need from the guy out on the highway. We buy out Malick and his son which gives us contracts with a quarter of the casinos. We hire the best of the crews that come here each week and best of all, we get these babies:" Bernie held up the lightbulb. "Made by a guy that Milton knows in Jersey for a third the price and they last twice as long. With your contacts and mine, we give everybody in town better service at a cheaper price." Bernie stopped talking again and waited. Tommy took a long sip of his scotch and looked up at Bernie.

"Yeah, Bernie, I get it, a lighting company. Give me one good reason why I should do this." Bernie smiled down at Tommy and with his arms supporting him on the back of the chair he leaned forward toward the mobster.

"Three times a week, fifty-two weeks a year, there will be two vans and two cherry pickers in front of the Sands Hotel with your name emblazoned across the sides." Tommy chortled.

"That is a very good reason, my friend. I like that idea very much." Tommy's eyes narrowed to slits.

"But how does this get me into the casino business?" Bernie rolled up the paper, replaced the rubber band and handed it to Tommy.

"After we run this company for two or three years, we create a holding company that holds the lighting company and the new hotel and casino we buy or build. Clifford Jones is pretty sure that by then corporations will be able to own casinos. The Sahara is almost a de facto example of a corporation owning a hotel, because the Del Webb corporation is the main player. He and a few others have been pushing this to the Commission as a way to get guys like you out of the casino business. Certify corporations, not individuals. So I say, yeah, why not? You want corporations? Presto. We make Tommy Carmino a corporation. Simple as that. Clifford has all the paperwork ready to go, all I need is your John Hancock and your hundred thousand." Tommy chuckled and pulled an envelope out of his pocket. Steve recognized it as the same one that Tommy had tossed on the table at the diner two nights ago.

"There's half of it, and since Slick here doesn't like money, his half of that deal goes into the pot as well. Cash gonna work for you?"

"No problem. We can use that to buy all our equipment, probably get a discount for cash. Just one more piece of business to take care of and then we are done for now. We need a Board of Directors. I nominate you, me and Steve, here. That way Steve will be the tie-breaker in any disagreements. Has does that sound?" Bernie chuckled at the expression on Tommy's face.

"How does it sound? It sounds like a set-up to me. Like I should ever live to see the day that Slick here will side with me against you." Bernie held up his hand and cocked his head.

"I figured that would be your take, Tommy, so how about this: Steve stays on the board, I nominate two other people, and you do the same. My guys are Clifford Jones and Marvin Littlejohn. You shouldn't have any objection there. You are closer to Clifford than I am and your boss does projects using Marvin's firm." Tommy nodded thoughtfully.

"Fine, that works for me. But how you gonna convince them to come on the board?"

"Simple. Every board member gets a $10,000 a year stipend." Steve grunted to get Bernie's attention.

"Are you sure about that Bern? I think all of us would be happy to be on a board of anything with you. I don't need compensation." Bernie scowled.

"Of course you do. There are going to be monthly meetings and a lot of decisions are going to have to be made and made right the first time. I am also looking ahead to when the holding company is formed. Those guys and the two guys Tommy gets are going to be the seed money and the shareholders that are going to get Tommy his own casino to run." Tommy stood up from the table.

"I'm in Bernie. Tell me where and when you want to sign the

papers. I will call you with my two names tomorrow. We're gonna need a building right?"

"Yes, we are and I will let you take care of that. I will have Malick senior call you with the specifications." Bernie stood and held out his hand to Tommy. Tommy shook it briefly and smiled down at Bernie's beaming face. Bernie released Tommy's hand and held his out to Steve. Steve shook it and they both looked at Tommy. Tommy grimaced.

"I don't believe this. I will probably wake up in the middle of the night and wonder what I have gotten myself into." He shook his head as he grasped Steve's hand and then turned to go. Steve turned to Bernie.

"I am taking Remy out to dinner, so I better get going as well. It has been very entertaining to say the least. Thanks for everything." Bernie laughed and followed him to the door. Steve patted his old friend on the shoulder and quickly weaved through the tables and out the front door. He caught Tommy's eye and waved to him as he was stepping into the big red Cadillac. Tommy stopped and waited as Steve came up to the car.

"What now, Cannon? I thought you had a hot date."

"Tommy, I need to talk with you about a few things. Get in the car." Tommy sighed and sat down in the drivers' seat. Steve closed the door against the cold air. Tommy looked over at Steve with an impatient expression on his face.

"What gives?"

"I heard from very good sources that there is a new agent assigned to the field office here by the name of Jacob Hurley and that you are his pet project. They also have a tail on you and I don't know, nobody said, but I would assume a wiretap as well." Tommy's gloved fingers drummed softly on the steering wheel.

"Who are these impeccable sources?"

"Nick Montero and Tam Polhaus. Tam had to file a report when you showed at the diner. Agent Hurley is also DA Larsen's brother-in-law. This looks serious, Tommy." Tommy snickered.

"Well, I'm surprised at you Slick. Only partners but two minutes and already you got cold feet." Steve ignored the remark.

"Easy to find out, Tommy. Go back into Foxy's, call Jack and Little Moe and have them drive out here. Once you leave, should be pretty obvious if there is a tail." Tommy thought for a few seconds.

"You're right, Cannon, should be easy to tell, but I got you here to do that for me. I will drive around the far side and come back down this lane. You get in your car and see if I am being followed. If I am, keep on going. If not, follow me over to the hotel and let's have a drink before you pick up your lady friend." Steve buttoned up his coat and opened the door.

"Fine, give me a minute to get into position." Steve closed the heavy door of the caddy and walked the twenty yards to the Jeep. He got in, started the engine and waited. Tommy slowly backed the Cadillac out of the parking space and cruised in a slow arc through the parking lot and back down the lane where Steve was parked. Tommy stopped at the entrance to the strip and then eased into the rush hour traffic. Six cars down in the row behind him, Steve saw the lights of a car switch on and a gray sedan with two men inside, speed quickly to the entrance and turn in the same direction that Tommy had gone. Steve did the same and two blocks later he pulled his car alongside, keeping back just far enough to not be seen. Neither of the men was Jacob Hurley, but one was Agent Molini, an FBI agent Steve had dealt with last summer. Steve pulled ahead and caught up with Tommy. When he was even with the car he looked over. Tommy winked and smiled. Steve pulled quickly ahead and made a U-turn one block down. Tommy nodded his head as Steve passed by him going in the opposite direction.

A half hour later, Steve and Remy stepped up to the maître 'd's podium at the House of Lords, a restaurant inside the Sahara Hotel and along with the Sultan's Table at the Dunes, one of the best dining spots in Las Vegas. As they were escorted to their table, they could hear the dance music coming from the Don the Beachcomber, another restaurant and dance club in the hotel. Steve sat back and looked across at Remy as she leaned forward, her hands folded under her chin.

"This is what I always missed, Gem. You and I going out together and having a good time just like regular couples." Remy smiled and reached out and put her hand on top of Steve's, her diamond earrings sparkled in the candlelight.

"Do you think if I had met you first, before I met Nash, that you and I would still be together?" Steve put his other hand over hers and stroked it gently.

"I don't know how those things work Gem. All I know is that the first time I saw you, I knew you were the woman I was meant to be with. Sometimes those things work out and sometimes I think about all the people that for one reason or another are fated to never be with that one special person. You and I got lucky and I am never going to let you go."

She squeezed his hand and murmured, "I love you," as the waiter approached the table and handed them both menus. Steve smiled into the deep brown eyes for a few seconds before he dropped his gaze to the wine list. He ordered a bottle of French Champagne and caviar. When the waiter had placed the open bottle in the ice bucket by the table and left, Steve held out the small champagne glass, and watched while Remy tipped her glass gently forward, the small clink barely heard in the ambient noise of the large room.

An hour later, at the end of the meal, they sipped the last of the champagne. Remy had just finished recounting her efforts to recruit dancers for the revue that she was putting together for Bernie's hotel, the Casablanca. Steve waited until there was a lull in the conversation.

"You never told me, Gem, what is was like growing up in France under the Nazi occupation." He watched as she looked down and ran her fingers up and down the stem of her champagne flute. She shrugged.

"It was harder on my parents than it was on me. I was just ten years old when the Germans marched into Paris. My parents sent my older sister to live with my father's brother and his wife in the south of France. My parents owned a cafe that turned into a nightclub at night. My mother sang and my father played in the small house band. My father decided that he wanted no part of the Germans and when they started coming into the club, he shut it down and we joined my sister. My father had a hard time finding some way to earn money. After the war, we returned to Paris, but he had lost everything and it was many years before he and my mother were able to open another café." She looked out over the well-heeled crowd enjoying their dinners.

"In many ways, Steve, it is like a world I visited a long time ago. My life has been so different since then. I know a little of what my parents felt. I have had to start over and sometimes it is the last thing you ever expect to do." Steve reached for her hand.

"But look how much you have accomplished so far. As far as I know, you will be the first woman to produce a first line show at a Strip hotel. Who knows where it will lead?"

"You are right, but it is still a lot of responsibility and the last thing I want to do is to let Bernie down." Steve scoffed.

"Let me tell you something about Bernie. I don't care how much he likes you, and I know for a fact he adores you, he would not put his money and the investor's money in jeopardy. He wouldn't have asked you unless he was sure that your show will put all the others to shame." Remy squeezed his hand.

"I like how you see me, you should tell me that every day." Steve leaned forward and whispered.

"How about I tell you bright and early tomorrow morning, after we go next door and dance?" Remy smiled as she took the arm that Steve had extended to her as they stood from the table. Their heads were touching lightly as they left the restaurant arm in arm.

January 8

Tam was fifteen minutes late when he spied Steve in one of the orange vinyl booths in the back of the Bob's Big Boy restaurant. He shoved his coat over the top of the back cushion and slid into the seat across from the private detective. Steve looked up from the menu, his left arm resting on the file that DA Larsen had given him.

"You're going to have to be a little more punctual if you want to be my partner." Steve held the menu up in front of his face to hide his grin. Tam ignored the remark but took the opportunity to slide Steve's cup of coffee over to his side of the table. He lifted it to his mouth and made a show of taking a loud sip. Steve lifted up the menu and seeing his cup was gone, slid out of the booth and helped himself to another cup from the coffee station. When he returned, Tam had his own file out on the table and was taking notes. Steve snickered.

"I bet you were one of those kids in school who tried to cram in their homework during their homeroom period, right?" Tam stopped and looked at him with tired eyes and a blank expression.

"If I had tried that, I still wouldn't be able to sit down after the nuns got through with me." He looked back down at the yellow legal pad and crossed out something he had just written. Steve took a sip of the hot coffee. He put his cup down in the empty saucer and tried to read Tam's notes from his side of the table.

"So let's assume for the sake of argument, Tam, that you reviewed the file last night like we agreed. What is your gut telling you about this crime?" He cocked his head to one side, watching as the detective sat back in the booth and let out a large sigh.

"Well, if Harris McCord didn't do it, I think he knows who did or knows more about it then Samuels was able to get out of him." Tam reached over and poured some cream into the coffee from a small silver pitcher.

"Yeah, Tam, that is pretty much how I see it. It makes more sense than not, but it doesn't fit entirely. The room and the condition that Rowena said it was in, don't jibe with a street thug druggie looking for money and things he can pawn for quick cash." Tam looked at him over his cup.

"I agree, but maybe there was something there that we don't know about and that was what he was after."

"Maybe, but that would mean that Desmond had kept it from Rowena and while possible, it is a little bit of a stretch. On the other hand, it seems she wasn't aware of this windfall that Desmond was expecting. Maybe he got it, Harris found out about it, and that was the motive." Both men looked down at the files spread across the table, and were silent. Their contemplation was interrupted by the waitress who came to take their breakfast order. Tam ordered eggs and bacon, Steve ordered buttered rye toast and orange juice.

When the breakfasts came, the men ate in silence and pored over all the information the files contained on Harris McCord. Steve lit a cigarette and watched through the smoke as Tam finished his breakfast and his reading. When he was done and the waitress cleared the table and poured more coffee, they spread out everything they had on the suspect and went back through it several times. After a few minutes, Steve cleared his throat.

"Tam, this guy was a small time pimp. You worked vice for several years, I think we need to start tracking him down in that direction. If he is indeed on the run, I think that is where he may go to lie low. So, women that worked for him, other druggies, anybody that you can think of that he may know or was associated with in the past. I will get with Larsen and see if we need a warrant and hopefully I can get into his apartment and be back at your office by noon." Tam raised his hand and reached into his pocket and then put a small brass key on the table and slid it across to Steve.

"What is this?" Steve picked up the key and held it up in front of his face.

"It's the key to the slime balls' apartment. I saw it on Samuels' desk and pocketed it." Tam smiled slyly. "When I get back to the office I will get with Larsen and make sure there is a warrant out today on McCord. That way you should be covered when you turn the place." Steve slipped the key onto his key ring and smiled. "See, I told you partnering up would be a good idea." Tam didn't reply, but began putting the stacks of paper back into the file folder.

"I already have several ideas on some people we should look up. I will get with the vice detectives and see which of them are still around. I assume since you are getting expenses from Larsen's office that you will take care of this?" Tam slid the check over to Steve's side of the table. Steve picked it up and looked at the total.

"I'm only getting twenty a day for expenses, so maybe you better pack a peanut butter and jelly sandwich a couple days a week." Steve slid his file off the table as he stood up. He waited until Tam had put on his coat and they walked together to the entrance. "See ya around noon, Tam." Steve turned up the collar of his coat and headed in the opposite direction from the restaurant to where he had parked the Jeep a half block away. He made a U turn on the wide street and headed out to the valley and the Westchester apartments.

Steve closed and locked the door of apartment number 20 carefully behind him. There was no response when he tried the light switch and deciding not to pull open the curtains, Steve waited until his eyes became accustomed to the dark interior. When he could see to make his way, he walked to a back bedroom and drew open the curtains. He repeated the same process in the other bedroom and the small bathroom. There was now enough ambient light to search the rooms. The floors of both bedrooms were littered with papers and old clothes in little piles on the green shag carpet. Steve kicked the clothes into a bigger pile in the largest bedroom and quickly searched all the pockets. Finding nothing he scooped up the papers from the floor and carried them to the kitchen, depositing them on the small linoleum covered bar that separated the kitchen from the living room. He repeated the process with the second bedroom and then turned his attention to the living room. He was going through the pile of papers that stood in two tall stacks on the bar when there was a knock on the door. Steve moved quickly next to the kitchen window where he could see the reflection of the apartment manager in the glass.

Steve opened the door and looked blankly at the woman who by her lack of surprise at seeing him in the opening of the door, meant she had likely seen him enter the apartment ten minutes ago. She stood with her hands on her hips.

"I suppose you have permission to be in there, right?" Steve did not change his expression.

"This is an ongoing police investigation and I am here at the behest of the District Attorney's office." She took a step forward and folded her arms across her chest. The blue mascara covered eyes narrowed.

"Last time you were here, you were just a private investigator poking around. I don't suppose you got a warrant?" Steve pulled his notebook from his back pocket and slipped the small pencil from the silver spiral top. He wrote quickly and tore the page off and handed it to the woman.

"Call DA Larsen if you want more information, I'm busy here." Steve shut the door and locked it, sliding the gold button of the safety chain into position. He heard her descending the steps and went back to work sorting through the papers. When he was done he carefully folded four of the sheets and put them into his inner coat pocket. He stepped out onto the concrete walkway and locked the door behind him. He walked the few steps to the next door apartment and rapped sharply against the brown wood. After several minutes the young girl he had met before opened the door. Steve noted that she wasn't holding a baby and that she had removed the chain and now held the door almost fully open.

"Did you know it was me knocking?" Steve indicated the front window between the two apartments.

"Yes. I saw you when you got here. I figured that you would want to ask me more questions."

"Only one. Have you heard anyone in that apartment since I was here last?" The young girl shook her head.

"Well if you do, call this number." Steve handed her one of Tam's cards with the switchboard number and Tam's extension.

"OK, mister, I will." Steve smiled and waved as he turned toward the stairs. He had just started down when he saw Samuels waiting at the bottom of the steps, blocking the way, his hand resting on the guardrail. The manager stood several yards behind Samuels by the gate that lead to the pool. Steve smiled and slowed his steps to a steady cadence as he spoke.

"If you aren't out of my way by the time I get to the bottom, Samuels, you and your little fedora are going for a swim." Steve took one more step and jumped through the air right at the startled detective. Samuels caught the heel of his shoe on the edge of the sidewalk as he scrambled to get out of the way. The cuff of his raincoat snagged on the end of the guardrail, tearing the sleeve completely away at the shoulder as he crumpled to the ground, hitting the back of his head on the chain link fence that surrounded the pool. Samuels had moved a split second before Steve landed flat-footed on the ground right in front of the prone detective. Steve laughed loudly.

"Well, you almost made it Samuels, but I think you might need a new raincoat." Steve started toward the hallway leading to the parking area, but stopped and turned toward the manager who was looking down at Samuels, still lying stunned on the ground. Steve waited until she looked up.

"Next time, when I tell you to call somebody, make sure you follow directions." He turned and was on his way before he saw or heard her reaction. He drove to Bernie's and used the phone in a booth two doors from the deli. He waited several minutes until Tam picked up.

"I got a couple of leads from some papers I found in the apartment. I will drop them by later. Nothing much of interest in the place. The girl next door who seems to babysit around the clock hasn't heard anyone in there since the night after the murder. Have you found anything we can follow up?"

"Yeah, I have a couple people we can go talk to that might know where this character is. When you get here, we can make the rounds."

"I'm here at Bernie's for a little while, then I will head your way. See ya."

Bernie sat quietly after Steve briefed him on the conversation that he and Tam had over breakfast. He played absentmindedly with a spoon on the felt tabletop for a few seconds before he spoke.

"You mean that it might turn out that Desmond had to die because some junkie needed money for a fix?"

"I'm sorry, Bern, the more we know, the more it looks that way. I personally think there is more here than meets the eye, but we have to go where the evidence takes us. Tam and I still have a lot of footwork to do. In my experience, if you follow some of the side routes, a much fuller picture emerges, and sometimes you even get a whole different story. The important thing now is to find this Harris character and arrest him or eliminate him from consideration, so we can get closer to the truth."

"The important thing, Steve, is to find out what happened, regardless of how it looks. If Desmond was involved in something he shouldn't have been, well....."

Bernie rose from the table and went over to his desk. When he returned and sat down again, he placed a small flat box in the middle of the table.

"This was dropped off this morning. It's from Monari. It's over two hours of Desmond's own compositions, most of them played by the man himself. Wouldn't know anything about this, I suppose?" Steve picked up the box and turned it over. The back of the box had two columns of horizontal lines that were meant to hold a description of the contents of the tape. There were so many entries that Monari had double and tripled up in small writing to list them all.

"He did fast work, Bernie. I hope you like it."

"Like it? Are you kidding, there is stuff on here I never heard of, let alone heard. I can hardly wait to get home tonight and put it on." Bernie held the box in his hands and smiled.

"My pleasure, Bernie, and I am glad you were able to get him into the show, after I opened my mouth about it." Bernie waved him off.

"Naw, nothing to it, they would have included him anyway. Quincy told me that he has worked with Buck many times in LA and he was going to tap him for arranging some of the horn parts. He says with so many horn players on stage, he needed someone who knew the strengths and weaknesses of everybody involved. Plus, some guys like Frank, like a lot of horns, the more horns, the better, some others, not so much. So, it looks like it is working out like it is supposed to."

"Well, you've had quite a week my friend. How you were able to get Tommy to completely forget about running your new casino was pretty impressive." Bernie screwed up his face derisively.

"It wasn't that big a deal. He's a businessman, dyed in the wool, and once I saw the opportunity, I knew he would go for it. But Tommy is nobody's fool, he will check with Clifford Jones to make sure that everything is on the up and up." Steve hesitated, but then spoke.

"Tommy has some trouble ahead of him, Bern. I found out yesterday that there is a new FBI agent in town that has been assigned here just to investigate Tommy and by extension, I presume, his boss. Some of the things that came to light last summer have piqued their interest. They tail him everywhere, and if experience is any guide, they will eventually want to know our connections in the deal. So, protect yourself."

"Thanks, for telling me, Steve, I had heard some noise to that effect. My hunch is that if you were to follow the trail back far enough, it leads to the Sands, but it doesn't matter much one way or the other. It is not in anybody's best interest to rock the boat too much. It's just a way to cause Tommy some inconvenience and slow him down a little."

"Maybe, but on another subject, Bern, I am taking a little trip this weekend to Arizona." Bernie looked up quickly from perusing the back of the tape box.

"Arizona? What's there that you have to see so badly?" Steve looked Bernie in the eyes.

"There is a place there that Angelo Sorelli stayed for a while when he got out of prison a few years back. I am going to check it out and see if I can pick up his trail."

"Alone. You're going alone? Can't you take someone with you? I would feel a lot better about it all if you would."

"I know, Bern, but this I have to do alone. Too many people draw too much attention. It will be alright, it is just mostly reconnaissance, I wouldn't worry about it, I'll be home Sunday night." Bernie was not mollified, but let the subject drop.

It was just after noon when Steve walked across the large granite slabs of the plaza that led to the police station. He found Tam in the break room talking to two other detectives and a uniformed cop. They were laughing when Steve came in the door, but quickly fell silent. Steve stopped and surveyed the scene.

"What's so funny?" Tam pointed to a chair in the corner where a gray raincoat was slung over one of the arms. A detached sleeve to the coat was laid out on the table.

"Samuels is down in the infirmary getting one of the nurses to patch up a bloody bump on the back of his head. Won't tell anyone what happened. Carl here thinks that our boy pushed a suspect a little too far." Steve jerked his head toward the door.

"I don't have time to wonder why Samuels can't get out of his own way. Let's go to your office and figure out what to do next." Tam's eyes narrowed as he fell into step behind the private detective.

"Out of his own way? What do you mean by that?" Steve didn't stop.

"Nothing. It is just a figure of speech. Let's get busy." Steve turned into Tam's office and sat in one of the chairs, laying his file on the desk. Tam closed the door behind them and watched as Steve lit a cigarette.

"Any luck at the apartment?"

"Some." Steve dropped the Pall Mall into the ashtray, pulled the four pieces of paper from his coat pocket and smoothed them out on top of the file. He handed the first one to Tam who looked at the front, turned it over read something on the back and handed it back to Steve.

"What do you make of that?" Steve held the paper up to the light.

"Well, it is a note, likely written to Harris. It is in block print and pretty illiterate, looks like a man's writing. 'Meet me at 6th and Ogden right where you know where. Be there at eight tonight.' There is a small hole in the top where it was probably tacked to the door of the apartment. There's no signature." Steve turned the sheet over, the back was an invoice for a storage space that listed an address on 23rd Street. There was no name associated with the invoice. Steve set the paper aside and looked up at Tam.

"What's at 6th and Ogden?"

Probably a flop house, that area is full of them. One of the peo-ple we are going to contact today lives on Sixth just above Ogden."

"And the storage company?"

"Never been in there, but I have been past it many times." Steve nodded slightly and picked up the cigarette, took a drag and replaced it. He shuffled through the other three pieces of paper.

"Don't know if these are anything at all. This one has a list like a grocery list, but I don't recognize any of the items. Tam took the sheet and read the names.

"'Black Araby', that is a street name for a specific type of black tar heroin. The others are just names for types of regular heroin. He seems to like brand names. The numbers beside them are probably grams, so this is either an inventory list or an order that someone has placed with him. If it is an order, it is a pretty large one. If his inventory can support these kinds of numbers, he is a bigger dealer than we gave him credit for. What are the other two?"

"Another list like that one, all the same names appear, different amounts and this one is dated, December 10th. But take a look at this." Steve placed a yellow sheet of lined paper on the desk in front of the detective. Tam looked at it without picking it up.

"A diagram, but of what?" Steve stood and bent over the desk. He pointed to three areas on the page with the hand that held his cigarette.

"I wondered that too, when I first saw it, but as I drove away, it came to me, I pulled over and looked again. This is a diagram of the apartment complex. See how each apartment is one of the boxes and how the hallways lay out?" Tam leaned closer and squinted at the page.

"I'll have to take your word for it. The one time I was there, I didn't pay much attention to anything but the crime scene. Why do those boxes have an 'X' in them?" Steve sat back down in the chair.

"If I'm right and it is a diagram of the complex, then those two boxes correspond to Desmond and Harris's units, and the other one is the apartment of the guy who said he saw someone running past under his balcony that night. Of course it could just be doodling, but the haphazard way it is drawn, suggests it was a quick sketch to show someone a plan." Tam rubbed his chin and looked across at Steve.

"Suggests more than a simple drug deal or a strong arm robbery, doesn't it?"

"Yes, it does, but like most of what we know, it is only a suggestion." Tam stood up from the desk and grabbed his jacket from a rack in the corner.

"Well, we aren't learning anything here. Let's go talk to some of the upstanding citizens that know this guy." Steve followed Tam out of the office, closing the door behind him. Just ahead, Steve caught sight of the bandaged back of Samuels' head as he turned into the breakroom. He smiled as he walked by the open door, but kept his gaze straight down the hall. Tam waited for him at the bank of glass doors that led to the plaza.

"Let's take your car, nobody in that neighborhood knows it, so we should be able to work there for a while before the word gets out and everyone goes to ground."

"Fine by me, I assume the most likely character is first on the list?" Tam led the way out to the parking lot.

"Yep, and you are going to knock on his door. You'll drop me off at the corner and I will move up the alley and in position behind the building. Are you packing?"

"No, but if you have an extra, I'll carry it." They reached the Jeep and Steve unlocked the passenger door for Tam.

"You shouldn't need one. This guy is violent, but knives are more his weapon of choice." Steve snorted.

"I don't have one of those on me either, but if I stay far enough away from him, I guess I can duck if he throws it at me." Tam grinned out the window as Steve pulled out of the parking lot and two blocks later turned onto Fremont Street.

As Tam had indicated, both sides of Sixth Street above Ogden were lined with one and two story flophouses and small homes, most built in the twenties. At Tam's suggestion they drove at normal speed through the neighborhood before circling the block and stopping at the entrance to the alley, thirty yards from the corner. Tam handed Steve a five by six picture. It was another booking photo, this time of a rough looking man that looked of Mexican descent.

"Juan Ramos. They were arrested several times together. Drugs and break-ins of businesses mostly, but Ramos would go down to Mexico occasionally, and bring back women that would turn tricks for Harris. He is a little taller than you. Halfway up the block, the small gray house number 610. Belongs to his sister. If he isn't there, she usually knows where he is. If he is there, get him to come out on the porch to talk, I will able to see the two of you from where I'll be. Be prepared that when he sees me, he will most likely try to bolt. Got it?"

"Yeah, I got it." Steve looked at the picture in his hand. "You're right, I wish I was packing." He watched as Tam got out of the Jeep, closed the door quietly and started up the alley, keeping close to the sagging wooden fence that ran part way down the narrow two track road. Steve locked the car and walked as casually as he could around the corner.

The unpainted boards of the porch at number 610 squeaked loudly under Steve's weight as he stepped up from the sidewalk. His footsteps made even more noise as he approached the screen entrance. The white paint was peeling in long strips off the front door, as Steve opened the screen and knocked sharply on one of the two panes of glass on the top of the exposed wood. He stepped back and kept the corner of his eye on the curtained window to his right.

Steve heard a movement behind the door just before a female voice said something in Spanish that Steve did not understand.

"I need to speak to Senor Ramos, por favor." His voice was elevated, but the mixture of Spanish and English was not responded to. He knocked again.

"Por favor, Mr. Ramos." Steve stepped back and turned to his right to see if the curtains on the front window had been disturbed. Just as he turned back to the door, he heard a noise coming from around the right side of the house that sounded like a door being shut and rapid footsteps. He took two long strides, vaulted a low wooden handrail and with three more steps rounded the corner of the house. He took in the scene even as he crouched low at the waist and rushed forward. Juan Ramos was holding Tam at gunpoint. Tam's hands were held out at his waist and the calm expression on his face registered somewhere in Steve's brain as he hurtled forward. The large Mexican turned as he heard Steve's approach from twenty feet away, but as Steve had expected, he didn't look down immediately, and in the spilt second it took him to begin to swing the gun around, Steve's left shoulder slammed into the back of his knees. Steve drove his hips through the contact, and pushing violently upward with his arms, threw the man back over his left shoulder and heavily to the ground. The small .38 revolver clattered on one of the red stepping stones that lined the narrow passageway between the house and a neighboring fence. Steve turned quickly and knelt down forcefully on the back of the prostrate man. Juan Ramos' face was bloody where it had contacted the paving stones and Steve could tell from the angle of his right arm that his shoulder was dislocated. Tam had picked up the gun and was now standing over both of them with the handcuffs.

"I've rousted this guy several times, never pulled a gun before. I wonder who he thought you were?" Steve stood as Tam, aware of the man's pain, retrieved a second pair of cuffs and gingerly fastened them together around both wrists. It took both of them to get the man on his feet. Tam reached down for the gun and placed it carefully into his jacket pocket and then pointed toward the alley.

"Best if we go this way, we will attract less attention in case someone wants to be a hero." Steve held Ramos by the back of his shirt as they marched him back down the alleyway to where the Jeep was parked. Steve unlocked the back passenger door and Tam lined the suspect up with the opening, forced him to lean over and with Steve's help pushed the groaning man on his belly across the seat. Tam folded the man's legs in the air and closed the door, holding it while Steve relocked it. Tam got in the front seat and pulled his own revolver from a holster on his hip and turning halfway around in his seat, held it above the seat, making sure that Ramos could see it. Steve clamored into the drivers' seat, made a quick U-turn and sped quickly out of the neighborhood. Less than five minutes later, Tam directed him behind the police headquarters and into the underground parking lot that led to the booking rooms. Tam handed the gun to Steve and ran inside the double glass doors. Steve moved across the bench seat until he was sure that Ramos could see him and the gun.

Tam reappeared thirty seconds later, a uniformed Hispanic officer trailing behind him. Tam opened the back door on the drivers' side and then stepped aside as the officer began to pepper the suspect with questions in rapid fire Spanish. Two more officers emerged from the entrance and slid Ramos from the back seat and stood him up. They held him on either side and marched him into the booking area. The Hispanic officer approached Tam and Steve, looking quizzically in Steve's direction before speaking to Tam.

"I have told him that he is being arrested for assault on a police officer and resisting arrest. I also told him that he may be facing attempted murder of a police officer if he doesn't cooperate. I suggest we let him think about it for an hour or so, get his shoulder looked at, and by then he may be ready to talk."

"That sounds good, make sure you are here in an hour when I get back, I want you to be the translator on this one." The officer nodded, closed the door of the Jeep and went back through the double glass doors. Tam turned to Steve and smiled.

"How's your expense account looking now? Let's get some

lunch." Steve snorted quietly to himself, and climbed behind the wheel and waited until Tam settled into the passenger seat and closed the door.

"Nugget OK?" Tam nodded and pulled a notebook from inside his jacket and began to scribble notes across the first page.

"You got it easy, Cannon. You get in a dust-up with someone, once it's over, it's over. You can go home and have a beer. Me? I got three hours of paper work ahead of me if I'm lucky." Tam sighed and continued writing. Steve looked across at the older man.

"You seemed pretty calm back there, looking down the barrel of a gun." Tam stopped writing and looked up with a blank expression. He reached in his right coat pocket and pulled out Ramos' pistol. The cylinder was open and Tam held it with a pencil through one of the chambers. He held it at an angle, so that while it wasn't pointed at Steve, he still had a frontal view of the weapon. All the chambers were empty.

"Trick I learned from my old man. Most of the career criminals know that if the gun is unloaded they can sometimes catch a break if they are caught. If the gun is empty and the cop doesn't know their tricks, well, they at least have a fighting chance of getting away. Nine out of ten revolvers are easy to spot. The semi-automatics you can usually tell because they swing 'em around real light." Tam put the gun back in his pocket and continued writing as Steve eased into his usual parking spot behind the Golden Nugget. He turned and waited until Tam had finished writing and put his notebook back into his pocket.

"How about a nice steak? They do a great one in the dealers' canteen just off the casino floor.'"

"Sure and I bet that because you have privileges in there, it's free, right?" Steve waited for a few seconds until Tam looked over at him, and then spoke in a serious tone.

"I leave the full price of the meal as a tip for the wait staff." He watched as Tam shrugged and opened the door.

The canteen was crowded as the dealers and box men waited for the two o'clock shift to begin. Steve and Tam found a table behind a group of cocktail waitresses that were just finishing their lunches and were chatting and reapplying their make-up. Tam leaned in close to Steve.

"Is it always this noisy?" Steve looked at his watch.

"It'll be like a graveyard five minutes from now." Tam nodded and sat back in his chair.

By the time the waitress made her way to their table and had taken their order, Steve and Tam were the only ones in the large room except for a crew of busboys clearing the tables. Steve had greeted the woman by name and then ordered for both of them. Steve picked up the salt shaker and pouring a little into the palm of his hand, tossed it over his left shoulder. He stared evenly at Tam.

"Why didn't you process that gun as evidence?" Tam watched an empty coke bottle that had fallen loudly from one of the bus boy's trays roll across the floor and under a table.

"It'll get done, when I get back. You turn in an empty gun right away, might be a clean deal, might not. Turn it an hour later, still empty, when you could have easily loaded it in the meantime?" Tam opened his hands and shrugged.

"Know what?" Tam was now smiling at Steve. Steve shook his head slowly from side to side.

"No, what?" Tam laughed as he spoke.

"I guess I should be grateful you played football instead of base-ball." He continued laughing and sat back as the waitress arrived at the table carrying two platters with the steaks that Steve had ordered plus baked potatoes and grilled vegetables. A bus boy stood behind her holding two large mugs of lager. When they left, Steve leaned over the table closer to Tam, his knife and fork in his hands.

"It wouldn't have mattered what I did, if the gun was empty." Tam cut a piece of the steak and hesitated with the morsel in midair.

"Maybe, but he knew from my reaction I had made the gun, his next move was to run right over me. I have had that happen a few too many times, so I was glad to see your Johnny Unitas act."

"Unitas is a quarterback." Tam waved his knife dismissively in Steve's direction.

"I don't care if he is a water boy, I was just glad to see Mr. Ramos hit the ground."

"What next, Tam? You've dealt with this hombre before, he likely to give us what we want?" Tam stopped chewing and took a long draught from the beer stein.

"Depends. He has visa problems and hates the idea of going back to Mexico. So unless he has become a citizen when I wasn't looking, it should be easy to get him to spill what he knows. That is why I have Rivas doing the translating. He takes no prisoners and doesn't put up with a lot of guff. Some of these guys rattle on for ten minutes and then you get a one word answer from the translator. But I guess the real question is: Does he know anything, or was he just running for some other reason. We'll find out." Tam looked up over Steve's shoulder as someone approached the table from behind. Steve turned and looked up as Nick Montero slipped into the seat next to him.

"Twice in two days? What happened? Did Bernie get enough of you?" Nick laughed good naturedly and held out his hand to Tam. Tam wiped some grease from his fingers with a napkin and took the firm grip.

"Hi, I'm Nick Montero." Steve pointed at Tam.

"This is Detective Tam Polhaus, one of Las Vegas' finest. Tam, this is Nick Montero and he owns this joint." Nick held up his hand as Steve finished speaking.

"Runs the joint. Which means less money and more headaches. What brings you two down here, nothing official, I hope."

"Naw, Nick, nothing like that. Tam here got his feelings hurt by a suspect this morning and I'm just helping him get his strength back." Tam shook his head and turned his attention to cutting his steak. Nick looked at Steve.

"But everything's OK, now, right?" After Steve nodded his assent, Nick stood up.

"I just dropped by to tell you that just after you left yesterday, Jack Cathay called looking for you. Said he needs to talk to you, just thought I would pass that along." Nick extended his hand once again to Tam.

"Nice meeting you detective, drop by any time and have lunch on me." Tam stood up and shook Nick's hand.

"Thank you Mr. Montero, I will make sure that Steve here and I make it back soon." Steve stood as well and wrapped his arm briefly around the Basque's shoulders and patted his arm.

"Good to see you, Nick. Tell Margaret, I will see her on the 24th, and that Remy is looking forward to it as well." Steve watched as Nick moved through the tables and disappeared into the casino. When he sat back down, Tam was looking intently at him.

"You do know who is involved in this place, don't you?" Tam pushed his plate away with his steak half eaten. Steve took a sip of his beer and fished a pack of Pall Malls out of his breast pocket, and lit it.

"Yeah, I know. But here is something I know as well, and maybe it is time you should know it too. Nick is a decent, stand-up guy. He treats his employees better than anyone else in this town and he raises almost as much money for charitable causes as Bernie does." Steve let out a long stream of smoke and looked across the room where several dealers had just sat down on their break. He listened to Tam without looking at him.

"I didn't say he was anything one way or another. I was just pointing out that this place is crawling with wise guys as bad as any in town, that's all." Steve turned back and took a second drag on the cigarette, his eyes fastened on the detective across from him.

"How many times are we going to have this argument? Are there some very bad people in the mob who do unspeakably bad things? You bet there are. Does this town work better because everyone knows their place and the wise guys impose discipline on a cash rich business? Yes, it does. Are there so called 'upstanding citizens' that weasel and chisel their way through and corrupt everything they touch? Yeah, there are, and you and I have put a few of them away. Do I have to put up with a crooked cop pushing me around every time I take a case? Yeah, I do. That's rough and that's tough, my friend, but that is life in the big city. So why not get past all that and realize there are worse things to deal with than a few organized criminals siphoning money out of casinos that play games that the suckers are always destined to lose? Nobody holds a gun to anybody's head and makes them come here and lose all their money, right?" Steve took another quick drag on his cigarette and crushed it out as he stood up.

"Finish your steak, I'm going to make a phone call." Steve slipped a ten dollar bill under his plate and looked across at Tam who was busy examining his fingernails.

Steve stood in a small alcove just outside the canteen and dialed a number followed by an extension. The line crackled for a minute and then Steve heard the unmistakable voice of Jack Cathay.

"Jack, this is your buddy, Steve Cannon. How ya' doing today?" Steve heard Jack mumble something under his breath.

"I got no buddies, wise guy, and if I did, you wouldn't be one of them." The wheezy raspy voice sounded even more irritated than usual.

"Are you sure, Jack? I heard you been trying to find me all over town."

"Well, now that you have found me, I'll make it short and sweet. I found the quack that patched up Sorelli after he got roasted in the desert. He lives way out in Jean. He's a veterinarian. Guy said he stayed there two weeks, doesn't know how he got there or where he went when he left, but some guy flew a small plane into an airport near Jean and that's how he skidaddled. So there's that. The only other information I got from him is that Sorelli is scarred heavily on the left side of his face. In his opinion, he took off way too early and was risking infection. So there you have it, goodbye."

"Goodbye, yourself, Jack," Steve said to the dial tone. He replaced the white phone and poked his head around the entrance to the canteen and catching Tam's attention, motioned for Tam to join him outside. When Tam arrived gnawing on a toothpick, Steve waited until a small group of diners passed their position before he spoke.

"I just got off the phone with Jack. Sorelli skipped out of some kind of vet's office or make shift surgery out in Jean two weeks after the fact. He got somebody to fly in, land nearby and fly him somewhere. This weekend, if you're not doing anything more important, I think it would be a big help to check this guy out and find this airstrip wherever it is and ask around. Maybe somebody saw something the day he flew out. You know, maybe a cop will scare more information out of him." Tam looked around and shifted the toothpick to the other side of his mouth.

"Yeah, I guess, where you gonna be?"

"Sedona, where else." Tam nodded.

"Solo?"

"Yeah, I'm going to come from the west and cross ten miles of desert. The BLM maps show an airstrip near the location you gave me, and if Sorelli is there or has used the place, it is probably better I not march through the front gate." Tam looked at his watch.

"Let's go, our friend should be sweating up a storm by now." Steve fell in behind the detective as they made their way out of the casino and into the parking lot.

Juan Ramos sat in one of the drunk cells that had been converted into an interrogation room by the addition of four uncomfortable chairs and a metal topped table. His left arm was in a sling and he held it tightly against his chest. He watched as his lawyer paced up and down in front of the bars. The lawyer looked at his watch for the tenth time since he had arrived thirty minutes before. Steve and Tam watched the two from several yards down the hall and out of sight as they waited for officer Rivas to finish a phone call in the booking room. Tam spoke in a low whisper with his head inclined toward Steve's.

"I don't like the looks of this, where'd this guy get a lawyer? We probably only got one good shot here. In my experience, we keep it short and to the point until we figure out what this guy's angle is." Steve nodded just as Rivas came up behind them.

"Ready, Senoritas?" Rivas laughed at his own exaggerated accent and led the trio to the door of the cell, unlocked it and went to one of the chairs facing Ramos and sat down without looking at the lawyer. Tam did the same and sat beside Rivas. Steve brushed past the lawyer and leaned up against the wall nearest Ramos and stared at the prisoner. The lawyer cleared his throat. He was an overweight Hispanic man in his early thirties. He had loosened his tie in the warm cell and he reached down and picked up his briefcase before he spoke.

"I demand that you release my client immediately." He stomped to the table and throwing his briefcase on the surface, sat down behind it in the only empty chair. Tam stared at him coldly.

"And just who are you, and who called you?" Rivas started to translate into Spanish.

"I speak English, you idiot." Though the word he used was in Spanish and Steve guessed it was stronger than the word; 'idiot'. Tam reached in his pocket and withdrew the revolver, still holding it by the pencil. He placed it on top of the briefcase. The lawyer looked down at the pistol as if he had never seen one before. Tam snickered.

"Well, if you comprende so well, why don't you answer my question?" The lawyer pulled a business card from his pocket and slowly handed it across to Tam, his eyes still on the gun. Tam looked at it and held it at an angle so Rivas could see it. Steve read over Rivas's shoulder.

'Almedo Guitterez, Immigration Attorney.' Tam looked up at Guitterez with the same hard stare as before.

"His sister called me." The lawyers voice was quiet. Tam stood from the table and walked over to the door and leaned back against the bars.

"Mr. Ramos, here, is not a United States citizen, at least he wasn't last I heard. But I don't care about that right now. This is not an immigration beef. This is a murder inquiry and your client may be implicated in that, we are about to find out. But he will go down for deadly assault on a police officer and resisting arrest, passport and birth certificate or not. So I guess my question to you, Mr. Guitterez, is this: Do you want to pitch in this league, or do you want to shove off and let us handle it?" Tam folded his arms and gazed across the room at the perspiring attorney. Mr. Guitterez said something in Spanish to Juan Ramos and grasping the pencil gingerly, lifted the snub nosed .38 from his briefcase and put it down carefully in front of Rivas. He stood up and crossed in front of the table and stood in front of Tam. Tam, who was three inches taller than the lawyer, looked down at him for several seconds before he stepped to the side and let him pass. Juan's black eyes watched the lawyer walk quickly down the hall until he disappeared around the corner. Tam slid off the bars and stood behind Rivas.

"Let's get this underway, shall we? Ask him if he knows why he is here and also ask him if he wants another lawyer." Tam waited until the exchange was over. Rivas leaned back in his chair and spoke to Tam over his shoulder.

"He doesn't want a lawyer and he says he wasn't going to shoot you and that you should forgive him."

"Tell him that depends on how cooperative he is and show him this picture and ask him where we can find his running partner." Tam handed Rivas the photo with the back to Ramos. Rivas spoke a few sentences before he tossed the picture in front of the prisoner. Ramos's eyes grew large when he saw the picture of Harris McCord. He spoke several sentences in rapid fire Spanish and then pointed at Steve. Rivas wrote a few lines in a notebook he had just opened as he spoke.

"Mr. Ramos says that he saw the man in the picture two days

ago. They met briefly and Harris gave him some money that he said he stole from somebody. When he saw Cannon, here, he thought he was the guy coming to get the money back."

"Where is Harris now?" Rivas barked the question across the table and started writing again as the prisoner spoke.

"He says he doesn't know, but he is supposed to meet with someone Monday night and that man is going to take him to Harris and they are supposed to pull some kind of job."

"What kind of job?" Tam paced around the cell as a long exchange ensued. Finally Rivas sat back, sighed, and started writing in his notebook again.

"He says that he came back from Mexico a week ago with a woman that has been staying with Harris since then somewhere in North Las Vegas. Next week they have a rich customer lined up for her services and when he shows, they are going to rob him and maybe hold him for ransom, or maybe just take pictures and blackmail him." Ramos spoke several more sentences in Spanish and indicated to Rivas that he should tell Tam.

"What did he say?" Tam walked behind Juan and looked down at Rivas.

"He said that Harris had a lot of money and was expecting more. That was why he was so generous with our boy Juan, here." Tam paced back and forth behind the prisoner glancing now and then at Steve.

"Whaada you think?" Steve shrugged and still leaning against the wall folded his arms across his chest.

"I think it is worth a shot. You got somewhere we can stash this guy until Monday night?" Tam nodded and looked at Rivas.

"You want some overtime just hanging around your house this weekend?" Rivas laughed.

"And just who is going to authorize that, gringo?" Tam smiled and with arms straight on the back of the empty chair, he looked down at Rivas.

"The Assistant DA, how about that? You in?" Rivas looked at Ramos for a long moment.

"Yeah, I'm in, but I want to hear it from the DA himself." Tam straightened up.

"Fine, wait here." Steve and Tam walked down the hall to Tam's office. Tam picked up the phone and put a call into DA Larsen's office.

"He's out, won't be back until four. Meanwhile I'll get the paper work done on Ramos. I need to get him a lawyer so he can sign off on our plan. Once we outline the advantages to his client, he will play ball. If we keep him in the stir, Harris will find out about it, and the deal will be queered." Steve moved from his place just beside the open door.

"I've got to get things together for Sedona. I'll be home for the next several hours, so if need me to do anything, give me a call." Steve turned to go, but stopped when he heard Tam call out his name.

"Steve. No hard feelings on the Nick Montero conversation, right? I may have been a little out of line there." Steve smiled.

"It's all water under the bridge and forgotten, Tammy boy." Steve laughed when he saw the detective's reaction to the use of the diminutive version of his name. Steve walked down the hall singing: 'Tammy Boy', to the tune of 'Danny Boy' in his deep baritone. He heard Tam's door slam behind him.

Steve pulled a medium frame pack from the back of his hall closet. He opened a box and selected four canvas rucksacks of various sizes and strapped them to the ash wood frame. Into the four sacks he loaded all the things he could anticipate for a two day, one night, trip to the desert. One of the rucksacks contained items that went on every trip. Besides two compasses, a small survival kit that contained a candle and three ways to start a fire including a small vial of waxed matches, went into the smallest bag. Steve added a signal mirror and a bright chrome whistle to the bag. Even though it was midwinter, Steve packed small containers of water everywhere they would fit. If he found no water at all, he needed as much as he could carry. In the rucksack devoted to food, he put two thin white tins of DAK bacon, three small potatoes, two apples, a small bag of peanuts, a small jar of instant coffee crystals, and ten ounces of beef jerky sealed in cellophane. In the large rucksack that sat on the top of the frame he replaced the large set of naval binoculars with a compact spotting scope that had a small tripod folded into the underside. Two .38 caliber speed loaders each holding five cartridges for the snub nosed revolver he would carry at his waist went in next to the scope. The middle rucksack and the biggest, contained a mess kit that when unfolded was two kidney shaped pans connected by hinges and inside were several small empty containers, a hobo's knife and fork and a small leather bag full of dry condiments and a small vial of cooking oil. Steve fastened his tightly rolled eider down sleeping bag to the bottom of the frame with thin leather thongs. He then slipped his arms through the worn leather straps and jumped up and down a few times. After rearranging a few items, he walked briskly around the outside of the house several times and when he was satisfied that the rig made no extraneous noise, he locked it in the back of the Jeep Wagoneer. Back inside, he pulled out a small gray Swiss army bag that he would sling over his shoulders. In this he put his main supply of water and two small metal flasks of whiskey along with a green plastic collapsible cup. He entered his office and from a drawer in a wooden file cabinet in the corner he pulled out a new Pentax Spotmatic single lens reflex camera. He loaded a roll of Kodak Tri-X black and white thirty-six exposure film into the back of the camera, while three extra rolls went into the gray woolen bag. At the bottom of the drawer was a case containing several lenses. He lifted out the 40mm to 240mm zoom lens and after unscrewing the normal 50mm one from the camera body, he replaced it with the longer lens. He carried the camera by a long leather strap into the living room. He placed the bag along with his maps and the camera next to the door.

After a quick shower, Steve donned his tux for the second time in a week. He looked at his watch. He made a quick decision to leave and drop by the Sands. If the traffic was good, he would have an hour to help Bernie before he picked up Remy.

The big Jeep wove through the back parking lots of the Sands Hotel. Steve found a spot that was only twenty yards from the rear entrance to the showroom. There were men still unloading musical equipment and parts of the stage when Steve walked through the large bay door and into the backstage area of the Copa showroom. The first person he saw that he knew was Vic Damone, who was pacing around with a music score in his hand. Steve had played poker with the singer many times in the past, but had not seen him for over two years. Steve came up behind him as he squinted down at his lyrics.

"Hey Victor, how you been?" Steve chuckled at the frown on Vic's face when he turned around to see who was daring to call him 'Victor'. The frown inverted into a big smile and was followed by an immediate bear hug.

"Hey man, how you been, man it's been a while. You used to call me that when I was taking all the poker pots. We should get together, and play cards, I would like to hear you call me that again." Steve patted him on the back as he continued toward the front of the stage. He skirted behind the silver and black main curtain and descended three steps and entered the pit where two dozen musicians were warming up. In the middle of the cacophony, Bernie Gold was huddled with Quincy Jones and Jack Entratter. Steve sat on a low railing and listened to Dizzy Gillespie and Billy Eckstine rehearse one of the old tunes they used to play when Dizzy was part of Billy's big band. All around the small enclosure, the greats of jazz practiced, laughed, sang and caught up with bandmates some hadn't seen in twenty years. A few minutes went by before Bernie spied Steve and made his way through the assemblage to where Steve stood.

"Why are you here so early?" Bernie had to bend close and raise his voice to be heard. Steve turned sideways and bent down to Bernie's ear.

"Figured you might need me to do something for you." Bernie smiled and indicated that they should retreat to the other side of the stage where stage hands were setting up the seating for the various combinations of musicians that would be performing in two hours' time. When they could converse in normal voices, Bernie pulled two chairs to the side of the stage and they sat down.

"How you doing, Bern, this is a zoo." Bernie laughed.

"I told you I would regret this. But if I am honest, I would have to say, that there wasn't much for me to do once the musicians all got here and Quincy took over. The problem will be getting everybody on that wants to play and everybody has a list of who they want to play with, but I think Quincy got all that sorted out in rehearsal today, though there may be a few bruised egos here and there." Bernie spoke in the usual staccato cadence he lapsed into when he was excited about something.

"If you have a minute, there are some people I want you to meet."

"Sure, Bern, I have half an hour before I have to pick up Remy." Bernie pulled the chairs back where he had found them and led Steve off the stage and up the few steps to the showroom floor. As they approached the same table that Steve and Remy had sat at just three nights before, Steve saw several people already seated, one of them was Rowena. They all greeted Bernie warmly as he turned and indicated Steve behind him.

"This is the guy I told you about this morning. This is Steve Cannon." Steve nodded in the general direction of the assembled group. Bernie started with the women that were present first.

"Rowena you already know. This is Marilyn Rooney, Desmond's daughter, this is Howard, Desmond's brother and this is Darren,

Desmond's son." Steve stepped up and shook all of their hands and reached out and patted Rowena gently on her shoulder as he shook her hand. Marilyn spoke first.

"I hope you catch whoever did this, Mr. Cannon. Bernie says you have been working on the case since you heard about it on Monday. Do you have any news for us?" Steve had been listening carefully as the short brown haired woman spoke. Steve guessed she was in her mid-twenties and therefore younger than her father's girlfriend. Though all the seats were together, there was a noticeable gap between Rowena and Marilyn, who was definitely part of the group of three.

"Yes, I have been investigating the case this week, along with the police and also someone in the District Attorney's office. It has been a process of elimination so far, and looking for a possible motive. We have a definite lead that I will know more about next week. Everyone has been very cooperative so far." Steve glanced at Rowena who looked quickly down at her hands. "I am very sorry for your loss, and although I did not know Desmond as well as Bernie, I considered him a friend, a good man, and a great musician." Howard Rooney stood up as Steve finished. He was obviously older than Desmond had been and was slightly stooped, his hair was gray and thinning on top. His light blue eyes twinkled as he addressed Steve.

"I want to thank you Mr. Cannon for the generous contribution that you made to the memorial fund. We will never forget it." Mr. Rooney sat down after his formal show of appreciation. Steve felt his cheeks blush a little as he spoke.

"That was actually a contribution from Mr. Sinatra. He insisted I take money to help in the expenses for the investigation. My policy is always to not charge for work I do for friends." Steve stepped back as Bernie informed everyone that Steve would be returning shortly with Remy and that Bernie would join them all at the table. Steve said goodbye to Bernie a few steps away from the table and the two men parted going in different directions. Steve retraced his steps through the backstage area, stopping for a few seconds to listen to Quincy Jones run Count Basie and his band through some changes. The back area of the Sands was dark and almost deserted when he wheeled the Jeep from the parking space and started up the Strip toward Remy's house.

Remy and Steve returned to the Sands and a scene that was much like the one they experienced on Tuesday night. This time, however, the crowd was almost all royalty from the jazz world. Steve looked out on the sea of black and white and realized that a tux was one piece of apparel that most professional musicians owned at least one of, if not two or three. Steve escorted Remy to the table and introduced her to Rowena and the family. Remy sat with an empty chair between her and Rowena that Bernie had requested for himself. There were two empty chairs beside Steve that were constantly being filled and emptied by jazz musicians coming over to pay their respects not only to the family, but to Howard as well, who had been an alto saxophonist of note in several regional big bands in the Midwest and had played with many of the greats as they came up.

The memorial began a little after seven o'clock. Several of the family members walked up to the microphone just below the stage and told the assembled group what Desmond had meant to them. They were followed by Bernie and several of the musicians who were scheduled to perform in his honor. Most of the musicians had humorous stories to tell, but almost all of them described the many ways that Desmond had helped them become better musicians. When the last person to speak had taken his seat, the silver and black curtain slowly opened. Quincy Jones had realized early on in the three day project that he had at his disposal almost all the best jazz musicians that were still living, and he was determined to make the most of it. A small ripple of excitement spread through the crowd as they realized what they were about to witness.

The stage held forty-three musicians, most of them arranged in historically important groups. Just to the right of center stage sat a lone chair and on top of it sat Desmond's trumpet. Front and center, Billy Eckstine was surrounded by the surviving members of his big band and he stood side by side once again with his star trumpet player, Dizzy Gillespie. In between them was another chair that held a saxophone. Very few people in the showroom had to be told it was in honor of Charlie Parker. Billy Eckstine counted his men down and they eased into a medley of Charlie Parker songs that ended with his classic: 'Orinthology'. The spotlight shifted stage right to Chet Baker, Stan Getz, Gerry Mulligan and Paul Desmond. They took turns trading improvised solos within the chords of 'My Funny Valentine'. They did the same with two of Desmond Rooney's better known compositions: 'Dublin Three AM Blues' and 'Rainy Day Interlude'. As their mini set ended the stage lights went dark for several seconds and when the blue spotlight again cut through the smoky haze it illuminated six men. The audience murmured, then became quiet as Count Basie led the band into an intro of 'Round Midnight'. The group in the spotlight began to play one by one, and as each player came in, the Count took out another section of the band. John Coltrane was the first, followed by Paul Chambers on upright bass, who was quickly joined by Red Garland on piano. When Philly Joe Jones came in on drums, the music from the four men swelled and then faded as the two men in the middle started to play, their horn lines weaving in and out and in turn calling to the other instruments to take short solos. Sonny Rollins and Miles Davis then traded improvised solos for the next five minutes, both of them swaying in the center of the stage to the rhythm of the other man. When they were finished, the crowd was silent for a few seconds than erupted in waves of applause. The group then played two of Desmond's original compositions: 'Brooklyn Nocturne', and 'The Way I Love You'.

Next were the singers. Frank Sinatra and Vic Damone each spoke of Desy for a few minutes and after singing three songs each, left the stage and sat at one of the tables that was directly in front of the stage on the left. A white piano was rolled to center stage and Duke Ellington strode on dressed in a tux that matched the instrument. He and the band began a very up tempo, 'Take the A Train', that Quincy Jones had decided to stretch out, giving several of the musicians in Count Basie's band as well as the newly added members the chance to solo. As Duke stood up to accept the round of applause at the conclusion of the tune, the clapping and cheering suddenly swelled as the crowd spotted Ella Fitzgerald as she blew a kiss at Count Basie and stepped up beside the Duke's piano. Duke Ellington turned around and helped count off the band as they erupted into: 'It Don't Mean a Thing If It Ain't Got That Swing'. Ella scatted several bars after each verse, and when they had reached the end of the tune as they had rehearsed it, the crowd was so wildly cheering at every note that Ella sang and every solo, that the Count had them all just circle around and repeat the whole tune again. It was a full ten minutes before the crowd returned to their seats and stopped their ovations. When it was finally quiet again, the Duke played a few tinkling changes on the piano while the rhythm section of the band laid down a quiet moody layer of sound. After ten bars the sweet mournful notes of a trumpet was heard coming from off stage. Ella turned and smiled, her head bobbing gently with the beat. By the third note the crowd had stood again and was already clapping when the trumpeter appeared and kissed Ella lightly on the cheek between runs, his huge smile flashing at the band, the Duke and the crowd almost simultaneously. Louie 'Satchmo' Armstrong grinned and waved at everyone he recognized as the Count and the Duke kept the intro coming around until the applause subsided. Louie leaned into the microphone that Ella held up for him and crooned the first verse to 'La Vie En Rose'. Ella repeated the first verse and then the two of them finished the song as a duet. As the applause rose and fell several times long after the song had ended, Louie walked to the front of the stage and the microphone that stood beside Desmond's trumpet. He smiled broadly for the several minutes it took for the crowd to stop showing their appreciation.

When he finally spoke, his voice was quieter than normal.

"There are some cats who come along and you just know that God made them to do exactly what they are doing. 'Redness' was one of those cats. If you talk to any of us that blow on this lady," Armstrong held up his trumpet and then gestured at the lone horn on the chair beside him, "We all had the same feeling when we heard him play that he was speaking to us in a language that only the two of us could understand. In my case, it was like all of New Orleans was pouring out of his horn, the ghost of every note I ever heard in every dive and on every street corner was given to me as his personal gift." He stopped as several musicians in the audience expressed their agreement. "Over the last couple of days, several of us got together and put those feelings into the music. I would like to bring out those people right now." He stepped back from the microphone as Dizzy Gillespie, Chet Baker and Miles Davis joined him at the front of the stage. As Count Basie and Duke Ellington played the slow intro, Satchmo stepped back up to the microphone.

"This is called: 'We Will All Remember Desmond'. What followed was a threnody for the trumpet with each player melding his particular style into the languid melody that was at once melancholy and hopeful. One after the other, the four greatest trumpet players in the world stepped to the microphone and poured their soul into their interpretation of the music they had composed together in a paean to Redness. The notes soared and swirled and when they had finally faded, few musicians in the room doubted that they had heard a new addition to the jazz canon and that many of them would record and play the song for years to come.

The show ended with the family coming up on the stage and joining all the musicians that had participated. The Count Basie band played what was by now the theme song of the night as the musicians and friends of Desmond Rooney mingled in small groups. Steve and Remy were left alone at the table. As some of the musicians left the stage and began filtering back through the showroom, Steve and Remy walked down the stairs beside the stage and into the backstage area looking for Bernie. They found him in deep conversation with Jack Entratter and Quincy Jones. As Steve greeted the group, he noticed Buck Monari packing up his trumpet a few feet away. He excused himself and greeted the musician.

"I hope that sounded as fantastic to you up there as it did to us in the audience." He held out his hand as the Sicilian straightened up and smiled.

"It was the greatest, man. One of those nights everyone will talk about for years and there will be twenty times the people that were here that will claim they were." Steve laughed.

"I am sure of that. And while I have you here I wanted to thank you for making that tape for Bernie. I had to promise him that I would come over and listen to it with him this week. So I just want to say thank you." Steve reached out and patted Buck's shoulder.

"Man, I should be thanking you. You got me up on that stage and I will always be grateful."

"My pleasure, think nothing of it, but let me ask you something else. Do you think I could come over to your place this week sometime and take a look at your collection of Desmond albums? Something has occurred to me and I would like to check it out." Buck smiled as he swung his tux jacket over his arm and picked up his trumpet case.

"Sure, Steve, but we will have to make it after noon because I am subbing for one of the guys in Louie Prima's band and their last show doesn't end until six in the morning." Steve stepped back in mild surprise.

"That is burning it at both ends. Tell you what, I'll call you around three later on in the week and we can go from there."

"Sounds good, I will talk to you then." Buck waved goodbye as he walked through the musicians and stage hands that crowded the area. Steve turned around and rejoined Bernie and Remy who were standing alone and talking quietly. Steve gently took Remy's hand and put his arm around his old friend.

"Well, Gem, what do you think of our boy here? He pulled it

off like a trooper." Bernie squirmed away from Steve's grasp and laughed as he led the trio back out to the showroom.

"All I did was make a few calls. The third or fourth one was to Quincy Jones and I didn't have to do much after that."

The showroom was being quickly set up for the Sinatra midnight show and most of the musicians and friends had spilled out into the casino or left for their other gigs. Steve and Remy said goodbye to Bernie in front of the hotel as the valet brought his Thunderbird around. On the way home, Steve told Remy about his weekend plans.

January 9

The moon was in bright half phase in a clear cold sky when Steve pulled the front door closed and climbed into the Jeep, placing the canvas bag and his maps on the passenger seat next to him. His right hand went to his waist and the .38 snub nosed revolver in the small hip holster hidden beneath his flannel shirt. After letting the engine warm for a few minutes, Steve turned the tires from the slight incline at the end of his gravel driveway and headed toward the Boulder Highway. He glanced at his watch as the Jeep picked up speed on the deserted road. 4:30. He had two hundred and forty-three miles in front of him until he reached the point where he had decided to park the car and began his hike. He planned on stopping twice during the trip, the second time for gas and breakfast.

The headlights cut yellow beams through the blackness that had settled on the bottom of the deep canyon as Steve began the drive across Boulder Dam. Halfway over the span, he pulled from the road into a turnout area and parked in one of the ten spaces that butted up to the stone wall encircling the edges of the dam. He retrieved a flashlight from the glove box and walked the ten yards between the car and a bronze plaque set into a stone monument that was made from the same materials as the wall. There were ninety-seven names on the shiny brown surface of the monument. Ninety-seven men who had died building the dam. Steve held the light on the third one from the bottom. Leland Cannon. Steve stared at the inch high letters for several seconds before he stepped up on the sidewalk and leaning over the rock wall looked down into the black swirls seven hundred feet below. Back in the Jeep, he sat still and felt the faint rumblings of the machinery working inside the dam far below the surface of the road. A few minutes later as he drove to the end of the dam, he wondered if his father had ever hiked in the desert around Sedona.

Four hours later, Steve turned away from the rising sun onto a smaller highway and after three miles on the new road he pulled into a small truck stop that housed a diner in the bigger building of the three that sat on the flat dusty lot. The small dining room was almost full as Steve sipped his coffee at the counter and listened to the early morning chatter around him as he waited for his breakfast. There were at least two groups of locals in the four booths across the room and a group of farmers sat two stools away from Steve as the counter curved toward the kitchen. Steve only half listened to the weather talk and the comments on the morning's crop report as he ate his bacon, eggs and pancakes. He had also ordered a double portion of biscuits to go. He was sipping his second cup of coffee and waiting for the waitress to bag up the biscuits, when a piece of conversation floated over from one of the stools and caught his attention.

"Yep, its' being flown in today. Leroy said he would hold it until tomorrow and that's when I'll drive over and pick it up." A few minutes later, the farmer put down his cup and waved goodbye to his seat mates as they filed out of the door and climbed into a '56 Chevy pickup. Steve looked casually in the farmers' direction, and smiled when he caught the man's eye.

"You think the weather will hold this weekend?" The farmer nodded.

"Yep. No rain 'til Tuesday, the earliest, and precious little then, I bet. You passing through?" Steve nodded back.

"Just doing some sightseeing. I thought I overheard you mention an airport a minute ago. Is there one around these parts, I don't remember ever hearing of one?" The farmer took another sip of his coffee and looked at Steve in the large mirror that hung on the back wall across from the two men.

"Wouldn't call it an airport on a good day. Short boondock runway is more like it. There are two hangars there that some of the locals keep their planes stored in, and there is a place where you can buy aviation gas, but that's about it."

"Is there a charter service there?" The farmer looked over at Steve and for the first time, looked him up and down. When he spoke it was with a very noncommittal tone.

"Leroy Blevens can make those kinds of arrangements, but I wouldn't waste your time, if I were you."

"Why not?" Steve picked up the bag of biscuits from the counter and slid off the stool to face the farmer who was staring straight ahead.

"Because he ain't likely to do it unless he knows you." Steve repeated the question. The farmer shrugged.

"Ask him yourself. Three miles down the road, the Socony Mobil Oil station." Steve started toward the door.

"Thanks, I'll do that." Steve climbed into the front seat and sat for a few minutes smoking a cigarette. When he was done he pulled back onto the two lane road and three miles later saw the large red winged horse on the sign above the gas station. He pulled into the pumps and nodded to a young man watching the gas flow into a station wagon that was loaded with camping gear.

"Leroy Blevens around?" The youth didn't look up from the spinning numbers on the pump, but jerked his head in the direction of an open garage door. Steve locked the Jeep and crossed the oil stained pavement, then onto a patch of gravel in front of the garage. He ducked under a pickup that was hoisted on a rack and stood before a pair of overall clothed legs that stuck out from under a '62 Chevy. When the owner of the legs realized Steve was standing there, he slowly slid the creeper sled he was on out from under the car. When Leroy stood up he was nearly as tall as Steve and looked to be close to the same age. He looked Steve in the eye, but Steve had the distinct feeling that Leroy was taking in more information than that. The sandy haired man pulled a red rag from his back pocket and rubbed a patch of grease from his face revealing a row of dark red freckles across his cheeks.

"Can I help you?" He was now trying in vain to remove the grease from his hands with the rag.

"My name is Steve Cannon, Mr. Blevens, and I understand that you handle plane charters." Leroy shook his head.

"Well, if someone told you that, then they probably also mentioned that I only do it for people I know real well." Leroy wadded up the rag and threw it into a fifty gallon drum five feet away.

"Yeah, they mentioned that fact, but they wouldn't say why. So I'm asking you." Steve smiled and leaned back carefully on the two door coupe. Leroy turned and spit a brown stream of tobacco into the pit below the pickup truck.

"I'll make you a deal. You tell me why you're carrying a pistol on your hip and I'll tell you why I don't get involved with strangers and airplanes." Steve smiled once more and patted the grip of the small pistol under his shirt.

"You are pretty observant, Mr. Bleven. I am a private detective from Las Vegas and I am here following a lead on a fugitive from justice." Leroy snorted, but Steve noticed the half smile that played across his face before he turned to send another stream to the bottom of the pit.

"A bounty hunter, right."

"No, this is personal. This guy killed four people including the wife of a friend of mine." Leroy leaned back on the hood of the Chevy and folded his arms.

"Sorry, no offence meant."

"None taken, Mr. Blevens."

"It's Leroy." The man held out his hand to Steve. Steve motioned toward the open door of the garage office as he grasped the oily calloused hand.

"Somewhere we can talk in private?" Leroy nodded and turned toward the door. Steve followed him into the small grimy room and closed the door behind him. Leroy sat behind a small desk that was covered with auto parts soaking in pans. Steve leaned up against a filing cabinet. Leroy pulled a small bottle of whiskey from a drawer at his elbow and pulled down two paper cups from their holder on the side of a water cooler. He poured the small cups half full and handed one to Steve.

"Might be a bit early, but from one cop to another." Leroy hoisted the cup slightly above his head before he downed it in one gulp. Steve did the same and immediately wadded the cup up in his hand and tossed it into a garbage can at his feet. He looked quizzically at Leroy as he poured another shot of the whiskey. He held the bottle up to Steve, but Steve shook his head.

"Twelve years a cop in Phoenix." He downed the second drink and likewise threw the wadded cup into the trash. He leaned back in the chair and looked evenly across the desk at Steve.

"I had only been chartering planes for a month when the federal narcotics boys and Border Patrol were swarming all over this place. I was so green I didn't know it is a favorite ploy of the drug smugglers, so no more of that for me." Steve nodded and reached into his jacket pocket. He placed the dog eared picture in front of Leroy.

"Ever seen this man?" Leroy picked up the photo and held it to the light that came in through the window.

"Nope. Is this the guy you're looking for?" Steve nodded and took back the photo and replaced it into his pocket.

"I am more interested in the airstrip that is in the vicinity of Crows Canyon. You ever seen it or flown into it?" Leroy shook his head.

"Nope. Never have. It's private. Belongs to two of the big ranches there. All I know is that even the smugglers don't try to land there without an invitation, for what that is worth. Is that where you are headed?"

"Yes. If the map is right, I can get close to the airstrip by staying on BLM land." Leroy shook his head.

"Wouldn't try it, were I you. Cameron Vanderhof thinks the BLM land is his just because his father used to have grazing rights." Steve pulled his notebook and short pencil from the back pocket of his heavy canvas pants and began to scribble, pressing the notebook up against the cabinet.

"Who owns the other ranch?" Leroy shrugged his shoulders and waved his right hand.

"Nobody knows and Joel Vanderhof, the brother who sold it ain't saying. All anybody knows is that whoever owns the place, they don't run cattle anymore." Steve scribbled in his notebook. When he was done he stood away from the file cabinet and looked down at Leroy.

"I am going to let you get back to work, Leroy. I appreciate the information. Let me ask you a favor before I go."

"Sure, if I can." Steve tore a page from the notebook and handed it to Leroy. Leroy looked up after reading from the page.

"Who is Tam Polhaus?"

"He is a police detective in Las Vegas. If I don't stop back in here for gas by five o'clock tomorrow night, call him and tell him so." Leroy folded the small piece of paper and put it in the pocket of his coveralls.

"No problem, but I may be up at the house." He opened the top drawer of the desk and handed Steve an oil smudged business card.

"That's my home number. Call me when you get here." Steve waved the card in Leroy's direction.

"Thanks, Leroy, I will."

The highway continued flat for the next ten miles and then began twisting through a series of low hills. After another five miles, Steve pulled over to the side of the road and checked his map. When he pulled back on the highway he had only gone a half a mile when he found what he was looking for. A faint two track trail led off the back of a gravel turnout. It meandered over a large hill and looked to have had no recent traffic. Steve shifted the Jeep into low and waited until a car passed by before following the narrow road to the top of the hill. From the crest of the hill, Steve could see for several miles. Even the sparse vegetation that surrounded him on the small knoll vanished three hundred yards ahead as the hills flattened out onto an arid desert. He could see several deep arroyos that began at the bottom of the hill and all ran in the general direction he needed to go. He also saw a little cleft in between the hill he was on and the one next to it. It was only fifty yards off the trail, but if he could nudge a little deeper into it, the Jeep could not be seen by anyone staying on the track.

Twenty minutes later, Steve had obscured the back of the vehicle with some dried brush from the hillside. He shouldered his pack and then moved into the shadow in front of the Jeep. For ten minutes he stood and listened, watching the direction he had just come and the small portion of the trail he could still see. Satisfied there was no one about, he skirted the bottom of the last hill and walked down a steep slope into an arroyo about thirty yards wide. Steve avoided the middle of the wide gully where the sand was several inches deep and the walking was easier. He chose instead, the rockier portion along the edge, where footprints were less likely to be left and a solitary walker was less visible. The only vegetation over two feet high was along the sides as well. Whenever Steve came upon a clump of bushes that offered enough cover, he would duck behind it and watch his back trail for several minutes. At least once every half hour, he would find some cover that allowed him to climb out of the arroyo unseen. With a small pair of binoculars he carried in his shirt pocket he would glass the surrounding area paying particular attention to the portion of the arroyo immediately in front of him as well as his back trail. Though these frequent stops and excursions to the top of the arroyo slowed his travel time down significantly, they were a critical part of travel in the desert. Steve had hiked in the desert with his father and his older brother from the time he was five years old. His father used every opportunity to illustrate the point that even though the desert seemed empty to the casual observer, in reality, a host of people lived there, considered it their home, and looked upon any outsiders as resources to be exploited. Steve knew that almost every event that occurred in this wasteland was observed by someone, usually by several people. Steve had often used this little known fact in his work and had even cultivated relationships with several of the denizens of the Mojave Desert around Las Vegas. Today, he had gotten lucky with the weather. A low bank of gray clouds had moved into the area since he left the gas station. The breeze had stiffened and small local dust storms moved along the flat mesas. No shadows and limited long range visibility would make Steve harder to detect, but it would also make it harder for Steve to locate potential trouble. That trouble was not long in revealing itself.

Steve had just finished eating one of the biscuits and drinking a small quantity of water behind a three foot high clump of cactus on the ridge, when he detected something moving in the arroyo just next to the one he was traveling in. Whatever it was, it was moving slowly as well, and appeared to be employing the same tactics as Steve. It took the figure several minutes to emerge from behind the bushes that had first attracted Steve's attention. It quickly moved fifteen yards and disappeared behind a similar clump of vegetation. Steve wriggled out from under his back pack and pulled the spotting scope from the top rucksack and using the pack as a rest, he got as low as he could on the exposed ridge top, adjusted the scope on the bushes two hundred yards away and waited for the figure to reappear. A long several minutes later, Steve watched as the man emerged from his hiding place and climbing quickly from a crouched position, crested the side of the arroyo and lying flat on the ridge top, peered down into the arroyo where Steve had been walking minutes before. When he realized that Steve was not where he should have been, the man froze and then inched his way back behind a medium sized rock that afforded the only cover on the red dirt ground. Steve could see the upper half of the man and studied him for any details he might learn.

The man was in his mid-fifties, taking into account a life spent out in the elements. From his clothes, Steve guessed he was some sort of prospector, but the fact that he had a newer model pair of binoculars and that his clothes were only normally worn and dirty, suggested he either didn't live in the desert full time or had some type of steady income. Most desert rats, never knowing when they would see their next dollar, tended to wear an item of clothing to shreds before seeking a replacement. Steve inched down below the crest of the ridge, dragging the pack behind him. When he was no longer in danger of being observed, he used the binoculars to glass the area in front of him for whatever options were open to him. Steve had been walking down the center part of three parallel arroyos. The one that the intruder occupied was the smallest. The one Steve was now looking into was the biggest and offered the least amount of cover between the three. It was obvious to Steve that the man was planning on intercepting him at some point farther along the trail he had been following. Steve moved his head over the ridgeline just enough to get one side of the binoculars on the man's position. He was still there and looking down the arroyo back along the trail that Steve had already covered. Steve figured he had at least ten minutes to get out in front of the man as it would take that long for him to convince himself that Steve was not coming down the arroyo. Steve dragged the pack behind him as he slalomed through the deep sandy dirt on his way to the bottom of the gully. Once he hit the rockier surface of the old stream bed, he quickly readjusted his pack on his back and began a slow jog straight up the arroyo.

Fifteen minutes later he spied a small offshoot gully that led back into the original arroyo he had been traveling in. He slipped the thirty yards through the narrow opening and stopped and glassed the ridges on both sides before moving quickly across the flat bottom and stopping behind a clump of manzanita bushes. He had traveled at least five hundred yards from his original position. After catching his breath, Steve climbed slowly to the top of the ridge and after getting as flat as he could, he turned the binoculars up the third arroyo. He gave himself thirty seconds and when he didn't see anything moving his way, he crawled the steep twenty yards down to the bottom. The arroyo narrowed quickly where he was and he realized anyone coming through would have to pass within five yards of his concealed position behind a dead cottonwood tree that a winter flood had pushed up against the side of the slope. He took off his pack and stashed it under the branches of the tree and then pulled the revolver from its' resting place, slipping it into the front pocket of his heavy jacket. From his hiding place he could see all the way up the arroyo to where he first spotted the man. He could also view both ridge lines without being seen. He looked up at the sun, hazy behind the cloud cover and calculated that there were only three more hours until sunset. He was still at least two miles away from the airstrip and he had wanted to reconnoiter the area and then find a comfortable place to camp before heading back early in the morning. But caution was the rule he had been taught well by his father, and if someone was following you, it paid to find out why, sooner, rather than later.

It was no longer than five minutes before Steve spotted the man approaching. He was moving quickly and Steve figured that he must have panicked when Steve did not appear where he was supposed to and was now trying to escape, or more likely, trying to get out in front again, to reacquire the element of surprise. Steve was a little confused with the strategy. The safer move would have been to immediately change the direction of travel and carve a large arc away from the area and work to establish contact at another point. Steve lowered his profile as he heard the sound of labored breathing coming toward him. Thirty seconds later, the man appeared in front of Steve, slowing down appreciably from the pace that he had been moving when Steve had first seen him two hundred yards away. Steve waited until he had gone several yards past his hiding place. Steve stepped out onto the trail behind the figure.

"Hey!" Steve's voice was loud and strong with the breeze behind him. The man froze for a split second and then wheeled quickly around to face Steve. The element of surprise was usually the key in these types of confrontations, and once startled, it would hard for the man to gain the upper hand. The man looked at Steve's hands pushed deep into the slit pockets of his jacket. He wiped his hand nervously across his face, pushing his wide brimmed hat back on his head. Steve pressed his advantage.

"I think you better tell me why you are following me and you better make it quick." Steve took two deliberate steps toward the man, who retreated the same distance, looking to the sides of the trail for an escape route. Seeing none, he turned toward Steve and raised his arms up halfway. When he spoke, his voice cracked from fear.

"I thought you were following me. I wasn't following you, I swear."

"Sit down right where you are." Steve indicated a large rock halfway between the two men. The man slowly lowered himself onto the rock, his hands still in the air and his eyes locked on Steve's. Steve moved slowly to his left so that the sinking sun was behind him and in the eyes of the man seated before him.

"If you weren't following me, what are you doing out here, then?" The man slowly lowered his hands and rested them on his knees, making sure that Steve could still see them.

"It's a free country, I can roam around all I want." The man's tone betrayed his fear.

"I watched you from the top of the ridge back there. You were expecting me to come up that wash. I have been hiking the desert for almost forty years. I know when I'm being followed." The man squinted at Steve.

"Look, this is no big deal. Just let me go, and I will go back the way I came. I don't want any trouble, I wasn't even heading toward the ranch." Steve moved a little closer.

"And what ranch would that be?" The man's brow furrowed.

"What do you mean what ranch? Say, who are you anyway?" The man shaded his face with his hand, even though his hat had a wide brim.

"No, hombre. The real question is: Who do you think I am?" The man dropped his hand and stared at his boots while he turned something over in his mind. He removed his hat to mop his brow with a red handkerchief, revealing a thinning head of gray hair.

"So, if you're not one of the ranch goons, who are you, and why are you here? Can I stand up? It's getting real uncomfortable on this rock." Steve stepped back but kept his hand in his pocket.

"Sure, but don't try anything. We may get around to who I am and what I might be doing here, if things go the right way. But first, you are going to tell me about the ranch." The man brushed off the seat of his heavy khaki pants with his hat and gazed at Steve.

"Let's start with your name." Steve's tone had not softened.

"Harvey. Harvey Chandler."

"What do you do for a job, if you have one?" The man coughed.

"I'm a petroleum engineer." He waited for the next question.

"So you are out here exploring this area for signs of structure, right." The man half smiled.

"Seems you now a little about my field. You wouldn't be from a rival company would you?" Steve matched the half smile.

"No, that's not my field. I just know a little about it, that's all. So my guess is that this is unauthorized as far as the land owner goes, right?" The man nodded.

"We have the ability to drill under here from adjacent lands."

Harvey swept his arm in a large circle. "But first we have to prove that there is oil here, so that job was handed to me." Steve nodded.

"You don't look prepared to spend the night out here, where's your rig." Harvey pointed back the way they both had come.

"About a mile beyond the highway. I got my truck and I pull a small camper. I was just heading back when I saw you. Figured you must be a new one or something. I was just trying to get a good look at you, that's all." Steve snorted.

"Maybe. Didn't look like that to me, I usually go with my gut feeling in my business and it looked to me like I was about to get waylaid. You ever see an airstrip up ahead?"

"Sure, even flew in there a couple of times. But that was before the mafia guy bought the ranch and put the kibosh on any oil exploration." Steve ignored the remark about the new owner.

"From the map it looks like we are on BLM land. I got that wrong?" Harvey shook his head.

"No. You got it right, except in this state they recognize a ranchers' claim to land if they have held grazing rights on it over several generations. Finding oil here would vacate that claim, so that is why they try so hard to keep us out of here." Steve nodded and turned to gauge the sun that was much nearer the horizon than when he had first spotted Harvey Chandler.

"How long would it take us to get to the airstrip from here?" Steve watched as the man looked around him.

"An hour, more or less. But you were heading in the right direction, you don't need me." He looked over at Steve with a slightly imploring expression on his face.

"You're wrong there, Mr. Chandler. If we get rousted, I am just your assistant. We get kicked off and that will be that. Besides I might have some questions about what I am looking at. Comprende?" Harvey shrugged and pointed.

"This way. They don't usually check this arroyo. Too many snakes to spook their horses. We can get within three hundred yards of the ridge overlooking the airstrip without leaving the gully, but that last stretch is pretty exposed."

"We'll worry about that when we get there. The faster we move, the quicker you can get back to your rig, but if I were you, I would plan on spending the night out here. That prospect scare you, Mr. Chandler?" Harvey shook his head.

"Done it before. Just a little more uncomfortable that's all. The goons never leave the ranch at night." Steve nodded and indicated to Harvey that he should lead the way. Harvey kept to the rocky side of the arroyo and Steve followed ten feet behind, keeping his eyes on the tops of the ridges.

Forty-five minutes later, the wash narrowed and opened into a flat open area about the size of a football field. It was covered with a grove of cottonwoods. Steve figured that most of the year an underground stream must run under the area. Harvey stopped and pointed beyond the cottonwoods to where a large hill rose to a flat mesa top. The slope was bare red dirt and though not steep, was at least one hundred and fifty yards long. Steve indicated that they should continue. They double timed it through the easy walking below the trees and caught their breath at the bottom of the long slope.

"We are going to be exposed all the way up there and while we are looking over the top. Anybody riding to or from the ranch will spot us quick." Harvey stopped speaking and waited for Steve's reaction.

"How far away is the airstrip from the top of that slope?"

"It lies about one hundred yards below the crest and about three hundred yards away."

"Any chance of getting closer?"

"Not without being seen." Steve looked up the slope and back down to where they stood. There did not seem to be any better place to start from. Steve took off his pack and stashed it under the roots of a nearby cottonwood. He held the spotting scope in his hand while he wrapped his flannel lined khaki jacket around the instrument. He slung the camera strap over his shoulder and positioned the camera against his back. Holding the bundle under his arm, he turned to Harvey.

"I'll go up first, you wait here. If the coast is clear, I will give you the high sign. If not, you wait down here until I get back." Steve looked into Harvey Chandler's eyes. Harvey nodded.

"I'll wait for you here unless you wave me up." Steve turned and crouching as low as he could, began scrambling up the soft red dirt of the slope. Halfway up there was a shelf of hard red soil that crumbled easily under the weight of a man. Steve laid the bundle down while he excavated a small corridor through the crusty dirt. Fifteen minutes later he reached the edge of the mesa. He looked back to make sure that Harvey was still there, and then moved several yards to a small notch in the sandstone he had seen on the way up. He pulled a tumble weed from the small crevice and using his large folding knife, removed enough dirt to make room for two men. When he was done, he raised his head up little by little and peered over the edge.

Below him the mesa gently rolled down to a small basin. At the west end, a group of four buildings was nestled up against a dry river bed that was lined with cottonwoods. Directly in front of Steve and half a mile away lay the airstrip. It was not much more than a dusty road cut through the salt brush. At the far end was a hangar that Steve guessed could hold two planes and looked like it had been recently built. Steve glassed the largest building through the binoculars. It was the main ranch house and in the five minutes that Steve swept the binoculars back and forth between the buildings, there was no movement at all. He lowered himself back below the crest and waved for Harvey to come up. Harvey waved back with little enthusiasm and started the arduous climb up.

Steve waited for Harvey to catch his breath before asking him to join him in the cramped quarters of the notch. While Harvey had been climbing, Steve had used several rocks he was able to reach to set up and steady the spotting scope. It now was able to pivot freely in all directions. When Harvey had squeezed into the small space, Steve gave him the binoculars and pointed toward the ranch house.

"Take a careful look at that whole area and tell me if anything looks different from the last time you saw it." Harvey bent over from his crouching position and leaned on his elbows as he carefully glassed the compound. Steve kept his head swiveling slowly in all directions keeping an eye out for any trouble headed their way. With the exception of three horses in a pasture five hundred yards to the east, there was nothing moving. When Harvey was through with the binoculars, he lowered himself back down into the hole out of the wind.

"The last time I saw this place there was a lot more activity." Harvey pointed toward the horses. "I was over there way beyond that large corral. They had riders all up and down the arroyo that day and I had to move as fast as I could to the east to avoid them."

"How many were there?" Steve had his notebook out and pressed against his knee.

"Five. There's a foreman that lives by himself in the small white house just beside the ranch house. Some of the others live in the long building that I am guessing is some type of bunkhouse. On this particular day, there were two men I hadn't seen out here before and they didn't seem too familiar with riding through country like this. I saw them coming toward me from quite a ways off and I was able to avoid them pretty easily and I got the impression that they were out there to see something and it wasn't me." Steve wrote a few lines in the notebook.

"I'm going to use the scope for a few more minutes and then we can get out of here. Keep your eyes open, especially behind us." Steve rose up a few inches and stretched out along the edge, pushing the scope carefully in front of him. With the high powered scope many more details of the ranch came into view. There was a gas pump just beyond the corner of the airplane hangar and there were three saddles and saddle blankets side by side on a fence just behind the bunkhouse. Steve was just about to swing the scope toward the area where the horses were grazing, when he saw the door to the bunkhouse open. A stocky man of medium height and wearing a gray Stetson walked out onto the board porch and tossed a cigarette butt into the dirt. He was wearing a denim shirt, blue jeans and cowboy boots. He turned and said something to someone still inside the door and then turned and moved off toward the main house. Steve's view of the front of the house was partially obscured as the man knocked on the door and waited. Steve saw the top half of the door open, but could not see the person who opened it. After a few seconds, the door closed and the man walked the length of the covered porch and turned at the side of the house, and after disappearing from view for a few seconds, emerged onto the expansive deck that was attached to the back of the house and overlooked the dry creek bed and the cottonwoods. The man paced back and forth on the deck smoking a cigarette he had rolled himself. After several minutes he turned and greeted someone that had come out onto the deck, but was out of Steve's view behind the side of the house. Presently the man turned and pointed to something beyond the creek bed. The other man moved out on the deck and stood next to the man as he gestured, the hairs on the back of Steve's neck rose and he felt a chill settle over him. Even with his back turned, Steve recognized Angelo Sorelli.

Steve slowly eased the camera from its' resting place on his back around to the front. He peered through the lens and after turning on the light meter, adjusted the focus and brought the back view of Angelo Sorelli forward until it filled the small screen. Steve could see the angry purple scars on the back of his neck. Steve methodically snapped as many pictures as he could, before Sorelli turned abruptly and disappeared from view. Steve would have to wait to see if he had caught a frontal shot of the killer. Steve took several pictures of the man as he returned to the bunkhouse. He also used another roll of film on overlapping shots of the compound and then secured the camera and the scope and motioned for Harvey to start down back down the slope. The sun had dropped below the clouds and was sitting just above the purple ridges to the west as the two men started back through the grove of cottonwoods. Steve sent Harvey ahead and watched their back trail. He then caught up to his companion by double timing it through the trees and then repeated the process back down the long arroyos. When they had moved two miles from the ranch and were stopped just below the edge of an arroyo and could see all around them, Steve held up his hand and called a halt. He pointed a hundred yards to the west where the arroyo turned sharply out of sight.

"There is a carved out section of the arroyo over there where the flood waters gouged it out. That is a perfect spot to camp. We can build a fire just outside the overhang and stay warm all night. Unless someone is walking or riding the arroyo at night, they won't be able to spot us." Harvey looked southward toward the highway and his comfortable trailer. It was still four hours away in daylight, impossibly dangerous to reach after the sun went down. He sighed as he sized up the under packed rucksacks strapped to Steve's back.

"I guess I have don't have much choice, now do I?" Steve laughed.

'No, you don't. We are going to have to move pretty fast to gather enough firewood to last the night. I figure we have forty-five minutes before it will be pitch black. I suggest we get to it." They both clamored down the side of the arroyo and jogged quickly around the bend.

An hour later, Steve unfolded the sleeping bag and laid it flat out on the soft sand between the sandstone overhang and the fire that was laid out and burning in a line just three feet from the bag. Steve began to carefully unpack each rucksack while Harvey arranged the wood they had gathered into small piles that would be easy to reach during the night. Steve rearranged several rocks in the middle of the fire where the wood had already been reduced to coals. He opened the mess kit and balanced the hinged pan carefully on the rocks. When he was confident that he had a stable platform, he poured a little of the cooking oil in one side and sliced the potatoes into the pan. After sprinkling a few of the seasonings from his small bag over the potatoes he turned his attention to securing the camera and the spotting scope in a dry portion of the shelter. He handed the rucksacks containing the water vials and the survival gear to Harvey to secure. Harvey looked over at Steve quizzically when he pulled out the two flasks of whiskey, but then shrugged and lined them up in the sand beside the water bottles. When the potatoes were close to done, Steve opened the tin of bacon and draped all eight slices over the other half of the pan. As they sizzled and shrank, he moved them all the way into the pan. When the bacon was cooked, Steve sliced open one of the large biscuits and placed four strips of bacon and several slices of potato on the fluffy halves and handed it to Harvey. After he had done the same for himself, the two men sat side by side and ate in silence.

After dinner, Steve took one of the whiskey flasks and a small bottle of water and leaned back against the warm wall of the rock shelter. Harvey sat cross legged on the sleeping bag, his back to the fire and looked down at the flask of brown liquid that he had just been handed.

"I figure you for a non-drinker, Mr. Chandler, am I right?" Steve took a small sip of the fiery whiskey and let it burn the inside of his mouth before he slowly swallowed. Harvey nodded.

"Never liked the taste. I know that isn't the point of the exercise, but I just never could seem to get it down even in college." He placed the flask to one side and took a small sip of water as he contemplated Steve and the large shadow he threw on the wall.

"I don't suppose you are going to tell me what you were so frantically taking pictures of today? My guess is that you found what you came for." Steve took another sip from the flask and shifted his eyes toward Harvey. He could not see his features because of the backlight from the fire.

"Yeah I did, and under normal circumstances you would be right in assuming that I would keep mum about it. But since you seem determined to keep traipsing around out here, I think it is my responsibility to tell you that you are in mortal danger." Steve looked out beyond the fire and let his words take effect. When he looked back at his companion, he could see fear in the way his body moved, even though he could not see his face.

"The man who you referred to as the 'mafia', is one Angelo Sorelli, and you would be a whole lot safer if he was just one of your typical Mafiosi wise guys. He is a psychotic and sadistic killer who has murdered and maimed many people." Steve took a bigger swig of the fiery liquid. Harvey's voice was quiet when he spoke.

"How did you know he was there?"

"I didn't. Investigating things is my work. I came out here on a hunch and it has paid off, that's all." For several minutes both men sat quietly. Harvey broke the silence.

"So, Mr. Cannon, what are you going to do about it, now?" Steve could feel the large brown eyes gazing at him from under the gray shaggy brows. Steve leaned to the side and tossed a large mesquite branch into the part of the fire that lay nearest him.

"I will go back to Las Vegas, Mr. Chandler, and I will come up with a plan to return here and kill him." The newly added branch popped loudly in the cold desert air. Harvey shifted around on the sleeping bag until he was looking into the fire and Steve could see his face.

"I've no doubt, Mr. Cannon, that this man has wronged you and others greatly. But that is for the law to decide. We do not have the right act on our own in these matters." Steve took another sip from the flask and followed it with another one from the water bottle.

"Don't you think, Mr. Chandler, that there are some creatures among us that are so truly evil, that it is the responsibility of all of us to make sure that evil is buried?" Harvey pushed a stray coal back into the fire with a small branch and waited for a long minute before he replied.

"I think, Mr. Cannon, that you are good at what you do." Harvey stood and walked carefully around the fire and out beyond the circle of light. When he returned several minutes later, he stretched out on the sleeping bag with his back to Steve. Steve finished the whiskey, put several more branches on the fire and pulled his coat up over his chest. He watched as large sparks escaped the inferno and rose to the ceiling of the cave, falling back down as small spots of soot.

JANUARY 10

Steve Cannon rose at five thirty in the morning, an hour before first light. His companion snored softly by the fire, cocooned in the sleeping bag and just a few inches from the smoldering coals. Steve put the last of the small wood piles on the edges of the fire away from the slumbering form. He was preparing breakfast, when Harvey rolled over, his eyes blinking up at the ceiling of the rock shelter with a blank expression. After a few minutes he rolled onto his side and watched as Steve poured dark thick coffee from one side of the hinged pan into two small tin cups. He grasped one cup by the three inch aluminum handle and set it down carefully in front of Harvey. He set his own cup to one side and began to make the same meal as the previous evening but this time without the potatoes. When he was done, he turned to Harvey who was now sitting up and sipping the coffee with the sleeping bag pulled up over his head like a thick hood. He waited until Harvey put the cup down and then handed him the large biscuit sandwich and an apple. As before, they ate in silence, until both were crunching into the last of their apples.

"You don't seem to be a morning person, Mr. Chandler. I hope it is not the company." Harvey took one last small bite and threw the apple core into the fire.

"No, Mr. Cannon, I don't generally sleep well without a roof over my head." Steve grunted a reply and threw the last drops of his coffee into the fire.

"Well, by the time we get packed up, it will just be light enough to travel." Steve wiped the cooking utensils as clean as he could and placed them into their rucksack. Ten minutes later the pack was ready to go. With Steve's knife and several large branches, they moved enough dirt over the fire to smother it and when they were done, there was no trace that anyone had camped there recently.

"I appreciate you taking care to conceal our traces, Mr. Cannon, especially since I will no doubt be returning soon." Steve scoffed.

"Not just for your sake, Harvey, I will be coming back myself. Kind of self-preservation for both of us. If you're ready, let's go."

For the first thirty minutes the two men moved slowly in the half light. The cloud cover from the day before had vanished and the sun rose brightly to their left as they made their way through the arroyos. At each rest break, Steve tried to commit the terrain to memory and asked Harvey numerous questions about what other approaches to the ranch looked like. When they had stopped for the third time, they had seen a rider three hundred yards in the distance quartering away from them. When the man and horse had dipped below the lip of one of the mesas, they were able to make out his features below the sunlit terrain. Harvey was convinced that it was Cameron Vanderhof out for his Sunday morning ride. They waited until he was out of sight before they descended back into the arroyo and continued their journey. For the next hour, Steve made sure that one or both of them scrambled to the top every ten minutes or so, and glassed the terrain in the direction they had seen the rider. It was just past noon when they reached Steve's Jeep. They both drank several pints of water while they rested in the shade in front of the vehicle.

"It's still at least a half hour walk to your truck. I will give you a ride." Harvey nodded assent and Steve backed the Wagoneer carefully out of the narrow space and turned it back toward the highway.

Ten minutes later, Steve was mildly surprised when he saw

Harvey's white Ford pickup and the small teardrop aluminum trailer sitting out in the open just yards off a well-traveled dirt road. He pulled around and parked facing the rig that was covered with a thick layer of red dust from passing vehicles. Steve looked over at his hiking companion.

"Sure I can't buy you some lunch down at the café?" Harvey climbed out of the passenger door and looked back into the Jeep at Steve.

"No thanks, Mr. Cannon, I want to get some of the core samples I took on Friday back to the company lab." Steve looked over to the bed of the truck where a lightweight coring rig could be seen lashed to the sides of the vehicle.

"I'll wait here while you make sure your rig starts." Harvey waved assent as he closed the door and patted his pockets for his keys on the way over to the truck and trailer. A few seconds later, Steve heard the engine start strongly and settle into a smooth idle. Harvey climbed from the cab and made his way to the driver's side of the Jeep. Steve rolled down the window, the still cool midday breeze swirling through the cabin. Harvey held out a card. Steve quickly pulled out his wallet and extracted one of his own. Steve looked at the beige card he had just been handed.

'Harvey Chandler, Petroleum Engineer, Richland Oil Co., Denver, Colorado.'

In the corner of the card was the company telephone number and Harvey's extension. Steve started up the engine of his car.

"Well, Mr. Chandler, thanks for your help back there. Perhaps we will see each other again. Remember what I told you. Finish your work out here quickly, and don't come back." Harvey took several steps back from the side of the Jeep.

'I appreciate your concern, Mr. Cannon, and I will follow your procedures through the arroyos from now on." He waved and turned back toward the pickup that was still idling five yards away. Steve shifted into low gear and moved back down the dirt road toward the highway.

Leroy Blevens had his head under the hood of a Dodge truck when Steve's tires rolled over the rubber tubing by the red and white gas pumps and rang the service bells. He didn't look up, so Steve waved off the young kid who had emerged from the garage and was sauntering out toward the pumps. Steve pulled the Jeep around and parked fifty yards away from the pumps. Steve waited several feet away while Leroy finished tightening something deep under the hood. Most of the upper half of his body was prone over the greasy engine.

"Wouldn't it more comfortable to put her up on the lift." Leroy grunted as he used most of his body to turn the wrench.

"Yeah, maybe, but not nearly as quick. You seem to be still among the living this morning." Steve stepped up to the truck and leaned on the fenders and peered down into the engine bay. A few seconds later, Leroy slid back down onto the ground and waved a large socket wrench in the direction of the highway.

"Got time for lunch?" Steve pulled down on the hood snapping it into place the last two feet.

"Yeah, sure, if you let me buy." Leroy's smile had extra creases from the grimy dirt that covered most of his face.

"Just let me clean up, I will be out in a few minutes."

Steve was leaning on the side of the Jeep when a new red pickup pulled off the highway at a high rate of speed, streaming a cloud of dust behind it and came to a sudden stop behind Steve's car. When Steve glanced over he recognized the man who was climbing from the driver's seat as the same one he had seen riding earlier: Cameron Vanderhof. The tanned face stared at Steve across the hood of the Jeep from under a white straw cowboy hat. The strong smell of horse sweat reached Steve's nose. The mouth of the man contorted as he spit out his words.

"Who the hell are you and what were you doing on my land?" Steve looked back passively and said nothing.

"I saw you coming off the dirt access road and then ten seconds later that jackass petroleum engineer came out too, right behind you." Steve took a step forward and put his hands into the front pockets of his jacket. He shrugged and looked deep into the pale gray eyes as he spoke.

"I thought your ranch ended on the east side of the highway. A lot of BLM land around there, and I am pretty sure I was on it when you saw me." Steve pulled a pack of cigarettes out of his front pocket and cupped his hand over the zippo lighter as he lit the Pall Mall and squinted across at the angry cowboy. Vanderhof sputtered again and leaned across the hood.

"You think I don't know that the two of you had just come from trespassing on my land?" Steve looked down and moved the toe of his hiking boot in a circular pattern on the soft gravel.

"I was led to believe, Mr. Vanderhof, that your ranch is on the other side of the mesa and that the land in question is BLM tracts that lie between the highway and the ranch your brother sold three months ago. In addition to those facts, Mr. Vanderhoff, I don't think I much like the manner in which you are addressing me." Steve threw the cigarette butt onto the ground and pulling his hands from his pockets took another step forward. The surprised cowboy took several steps toward the front of the Jeep.

'Why you....' A deep voice behind Steve stopped Cameron in his tracks.

"Stop it, Cam. Back off or I'll back you off." Steve turned to see a clean faced Leroy with a freshly laundered flannel shirt and Levis standing just behind him.

"That's OK, Leroy. Mr. Vanderhof and I were just comparing notes on the local geography." Leroy snorted and spit a gob of tobacco six inches from Cameron Vanderhof's boots.

"This whole county is rooting for the day that the state takes that land back, Cameron. So as I have told you before, the less you show your face off your property, the better everyone likes it. Now, if you don't want to buy any gas, git on out of here." Leroy threw his right arm up in the general direction of the highway and the Vanderhof ranch. Cameron stared venomously at Leroy for several seconds before he turned on his heel, swung open the door of the truck and slammed it as hard as he could. When he had pulled back onto the highway and the dust had started to settle, Steve looked over at Leroy's grin.

"I told you that wasn't a great idea you had." Steve snickered and waved dismissively.

"He just got lucky. He was out for his Sunday morning ride and just happened upon us as we were leaving. If he hadn't seen the petroleum engineer, he wouldn't have been any the wiser. Ready for lunch?" Steve opened the passenger door for Leroy and then slid behind the wheel. As they drove to the diner, Leroy pointed out some of the more prominent landmarks as they slid by the window. They had almost finished their lunch when Leroy grew silent for a few moments before he spoke again.

"So, Steve, I don't think that you would drive all the way out here and risk the wrath of Cameron Vanderhof and who knows what else, unless you were pretty sure that you were going to get what you came for. Am I right?" Steve pushed the last of his hamburger around on the plate with the point of his knife.

"If you are asking me if I was successful in my endeavors, I would have to say yes. If you are asking me for more information than that, I would have to ask you, why?" Steve looked up and Leroy saw in his eyes that he was being anything but casual. Leroy nodded.

"Yeah, I get it, Steve, but you already showed me his picture, so I would have to assume that you saw him or have reason to believe that he is where you thought he would be." Steve kept a steady gaze on the ex-cop, and now he replied without blinking.

"I want you to look back on this conversation, Leroy, as something that was done for your own good. A man doesn't have to hide what he doesn't know in the first place." Leroy sat back in the comfortable vinyl booth and pulled a nearly empty package of Beechman's chewing tobacco from his shirt pocket. He placed a small wad in his mouth and rolling it into a ball with his tongue, smiled as he deposited it between his cheek and gum.

"Yeah, I get it. A need-to-know basis only. I guess if I were in your shoes I would play it the same as you. I guess we both know what's between the lines here. One of the reasons I quit being a cop. Too many parallel scenarios running through my head every day. I was afraid that one day I would act on one of them. I don't need the particulars of what this scumbag did, hell, I could fill in the details from a hundred cases and I bet I would be close. Justice comes in many guises my friend." Leroy winked and finished the last of his beer, before shifting forward in his seat.

"Let me change the subject, Steve. You ever do any deer hunting?" Steve nodded as he looked at the check the waitress had just laid upon the table.

"Yeah, why?" Leroy's mouth grinned with brown speckled teeth for a split second before his face grew serious.

"Well, you should come back out here and go with me sometime. But I have to warn you, around here, you need a pretty big scope and a rifle that can shoot flat out to four or five hundred yards. Got one of those?" Steve snickered.

"I probably do, but something tells me you have something that fits that bill even better. And I thought we were changing the subject." Leroy was grinning again.

"And about four hundred rounds of custom hand load to go with it. A guy like you, where you live, could set up his own five hundred yard range out where nobody would ever hear or see anything. Practice for several months under all types of wind and visibility conditions and get so good that anything was possible. Know what I mean?" Steve pulled several one dollar bills from his pocket and left one under his coffee cup as he looked down at Leroy.

"Yeah, I know exactly what you mean, and I appreciate the offer and if I decide to take you up on it, I know where to find you." Leroy motioned for Steve to sit back down in the booth. When Steve was seated again, Leroy's voice was hushed but earnest.

"Let me give you a piece of advice. Many times the cops I knew and the detectives that we worked with would bust our humps for long hours building a case against big drug kingpins that operated between Phoenix and the border. Then all that would get turned over to the Feds and they would plan a big operation. Know the result?" Leroy held up his hand with his forefinger and thumb in a circle. "Zilch. Those big operations always get compromised. The bigger the criminal, the more money he has to spend to make sure that information like that flows his way. Sometimes justice comes out of the business end of a 30.06 in the hands of a determined man. No disrespect or any connection intended toward our late president, but just remember that." Leroy looked directly into Steve's eyes as he put a napkin to his mouth and deposited the wad of brown tobacco into it. He picked up his hat and stood up from the booth. Steve remained motionless for a few seconds and then stood up and followed Leroy Blevens out of the door of the diner. They were almost in sight of Leroy's gas station before Leroy spoke again. He looked straight out the windshield.

"The word I get is that the runway you saw is being used to fly in drugs from Mexico and South America. Cameron Vanderhof is being paid to look the other way and raise a stink about anyone snooping around. His cattle business has been shrinking for years. Unlike his brother, he wants to keep the ranch. This comes from a source I trust in Phoenix. I just thought you should know, for what it is worth."

"Thanks, Leroy, I appreciate it. I hope I can return the favor sometime." Steve had pulled the Jeep off the highway in a big arc stopping just in front of the garage door. Leroy stepped out of the car and stood holding the door open and looking back in at Steve.

"You know, Cannon, someday I think you will do just that." Leroy shut the door and waved as Steve completed the arc and pulled back onto the highway, accelerating quickly and passing the diner two minutes later.

It was dark and past seven o'clock when Steve finally pulled into his own driveway. He wearily dragged all his gear into the small space just inside the front door. All he wanted to do was take a hot shower and sip a cold beer, but he dialed Remy first to tell her he was back and OK, and then meticulously unpacked his back pack and returned everything to its' rightful place. Only then did he take a shower and allow himself the luxury of a cold beer and some soothing music before he headed off to bed.

January 11

Steve awoke at six o'clock. It was still dark as he made a quick breakfast and drank two cups of coffee. He picked up the gray Swiss army bag and the camera that he had left on his desk in the office the night before. Outside, he slid open the metal doors of the garage, and slowly backed his '61 Corvette onto the gravel. Closing the silver doors behind him, he pulled the chain on the solitary light bulb that hung down in the middle of the space. From a shelf above the workbench he pulled down several cardboard boxes and lined them up on the surface. Steve unfolded a long metal table that had been leaning against the far wall of the garage. Snapping the metal legs into place, he removed several metal pans and four plastic bottles of chemicals from the boxes and placed them on the table spacing them out in a neat row. Next, he strung a piece of cord that had been coiled along the shelf across the space and secured it to an eye hook that was screwed into the far wall at the same height. He pulled out a thick padded blanket and carefully pushed the edges into the small space between the garage door and the concrete floor. When he was done, he turned off the light to make sure that no light seeped into the garage. Satisfied, he set to work.

A half hour later, Steve had a dozen negative strips pinned to the cord and drying in the darkness. While they dried he set up the enlarger and prepared the pans with the chemicals he would need to develop the pictures. From a lightproof box under the workbench he pulled out twenty sheets of Ilford high resolution photographic paper. He adjusted the red light that he propped up on the workbench and waited for the negative sheets to finish drying.

An hour and a half later, Steve stood in the middle of his office. He crossed over to a large cork board that covered the long wall of the narrow space. He removed all the pictures and notes from the board until it was completely bare. He then began to pin up the 8X10 photos he had shot the day before in the Sedona desert. The series of overlapping shots he had taken of the property he stretched across the top in a panoramic 180 degree view. He pinned the shots of Sorelli below that in a rough sequence. The last two showed the broad ugly countenance that now had a large set of scarred purple ridges on the left side of his face as well as several patches above the misshapen ear where the hair had refused to grow back in.

Steve sat back in the chair behind his desk and studied the pictures. If one had not been there and seen the terrain and Sorelli, the scene was almost bucolic. Steve pulled his notebook from his pocket and spent the next hour adding to the notes he had taken in the field. Several options were becoming clearer as he wrote. He realized the next meeting with Jack and Tam would have to be in front of the black and white pictures that now covered nearly the whole wall of his office.

Tam Polhaus was not yet in his office when Steve knocked on his door a little after eight. As he was deciding what to do next, he saw Samuels come around the corner reading a piece of paper he was holding in his hand. He was wearing what appeared to be the same raincoat he wore when he had tried to block Steve's way on the apartment stairs. Steve was looking to see if there were signs of repair on the sleeve when Samuels became aware of Steve's presence and turned quickly on his heels and scuttled around the corner without looking up.

"Well you sure have him spooked." Steve turned toward the voice that came from behind him. Tam smiled and shook his head.

"I should have figured you were involved in his little fracas, but spare me the details, the less I know around here the better." Steve shrugged as Tam turned a key in the door lock and entered the office. Steve closed the door behind them and settled into one of the chairs and pulled out his pack of cigarettes. Tam sat behind the gray metal desk and shifted a stack of papers from the center of the desk and leaned the chair back against the wall as he watched Steve light the cigarette.

"So, how was your little camping trip?" Steve reached over and pulled the half full ashtray to his side of the desk before looking up at Tam.

"Productive. And that is all I want to say at this point until you and I and Jack can get together. Hopefully you will have something to add to the discussion." Tam shrugged.

"Sure I did like I said I would. Made two trips out there, so, yeah, I have some information that might help piece things together." Steve nodded and took another long drag on the Pall Mall.

"Let's get together, Wednesday night, provided we aren't still tied up with tracking down McCord. Speaking of which, how is our boy Ramos doing?"

"I checked on him Saturday night and called Rivas today. He is behaving himself. I made sure he called his sister and told her he was out of jail. On his lawyers' advice, he even called the guy he is supposed to meet to tell him everything was still a go, so unless we got unlucky, nobody is any the wiser that we got our hooks in him." Before Steve could answer, there was a knock on the door. Tam raised his voice a few decibels and called for whoever it was to come in. The door opened quickly and DA Larsen stuck his head around the corner and leaned on the sill.

"I was in the building and thought I might catch you two together and save you a trip across the plaza." Tam motioned him to come in and went around to the front of the desk and removed a stack of files from the other chair. The lanky DA folded himself into the chair and looked over at Steve.

"What do you have on this guy McCord and what is the plan for tonight?" Steve snuffed out the butt of his smoke in the ashtray, sat back and folded his arms across his chest.

"A lot of circumstantial facts that all add up pretty strongly. If we can bust him on the job he is planning for tonight, that may give us some leverage to keep him on ice while we work on the story he gave us about where he was and what he did on the night that Desmond was murdered." He looked over at Tam as he finished. Tam stood behind the desk and leaned forward on his knuckles as he spoke.

"We already have Ramos' attorney primed in the right direction. He got on board quick when he saw the opportunity to get his boy off on some lesser charges. Unless someone is wise at this point, we should be able to collar McCord and get him off the streets." DA Larsen nodded his head slowly.

"That sounds OK to me, but now how about running down the evidence you have against him right now?" Steve pulled Tam's file from the top of the stack on his desk and began to pull each piece of evidence out and explained the significance of each one as he handed it to the attorney. When he was finished, he sat back in the chair and watched as Larsen looked again at several of the pages in the file. When he was done he handed it back to Tam and sighed.

"You are right, pretty circumstantial, but I agree that his statements strongly suggest that he is hiding something and his actions on the night of the murder and subsequently are suspicious as well. But I also think we have quite a way to go on this one." Steve nodded and Tam grunted. Tam spoke first.

"Once we get a collar on this guy, we can get him in the room with Ramos and see what comes out." Steve interrupted.

"I also think that we should bring in the guy that claims to have seen someone running down the sidewalk below his balcony that night. Might be interesting to put them both together and see who knows what about whom. Tell him we need him for a line-up, might work." DA Larsen put his hands on his knees as he stood up to go.

"Well, gentlemen, let's hope our luck holds tonight and go from there." Steve stood as Larsen opened the door to the office. The Assistant District Attorney hesitated for a few seconds and then stepped back in the office and closed the door. His brow was furrowed as he looked over at Steve.

"Maybe not the right time for this, but you and I need a little sit down about Tommy Carmino." Steve looked over with an expression he hoped was as blank as he was trying to make it.

"Sure, Jim, let me know when and where." He watched impassively as Larsen studied his face for a few seconds before nodding and leaving the office. After the door closed, Steve busied himself lighting another cigarette and avoiding the gaze he knew was directed at him from across the desk. When he finally looked up, Tam snorted.

"Well isn't that a surprise. Lay down with vipers long enough, and eventually you are going to show up with fang marks on your little heinie." Tam chuckled to himself. Steve shrugged.

"Most likely, a whole lot about nothing. The Justice Department gets heat from the Attorney General, so they fire up the FBI and their task force, and a lot of people get to work on their tans and their golf games in the desert." Tam began to rearrange the file back into the order it was when Steve picked it up to show to Larsen.

"Maybe. But Tommy has been pushing a lot of people around for years. Doesn't take much imagination to figure someone would drop a dime or two on him."

"Be cutting their own throat as much as his. This is an open city. Everybody can open a casino, and if there are any crybabies, they don't get much sympathy from the bosses back east. Plus,

Tommy's boss is bigger than most of those guys anyway and he also lives here, so I don't see anyone bucking that system." Tam decided to change the subject.

"I got the layout for tonight figured out if you are interested." Steve nodded and pulled out his notebook. Tam continued.

"I will have two uniforms in an unmarked patrol car stashed just off Ogden where no one can see them. I can radio them in quickly if we need back-up, but most likely you and I can handle the situation and they can come in and help with transport. I figure the less the better." Steve thought back to his conversation with Leroy Blevens and nodded his head. Tam sat on the edge of the desk.

"We wait just out of sight by the spot where Ramos and this other guy are going to meet. Most likely, McCord is somewhere else and we will have to follow them in your car. I also have another detective in his car we can hand the tail off to if we are made, or the distance is too far. Got it?"

"Yeah, so far, but what happens when you and I arrive at the scene? I count at least three of them and two of us, plus the mark and the girl. Things are likely to get a little hectic, don't you think?" Tam nodded.

"That's why the other detective will be on our tail and if it is a set-up, or someone gets the drop on us, he will back us up. Don't forget the two uniforms, the whole circus will be on the move with us." Steve nodded as he made a note to himself to bring at least two guns.

"The main thing Tam, is to take down McCord. If the others scatter, let them. Ramos' attorney will be able to round him up, and McCord and Ramos will happily give up the other guy. I just don't want McCord to get away in the confusion. What time does all this go down?"

Be back here at six. We will go over the plan with everybody. The meeting between Ramos and his contact is scheduled for eight in front of Ramos' house. We just make sure Ramos is out front on time and take it from there." Steve nodded and stood to go. He held the door for a few seconds and looked back at Tam before he stepped through it.

"I will call Jack and we all meet at my place around seven." Tam's features twisted into a frown.

"Why your place?"

"Because I have something to show the two of you and I don't feel comfortable moving it around." Tam snorted.

"Well unless it is an Angelo Sorelli mummy you stumbled over out in the desert, I don't see your problem, but if Jack agrees, I guess it's alright by me."

"Jack will agree. He wants Sorelli as much as you and I do." Steve saw a flash of something in Tam's eyes and suddenly felt a wave of sympathy for the Detective. He spoke quickly to cover for his friend.

"See ya tonight, Tam." Steve quickly closed the door before Tam had to reply and moved down the corridor and out the front door into the plaza. The biting wind was back and Steve pulled up the collar on his dark blue pea coat. He was almost to his car when he heard a female voice calling his name from across the parking lot.

Rita Malone strode quickly in her high heels to the spot where Steve stood in front of his Jeep. Her long light brown coat had a large fur collar that came almost up to her ears and looked plenty warm to Steve as he waited in the wind for her to arrive. Rita extended her hand as she came to a stop in front of Steve. Steve shook it and looked into the light brown eyes beneath the long black lashes.

"Steve, I saw you coming out and I thought if you had a minute we could talk." Steve gestured toward the Jeep.

"Sure, Rita. Let me buy you a cup of coffee. Hop in." Steve went to the passenger door and made sure that Rita got in safely before circling behind the vehicle and climbing into the drivers' seat. He started the engine and slid the heating lever as far to the right as it would go.

"Sorry, Rita, it may be a little cold in here for a while." Rita laughed softly.

"Don't worry about it, I had my mother send out all my winter clothes from Chicago, so I am one of the most warmly dressed people in town." Steve smiled as he steered the car out of the lot and headed for the Golden Nugget. A few blocks later, he thought better of it and turned to Rita.

"Ever been to Foxy's deli?" Rita shook her head. Steve took the next left he came to and headed toward the Strip.

"Well, then you have to meet my friend Bernie. He runs the joint and is real Las Vegas if you know what I mean."

"I have only been here six months, but I think I am beginning to know what that means." Rita snuggled down into her fur collar and watched the downtown part of the city slowly give way to the more glamorous beginning of the Strip.

Bernie was working behind the counter when Steve held the door open for Rita and helped her with her coat, hanging it up near the door. Walter approached them with two menus and waited formally for them to acknowledge him.

"Hi Walter, this is Rita Malone." Walter nodded his head and held out an arm toward an empty table away from the usual breakfast crowd. Steve pulled Rita's chair out for her and sat down just as Bernie came up from behind and slapped him on the shoulder. When Steve turned to look at Bernie, he was already smiling and extending his hand toward Rita.

"Hi, I'm Bernie. I don't think we have met." Rita nodded her head and accepted Bernie's dish pan reddened hand.

"No, but Steve told me that I was going to meet real Las Vegas when I met you." Bernie laughed and slapped Steve's shoulder.

I don't know about that, Miss Malone, but I won't hold it

against you that you walked in here with this guy." Bernie turned and took two coffee cups on saucers from a tray Walter was holding and after placing them on the table, turned for the silver carafe and the small pitcher of cream. Steve pushed the other chair out slightly from the table and motioned toward it.

"Bernie, why don't you join us?" Bernie was already moving back toward the counter.

"Maybe in a little while. We are short-handed today." He waved as he turned back to the counter and standing behind the cash register began to take money from several patrons who were ready to pay their bill and leave. Steve turned back to Rita.

"So to what do I owe this pleasure?" He watched as Rita pulled a large notebook from her purse she had placed on the empty chair.

"Actually, Hank Greenspun sent me. I was going to call you tonight at home, but when I saw you outside the police station, I figured that maybe I should do this now." Steve noted that her voice had taken on a more serious tone. Steve took a sip of the coffee and waited until Rita was ready to speak.

"Do you know who Clifford Jones is, Steve?" Steve nodded.

"Well, then I am sure that you also know that he has been a very important figure in the politics and inner workings of this town and the whole state for a long time." Rita waited for a reaction from her tablemate. Steve stretched out a stiff leg under the table.

"I am not sure what you are expecting me to say or what you want me to say at this point. You really haven't said anything I can comment on yet." Rita nodded.

"I know. Like I said this comes from Hank, so here it is: Hank has tapes of Mr. Jones implicating himself in illegal activities involving gaming licenses and skimming from several casinos, here, and in Reno." Steve shrugged.

"Why does he think I should be told this. What does this have to do with me?" Rita took a long slow sip from her cup and looked at Steve and shook her head slowly.

"Because he also implicated Tommy Carmino, and also implied

that Tommy was involved without the knowledge or permission of his boss." Steve slowly stirred his coffee and thought for a moment.

"Well, Rita, that is interesting information. But I still don't see why I have to be informed." Rita interrupted.

"Because Hank saw in the public records that a new corporation has been formed by Tommy and you are on the board of directors, and Clifford Jones is also on that board and is the attorney of record." Steve held his hands open.

"And Bernie Gold, who you just met, is the other partner and I say so what? If Tommy and Clifford have crossed some line that the Feds think shouldn't be crossed, then they will have to answer for it, right? I still don't see why Hank thinks I should be so concerned with this news. He, of all people should know that most of these types of inquiries eventually come to nothing." Rita's face grew serious and she looked down at her coffee cup. Steve frowned as he spoke.

"What else is there?" Rita looked up slowly and looked in Steve's eyes as she spoke.

"Hank is the one who set up the concealed wire on a low level casino owner from Henderson. He wanted you to know that from him before you heard it from someone else." Steve sat back heavily in his chair. He didn't speak for a few minutes but watched as Rita stirred her coffee and took a few nervous sips.

"You can tell Hank for me that I understand why he used you as a go-between. You can also tell him that I understand why he did what he did, and though I may not agree with his opinions of this town and some of the people who run it, I respect that he is doing what he thinks he has to." Steve finished the rest of his coffee in three quick sips.

"I am sorry, Steve, it seems like I am always delivering bad news."

"Don't worry about it, you'll get used to the way things work in this town. I appreciate you taking the time out of your day to let me know. Is there anything I can do for you?" Rita shook her head.

"Well, then let me drive you back to your car, and we can both get on with our work." Rita nodded and stood up to go. Bernie intercepted them at the door.

"Don't be a stranger, Miss Malone, now that you know how to get here." Rita smiled down at the beaming face before her.

"It's Rita, Bernie, and I will make this one of my special places, goodbye." Steve held the door for Rita and then held the door open for a few more seconds and looked back at Bernie.

"I will be back in twenty minutes. You and I need to talk." Bernie nodded.

'I'll be here. I have more help coming for the lunch hour, so I'm all yours." Steve forced a weak smile and let the door close behind him.

By the time that Steve returned from dropping Rita Malone back at the police station, Bernie had set up a table for them in the back room. Steve poured the coffee for both of them from the silver carafe and sat down across from his old friend. Steve smiled as he watched Bernie tentatively sipping the hot liquid.

"Gotta thank you again for including Remy and I in Desmond's memorial. You did a great job and everyone I talked to thought so as well." Bernie waved Steve off as he attempted another sip but decided it should wait and placed the cup back onto the saucer. When he looked back up at Steve, his expression had become more serious.

"That isn't what you came all the way back here to say is it? So out with it." Steve stretched his arms out onto the table with his palms down and sighed. He then relayed everything that Rita had just told him. When he was done he sipped at his cup and waited for Bernie's reaction.

"Actually, I heard something about this several weeks ago, but I thought it was about the guy from Henderson that owns that brothel." Steve nodded his head.

"I got a few more details on the way back to Rita's car. Seems this guy was pretending he wanted to set up a casino in conjunction with his other endeavors and he wanted to give Clifford 50k to get him a gaming license, no questions asked. Tommy comes into the deal, because the guy also wanted someone to run the casino that would offer him an extra layer of protection. Since we both know how much Tommy wants to set up his own gambling empire, it doesn't take too much imagination to figure Tommy jumped at the chance. I figure the guy got himself in some kind of hot water with his brothel and either he or somebody else came up with the bright idea of the wire to reel in bigger fish."

Bernie looked down at the table for a few minutes, before speaking. "How do you see this going down, Steve?" Steve leaned back in his chair and folded his arms. Just as he was about to speak, Walter came through the door carrying two plates of food. He set them down in front of the two men. Steve saw that the menu today was corned beef and boiled potatoes. Another waiter was right behind Walter and he put two small bowls of dinner salad beside the plates. When they had left, Steve cut up the thick piece of corned beef as he spoke.

"Well, Clifford's been caught doing this type of thing before. They don't call him, 'Mr. Juice' for nothing. The thing that Hank doesn't understand or figures he can get around is that almost all the people he thinks should care and step up and do something have all made deals just like this one, if not with Clifford, then someone else. And you and I both know that Clifford knows where all those bodies are buried. Clifford is the last guy anyone wants to see in the docket. I don't think this hurts Tommy at all, because it was just talk as far as his name is concerned, and Hank doesn't know what we know, which is Tommy's boss has given him permission to start setting up on his own. Anyway, that is how I see it." Steve took a bite of the pink beef and looked across at Bernie. Bernie chewed in silence for a few minutes.

"Yeah, I think you are right. I don't think this has any bearing on our lighting deal." He was about to take another bite when he sensed something in the demeanor of his lunch companion. He put down his fork and waited. Steve used his napkin to wipe his lips, then spoke.

"DA Larsen says he wants to have a meeting with me about Tommy. I am sure that this involves the case that the FBI are trying to put together and either it has reached the level where he is being brought in on the case, or he has heard something that he thinks I need to know. Either way, I think this is the bigger threat to Tommy. The FBI and the Feds have no stakes in this game, other than enhancing their reputations. We'll know more after I talk with him, but if I were you, I would use the Hank rumor to get Clifford to convince Tommy that you need a power of attorney in case he gets put on the black list or even gets put on ice for several years." Bernie nodded thoughtfully.

"Great minds must think alike. I mentioned that when Tommy and I signed the papers on Saturday morning in Clifford's office. Tommy didn't seem to have a problem with it as long as I sign one too, and Clifford holds on to them. I am supposed to play cards with Cliff tomorrow afternoon at the Desert Inn Country Club, I'll check with him again on that and maybe get his take on what Hank is up to."

"Meanwhile, I'll see if I can wrangle an audience with Tommy and bring him up to date. If you have a few more minutes, I would like to tell you what's going to happen next in catching the guy we think is Desmond's killer." Steve outlined the plan that was going to be put into action later that day. By the time he was done, they had both finished their lunches. As Bernie was helping Walter clear the table, Steve used the phone on Bernie's desk.

"Mr. Carmino's office, this is Miss Horvath speaking." Steve shook his head as he heard the grating school teacher voice come over the line.

"This is Steve Cannon, I need to see Tommy this afternoon, preferably in twenty minutes."

"Mr. Carmino has a full schedule this afternoon, what is this in reference to?" Steve groaned quietly to himself

"Tell him, Miss Horvath, that it is in reference to Hank Greenspun and a casino in Henderson, and by the way Miss Horvath, I would tell him in those words exactly, especially if you want to still be employed three months from now." Steve smiled as Miss Horvath huffed and placed him on hold. She came back to the phone three minutes later and Steve thought he detected a more polite tone.

"Mr. Carmino will see you at one o'clock."

"Tell Tommy I will be there." Steve hung up the phone and looked across at Bernie.

"I was thinking you should come too, but maybe it is better just me, since I seem to be the one everyone comes to with their Tommy troubles." Bernie chuckled.

'Yeah, Tommy has this way of thinking everyone works for him. In your case, he's even got other people believing it." Steve smiled and shook his head.

"Tommy is a unique guy in a town known for unique guys, that is for sure. If I learn anything new from Mr. Carmino, I will let you know. Thanks for lunch." Bernie waved to him from the back-room door as Steve swung open the front door and walked the six spaces to his car. He drove the three long blocks to the Desert Inn and parked beside Tommy's red Cadillac in the valet lot. He barely had time to lock his car before a burly security guard was blocking his way.

"Move it, pal, you can't park here." Steve smiled.

"I am on my way to see Mr. Carmino, and he gets real upset when people are late, especially if one of his employees is responsible." Steve watched as the information was taken in. He expected the guard to immediately get out of his way, but the man held his hand up in front of Steve's face.

"Stay right there." The guard returned to his golf cart and pulled a handset from a radio beneath the steering wheel and keyed a button on the side of the device twice. A laconic voice crackled through the small speaker.

"Yeah, I got a guy here, named..." He looked at Steve and impatiently gestured with his fingers. Steve shook his head.

"Steve Cannon."

"Cannon or something like that. Says he has an appointment with Mr. Carmino. Check that out and get back to me. Yeah, thanks." The guard replaced the radio and taking two steps forward rested his right hand on the butt of his pistol and squinted at Steve. Steve leaned back against the Jeep and folded his arms and whistled softly. A few minutes later, a golf cart came around the corner of the hotel, and moving in a swift arc it stopped just behind the security guard. The gray haired gentleman behind the wheel looked past the guard and smiled at Steve.

"Hi, my name is Earl. Mr. Carmino is in the steam bath and he sent me around to pick you up."

"The steam bath?" Steve unfolded his arms and walked past the guard without acknowledging him and climbed into the seat beside Earl. He had to quickly grab the side of the seat as Earl retraced the long arc as he sped the cart down behind the main building of the hotel and toward the back entrance to the country club.

Ten minutes later, Steve stood dressed only in a white terrycloth towel as he watched Earl open the locked door of the private steam room. Earl smiled and held the door open as a large cloud of steam poured over both of them. Steve walked into the semi-darkness and squinted as Earl closed and locked the door behind him. The room was long and rectangular and a bubbling cauldron of water and hot rocks lay in a long strip down the center. The walls were all wooden and there were two rows of benches down each side. On one of the benches Tommy Carmino sat with a scotch in his hand and a towel over his head. He was the only person in the room. Steve walked down the opposite side of the room and sat down across from Tommy. Tommy glared at him from under the towel.

"This is my steam hour, Slick, and I have had to answer that phone twice on account of you." Tommy indicated the phone that was on the wall above his head behind a fogged up plastic bubble. Steve leaned gingerly back against the hot wooden wall.

"This isn't my idea of a good time either. At least you seem to enjoy this torture." Tommy chuckled and took a sip of his drink.

"Relax, Cannon, a few minutes of this, a cold shower and you will feel like a new man. You should get out in the sun more, you look all pasty. I hope you don't want a drink, because I don't want to have to use that damn phone again." Steve shook his head.

"None for me thanks. This is not a social call. All I get lately is people wanting to pull me aside and talk about you. Why I am the lightning rod for all this, I don't know, but for what it is worth, there are some things you need to be aware of." Tommy snorted.

"Like what? I'm being followed? We already covered that so what else you got?" Steve felt the steam penetrating his lungs and he found it harder to breathe than he had just a few minutes before. A wave of panic rose up in his chest and he realized where he was the last time he felt this much humid and stifling heat: Guadalcanal. He sat more upright and began to breathe slowly through his nose, forcing the calmness down through his muscles. He looked across at the mobster.

"Hank Greenspun put a wire on some guy who offered Clifford 50k to get him around the Gaming Commission. Evidently Clifford went for the deal, mentioned you as a possible guy to run the casino. My guess it will be another one of Hank's ten part series on corruption in Las Vegas, so there's that. I will be having a talk soon with the Assistant DA concerning you, which again, I'm guessing, will have something to do with the fact that they have FBI agents brought here expressly to bring you and yours down. Other than that everything is peachy." Tommy stood up and poured a glass of water from a carafe that was inside a small refrigerator built into the wall. His tan body was only just now starting to thicken noticeably around the middle. He sat down carefully on the hot wooden slats and drank some of the water as he looked across at Steve. When he was done, he took another sip of the scotch.

"The Feds been trying for years to collar us for something. They've tried everything including income tax fraud and nothing has worked. This is a cash business and they can't prove anything unless they have a paper trail or someone that is willing to talk to them, both commodities in short supply in this town. Hank has had it in for my boss for years. If he didn't take it so personally all the time, he might actually make some headway, but he is always too obvious, and also overlooks the obvious. He can write all he wants about Cliff. Cliff will resign from one commission or other and that will be it. You want to hear something funny? Yesterday, Hank was in the boss' office and you know what they were talking about?" Steve shook his head carefully, trying not to interrupt the regularity of his breathing. "They were making plans to build a big new country club where the old Las Vegas Downs sits. Hank has signed on to be an investor and charter member. That is how this cock-eyed town works, Cannon." Tommy took another long drink of the water and squinted across at Steve. "Well?"

"Sure if that is how you say it is, Tommy, but I don't think it pays to be too cavalier about all this. DA Larsen is no dummy, and the fact that his brother-in-law is the head agent on the investigation does not bode well. I just hope for your sake that you didn't start your legitimate gimmick a few years too late." Tommy laughed.

"If I didn't know better, Slick, I might start thinking you care more than a flying rat about what happens to me." Steve shook his head.

"It pays to have friends in this town, Tommy. You and I both operate on that principle, but I don't see us together somewhere rocking on a porch in our old age." Tommy snickered at the image and swept his arm toward the door, indicating the room they were sitting in.

"Every month I have this room, my office and my personal suite swept for bugs. They are going to have to bring in more smarts than I have seen from them so far to get something on me." Steve stood to go.

"I hope my clothes are where I left them Tommy. Otherwise, Miss Horvath is going to have to do some shopping at the men's store beside the casino and deliver them to me personally." Tommy stood up and laughed.

"You tickle me, Slick, you really do. All you have to worry about is keeping me informed about any developments your law enforcement friends pass on to you. Capice?" Steve laughed as he started for the door.

"Sure, Tommy, that is my upmost worry. Keeping you informed. Don't shrivel up and die in here, OK." Steve pushed on the door which opened from the inside. He took a cool shower and dressed quickly. He cut through the card room and continued through the locker room and then along a short corridor until he came out near the casino. He circled the floor looking for Jack Cathay and made two full circuits of the large casino before he spotted him entering the cashiers' cage. He moved to the window and waited until he got the attention of one of the cashiers.

"Excuse me, could you tell Jack Cathay that Steve Cannon is out here to see him, please?" He smoked a cigarette as he waited for Jack to appear. After a few minutes, he saw Jack poke his head around and look at him through the window of the cage.

"What you want?" The gruff voice cut through the noise of the coins flowing through the counting machines that were behind him in the cramped room.

"Just a minute of your time, Jack." Jack grimaced and two minutes later let himself out of the heavily fortified door.

"Yeah, what is it?" Steve smiled and shook his head.

"I saw him." He stood with his hands on his hips and looked hard at the older man.

"Saw who, where? I got no time for riddles, Cannon." Jack turned and started for the door.

"Sorelli." The single word stopped Jack in his tracks. He turned back and Steve could see that several shades of color had drained from the craggy face in just a few seconds. He opened his mouth, but nothing came out. He closed it and tried again.

"Where....where...how could that be?" Steve stepped forward and grabbed Jack by the shoulders and shook him gently. The pale blue eyes suddenly focused and the usual hardness in them came back. He roughly removed Steve's hands from his shoulders and took a step back.

"Are you on the level with this?", he demanded as his lower lip curled into a sneer.

"Yeah, Jack I saw him. But you are going to have to wait for the details until Wednesday night. The three of us are meeting at my house at seven sharp. There won't be any hors d 'oeuvres. See you there." Steve spun on his heels and walked swiftly away through the twenty-one tables without looking back.

*

It had been dark for over an hour when Steve parked his Jeep as close to the entrance to the police headquarters as he could get. A light rain had fallen, leaving the streets slick and large golden halos around the lights in the parking lot. He heard Tam's voice call out to him as he walked past the breakroom on his way to the detective's office.

Tam was standing in front of a large table that was covered with deli sandwiches, soft drinks and small bags of potato chips. There were two uniformed officers with him as well as Rivas, the Hispanic officer he had met the week before. Across the room another detective that Steve didn't know sat at a table and was fiddling with several small hand held radio sets. Tam motioned to the food.

"Go ahead, eat while you can, who knows how long we are going to be out there." Steve shook his head, but sat down and opened one of the sodas. Tam sat across from him. Steve took a long drink before he spoke.

"Everything still as planned?"

"Yeah, we got Ramos stashed in the holding cell, I got Rivas to come along in case we need a translator. Figured he could ride with us." Tam jerked his thumb in the direction of the detective in the corner. "That guys' name is Resnick."

"Rivas and I had Ramos call his man today, to make sure everything is still a go. Turns out the guy's name is 'Calexo', a drug dealer we have dealt with several times over the years. He is a little higher in the food chain than McCord, so that is a new twist. He also has a reputation for violence against police and strongly objects to being arrested, so we have to be doubly sharp out there." Steve nodded and finished his soda.

"When do we go?"

"In a little while. I am having some plainclothes guys cruise through the neighborhood as we speak. When they get back here and report that everything looks cozy, we will roll." Steve nodded and stretched his legs out under the table and watched as Tam walked over to the corner and began to gather up the radios.

Forty minutes later the small convoy pulled out of the parking lot. Steve and Tam lead the way with Rivas and Ramos in the backseat of the Jeep. Four blocks below sixth and Ogden, Steve stopped the car and let Ramos out. The three remaining men drove to the observation point one block below the meeting point. Rivas turned around in the seat and kept a pair of binoculars trained on the lone figure as he walked up the street toward them and the meeting place. Ramos crossed a half block behind the jeep and continued on the far side of the street until he came to the corner where he was to meet Calexo. Ramos stood under a street light and lit a cigarette. It had started to rain again and Steve could see the drops as they fell out of the blackness and into the arc of light above Ramos's head. Tam had chosen their observation point because there were no streetlights anywhere near and with the rain on the windows, the men's dark clothing would be less likely to give them away. Steve felt for the small .38 on his hip and then the larger Browning 9mm under his left armpit in a shoulder holster. He settled back into the seat for the long tense wait. Tam chewed on several pieces of gum and stared out the windshield through the raindrops.

It was ten minutes past eight when a dark blue pickup with shiny chrome wheels cruised to a stop several yards past Ramos. He quickly flicked his cigarette butt into the street and jogged to the truck and climbed into the cab. The truck pulled away from the curb and picked up speed as it headed east down Ogden.

Steve waited for the count of five and then pulled the Jeep to the corner and turned onto Ogden. He purposely left the headlights off until he saw the pickup's brake lights flash as it slowed to make a right turn. Steve switched on the lights and made the same turn ten seconds later. Tam radioed the other two cars their location and direction of travel. He instructed the black and white unit to stay three blocks behind them. He radioed Resnick and made sure that he was out in front of the blue truck on a parallel street. Steve could see the taillights of the truck two blocks ahead of him and still heading straight. He slowed down until he was almost three blocks behind. Tam grunted.

"If he doesn't turn soon, so we can hand him off to Resnick, he will make us for sure." Just as he spoke, the truck made a left turn onto Eastern Ave. Tam quickly radioed Resnick and advised him of the change of direction. Steve turned left as well and three blocks ahead he saw the detectives' car two blocks behind the pickup. The suspect car made a right turn onto Stewart Street and traveled several blocks before it turned right again onto Pecos. A few minutes later, Resnick radioed that the truck was on a dirt road and cutting through a large tract of undeveloped desert. He requested that Steve and Tam pick up the trail. By the time they arrived at the spot, they could see the taillights of the truck several hundred yards away in the desert. Tam signaled for Steve to stop the car. Steve turned off the headlights, but kept the engine running as he glided to a stop.

For several minutes the trio watched as the truck didn't move. Tam had just suggested that they drive to the corner and try to intercept them as they came out, when the pickup's lights snapped on and off three times. Immediately another set of car lights came on and shone through the darkness fifty yards in front of the truck. Tam put his hand on Steve's arm to stop him from moving forward. The new car made a slow turn and the truck began to follow it toward a line of streetlights two hundred yards away.

"What is that street over there?" Tam pointed toward the lights.

"Sandhill," Steve replied as he drove to the corner before switching the headlights back on. Tam radioed Resnick and told him where the two suspect cars were likely to come out.

Steve continued slowly down the street, while Tam anxiously waited with the radio poised near his face. Just before Steve reached the intersection with Sandhill, the radio crackled to life again. It was Resnick.

"They've just pulled into the driveway of a house on Camel Ave. Turn left on Judson and then right on Camel, third house on the right. I have just driven by and both cars are there." Tam acknowledged the call and passed the information on to the black and white unit which was still on Eastern Ave.

Steve decided to approach the house from the opposite direction and turned on Cactus Way which ran parallel to Camel. When he had gone four blocks he made a right and then a left. From three blocks away they could see the lights of the pickup and the car still illuminating the small house from the driveway. Steve pulled over and killed the lights while Tam got busy on the radio and positioned the other two units. When Tam was finished he decided to wait for a few minutes to observe the house. Steve lit a cigarette and turned halfway around in the seat and looked at Rivas.

"Hopefully, Ramos knows what his role is here." Rivas was writing in his log book and looked up.

"Yeah, DA Larsen was pretty clear to his lawyer that any leniency or forthcoming deals were only going to happen if we got McCord into custody. He is scared to death to go back to Mexico." Steve frowned in the semi darkness of the car.

"I thought he went back to procure women for McCord?" Rivas shook his head and snapped the log book shut.

"Naw. He waits for them on this side of the border. He has someone else bring them across." Steve turned back around in his seat as Tam nudged his arm and pointed down the street. Ramos and another man that Steve assumed was Calexo had turned off the lights in the truck and were approaching the car parked in front of them in the driveway. Ramos hung back from the car and glanced around nervously as his contact bent over and spoke to someone inside the late model Ford. Steve looked over at Tam.

"This is your operation, Tammy boy, but I think they are in a perfect position for us to take them down. If that is Harris in the car, he can't go anywhere and we don't have to solve the problem of entering the house. Out here, we have the upper hand." Tam thought for a few seconds, rubbing his jaw and chewing slowly on the wad of gum. He looked over at Steve and then back at Rivas.

"Let's do it." He quickly radioed the other two units and directed them to start rolling toward the house. He looked at Steve and pointed down the street.

"Start driving normally until we get just past them and then hook in quickly behind the pickup. Rivas, get out fast with me on my side and use the truck for cover to get up and behind the car. I will take the driver' side, you take the passenger side and Steve, wait for a count of two and then try to separate Ramos and the other perp from the vehicle. Hopefully, Ramos knows enough to stay out of the way." Steve nodded and started the Jeep, turning on the headlights as he moved down the block.

Steve pulled the Jeep up behind the car at an angle so that the men in front of the pickup could not see the vehicle clearly. Steve waited for the count of two, pulled the .38 from his belt holster, flung open the door and quickly advanced toward the man who had been talking through the car window. By the time Steve cleared the front of the Jeep, the man had turned and was coming toward Steve at a high rate of speed. Steve was bringing the gun up to bear on him when Tam tackled him from behind the car and both men sprawled onto the grass. Ramos backed up quickly with his hands in the air. Steve ran to the drivers' side of the car and thrust his gun forward at the occupant. He could see Rivas pointing his gun through the window from the passenger side. Steve yanked the door open and grabbed the occupant by the neck and pulled him out of the car and onto the ground, straddling him and still holding him by the throat. The man had a watch cap pulled down over his face. Steve holstered his pistol as Tam bent down with a knee on the man's chest. He roughly yanked the cap from his face and snorted.

"Harris McCord. We have been looking all over for you, where you been?" Steve stepped back as Tam rolled Harris over and cuffed him. Rivas was standing over Calexo who was handcuffed and lay face down in the wet grass. Steve went over and quickly handcuffed Ramos and walked him to the curb just as the black and white skidded to a stop in back of the Jeep. Steve shook his head as he turned Ramos over to the uniformed officer who emerged from the passenger side.

"You guys timed it perfectly, a few seconds earlier and you would have actually been involved in this operation."

The officer scowled, but said nothing as he and his partner deposited Ramos in the back seat of the squad car. As Steve returned to help Tam and Rivas, he saw the other detective coming out of the front of the house leading a young Mexican woman. Steve pulled Harris onto his feet while Tam and the detective conferred. Steve walked Harris back to the squad car and watched as the two officers frisked him and shoved him in alongside Ramos. Steve backed up a few steps but decided to stay there for now and keep an eye on Harris. He stood back from the side window so that Harris would not see him as he watched. Harris was shaking his head and saying something to Ramos.

Steve grabbed one of the officers as he walked by.

"Hey, get in the car and keep them from talking to one

another." The cop scowled and pointed to the second suspect still lying face down in the grass.

"What about him?"

"Leave him for Tam, he's not going anywhere. Get in there and make sure they quit talking." The cop shrugged and returned to the car. Steve could hear his voice as he yelled something at the two handcuffed men but he couldn't make it out. Tam came back to the Jeep and pulled the radio handset through the window. After he spoke for a few minutes, he came over to where Steve was standing.

"I got another black and white coming to take him away." He pointed back over his shoulder at the prone suspect. Steve chuckled.

"Thanks for taking out that guy, he had the jump on me." Tam nodded and pointed into the squad car.

"When the black and white gets here, let's separate these two. We'll take Ramos out and put him in the other car with this guy once they leave with Harris. The detective is taking the woman downtown to get her statement. Rivas is going to be busy tonight. Harris is the only one that speaks English." Steve shifted his weight and looked away as Harris craned his neck around to look at the two men just behind the squad car.

"I'm following him all the way to the station. I can't take any chances on him getting loose." Tam nodded and spit out his gum.

"Yeah, we'll both follow him down in the Jeep. Here comes the other black and white."

Steve sat in the Jeep while the new officers picked Calexco off the grass and put him in the car where Ramos had now been moved. After they left, Tam and Steve followed the car that held Harris as it retraced the route back toward the station.

When all three were booked and assigned to separate cells, Steve and Tam sat alone in the break room and reflected on the operation over coffee and the leftover sandwiches.

"I am sure that Harris will have an attorney before we get in here tomorrow." Steve nodded as he bit into a turkey sandwich. He chewed for a few seconds before he spoke.

"We have to find a way to put some pressure on him. I think we swing by early tomorrow to that guys' apartment who was so eager to tell Samuels' about the man he saw that night. Bring him down here and see what he has to say. In the notes it said he was a dealer that got off at two in the morning, we should be able to roust him and get something out of him before a lawyer gets' involved." Tam grinned across the table.

"I think I know where you are going with this. I agree. I think it is our best shot. McCord is too streetwise to do anything but stonewall. We got warrants on Calexo, but we may have to cut McCord loose for the murder day after tomorrow unless we get him to talk, especially if we can't get the DA to see it our way on the charges we filed tonight." Steve stood up and tossed his empty coffee cup in a large trash barrel beside the table.

"I'm going home. Where do you want to meet and when?" Tam looked at his watch.

"Better if we take a black and white, so I will meet you here at 6:30 sharp." Steve nodded and swung his jacket around his shoulders as he made his way to the door.

"Thanks again for making us even with that flying tackle tonight." Tam grinned at Steve's back as it turned right and disappeared down the hallway.

January 12

The dark morning felt just like the six hours that came before it to Steve as he rose from his bed at 5:30. The nightmares would come back almost as soon as he had shaken off the last one and had finally fallen asleep again. Four or five times in the night he had been awakened by the same stifling, panicky feeling he had felt the day before in the steam room. Though he didn't feel rested, it was a relief to finally turn on the bathroom light and look in the mirror at a face that belonged to a living person.

He filled a thermos with coffee and once outside, he let the Jeep warm up at idle for several minutes before making the twenty minute trip downtown. The black and white was parked in the loading zone just in front of the plaza when Steve turned into the large empty parking lot. He saw the car was unoccupied as he approached it after parking the Jeep several spaces away. He leaned up against the cold metal and smoked the first Pall Mall of the day and was just finishing it as he saw Tam walking along the edge of the lot on the adjoining street, carrying a small white bag in one hand and a pink donut box in the other. Steve ground out the butt on the pavement just as Tam reached him.

"Got us some stakeout grub." Steve grunted a reply as he waited for Tam to pop up the button on the passenger door before he climbed inside, tossing the thermos on the seat between them. Tam stood outside with the door open and carefully handed two white cups of coffee into Steve. He put the pink box next to Steve's thermos and settled behind the wheel.

They drove toward the Westchester apartments saying little. When they reached their destination they parked just south of the enclosure that held the dumpsters. From their vantage point, they could see the back of the building and the likely route of anyone that might be going in or out of the suspect apartment. Tam wolfed down three donuts and his coffee, in as many minutes. Steve poured more from the thermos into Tam's empty cup. Steve ignored the donut in his hand, preferring to take small infrequent sips of coffee in an attempt to settle his queasy stomach.

"Whaddya think?" Tam spoke softly as he clapped his hands together brushing the donut crumbs onto the floorboards.

"I say we go see if he is home. I will let you do the talking in case his lawyer tries to get him out on an invalid arrest." Steve flipped several pages in his notebook. "Kevin Shirley." Tam nodded.

"OK, but let's make it as loud as we can, I don't think he is expecting any trouble at this point."

Two minutes later they were in position outside the second story door. Tam nodded at Steve and Steve kept his fist and forearm stiff as pounded several times into the door, the loud thumps reverberating around the stucco walls of the complex. Tam put his face near the door.

"Las Vegas police, open up!" Steve pounded three more times. Tam looked around and saw several curtains jerk open in the apartments below. The men could hear a slight commotion behind the door. When it opened two inches, Tam rammed his shoulder against the wood sending a half-naked man spinning to the rug as the door hit something and boomeranged back into Tam's side. Steve caught it and realized that someone was behind the door pushing back. Steve leaned his weight into it as Tam squeezed his way through the gap. Steve heard a small feminine gasp as the door opened three quarters of the way. He let up on the pressure and followed Tam into the apartment.

Kevin Shirley lay sprawled with his body halfway under a chrome dinette set. He was wearing a striped pair of pajama bottoms and a cast on his left wrist and forearm. Tam stood over him and watched as the man shook his head groggily. Steve turned halfway toward the door and pulled it back revealing a young blond woman wrapped in a flowered bedsheet. Steve nodded for her to go into the bedroom. She wrapped several more folds of the material around her body and quickly moved around the prostrate figure of Mr. Shirley and closed the bedroom door behind her without looking up at either intruder. Steve pulled a chair from the chrome and formica table and sat down, with his hands on his knees and watched as Tam pulled Kevin up from the shag carpet and deposited him into another of the small chairs. Kevin Shirley looked from one to the other.

"What do you guys want? You scared my girlfriend half to death." Tam pulled out his kerchief and mopped his brow and looked down at the suspect.

"She'll live and if you were really that concerned about her, you wouldn't have lied to the police about what you saw the night Desmond Rooney was murdered." He waited while Kevin pushed his hands through his thick brown hair and looked at both of them in turn.

"I didn't lie, I swear. I saw the guy just like I told you." Tam straightened up and stretched, stifling a small yawn with the back of his fist.

"Fine. We can continue this conversation down at police headquarters. Get dressed, and no funny business, leave the door open while you do it. Send your girlfriend into the bathroom." Kevin shook his head and moved to the bedroom door wiggling the locked doorknob until the girl opened it from the other side. Tam stepped into the opening after the girl had gone into the bathroom and watched while Kevin pulled on his socks and some pants. As he was buttoning his shirt and putting on a pair of shoes, Tam walked around the bedroom opening drawers and shuffling through papers.

Ten minutes later, Tam put Kevin into the backseat of the cruiser and locked the back doors. Steve sat sideways across the seat so that Kevin was always in his field of vision. Tam pulled onto Flamingo Road and looked into the rear view mirror.

"Tell you what, Kevin, when we get to the station, there are two ways this can go. You can cooperate and tell us what we already know to be true, or we can charge you as an accessory to murder. We got the creep who did it sitting in one of the cells just like the one you are going to be in, so think about that. And while you are thinking about that, think about this: You can do yourself a whole lot of good by coming clean. If not, you are going away for quite a while. Don't say anything now, just think about it." Tam sawed the wheel back and forth as he passed a slower car and winked over at Steve.

Steve poured himself a small cup of coffee using the metal cup attached to the thermos. His stomach was not as rocky as before, but he was beginning to feel the effects of little sleep.

Steve was finishing his second cigarette of the day when Tam walked into the breakroom after booking Kevin into jail. He slumped down on a plastic chair and looked across the table at Steve.

"Guess what? The kid's got a lawyer already. And not just any one, it's Lloyd Torgenson." Steve frowned and shook his head.

"Did he get his phone call?" Tam shook his head.

No, I think that he had the girl call for him as soon as we left the apartment. Only way he could have gotten here that quick." Steve snorted in disbelief.

"He's already here? How does a guy like Kevin even know a lawyer like Torgenson, let alone get him to come down to the police station at seven-thirty in the am?" Tam lifted both of his hands a few inches off the table and shrugged.

"Well I guess we both know the likely answer to that question and the routine we have to go through. I still have to clear it with the attorney to let you sit in, so let's give it a few minutes." Tam looked at Steve quietly for a few seconds before he spoke again.

"So, tell me again, why all the secrecy, and why do Jack and I have to haul our backsides almost all the way out to the Nellis Air Force Base to compare notes on Sorelli?" Steve looked into the bottom of the empty Thermos cup. He didn't look up.

"No big mystery Tam, I just have something you and Jack need to see, and it is more convenient if you see it there." Tam sighed and placed his hands on his knees as he stood up.

"Let's see if we can get this show on the road. I'll be back for you in a few minutes.

It was almost an hour later when Steve and Tam sat across a gray metal table from Kevin Shirley and his lawyer. Torgenson had made them wait until he could speak with DA Larsen personally and satisfy himself that Steve's presence at the interrogation was sanctioned officially. Torgensons' steely gray eyes looked from one interlocutor to another as he made some notes on a legal pad. When he was done he placed the gold pen into a small pocket of his gray woolen suit vest. He was cleaning his gold rimmed glasses with his pocket kerchief when he finally spoke.

"I assume that you will keep your questions brief, gentlemen. I want my client released within the hour." Tam noisily pushed his chair back a few inches and crossed his legs, his left hand sliding a black fountain pen continually through his fingers. He looked at Kevin and waited until the unshaven face had turned in his direction.

"Mr. Shirley, where are you employed?" Kevin quickly looked over at his attorney who was adjusting his glasses on his face.

"I worked at the Frontier Hotel."

"You don't work there presently?" Kevin shook his head.

"I need a yes or no, Mr. Shirley."

"No."

"How long have you been unemployed?"

"Three months since I broke my wrist waterskiing at Lake Mead."

"You're a dealer. Right? Blackjack if I'm not mistaken?"

"Yes, sometimes craps as well." Kevin shifted uncomfortably in his seat as Lloyd Torgenson shook his finger at Tam.

"He's a dealer, so what? I don't see what this has to do…" Tam cut him off without taking his eyes off of Kevin.

"How have you been supporting yourself, Mr. Shirley? I would think that at least a month ago you must have been strapped for cash. Might have listened to a proposal from Mr. Harris about how you might make some easy money?" Torgenson sputtered as he leaned forward. "I object to this line of…" Tam slammed his hand down on the table and glared at the lawyer.

"We got a collaborative witness on that! You know what he says? He says that your boy here took money to lie to the police about someone running under his balcony that night." Torgenson sat forward in the chair and began to waggle his finger at Tam again. Before he could speak, a low wailing moan came from the seat beside him. All three sets of eyes turned toward Kevin Shirley as he put his forehead down on his cast and began to sob loudly. Tam reached across and gave his shoulder a fatherly pat.

"That's OK, son, just tell us the whole story, it will make you feel better." Jorgenson found his voice and stood up, his loud words echoing off the cement walls.

"This interview is over! I want Mr. Shirley released immediately!" Tam stood up as well and smiled at the attorney and waited for him to take a breath. Jorgenson stopped.

"Why are you smiling detective?" Tam pointed to Kevin.

"He stays. I am arresting him for accessory to murder. Now you can stay here while I do that, or you can run along to the judge and tell him your sad story, we are done here, Mr. Torgenson." The red faced attorney slammed his writing pad into his briefcase and without looking at his client or the two men sitting across from him, left the cell.

Twenty minutes later, Tam joined Steve in his office. "How did it go?" Steve watched as Tam hung up his suit jacket.

"Fine. He isn't going anywhere for a while." Steve snorted.

"I think the next question out of Torgenson's mouth was going to be how much money? Boy, you rolled the dice on that one." Tam sat down behind the desk and looked carefully at Steve.

"I was just going with what you came up with. After you showed me that little schematic thing I got to thinking. I went back to the files, talked to both of the officers that canvassed the apartment building that night, and that was when I knew you were right. Our boy Kevin, couldn't wait for them to knock on his door. He came over to Desmond's apartment while they were moving the body to deliver that little nugget of information. One of the guys also remembered Kevin being visibly upset when Samuels cuffed Harris and took him downtown. It struck him as funny since Kevin had denied knowing Harris. So there you are. If we had crashed and burned in there right now, I figured it would have been on you." Steve shook his head at the half smile on the detective's face. Steve stood up.

"Well I guess now we run the same play on Harris, only in reverse." Tam gestured for him to sit down again.

"This one might not be so easy. His attorney is Hildebrand, out of Clifford Jones' office. Harris is too street smart to not figure there is a good chance that Kevin would fold like he just did. We got a statement from the woman and also Ramos. We now have the pleasure of Mr. Harris's company for as long as we please. I think we would be wiser to nail down Kevin's story and then plop it down in front of Harris's high priced attorney. Guys like Harris are too dumb to figure out that lawyers like Hildebrand see themselves as winners , not losers, and they let them twist in the wind rather than risk their precious reputations in front of a jury." Steve sat back and pulled out his notebook and read to himself from several pages. When he didn't say anything for several minutes, Tam lit a cigarette and waited. Steve put the notebook away and stretched out his legs, propping them up on the corner of Tam's desk. He put his hands behind his head and looked up at the ceiling tiles before he spoke.

"Don't you think it's rather queer that Hildebrand is involved in this case? He is the criminal litigation guy in Cliff's office, but I bet if you went through the files, you would find that he is more likely to be defending someone like Tommy Carmino. No, I think that Harris didn't pick his own lawyer, Mr. Hildebrand was picked for him." Tam snorted smoke through his nose.

"So, we're back to someone else other than Harris?" Steve shook his head and continued to look up at the tiles.

"No, Tam, you'll get to see your boy doing some big time for this crime, the only question is who else might end up there right beside him, along with Kevin." Tam grimaced.

"Oh, yeah, the motive thing." Tam swiveled in his chair and pointed at the three tall file cabinets that took up most of one wall in his office. "You know how many cases are sitting over there where the guy is doing time and we have no clue why he did the crime. It is one of the occupational hazards but I don't let it keep me up at night, that's for sure." Steve nodded absentmindedly. He whistled a short tune and then spoke.

"That's just the way you look at the world, Tam. There's no right way or wrong way, just different ways. For my part, I always have to know why someone does what they do. This case has been funny that way from the start. So since we have some time right now, let me get your take on some things since you and I are the only ones that have had access to the whole file." Tam's brow furrowed.

"I don't know where you are going with this, but if you think it is that important, shoot."

Steve sat forward in the chair and looked at Tam with his elbows on his knees.

"There are a few discrepancies. I want to see if you picked up on them too. For one, Rowena told me that she didn't know who Harris was when she saw him banging on the door, yet when the cops interviewed her two brothers, they seemed to know who he was. Now, it could have been the way that the officer wrote it up, but it is one of those things that stick in your mind. The other thing I find at least mildly curious is that Desmond confides to a guy he sees once every few months that he is coming into some dough, but he doesn't mention that fact to the woman he lives with. In themselves, not much, but I think you see where I'm coming from here." Tam's face screwed up into a frown.

"Yeah, unfortunately, I do. So now you suspect that it was Rowena or her brothers that killed the guy?' Steve shook his head.

"No, that is not what I am saying, at least not right now. My point is that there is more to this than the simple fact that Harris McCord ran a knife through one Desmond Rooney. I just need to know the whole story, and that story usually lies in the small details like the ones I just mentioned." The older detective threw up his hands.

"If that is how you want to spend your time, it's a free country, I guess." Steve stood to go.

"Well, Tam you are right about that and it looks to me like you have this end covered, so I need a couple of days to run this thing over in my mind, that's all." Steve walked to the door, then out into the hall before he turned back toward the room.

"I will check in, from time to time. If I don't see you tomorrow, I will see you tomorrow night at my house, right?" Tam nodded as Steve closed the door and walked down the hallway. As he neared the front door he saw Hildebrand and Torgenson sitting together on a bench near the door. They stopped their conversation when they saw Steve. Steve smiled as he leaned into the heavy glass door and walked out into the crisp air.

Steve and Remy drove through the gates to Bernie's townhouse complex just before five. They parked in the narrow driveway beside a white panel van. Steve had just opened the door for Remy when two men dressed in chef's coats came out of the side of the garage and began removing equipment from the back of the van. Steve looked at Remy.

"What do you think this is all about?" Remy laughed and took hold of Steve's arm.

"If I know Bernie, we are not coming over just to listen to his new Desmond Rooney tape."

"I am sure you are right." Steve rang the doorbell and they waited for a few moments until Bernie opened the door. He wore a big smile and a light blue shirt and gray slacks under a dark blue sweater. He stepped out onto the porch and wrapped his arms around Remy and then kissed her on both cheeks.

"I have been looking forward to this for a long time. The two of you together. Don't worry about all the coming and going here. I am auditioning head chefs for the hotel and I thought: Hey, why not? Perfect chance with you two coming over, so we are going to have a six course meal tonight and you can tell me what you think. This hotel business is hard work. All these details. With a deli, it's just: How's the meat? After that, pretty much everything else is gravy." Bernie led them into the spacious living room where he had a special bar set up by the long curving black leather couch.

"Let's have a drink. Dinner will be ready in a half an hour. What are you two drinking?"

A few minutes later they were settled on the couch. Steve and Bernie were sipping their scotches and Bernie had the bartender for the night mix Remy a Tom Collins. Bernie held up his glass.

"To my two favorite people. Thank you for coming." He took a quick sip and looked up as Steve and Remy still held their glasses aloft.

"And to Bernie, the best friend anyone could ever have." Steve and Remy clinked their glasses together and waited for Bernie to hoist his before they repeated the action. Bernie settled back and smiled at Remy.

"How does that space look to you, Remy?" Bernie looked over at Steve. "Milton did a survey on the existing structure from the Three Coins and he convinced me that we can use it as the basis for that whole wing of the hotel. So half the rooms are already there and it will cut construction time by at least six months. So I get the bright idea that he should remodel the showroom part first, which is what he has been working on all week. I thought maybe a perfect place for Remy and Donn Arden to put the show together." He looked over at Remy. "So? What do you think?"

"It is perfect, Bern. Milton says we will be in there by the middle of next week. And I love the ideas you have for the design." Remy patted Steve on the knee. "When we start the rehearsals, you can come down and see it. Bernie's idea is to make that space the smaller showroom, or a large lounge, but more like a large dance and bar space just like in the scenes at Rick's place from 'Casablanca,' right, Bern?" Bernie laughed and held up his empty glass to the bartender across the room. Remy waited until the man had given Bernie a new drink and retreated to the other side of the living room.

"Bernie found out that Oscar Aleman, the gypsy jazz guitarist is still performing, and opening night at 'Bernie's Place American', will be: Oscar, Stephanie Grappinelli and Josephine Baker. It will be like the hot jazz scene of Paris all over again."

"And." Bernie held up his hand. "The most beautiful woman ever to grace a stage in this town will open her new revue at the same time in the big room." He stood up and kissed Remy on the cheek.

The three friends laughed together and after a two hour dinner they assembled on the long black couch once again as Bernie spooled up the tape that Buck Monari had made for him. The chef and the bartender had departed, so Steve made them all drinks at the improvised bar. Bernie started the tape, pausing it once in a while to comment on the composition, the arrangements and some of the personnel that played on the recordings. Buck had included quite a lot of documentation on a handwritten sheet inside the tape box. Steve and Remy tested Bernie on his ability to pick out individual players. When the tape was over and they had rewound it several times listening to their favorites, some of which they had heard for the first time that night, Steve read again the titles on the back of the box.

"Bernie, let me ask you something. Do you remember when we sat here several years ago and you told me how you could tell which Duke Ellington compositions Billy Strayhorn actually wrote and those that the Duke may have written himself or in collaboration with Billy?" Bernie swallowed a sip of his drink and nodded.

"Sure, if you listen long enough, it is just like reading a book. I wouldn't say it to many people outside this room, but I think the Duke took way too much credit for Billy's stuff."

Steve nodded. Bernie and Remy decided to play the tape all the way through again. Steve sat back and studied the back of the box as the horn arrangements from song after song filled the large room.

January 13

It had been dark for several hours when a pair of headlights flashed across the window of Steve's small office. He had lit a fire a half hour earlier and put out some glasses along with a bottle of Jack Daniels and another of scotch. He closed the office door behind him as he opened the front door to greet his guest.

Tam Polhaus stepped into the dimly lit hallway, peeled off his heavy jacket and hung it on one of the coat hooks near the door. He followed Steve into the living room and accepted a glass of whiskey before he sat down on the couch. Steve sat across from him and after a sip from the glass, Tam sat back and groaned.

"Been a tough two days, Cannon." He shook his head and held up his glass watching the shadow of the fire dance through the orange-brown liquid. Steve sipped his scotch.

"Well, then you must have quite a bit to report." Tam sighed and shrugged.

"Not as much as I should have, that's for sure. Kevin came across with a statement that has all the earmarks of having been cooked up between his lawyer and Harris'. Says he saw the guy, but now isn't sure what night it was or even if it was a guy, now it might have been a woman. Still got Harris on the prostitution charge. The statement from Ramos and the woman are very strong and I got Larsen helping me to see what kind of deal can be worked out with

Harris on the Desmond murder. So far he is denying any knowledge of it. Right now we are pretty much dead in the water." Steve stretched his leg out and propped it up on a small ottoman.

"I guess we figured right when we saw who these two had representing them. There is some serious money flowing around in this case, and if I can figure out why, we will know the whole story." Tam snorted.

"I haven't seen you since yesterday morning. I figured it was all tied up with a bow just waiting for me when I walked in. You must be slipping." Steve stared into the fire.

"Yeah, maybe." Tam took a large sip of the whiskey.

"Where were you last night? I tried to call several times up until eleven." Steve chuckled.

"I was over at Bernie's place with Remy listening to music." Tam shook his head.

"Well, there is a productive use of time for a detective." Steve continued to stare into the fire without replying. Before Tam could add anything, one loud knock at the door echoed through the small house. Both men chuckled as Steve got up to answer the door.

"Who is it?" Steve called through the door.

"Just open the door, Cannon." Jack's gravelly voice was loud enough for Tam to hear from the couch in front of the fire. Steve opened the door a few inches.

"Oh, Jack it's you!" Steve feigned surprise as Jack pushed by him shaking his head. He headed over to the fire without taking off his coat and picked up Steve's glass and sniffed at the liquor inside.

"What is this crap?" He held out the glass like it was going to burn his fingers.

"That's a Highland single malt scotch, Jack. Try some." Jack ignored the reply and turned to Tam.

"What you drinking?" Tam pointed to the bottle of Jack Daniels. Jack snorted.

"I'll have some of that." Steve walked around the couch behind Tam and scooped up the bottle and a fresh glass.

"Sure thing, Jack, here you go." Steve sat next to Tam as the mobster settled back in the couch and looked around.

"Why do you live the hell out here?"

"So people don't come out to my house and annoy me." Jack nodded and continued to look around before taking a large gulp of the whiskey and fastening his pale blue eyes on Steve.

"Far be it from me to annoy anyone unless I am invited, but you're the one that said you saw Sorelli, so here I am." Tam sat up and looked over at Steve quizzically. Steve nodded at the detective and stood up.

"That's right, Jack, and seeing is believing. So if you gentlemen will bring your glasses and follow me…" Steve gestured toward the office door and then led the way across the room.

When they were all inside the office, Steve turned on two overhead lights that illuminated the far wall and pulled the sheet down that he had tacked up over the photographs. For a few seconds, nobody said anything. Jack walked closer to the wall of photos and squinted at the two frontal shots of Sorelli.

"Yeah it's that S.O.B., alright." Tam stood a little closer as well and swiveled his head slowly looking at all the pictures arrayed before him. Steve walked over and sat down behind the desk. A few minutes later, both men sat down on the small brown sofa. Tam spoke first.

"I don't even want to know how you shot those pictures. How did you know he was there?" Steve shrugged. "I didn't. I got wind of an airstrip and a ranch that had been recently sold to someone mysterious and I went looking. Could just have easily been a wild goose chase."

"Well, that sorta fits with what I found out in Jean. I had a talk with that vet that Jack came up with and from what he remembers and what I learned at the little airstrip they have, Sorelli has hooked up with this guy. After I heard the description, I went back and pulled several mug shots that fit, took them back and the guy confirmed it." Tam pulled a photo from his shirt pocket and after showing it to Jack, he passed it over to Steve. Steve looked at it briefly and then passed it back.

"Who is he?" Before Tam could answer, Jack grunted.

"Carlos Esquivel. Head of a drug gang that operates from Mexico across the border and into Tucson." Steve's brow furrowed.

"You know this, how?" Jack took the picture from Tam and looked at it for several seconds before he answered.

"My brother was involved in smuggling for him. When he got out of prison, he went back down there to work for him, never to be seen again. The word that came back was that Sorelli had murdered him. This is all the proof I need." Tam and Steve exchanged quick glances before Steve spoke.

"So now it comes down to what are we going to do about him? I think we should spend some time going over our options." Jack grunted again.

"Only one option. We figure the best way to get in there and kill him. What's the set-up look like?" Steve looked over at Tam and sighed.

"Not good. Twelve miles of open desert to get to where I took the pictures with riders looking out for intruders. Big ranch house with two hundred yards of open ground in front of it. Between seven to ten cowboys and guards always on the place. The only way to stealth our way in is up the dry creek bed that runs right behind the big ranch house where I got the shots of Sorelli, but you still have the twelve miles to get there. Steve tossed the topographical map he had on his desk over to Jack. Tam broke in before Jack could reply.

"Before we get all saddled up, I think there is another option here." He crossed over to the wall and pointed at the picture of the airstrip. "I think it is pretty obvious that Sorelli is smuggling drugs in from Mexico with his partner Esquivel. My guess is that the Feds in that area could put this info together with what they or their informants know and even a medium size task force could take him down." Jack interrupted.

"That ain't gonna get us nothing but grief. Ten percent chance tops that they catch Sorelli. Another ten percent chance that he goes to prison and at least fifty-fifty that he breaks out and we never see him again." Tam shrugged and looked at Steve. Steve sat back in his chair and looked at Jack for several seconds before he spoke.

"The word I got from a retired cop I met down there confirms our suspicions about what Sorelli is up to. However, there was also the implication that Sorelli might be protected by someone he bought off or has placed in a position to know when things move in his direction. He probably used the money from the Vegas Wash deal to buy into Esquivels' organization and he has set up the perfect conduit for the drugs. A big Fed operation is an option, and my guess is that they will stage one sooner or later, no matter what we do. So as far as I can see as we all sit here, it is a heads or tails deal. Big likelihood of failure with both options." Tam finished his drink in one throw and set the glass on the desk.

"So what was the advice you got from the retired cop assuming you gave him the lowdown?"

"You probably don't want to know."

"Surprise me." Steve looked at Jack and then shrugged.

"He thinks one guy, one rifle, in, 'boom', then out." Tam shook his head.

"Naw, I am an officer of the law, I can't sign up for that." Steve swiveled in his chair and looked at Jack.

"What do you say Mr. Cathay?" Jack snorted and finished his drink in one gulp as well.

"You know what I think. The only thing I wonder is if either of you got sand enough to do it." He stood up and held out his glass.

"More whiskey." Steve led the group back out to the couches and the fire. He poured everyone a fresh drink and sat down.

An hour later, everyone had left and Steve sat alone thinking about Desmond. The discussion had gone in circles with no new ideas or information traded among the three men. There was also no resolution on the course of action, or even if there was to be one. Steve had volunteered to bring the subject up with Assistant DA Larsen and see what he thought could be done on his end. Whatever was to transpire, Steve saw solving Desmond's murder as more of a priority.

January 14

The Westchester apartments were looking almost as familiar to Steve as his own house as he pulled into a parking space right beside Rowena's blue Corvair. He knocked several times and waited until she opened the door. The sun shone on his back with little warmth as he saw the door knob turn. When the door opened, he smiled.

"I waited until a decent hour Miss Vega, I hope you have a little time to talk with me." He waited again while she blinked back at him and the bright mid-day sun.

"Yes, I do, Mr. Cannon, but just a little while, my brother is coming over later and we are going out to eat." Steve nodded and walked through the door after she stood to one side. This time she closed the door a bit more softly. Steve sat down in the same chair as before and once again pulled out his notebook and pencil. Rowena stood behind the small bar that separated the living room from the kitchen.

"Would you like some tea, Mr. Cannon?"

"No thank you, Miss Vega. But I would like to know if there are any papers or records here of the recording contracts that Desmond may have had with any of the companies he worked for?" Rowena poured herself a cup of tea and sat down across from Steve.

"There is a file cabinet in his room that has quite a few folders in it, but I don't know what is in them. I was going to begin boxing them up tomorrow. I am moving at the end of the month." Steve casually wrote a few lines in his notebook before he followed up.

"Moving? Why?"

"I can't afford to live here now that Des is gone. They are closing down our show at the Castaways while they remodel the showroom. They won't tell us when we are going back to work and there are rumors they might bring in another show to replace us. Most of the money my brothers and I make, we send back to our family in the Philippines. It is crowded over there, but I will have to move in with my brothers." Steve watched her drink two sips of her tea as she looked around the small apartment.

"I am sorry to hear that, Rowena, maybe you can get an apartment with one of the other girls you work with." Rowena shook her head.

"No, they all have boyfriends, they wouldn't want me around." She put her hand quickly to her mouth as her small shoulders began to shake. Steve reached forward quickly and took hold of the tea cup and saucer before they spilled to the carpet. He put them on the small coffee table and pulled his kerchief from his back pocket. He put his arm around her shoulders as she sobbed into the white cloth. A few minutes later, her sobbing had slowed as she looked at Steve, large tears still streaming down her cheeks. She held his gaze for several seconds.

"I can't tell anybody." She buried her face in the kerchief again and began to cry harder. Steve held her until she was calmer. He raised the tea cup to her mouth and helped her take a few sips. When she had composed herself, she looked at Steve and then quickly looked away. Steve reached out and placed his hand gently on her knee.

"What is it that you can't tell anybody, Rowena?" She took a deep breath and looked down at her hands.

"Des and I were married six months ago." She gently blew her nose and looked at Steve.

"Why is that a reason to cry, Rowena?" He waited while she dabbed at a fresh torrent of tears.

"My brothers would be angry and they would tell my family. My parents would not understand." Steve nodded.

"Well, Rowena your secret is safe with me. As far as I can see, no one needs to know." He waited until she nodded.

"I am sorry, Mr. Cannon, I am being foolish. Please forgive me." Steve patted her knee.

"Nonsense. You have been through a lot. But I have an idea. Can I use your phone?"

Steve went into the kitchen where the phone hung on the wall just above the counter. He leaned forward on the speckled formica after he had dialed.

"Gem, this is Steve. If you have a minute, I have a question. Are you still looking to fill spots in the revue?"

"Well, I think Rowena would make a swell addition."

"The other thing, Gem, is that she having to move out of the apartment. I was thinking that maybe she could find a roommate among the other girls. What do you think?"

A few minutes later he hung up phone and rejoined Rowena in the living room.

"Do you remember my girlfriend, Remy DeMarche? You met her at the memorial." Rowena nodded as she wiped her eyes.

"Well, she wants you to audition for her new revue. Would you be willing to do that?" Rowena nodded again.

"And she says that you are going to move in with her until you decide where you want to live." Rowena looked up quickly, her large brown eyes red around the edges.

"Are you sure? Why would she do that for me?"

"Because, Rowena, she has been in hard places too, and like most good people, she doesn't forget what it was like when she sees others in trouble. You will have to dance very well to get into her show, but I think you have what it takes."

A half hour later Steve loaded a large cardboard box into the back of the Jeep. He had promised Rowena that he would sort through the papers, and return them as soon as he could. He looked at his watch: 3:10. He backed out of the parking space and headed for Desert Inn Road and the Blair House Apartments.

Buck Monari was leaning on the fence that surrounded the pool and was talking to some men that were cleaning the tiles as Steve approached. The big Italian straightened up and smiled when he saw Steve heading his way.

"Steve, how are you, man? I was hoping you were going to stop by this week." The two men shook hands and Steve followed Buck to his apartment.

"I don't want to take up too much of your time, Buck, I just need some information off some of the albums you have." Buck laughed as he shut the door behind them.

"No problem at all. Let me pull them all out for you and we can spread them on the table there and we can see what you need." Steve and Buck carried several armloads of albums out of the back room into the living room, being careful to keep them in the correct chronological order. When they had them all spread out and turned over, Steve began to read the backs of the albums and to make notations in his notebook. When he was done, he sat back and picked up the glass of wine that had been poured for him. They toasted and Buck studied his face for a few seconds before putting his glass on the table and leaning forward.

"There must be something important on the back of those albums, Steve." Steve took a sip of the Chianti and looked at the records that covered the table and were in several stacks on the floor.

"I know there is, but I don't know exactly what it is quite yet. Do you know if Desmond could have been in touch with any of these record companies?" Steve passed his notebook over to the musician. Buck flipped through the last three pages and handed it back.

"All those companies are either out of business or bought up by big conglomerates. I think the last record Desmond recorded was in 1958, and that company is now part of Warner Brothers. There was talk four or five years ago of bringing out a four album set of Desmonds' stuff, but I guess it was just a rumor, and I don't remember what label was involved. I asked him about it a couple of years ago, and he didn't want to talk about it." Steve turned the notebook over and over in his hand.

"What about publishing rights, tell me about how they work. Say you write several tunes you think might be worth recording, what would you do?"

"I would find a publisher that handles jazz and one I trust and have them publish them. If that was going to be a big part of what I planned on doing or was my main gig, I might start a publishing company myself."

"Hard to do?"

"No, not really. It can be a lot of work and headaches, but it is a good way to make sure that you get all the royalties every time something you wrote is recorded or used in some other deal for profit. Most publishing companies are pretty lax and the jazz world is even worse, so you find a lot of the big guys, especially the bandleaders with their own publishing company."

"Why the big band leaders?"

"Because you have a lot of musicians writing stuff and the players change a lot through the life of a band and it just makes sense that most of the creative output of that group would be in one publishing company. Most cats are way too loose about what they write and what happens to it, so I guess the system just evolved to meet those needs." Steve flipped back several pages in his notebook, found a page and handed it to Buck.

"A good portion of the pieces on these albums list the publisher as 'Sandeman Publishing'. You ever heard of them?" Buck looked down at the page and shook his head.

"Nope. But that doesn't mean much, there are probably hundreds of publishing companies, and where your song goes depends on a lot of factors including who you may have written it with, or who you were playing with at the time and their connections, a whole lot of things come into play there. But it is a little unusual that many of Des' songs would be with one publisher. I never noticed that before, and I never got the sense that he was really interested in most of the songs he wrote, which is a shame as you know having heard a lot of it. Most of the cats I know that play his stuff do it because they worked with him way back when and picked it up directly from him."

"How can I find more out about this 'Sandeman' company?"

"Well, I can tell you the quickest way. I have a good friend, Carl Fontana, who along with being a great player is also the head of the local chapter of the Musicians Union. He deals with these companies all the time, chasing down royalties and publishing rights for all the musicians in town. It will go smoother if I give him a call and see what he can come up with. Is that cool with you?"

"Yes, and I appreciate you doing that. If I call you about this time tomorrow, would that be enough time?"

"Sure. I'll call him before I leave for work. He will know right off the top of his head if he has any information you can use." Steve helped carry all the albums back to the shelves they were stored in. It was 4:30 when Steve threaded through the late afternoon traffic on the Strip and pulled into the parking lot of Foxy's.

He found Bernie in the small casino that was connected to the deli. Bernie had shut the games down for the day and was supervising the hiring of dealers for the new hotel. His idea was to expand his blackjack and crap tables, add a roulette wheel and take a part of the deli, wall it off and set up a small room exclusively for baccarat. He even hired a raft of shills to show up at midnight and play the games during the slow wee hours to make sure all the dealers were up to speed by the opening. Each dealer would rotate through all four shifts and through every game except baccarat, the dealers selected to deal that exclusive game would not deal other games. Steve grabbed a seat and watched as Bernie's pit bosses ran down the house rules for the dealers and the style in which they wanted the games to operate. The slots were still operating and Steve sat as far away from the noise as he could. Bernie saw him after a few minutes and came over.

"Give me a few more minutes here, and then we can go into the back and have a drink. It's been a long day and it isn't even five o'clock yet, jeez." Steve leaned over so Bernie could hear him.

"No problem, Bern, I am just fine here. Take your time. Meanwhile I will watch how your new bosses operate. Where is the tall guy from? I've seen him someplace, but I can't remember where."

"That guy? He's from the Desert Inn. Tommy sent him to work over here as a kinda gift. Thinks highly of him, thinks he may make a good casino manager someday." Steve pulled out his notebook and gestured toward the crap table where the man was instructing several dealers in the proper way to leave a shift and show the bosses that your hands aren't concealing chips. "What's his name?"

"His name is Rocky something. I'll be right back, let me ask Walter." When Bernie returned, the noise from the slots had increased to the point that he had to speak directly into Steve's ear.

"Pavina, Rocky Pavina." Steve nodded and wrote the name in his notebook as Bernie returned to the games.

A half hour later, Steve and Bernie sat together in the backroom and sipped at two full glasses of scotch. Steve's notebook was on the table and he was going over recent events with his friend.

"So, that's where we are, Bern, Harris is in jail and even though he hasn't confessed, the case is getting better against him and he is not going anywhere for a long time."

"I am a little scared, Steve, that he might get off, and at the same time, I want so bad that Desmond didn't die for some sordid reason. Sometimes I think that my fate is to have everyone in my life taken away by evil forces, kinda like they are following me around." Bernie's voice trailed off and he stared into the empty scotch glass. Steve reached across the table and closed a strong grip around his friends' wrist.

"Nonsense, Bernie. This was no senseless, mindless act, I know that now. Desmond had something that someone wanted and Harris McCord was just a means to an end. I can't prove that yet, and I don't even know if I am on the right path to finding out who or why, but I promised you that with your help I would find out why that man had to die. Now if you feel up to it, I want to ask you something." Bernie looked across at Steve and then back down at his glass before nodding his head.

"Tell me how you know just by listening if a particular jazz musician is likely to have written a song." Bernie stood up from the table and went to the bar and filled both of their glasses half full from the bottle of scotch. When he returned he sat back in his chair and nodded at Steve.

"Well for me it is pretty simple, I don't know about other people. All musicians have things they fall back on. Usually things they played when they were learning their instrument or little pieces of melodies they heard along the way that stuck, things like that. Eventually they turn those bits and pieces into licks and strings of notes that they tend to incorporate into things they are playing, especially when they are improvising. In addition, there are usually some chord progressions they like better than others, so when they sit around noodling or practicing, they tend to build on those elements and use them as the basis for the tunes they write. That is especially true, I think, of guys like Desmond, who don't consider themselves composers. They play tunes they made up, other musicians hear them, start playing them, ask what the name of the tune is, and 'voila', another song is born. So, if you listen to one guy long enough, you can hear a tune out of the blue and know he probably wrote it. In fact, one or two of the songs on that tape that Monari thinks Desmond wrote, I am pretty sure he didn't. But, hey, that's just my opinion." Bernie laughed and took a drink of scotch

"You shouldn't get me started on things like that, I can go on all night and bore everyone in the room." Steve laughed.

"Nonsense, Bern, that is very helpful. I listen to this stuff all the time, but I can never really get under the surface of the music like you can." Steve stopped talking as Bernie held up his hand and softly snapped his fingers.

"You know that reminds me of something I need to tell you. After you were in here the other day with Rita Malone, I couldn't get her face and name out of my mind. I knew I had seen her or something, somewhere before. Then it suddenly clicked. I called a guy I know back in Chicago and he confirmed it. When I went back there three years ago, I made the rounds of all the jazz and blues clubs. In one of the clubs there was a big poster up there when you came into the club with her face and name on it. I didn't catch her act because me and the guys I was with headed off to see someone else at another spot, but it was her. My guy confirmed it. So how do you like that? Our Miss Malone is a very well known blues singer, at least in Chicago." Steve took a drink and shook his head at his friend.

"Only you, Bernie, would come up with that. Somehow I'm not seeing her as a blues singer."

"No, I'm sure I'm right about this, Steve. And you know what? This guy says she is dynamite and he should know. So here is what I'm thinking: I got nothing against most of the entertainment they book into this town, I know that you have to appeal to all tastes, but outside of a few jazz guys, and Frank, very little serious music goes down around here. Take a guy like Monari. Do you think he likes playing behind Danny Kaye, as nice a guy as he is? No. He just does it to make a living until he can play behind Billy Eckstine or Sarah Vaughn. Guys like that want to be able to play the stuff in their heads somewhere besides their living room. So, in the hotel, I am going to have a nightclub that just showcases jazz and blues musicians. And I am going to ask Rita Malone, or better yet, you are going to ask her, to be part of the opening act. Whaddya think?" Steve threw up his hands and began to shake his head.

"No, no, no, not me my friend, not me, I barely know the woman, and even if I did, she hasn't mentioned it and maybe you ought to stop and consider why that might be? Maybe she doesn't want any…." He paused as he saw a blank expression spread across Bernie's face.

"I never thought of that. You might be right. Jeez what are we going to do?"

"What are we going to do, Bern? How about nothing? Nada?" Bernie nodded thoughtfully and sloshed the remaining scotch around in his glass.

"Maybe you are right. Yeah, maybe so. The guy says he has a record she recorded, gonna send it out to me. I guess we will see what's up then." He looked up and shrugged his shoulders.

"Don't think you fool me, my friend, this isn't over by a long shot, I know that. When the record comes in and you've had a chance to listen to it, let me know and I will think of something." Bernie's large smile beamed across his face.

"Thanks, Steve, I knew you would see what I see. I am also thinking of making Remy my assistant entertainment director in addition to her other jobs. Just what I have seen she has accomplished so far is great stuff, Steve. Even Donn Arden is impressed. She has great ideas and knows talent when she sees it. Think she will be OK with that?"

"You are going to have to ask her yourself, Bernie, but I don't see any reason why she wouldn't want to do it, but you take it up with her directly. I won't say anything in the meantime."

"Sure, Steve, sure, I understand, I think you are right. Jeez, look at the time, I better get back in there and make sure the dinner service is humming along." Steve walked with Bernie out to the dining room, where Walter was supervising the staff as they readied the bar and the tables.

"Steve, stay and eat."

"No thanks, Bernie, you have seen enough of me for one day, adios."

When the phone rang at 6:30, Steve was hoping it was Remy and that she had managed to stop work early. The voice on the other end was Assistant District Attorney Larsen.

"How are you this evening, Steve? I hope that I am not interrupting something. If this is not a good time, I can talk to you later." Steve sat down on the couch in the office and stretched the cord from the desk.

"No, Jim, this is fine. What can I do for you?"

"Well, Steve, there is a delicate matter I need to discuss with you that I don't think can wait. I am hoping I can get your cooperation." Steve slowly shook his head and waited until the attorney paused.

"Sure, Jim, go ahead."

"I think I mentioned Jacob Hurley, the FBI agent that has been assigned to the Las Vegas Field office. He is heading up the investigation of several people involved in the casino business here in town. Your name has come up several times in connection with one of the people under investigation and since Agent Hurley knows that you and I have worked together on a few things he came to me first. There is likely to be a Federal Grand Jury convened in the next month or so and a long list of people will be called to testify before it. I have gotten him to agree that if you were to come in voluntarily and answer his questions, there is a chance that you can avoid the formal proceedings. I have blocked out two hours of time tomorrow morning at ten o'clock for the meeting here in my office. If you agree, you are entitled to bring an attorney, but if you do, I have to tell you that the chances of avoiding the Grand Jury would be slim. I know this is a tough spot, but it is the best I can do. Before you answer, let me make it very clear that you will be under oath. Have you understood everything I have just said?"

"Yes, Jim, I understand, and I want to thank you for your efforts on my behalf. I will be there tomorrow morning at ten."

"Glad to hear it, Steve, that is a load off my mind. I am hoping this blows over for you quickly. I will see you tomorrow, good night."

"Goodnight, Jim."

Steve hung up the phone and stared at the wall for a few minutes. After a while he got up and put one of the Desmond Rooney records he had borrowed from Bernie on the turntable. He poured himself a stiff scotch and lit a Pall Mall as the first notes of 'Eastside Shuffle', a Desmond composition cut through the silent room.

JANUARY 15

S teve Cannon had just finished tying his tie for the third time when there was an insistent knocking at his door. He twisted the recalcitrant windsor knot as straight as he could as he walked through the front room and opened the door. He had to smile ironically in spite of himself. Tommy Carmino tipped his right hand off his forehead in a mock salute and walked into the house. He stopped at the back of the couch, slipped his coat off and laid it along the top of the green fabric. He put his hat on top of his coat and then turned to Steve who was standing with his arms crossed in the open doorway.

"Look at you, Slick, every time I see you now, you got on a suit. We won't count being naked in the steam room."

"Tommy, what are you doing here?" Tommy was looking around the room and didn't respond for several seconds. "So whatta ya call this motif, Slick: 'Early Mormon Chic'? It looks like some hole you stick Granny in, if you didn't like her. You got any coffee?"

Steve snorted and shook his head. "When I wondered yester-day what I would be doing today, I had no idea it was going to be a whole day devoted just to you, Tommy."

"What are you talking about? You don't even know why I am here yet."

"Sit down, Tommy, I will tell you later. Sit tight, while I get us both some coffee."

Steve came back quickly with two steaming mugs. "Sorry, Tommy, no milk or sugar."

"Figures. Serves me right coming out to the boonies." Steve sat in a chair across from Tommy and waited.

Tommy took a small sip of the coffee, made a face, and put the mug down on the coffee table.

"So, Cannon, where is Jack Cathay?" Steve jerked his head back slightly and snorted.

"He's your guy, Tommy, how should I know?" Tommy leaned forward with both of his hands clasped in front of him, his elbows on his thighs.

"Because the last anyone saw him, he was on his way out here to the lost forty to see you."

"Yeah, he was here. Wednesday night, got here at seven, left at eight thirty." Steve held out his hands and shrugged. Tommy shook his head and raised his voice as if he were talking to a person who was hard of hearing.

"He is missing, Cannon, am I talking to myself here?" Steve took a big loud slurp of his coffee and looked evenly at the mobster.

"What do you want me to do about it? As they say in the Navy: I don't have the hand receipt on the guy." Tommy snorted, shook his head and sat back wearily into the cushions of the couch.

"Let's start with you telling me what you talked about and I don't need chapter and verse from the minutes of the Sorelli Fan Club, just the highlights."

"Sure, Tommy. I showed Jack and Tam the pictures I took of Sorelli in Arizona. We discussed the situation and they both left. What else can I tell you?" Tommy sighed.

"So you told Jack where you saw this creep? Is that what you are telling me here?"

"Yeah, Tommy, that is exactly what I am telling you here. Jack is a big boy." Tommy moaned and shook his head. He looked up at the ceiling and spoke in a resigned voice.

"Little Moe is missing too." Steve sighed.

"Yeah I get the picture, Tommy. Tam and I were for thinking over our options. Jack was for…. well, you know Jack." Tommy nodded with a disgusted look on his face. Steve stood up.

"No sense us ragging on each other here. I have an idea, come in here with me." Steve walked into the office with Tommy close behind him. Tommy looked around the cramped room and shook his head as he sat down on the small couch. Steve sat behind his desk and pulled the small oil smudged card out of his top desk drawer.

"This is just a hunch I have here, Tommy. Probably a long shot, we'll see." Steve dialed the long distance operator, gave her the number and waited. A few minutes later, a familiar voice came on the line.

"Leroy, this is Steve Cannon from Las Vegas. How are you doing this morning?" Leroy laughed.

"Well pretty good, Steve from Las Vegas. I didn't expect to hear from you for a while, if ever, how is the target practice coming along?" Steve laughed back.

"Haven't popped a cap yet, Leroy, but I am curious about two guys that might have come through your place in the last two days. Probably Las Vegas plates, and these guys would be hard to miss for a guy like you if you know what I mean." Leroy snorted and Steve could hear the splat of tobacco as it hit the floor of the garage.

"Yeah, I saw them. Late yesterday. Older crusty guy and the other one so big he had the front seat cranked all the back to make enough room for his head. Said they were going hunting. I told them that nothing was in season, and the old guy like to almost jump out of the car at me. Seems to me you are consorting with a bad element." Steve looked across at Tommy.

"You don't even know the half of it, Leroy. Did you see them coming back the other way?"

"Nope. And if they were heading to where you were at recently, they are going to find a population boom. Word is that the Feds are going to mount a big operation against the ranch any day now. Maybe your friends will save them the trouble."

"Yeah, Leroy, maybe. You have my number, so give me a call if you hear anything I need to know. Thanks for the info, Goodbye."

"Bye, yourself, Cannon." Steve hung up the phone. Tommy held up his hands with a questioning look on his face.

"So?" Steve sat back in the chair and crossed one leg over the other.

"So, just as we suspected. They stopped at this guy's gas station near Sedona late yesterday afternoon. So now we know."

"A gas station? This is who you call? Slick, you need a better class of friends."

"I couldn't agree with you more, Tommy, but there isn't much we can do right now." Tommy nodded his head slightly and flicked a piece of lint from the couch onto the rug.

"You know what the set-up is that they are heading into. What are the chances I get my two guys back?"

"Fifty-fifty, Tommy, at best. It took me all day to hike there and I have been running around the desert since I was three. Plus, if a drug shipment is coming in soon, the whole place will be crawling with goons. Jack has made a bad choice."

"Well, Slick, that may be true, Jack has always been a hot head, but I blame you and I expect you to do something about this situation. Capice?"

"Two problems with that, Tommy. One, I am not responsible for what Jack does. Both Tam and I thought that trying to stealth Sorelli was a bad idea and we both told him so. Second, I am going to be a little busy for a while. I have to show up at ten this morning to answer some FBI agent's questions about why I associate with you. If I don't show or if he doesn't like my answers, then I get to talk to a Federal Grand Jury. Best I can do is talk to Tam and maybe he can get a line on the Fed operation that is being planned against Sorelli and his drug smuggling gang."

"I wouldn't worry your little head about that if I were you, Slick, I think a guy like you can handle himself around the Feds. If I didn't think so, I wouldn't be sitting here. This proves how little they got. Don't you think that if they really were on to something, I would be heading to some Federal pen right now? Even if they did, there are too many people getting rich on the system to let the Feds go down that road too far. They will print up some three inch thick report that will get thrown in a drawer somewhere and Larsen's son-in-law will get a big promotion and everyone will be happy. Just the way of the world, Slick, at least our little corner of it." Steve sighed and leaned back in the chair.

"Yeah, so everybody keeps telling me. I don't feel like getting grilled on an empty stomach. Let's go get some breakfast down at the Golden Nugget. I don't think you have ever met Nick Montero, he's a great guy." Steve wished he had been holding a camera to save the look on Tommy's face for posterity.

"What? Me losing two guys isn't enough for you? You want to start World War III, now?"

"Aw, come on Tommy, all I ever hear is how 'open' this city is. If you can't stroll into any joint in town for a bite to eat, I have to question the definition of 'open' here."

"'Open' means everybody can do business here, nobody owns the whole turf. Doesn't mean there aren't limits, it's just respect, that's all." Steve made a face and waved at Tommy dismissively.

"I don't buy it Tommy. I have seen plenty of cooperation when the mutual interest is threatened, you guys get like little schoolgirls with your cliques. I just thought you were moving in a different direction, Tommy. Maybe Bernie is wrong about you, maybe you are stuck in the past."

"What's Bernie got to do with this? If he was here he would agree with me."

"Maybe, but we'll never know. I'm leaving now so you have to go too." Steve led Tommy out to the living room and waited while he bundled up. Steve grabbed his pea coat from the closet.

"You wearing that? Why don't you just put a plaid flannel shirt over your suit while you're at it." Tommy rolled his eyes and walked out the door. Steve locked the door and when he turned around Tommy was still standing there.

"You know, Slick, I heard a story once. They said that two guys walked into Nick's casino back in the forties and grabbed a bunch of chips off a craps table and walked back out the door. Nick caught up with them in the middle of Fremont Street, knocked their heads together so hard they were out cold, took back his chips, took their wallets, their rings, their car keys and then took their shoes and socks and sauntered back into his casino. You think that really happened?"

"I don't know Tommy, why don't you ask him yourself?" Tommy gestured toward the big red Cadillac.

"You know, I just might do that. Wanna take my car?" Steve waved him off as he headed for the Jeep.

"I don't think so Tommy. I got enough explaining to do without you dropping me off at school." Tommy laughed and climbed into his car. Steve could still see the big red Caddy in his rearview mirror when he made the turn into the back parking lot of the Golden Nugget.

An hour and a half later, Steve stood in front of the frosted glass door that led to Jim Larsen's outer office. He entered and closed the door behind him. Neither of the two outer offices were occupied, so Steve rapped on the open door to Jim's private office. Agent Hurley came over to the door.

"Good morning, Mr. Cannon, I'm glad you could come." Steve shook the extended hand and smiled across the room at Jim Larsen who was sitting behind his desk. There were two chairs facing each other in the middle of the room. A large reel-to-reel tape machine lay on its' back on a table between the chairs. Agent Hurley directed

Steve to the one on the right. Jim Larsen got up and came around the front of his desk.

"Can I get you anything, Steve? Coffee, or water?" Steve demurred.

"No Thanks, Jim, I'm fine." Agent Hurley sat down with a note-pad and fussed about with the tape. When he was done he looked up at Steve. His countenance was not as warm and friendly as it was a few minutes before.

"This will be the procedure, Mr. Cannon. I will ask you a series of questions. After you answer them, we will take a short break while I confer with two other agents that are located in a room next door and are listening through Attorney Larsen's intercom." He pointed to a gray square box on the front of Jim's desk, just inches away from Steve.

"I will come back with a new set of questions. And we will repeat the process until we get the information we need. If all goes well, each round should contain fewer questions then the one before it. Is that clear?" Steve nodded.

"In that case, Mr. Cannon, I will have Attorney Larsen administer the oath and we can begin." After the oath, Agent Hurley dismissed himself from the room. When he returned he had a file with the edges of several photos visible. He sat down across from Steve and adjusted his glasses.

"Mr. Cannon, how long have you known Tommy Carmino?"

"Four or five years, give or take."

"Where did you meet Mr. Carmino for the first time?"

"At a card party thrown by Bernie Gold in the back room of his deli."

"Since then, would you say that your association with him is close?"

"No. I would say not, but he may disagree."

"How would you characterize the nature of that association?"

"We trade information from time to time. We may do each other favors on occasion."

"What type of favors, Mr. Cannon?"

"Like I said, we trade information."

"Mr. Cannon, in August of last year, did you or did you not transport seven hundred and fifty thousand dollars in skim money in the trunk of a car from Las Vegas to Los Angeles at Mr. Carmino's behest?"

"No. I just delivered a car."

"So you had no knowledge of the money in the trunk that was destined to help quell the workers strike in San Pedro Harbor?"

"News to me. No, no knowledge."

"In the same month, Mr. Cannon, were you arrested after a gunfight in a North Las Vegas neighborhood?"

"Yes, I was. But no charges were filed."

"Weren't you there with two accomplices, both of whom work for Mr. Carmino?"

"No, I was there on my own."

"How many phone conversations have you had with Mr. Carmino in the last three months?

"I have no idea, but I'm guessing you do."

"Twenty-seven, Mr. Cannon. How would you characterize those conversations, Mr. Cannon?"

"I wouldn't characterize them in any way. If you know how many there are, it is because you've tapped his phone, mine or both. So maybe it would save us all some time if you would characterize them."

"I think we will take a short break at this juncture, Mr. Cannon." Steve frowned and pulled out a pack of Pall Malls as Agent Hurley left the room. Jim Larsen came around and sat down across from him. Steve busied himself lighting up the smoke.

"Steve, I have to warn you as a friend, that the less you antagonize Agent Hurley, the better this thing will go." Steve exhaled and looked up at the attorney.

"With all due respect, Jim, this is a witch hunt, pure and simple. Tommy said something to me this morning that made a lot of sense. If there has really been a crime committed here, there would be plenty of evidence and the Feds wouldn't need to round up everybody that ever heard of Tommy, turn them upside down and shake them until something falls out. I have a lot of respect for the way you conduct your office and you know this isn't kosher." Jim sat back and scratched the back of his head.

"Off the record, I may have many opinions, but I am sworn to uphold the law. That is why we have Grand Juries. Agent Hurley can present his evidence and they can decide if there are grounds enough to proceed." Steve tapped the ash from the end of his cigarette on the glass tray with a backhanded motion of his right hand.

"You know, Jim, I don't agree with Hank Greenspun on many of his opinions and editorials. I think he is off base a lot. But at least he has to live or die in the court of public opinion. He has to put it out there for the average guy to decide. This cowardly, secretive stuff turns my stomach. So if you would do me a favor, when Mr. Hurley comes back, tell him for me that I would be happy to sit in front of a Grand Jury and answer this line of questioning. Could you do that for me?" Steve took one last quick drag on the cigarette and snuffed it out just before he stood up. Jim Larsen stood up as well.

"I think you are making a mistake, Steve, but I do see your point. I know Agent Hurley pretty well and I am afraid he will take this as a challenge to his authority." Steve walked to the open doorway before he turned to face the attorney.

"Like you said, Jim, this is why we have Grand Juries. Goodbye." Steve walked toward the outer office door just as Agent Hurley was coming in. The FBI agent stopped short with a startled expression on his face that quickly dissolved into a deep frown.

"Where are you going, Mr. Cannon?" Steve pushed past the agent, talking over his shoulder.

"You know where to find me, when you convene the Grand Jury, Mr. Hurley." Steve let the door to the outside office close behind him before he could hear the reply.

Five minutes later he was knocking on the closed door to Tam's office. When there was no reply, he opened the door and leaving it ajar, he sat down in front of the cluttered desk and lit a cigarette. He was studying the large wall map of Las Vegas when Tam walked in carrying a cup of coffee and a bag of sandwiches from the diner down the street. Tam snickered when he saw Steve.

"Well that didn't take long." Steve turned from the map and stubbed out the cigarette in the overfilled ashtray.

"It took even less than that." Steve sat back down in the metal chair and watched as Tam took the lid off the coffee and unwrapped two turkey sandwiches, placing them on top of the brown paper bag he had ripped open into a ragged tablecloth.

"I hope you are not hungry, I didn't know you would be here. Didn't expect to see you for another hour. At least that is over." Steve waved him off.

"No, not hungry. And it isn't over. I walked out of the interview." Tam stopped chewing and leaned forward so that he could see past the large stacks of files on the front of his desk.

"I am not sure that was the wisest move, Steve. You remember all the grief you gave Agent Brady last summer? They don't forget stuff like that, and now you got this new guy on your case as well. I hope you know what you are doing." Steve put his hands behind his head and waited until Tam picked up his sandwich again and took a bite.

"Well, we'll see what the future brings on that score, but that isn't why I stopped by. Jack and Little Moe have decided to take things into their own hands. Tommy alerted me that they were missing last night. I got on the horn and talked to the ex-cop I met and he confirmed that they came through his gas station mid-afternoon on Thursday. Jack must have left my house and swung into action. I don't see how he could have had the time to make the kind of preparations you need to cover that amount of desert. Even if he knew what he was doing, which he doesn't. I would be surprised if

Jack has ever been to a city park, let alone the boondocks like the area around Sedona." Tam had suddenly lost interest in his lunch.

"I don't believe this. Did you know about this?" Steve jerked his head back and looked incredulously at the detective.

"Did you hear what I just said? He didn't say anything to me, but it crossed my mind that he might react like that. That is the main reason that I kept it under my hat for a while. Doesn't look like it did much good." Tam shook his head and sipped at the coffee cup.

"I thought we had convinced him that it was suicide to go down there..." Steve interrupted.

"The other piece of information I got was that the Feds are supposedly planning some sort of drug task force raid on the ranch. You need to see if you can come up with anything on that. I don't know if that would be a good thing or not. I don't see anybody winning in this deal." Tam sighed.

"Why do the breaks always go Sorelli's way?" Tam turned toward Steve and his expression had the blankness that Steve knew from experience meant that Tam was thinking about something else. Steve could guess what that was, and spoke quickly.

"Well, his luck will have to run out one day. If there is one thing you learn living in this town is that if there is such a thing as luck, it disappoints everyone eventually."

When Steve arrived home he quickly changed his clothes and unlocked the deep closet in the corner of the bedroom. Twenty minutes later he was on Highway 15, the road that led to St. George, Cedar City and ultimately to Salt Lake City, three hundred and sixty two miles away. He drove for nearly an hour before he slowed and took a gravelly side road just before the small town of Mesquite. He drove along the dusty track for ten miles before the road climbed a long hill and dead-ended in the remains of an abandoned silver mine. He parked the Jeep on a small promontory composed of old tailings from the mine. From his vantage point he could see nearly all the way back to the freeway and anyone that might come up the same road would be visible for ten minutes before they arrived.

Steve opened the back tailgate of the Jeep and pulled out two sand bags laying them on top of one another on the hood just in front of the windshield. He pulled a canvas bag and a long leather gun case out as well and laid them alongside the sand bags. Returning to the back he lifted a heavy wooden frame with two metal spikes protruding from the edges, the rough-hewn wood enclosing a three foot diameter black bullseye target. He started down the side of the dusty hill, letting his boots slide over the broken shale as if he were skiing. He walked a hundred yards to a ten foot high mound of tailings. He pushed the spikes down into the soft ground in front of the mound and adjusted each side until the target was straight and angled directly toward the Jeep. As he walked back, his foot kicked up several empty rifle shell cases. He casually inspected them as he climbed back up to his vehicle. Though there were spots that would suffice closer to town, the abandoned mine was ideal. The land was still privately owned and shooting on it was preferable to shooting on BLM land, where often zealous employees of the sprawling bureaucracy would confiscate weapons first and ask questions later. They might be attracted to his gunfire here, but there was nothing they could legally do about it. He just had to make sure they had left the area before he traversed BLM land to get back to the freeway. But in the ten years he had been coming here, he had seen no one.

Back at the Jeep he slid the rifle from the soft sheepskin lining of the case, being careful not to snag the scope on the zipper of the case. The Winchester Model 70, 30.06 rifle had been recently cleaned and the smell of gun oil and Hoppes No. 9 rose from the gleaming dark blue barrel and the lightly checkered walnut of the stock and forearm. From the canvas bag, he unrolled the spotting scope from its' small blanket covering and lifted out a tooled leather bandolier that held twenty five cartridges that he had hand loaded himself. The 150 grain copper jacketed bullets gleamed in the weak winter sun as he selected three and loaded them carefully in front of the open bolt. He nestled the rifle on the top of the sand bags and slid the bolt home with a satisfying metallic clunk. From his pocket he took two 9mm shells and pushed them partway into his ears. He hunched slightly over the hood of the Jeep and adjusted his cheek on the stock until the thin black crosshairs of the scope lay directly across the center of the bullseye. He took up the small amount of slack in the trigger as the center of the crosshairs oscillated lazily over the center of the target. When his breathing was synchronized with the slight wavering, he squeezed the trigger just as the crosshairs moved gently toward dead center. The gun bucked against his shoulder at the same time that Steve saw a puff of dust rise up from just behind the target. He balanced the rifle on the sand bags and swiveled the spotting scope onto the target. The bullet hole was visible three inches above the center dot. Steve adjusted the small round rings on the side of the scope and fired two more times until the bullet hole was exactly six inches above the dead center of the target. At ranges three hundred yards and beyond, Steve would be able to hold on a man's head and the natural drop of the bullet would put the copper slug in the center of the body mass.

Leaving the rifle on top of the sandbags, Steve squinted back down the road for a few seconds before returning to the back of the Jeep and pulling out a six foot human silhouette, outlined in black. Instead of wood, the frame was made of a lightweight metal. Steve walked to the first mound and target and then paced off another two hundred yards beyond. He placed the target in the ground twenty yards in front of a large slope that formed the outer wall of one of the main pits. He quickly retraced his steps and again checked the road for activity before settling down once more behind the rifle. He waited for a full three minutes for his heart rate to level off. When he was again able to breathe easily through his nose, he lowered his head behind the scope. He repeated the same procedure as he centered the crosshairs on the black outline of the head. This time, though, he waited for five seconds after his finger had tightened as far as it could go before the trigger break. He let his breathing settle down through the muscles of his arms. A part of his mind projected his body through the scope, into and through the target itself. The loud crack and concussive force surprised Steve as it always did when he was truly zeroed in. The spotting scope revealed the hole to be in the middle of the heart slightly right of the mid line.

Steve fired five more shots from the same position, switched to the sitting position, the preferred one for many Marines and finished with six shots lying prone just in front of the Jeep. Aside from a small adjustment for an increase in the breeze, it had been relatively easy to put all seventeen shots in a grouping that lay within a six inch circle. As he cased the gun and policed up his empty shell casings, Steve was satisfied, but not impressed. Ideal conditions on the range were rarely if ever replicated when the shots counted, and unless one practiced relentlessly under every conceivable circumstance of weather and terrain, the element of luck was all too often the determining factor. Still, it was a start, and even more importantly, it felt good to do something even if it was at this point mostly symbolic.

Steve was only a mile from the freeway when he slowed as a sheriff's car crested a small hill fifty yards in front of the Jeep and approached in the center of the road, blocking Steve's way. Steve pulled the Jeep to the right as far as he could and stopped, rolling down the window as soon as his own dust drifted by. The sheriff deputy pulled his car even with the Jeep and rolled his window down as well.

"How you doing today?" The sheriff deputy was around Steve's age and wore a white straw cowboy hat above a face that was dominated by a thick black handlebar moustache.

"I am doing fine, Officer, can I help you." The cop spoke briefly into his radio before he answered.

"Got a call of a lot of shooting up at the old Clayton mine. Did you hear any shooting?" Steve nodded and gazed back at the deputy with a casual expression.

"I did hear it officer. About seventeen shots if I counted right." The officer snorted.

"Well, the call wasn't too specific, just that it was loud, probably large caliber."

"Yeah, I would agree, sounded like 30.06 to me." The deputy squinted up through his dusty windshield at the mine.

"Well I doubt if it is worth my time to drive all the way up there. Whoever it was, probably not up there anymore." He looked over at Steve. The moustache lifted up a little in front of a small grin.

"I suspect you are right, officer." Steve watched as the deputy stuck his head out of his window as he looked for a good place to turn around on the narrow track. He looked back over at Steve.

"You drive carefully, you hear?" Steve waved his hand in a small salute near his left ear.

"Thanks, officer, I will." Steve drove a little slower toward the freeway and when he stopped and was waiting for traffic to clear he saw the deputy's car a hundred yards behind him. Steve pulled onto the freeway and watched in his rearview mirror as the cop drove away in the opposite direction.

Steve turned onto a frontage road that ran parallel to the freeway and led into the small town of Mesquite. Steve drove the short three blocks that comprised the main street and pulled the Jeep into a large parking lot in front of a drive-in that advertised burgers and shakes on a faded sign above the weed choked car-hop lanes. Steve walked inside and ordered two cheeseburgers, a side of fries and a chocolate milkshake. He also got change for a dollar bill and walked out to the phone booth while the food was being prepared.

Buck Monari picked up on the fourth ring. Steve could hear talking in the background and someone playing notes on a saxophone.

"Buck, this is Steve Cannon, have I caught you at a bad time?"

He could hear Buck say something back into the room and the notes stopped.

"No, man, just a few guys over shooting the breeze. I am glad you called. I talked to Carl yesterday and he just called me back an hour ago. He made a few phone calls, let me get the piece of paper I wrote it down on." Steve waited and listened to the muffled chatter from the living room.

"Here it is, Steve. 'Sandeman Publishing.' Carl says it was set up by Sammy Sanderson in the mid-forties and he had it until 1958, when it was sold but nobody knows to who. Carl figures it got absorbed into another house, which got absorbed, etc. He said the last time he had to deal with publishing rights held by the company, it was for a piano player that worked with Sanderson in the early fifties. He dealt with a guy by the name of Herbert Sutherland, and I have his number here on another piece of paper. He said it has been two or three years since he called that number, but, it is all he could come up with. But he also said that every time he called that particular publishing company, he would eventually hear from Sanderson, so Carl thinks he is still involved in some capacity. I hope this will help you out." Steve wrote the number in his notebook next to the other information he had just been given.

"Thanks, Buck, this will help a lot. I will let you go, but I will be in touch."

"It was my pleasure, take care." Steve hung up the phone and over the burger and fries, he flipped back through his notebook and reread all the notes he had on Sammy Sanderson. The sun had dipped behind the clouds that hung on the horizon as Steve drove back down the highway toward the lights of Las Vegas, a few of which had already twinkled on and could be seen from several of the higher hills on the way back to town.

January 16

Steve was in his office by 7:30 on Saturday morning. He carefully removed every piece of paper and every file folder from the large cardboard box that Rowena had let him take from the apartment. He separated the contents into as many piles as seemed relevant, before he began to examine each one closely. After a half hour it was evident that there were four main categories: Letters and time sheets from the union detailing most of the gigs that Desmond had played in the last six years since settling in Las Vegas. Producer song lists and studio time sheets from several recording studios in LA, most within the last three years. Royalty payouts from record companies, the most recent was dated from late 1961, and a miscellaneous pile that held mostly pages with handwritten notes. It was the miscellaneous pile that Steve decided to tackle first.

Around ten o'clock, Steve picked up the phone and dialed the LA number that Buck Monari had given him. After twenty unanswered rings he hung up. On a whim he redialed five minutes later and a younger sounding male voice picked up on the third ring.

"Hello, I am looking for Herbert Sutherland, might he be available?" There was a short pause on the other end.

"Uh...no, Mr. Sutherland is gone for the weekend. I have a number where he can be reached but I can only call it if whatever it is can't wait." Steve waited for the young man to finish before he replied in a gentle matter-of-fact voice.

"Sure, sure, I understand. This was not that important, I just had a few questions about Sandeman Publishing." Steve stopped and waited.

"Oh.. Sandeman, yes, are you from the record company?"

"The record company?" Steve lightened up on the question mark at the end and let his voice trail down and off.

"Yes. 'Birdland Records'. This is about the four album retrospective isn't it?"

"Well it is, but I am not from Birdland Records." Steve held his breath.

"Oh.. I just thought…Anyway what did you need to know?"

"I was just wondering if the final details have been worked out between Birdland and Sandeman on the record deal."

"I don't know, I am just an intern here and Mr. Sutherland is handling all the details of that project. In fact, he is flying to Las Vegas on Monday to get some papers signed in connection with that deal." Steve decided to interject quickly.

"Oh that's great, do you know where he is staying? Maybe I can catch him there and meet with him face-to-face."

"I don't know exactly… I have only been here a few months myself, but I do know that the last time he flew there he stayed at a hotel called the Tropicana. Is that any help?"

"Sure, a big help. I would like to thank you for your time."

"Wait. What is your name so I can tell Mr. Sutherland?" Steve heard the question coming and quickly hung up the phone.

Two hours later the stacks on the desk had been shuffled and reshuffled as Steve had gone through each piece of paper one by one, some several times. If the answer was among them, it was proving elusive. He had just sat down with a cold beer when the phone rang. When Steve picked it up he found Tam Polhaus on the other end.

"Hi Tam, what do you have?"

"Not good news, my friend." Steve sighed, took a sip of the beer and sat back into the couch.

"Let's hear it."

"You were right. A big operation went down out in Sedona yesterday afternoon. Federal Drug Taskforce and FBI. I know a guy in the Phoenix office of the Narcotics Bureau and he filled me in. They used helicopters and dune buggies to surprise the guys at the ranch." Tam hesitated.

"What was the outcome, Tam, do I have to guess here?"

"They arrested a few people, none that match Sorelli's description, confiscated an airplane and forty pounds of heroin." Tam hesitated again.

"Why do I get the feeling there is more?"

"Because there is. One of the dogs they use for sniffing out the hard drugs led them to two fresh graves in the dry creek bed. When I talked to the guy this morning, they were still waiting for a team from Phoenix to get to the scene before they excavate. But I think we can assume the worst at this point." Steve ground his teeth together and silently pounded his fist against his knee.

"Nothing to say, Steve?" Steve took another large swig of the beer.

"What is there to say, Tam? We both knew this was the likely outcome. Now I have to break it to Tommy."

"Like I said, the team isn't on the scene yet." Steve snorted.

"Not likely they are still alive, or the Feds would have scooped them up in the raid. Keep me posted if you hear anything else noteworthy. Where are you on the Harris McCord deal?"

"Not much further along than the last time we spoke. Formal charges will be filed on Monday in the prostitution case. DA Larsen already has Ramos and Calexo and their lawyers chomping at the bit for deals, so the squeeze should tighten on Harris and Shirley next week. What have you got?"

"I don't quite know yet, but I may be close to finding out why Desmond died, and once I know that for sure the whole picture will be clear. I may need you in your official capacity soon, so stay in town." Tam snickered.

"Where would I go? Raising a ten year old by yourself pretty much determines how your free time is spent."

"I am sure that is true. I've got to go track down Tommy. Enjoy your rest." Tam laughed sardonically as he hung up the phone.

Steve had to place three phone calls to the Desert Inn Hotel before someone was able to tell him that Tommy Carmino had teed off on the hotel's golf course an hour before. When Steve arrived at the starter's shack there was no one there with the authority to let him borrow a golf cart. He had almost decided to start at the eighteenth green and walk the course backwards when he saw Earl's silver mane coming toward him at a high rate of speed in his souped up cart. Steve waved and Earl and the cart slowed quickly to a stop beside him.

"Earl, I have to find Tommy out on the course I need you to give me a ride." Earl took a puff on a cigarette and his tan, wrinkled face looked at Steve steadily over the plastic steering wheel. He pointed to a cooler in the back of the cart.

"Hop in. I have to deliver this booze to Tommy and his golfing buddies anyway," Steve quickly jumped onto the bench seat and braced himself, remembering his first ride with Earl. Even with the cart going flat out, it took twenty minutes to reach the seventh hole. Several times they had been forced to stop behind large trees as groups of golfers teed off and sent golf balls in their direction.

Steve watched from beside the cart as Tommy missed a three foot putt on the seventh green. He was wearing a mint green pullover cardigan, black polo shirt and green and black plaid pants. He recognized two of the golfers as regulars he had seen in card games around town, the fourth was Clifford Jones. When they came off the green toward their carts and Earl, the other three were laughing and joking, Tommy was fuming. His mood didn't improve when he saw Steve standing by his cart.

"I've bogied the last three holes, Cannon. I should have known you and your bad luck were around here somewhere." Tommy jammed his putter forcefully into the golf bag that was strapped on the back of his cart. Steve smiled broadly.

"Now, is that any way to talk to a hard working board member of Carmino Lighting?"

Clifford Jones overheard the remark and chuckled as he walked by on the way to his cart.

"Good afternoon, Mr. Cannon, care to play a few holes?" Tommy snorted.

"Slick, here is more an aficionado of games you play sitting down. Double or nothing from here on out, Cliff." Tommy stood next to Earl who was busy mixing rum drinks for the foursome. Steve sat down on the passenger side of Tommy's cart. Tommy frowned as he took a sip of the liquor.

"I don't need bad luck riding around with me, Slick."

"Just a hole or two, Tommy. I need to talk to you."

"Well, if it's about your little chat with the FBI, I already heard you walked out. Looks like you came around to my way of thinking." Steve put his hands in the pockets of his jacket as a cold gust of wind swept across a water pond to his right, roiling the calm surface.

"No, Tommy, not about that." Tommy's frown deepened and he caught the sleeve of Earl's jacket as he was turning to serve the other men.

"Give me another slug of rum." Tommy waited until Earl had poured from the small bottle, then took another large swig of the concoction and squinted toward the sun and Steve.

"I'm going to tee off and then we talk." Steve shrugged and watched as one by one the golfers sent the small white ball soaring into the pale winter sky. Tommy's game was an athletic one as could be guessed by his physique and the way he carried himself. Though his Achilles heel was a lack of touch around the greens he made up for it with a shot trajectory that was low and true; a big plus on the windy desert courses. On this occasion he hit a low draw that missed a large centrally placed fairway bunker that had trapped all but one of his companions, his ball rolling a hundred yards past the sand trap on the hard winter fairway.

He was not in a better mood when he slid behind the wheel and jerked the cart onto the narrow path.

"So, talk."

"Not good news, Tommy. The Feds raided Sorelli's ranch yesterday. Found two fresh graves, probably digging them up as we speak. Likely they will find Jack and Little Moe."

Steve braced himself just in time as Tommy swerved the cart violently off the path toward his ball. They slid to a sudden stop behind a four foot high palm tree to allow the others to hit their second shots. For a few seconds, nothing was said as the two men watched one of the balls fly low and weak out of the bunker and roll to a stop five feet away.

"The way I look at it, Cannon, your complete lack of ability in this little adventure has cost me two of my guys. Little Moe I can get along without, but now I gotta find a new cage man that can keep everybody in line." Steve snorted.

"I already told you that Jack was acting on his own, against advice. And here's an idea: Why don't you promote Rocky Pavina, if you're so high on him. That way, Bernie won't be saddled with a guy who is under investigation for tampering with slot machines." Steve turned and was met by a steady gaze.

"How about you quit telling me how to run my business?" Steve shrugged and watched as one of the other players pulled up in his cart and approached his ball.

"You said you had a problem, I was just making a suggestion as to how you might solve it." The golfer came toward their cart.

"Hey, Tommy. How far is it from here?"

"How the hell do I know? Do I look like your caddy?" Tommy

punched the gas and the cart rocketed over to where his ball lay. He pivoted out of the seat and grabbed a club as he passed behind the rear of the cart. He addressed the ball quickly, then hesitated and backed away. He looked to both sides of the fairway and then back at the green.

"It's two-twenty from here, Tommy, then forty more feet to the pin." Steve spoke casually. Tommy turned and peered back toward the cart.

"What? You some kind of comedian, now?"

"No, Tommy, just a guy who used to be out of work trying to earn a few bucks caddying on your nice course here. Use your two iron, start it out to the right, your draw should bring it back in close." Tommy stood still and stared at Steve before he walked slowly back to the cart and exchanged clubs. A few seconds later, Tommy's ball rolled onto the green and stopped five feet below the cup. He climbed happily back into the cart as Clifford Jones glided by. He pointed at Tommy and laughed.

"I never thought I would see the day when you had a shot at birdie on this hole." Tommy grinned and turned the cart in a long arc toward the green. He took a big gulp of his drink and smiled over at Steve.

"You know, Slick, sometimes it does pay to have you around. Not often, but sometimes. Now all you have to do is read this putt for me and I can take these guys for a cool five grand." Steve chuckled and shook his head as Tommy pulled the cart to a stop behind the others.

"I'm staying here. That putt breaks three inches to the left. But do me a favor, Tommy. Hit it and don't look up until you hear it drop into the cup. Think you can do that for me?" Tommy snorted and marched up to the green slapping Clifford on the back as the golfers spread out to look over their putts. Steve was a little surprised when Tommy followed his advice and was whooping it up on the green while his playing partners stood silent and dumbfounded.

When he returned to the cart the sour mood of ten minutes earlier had vanished.

"His talents to reveal. You do surprise me sometimes, Slick. How about we form a partnership? I tell these rubes you are my bodyguard because I have been getting death threats and you ride around and give me the lowdown on every hole. 50-50 split, whadd'ya say?" Steve stepped out of the cart and bent down to look at Tommy.

"I'm going to walk back. I can cut across the ninth fairway to the clubhouse from here. But I do have a request. I need to know a room number at the Trop where someone is checking in on Monday. What can you do for me?" Tommy smiled as he pulled on his mint colored leather glove.

"Tell you what, Slick. You ride with me and whisper in my ear on the ninth and I will make that call for you from the snack bar at the turn. Deal?" Steve looked over at Clifford who was busy adding up his scorecard. He climbed back in the cart.

"Aha! We got 'em now." Tommy pulled alongside the other carts and made an extra thousand dollar bet with each man that he could birdie the next hole.

Ten minutes later, Steve waited outside the small snack shop while Tommy collected the money from the other three golfers seated at the shaded picnic tables. He picked up a cocktail napkin and with a stubby green pencil wrote Herbert Sutherland's name in block letters. Tommy came over waving the stack of hundreds.

"Sure you don't want a taste of this, Slick? It's found money, the best kind." He laughed as he took the napkin from Steve and walked inside the small concession. Steve leaned up against the counter and watched as Clifford Jones sauntered toward him and casually tossed a hot dog wrapper in the garbage can five feet away. He pretended to read the menu placard beside Steve as he spoke.

"I think you may have forgotten, young man, that I worked beside your father on the dam. I have forgotten more about your childhood than you probably remember. The next time I see you out here, I want to see you packing your own set of clubs. We'll see how cool you are under pressure when it is your money and your white knuckles gripping that putter." He turned and smiled his genial smile. Steve smiled back.

"I'd love to accommodate you, Mr. Jones, but I'm afraid the dues for your little boys' club here are way too steep for the kind of money a private eye makes." Clifford smiled benevolently.

"Well then, Mr. Cannon this is your lucky day. Just so happens I know a guy who is selling his membership very, very cheaply." Steve smiled back and shifted his weight from his aching right leg to his left.

"I am sure he wants more than I am willing to pay." Clifford shook his head.

"All you have to do is handle a hundred and fifty dollar tab at the bar and restaurant each month. You can swing that, right? Then we can also have the pleasure of your company at the card tables. I have heard about your prodigious talents but so far I have been denied viewing them in the flesh." Before he could reply, Tommy came out of the open door and handed Steve the napkin. He folded it in half and put it in his back pocket. Clifford chuckled and caught Tommy's arm.

"Well, Tommy, we have a new member to add to the rolls. Mr. Cannon here has graciously consented to join our club." Tommy stopped and turned toward the two men.

"Since when?" He looked at Steve. Steve shrugged when Clifford turned his head toward Tommy. Clifford laughed and slapped Tommy on the arm.

"Always room for one more, right Tommy? And get used to the idea that any future outings will involve a partner rotation of Steve here, so that we all get the benefit of his advice." Clifford laughed again and walked back over to the table joining the other two golfers. Tommy looked intently at Steve.

"If you wanted to join, all you had to do was ask." Steve frowned.

"Not my idea, but in light of recent events, it won't hurt to develop new sources of information." Tommy was about to say something, but then stopped and considered for a moment.

"You're right Slick. This might do us both some good." Steve shook his head and turned to go.

"I will let you know what I hear about Jack and Little Moe."

"Right. You do that, Slick."

Steve was about to open the door of the Jeep when he remembered the napkin. He opened it up and turned it toward the sunlight to read Tommy's scrawl.

'Herbert Sutherland, due to arrive Monday night. Room 2064. You still owe me for two guys.'

January 17

"Mr. Cannon?" The voice on the phone was firm and controlled. Steve had just finished breakfast and was leaning against the counter in the kitchen after picking up the receiver which hung on the wall behind him.

"Yes, this is Steve Cannon, who is this?"

"Mr. Cannon, my name is Harlan Richland, I am vice president of Richland Oil Co. I am hoping this is a good time to talk." Steve stretched the phone cord over to the dining table and sat down.

"Sure, Mr. Richland, how is Harvey Chandler?" There was a slight pause before the caller resumed.

"That is what I am calling about, Mr. Cannon. I found one of your calling cards in Mr. Chandler's desk and I was wondering why he might have needed your services?"

"He didn't, Mr. Richland. I ran into him in the desert outside Sedona and we shared a campsite for a night."

"When was that?"

"A week ago, yesterday. Why are you asking, has Harvey gone missing?" There was another pause and the voice was not as self-assured when it spoke again.

"As a matter of fact, yes, Mr. Cannon, and I have to ask how you were able to come to that conclusion so quickly?"

"Because, Mr. Richland, that area is controlled, or was, by a sadistic killer who is using it to smuggle drugs in from Mexico. I was there trying to get a line on him and that's when I ran into Harvey out surveying. I told him in no uncertain terms that he should not go back on that land. Your call suggests to me that my advice went unheeded, am I right?"

"I don't know, Mr. Cannon, no one has heard from Harvey since last Tuesday when he went back out into the field. My father is very distraught. His father and Harvey's were boyhood friends." Steve sighed under his breath.

"Well, the best advice I can give you right now, Mr. Richland, is to call the FBI office in Phoenix, tell them about Harvey and where you suspect he was last week. They conducted a raid late Friday on the ranch and they might have some more information."

"Yes, Mr. Cannon, I will do as you suggest."

"And, Mr. Richland?"

"Yes?"

"Call me back if you find out anything one way or the other." The voice was quiet in reply.

"Yes, Mr. Cannon, I will. Thank you for your help."

Steve dialed Tam's home number and let it ring until Tam picked up.

"Tam this is Steve. What have you heard from Arizona?"

"I thought all this could wait until tomorrow, Cannon, it is Sunday for the rest of us you know." Steve laughed.

"Yeah, I know compradre, but no rest for the wicked, right?" Tam snorted

"Quick and dirty. They opened the two graves late yesterday. One description matches Little Moe, the other guy is definitely not Jack." Steve interrupted.

"Yeah, I think I know who the other guy is. Call your contact back and tell him to call a Mr. Harlan Richland at Richland Oil Company in Denver. I am pretty sure the other guy is Harvey Chandler, a petroleum engineer that works for the outfit."

"Why don't you call them?"

"Because I am going to Arizona to find Jack."

Steve hung up and rested his hand on the phone for several minutes as he thought ahead. An hour later, he drove over the dam for the second time in two weeks.

Leroy Blevens was on his back porch cleaning the last of the four desert quail from a morning hunt when a familiar red Jeep pulled into his yard. He walked over to the wooden railing wiping his bloody hands with a towel as he watched Steve Cannon approach.

"From the look on your face, something tells me I won't be spending the next two hours on my couch watching the Lakers." Steve didn't smile as he climbed the three wooden steps to the porch.

"I need your help finding a guy, Leroy." Steve looked the ex-cop in the eye. Leroy looked away and rubbed a two day old stubble as he looked off over the mesa.

"I don't suppose this will involve a ranch of local notoriety, now, would it?" Steve snorted.

"Of course it does, Leroy, and what better way to spend a Sunday afternoon?" Leroy turned around and they both laughed. Leroy shrugged.

"Well, let me go inside, put these birds in the freezer and break the news to Martha. I'll be back."

When Leroy returned to the porch, Steve was already in the Jeep waiting. Leroy opened the back door and threw in a large canteen of water before he joined Steve in the front. Steve pulled the Jeep in a large circle and headed toward the highway.

Leroy watched the scenery go by for several miles before he spoke.

"So, who is this guy, if you don't mind my asking?" Steve pulled the Jeep over to the side of the road and looked over at Leroy.

"Why we stopping?" Steve looked at Leroy for a few more seconds and then out of the windshield.

"Because you can be back at your house in a half hour if you don't like what I am about to tell you." Leroy said nothing.

"His name is Jack Cathay." Leroy snorted.

"The big one or the old grumpy guy?" Steve snorted back.

"The old grumpy guy." Leroy nodded thoughtfully.

"Well, who or what is he besides grumpy?"

"He works for the guy who is number two to the biggest mafia head in Las Vegas." Leroy looked out the side window at a small pile of beer cans some revelers had left in the dirt. Several of them had lipstick on them. Leroy sighed.

"Well, if he's been out there since Thursday, I suggest we stop jawing and get going." Steve pulled the Jeep back on the highway with a small smile on his face.

Steve stashed the Jeep in the same place as before. There were new sets of tire tracks on the faint trail. Steve figured some of the FBI elements had gone in this way. The two men stood at the top of the hill and looked out toward the ranch.

"How good a tracker are you, Leroy?"

"OK, I guess. A lot like hunting. What is your plan?" Steve pointed ahead.

"We have to search each of these arroyos. I will take the two on the right you take the one on the left, since I have never been in that one. Unlikely to be out in the open, so we concentrate wherever there is cover or someplace someone might hole up. If he is hurt or...." Leroy finished the thought.

"He will be in those types of places in that case as well." Steve nodded.

"Right. At ten minute intervals we climb to the top of the ridge we are under and make eye contact before we continue." Leroy nodded.

"Agreed. Let's go." Steve adjusted his backpack and trailed slightly behind Leroy as they threaded their way through the large clumps of manzanita bush. Before long, they were out of sight of each other.

Steve noted that there had been a recent rain that would have erased most of the footprints, but would actually make the task easier as there would be fewer false trails. Steve crisscrossed both arroyos several times each mile, checking behind every clump of bushes and every dished out section of wall where someone might hide. He used the trips to the top of the ridges to cross from one arroyo into the next. He figured he had walked five miles before they were even one mile closer to the ranch.

He must have walked by the first sign and wouldn't have seen it at all if he hadn't climbed right above it to wave to Leroy. As he started back down he saw the dark splotch against the light colored earth. From ten feet away he could tell it was dried blood. Steve stopped and looked carefully around the spot he was standing. He could see no footprints or even any signs of disturbance in the immediate area or around the stain. He spent the next ten minutes searching carefully in ever enlarging circles around the spot. Finding nothing further, he climbed to the top of the ridge and waited for Leroy to appear. Leroy spotted Steve first and was already sliding down the side of the middle arroyo when Steve caught sight of him. Seeing Steve in the same spot on the ridge as before had alerted Leroy to the fact that Steve had found something. Five minutes later, both men peered at the large patch of dried blood.

Leroy stood up, rubbing some of the dark red grains between his fingers.

"Impossible to tell from this whether it is human or animal, but any small animal losing this much blood in one go would be right around here or at least his remains would be, even if something ate him. Nothing much big around. Too far north for javelina pigs." Steve looked up and down the arroyo.

"Well, it is right along the side, just where we figured someone would travel if they were being pursued, so let's split up and search this side for a hundred yards each way and back again, meeting up back here." Leroy nodded and headed off toward the direction they had come. Steve started slowly up the arroyo, moving only twenty yards in ten minutes.

Fifty yards from where they had found the blood, Steve slowed and stopped. The hairs on the back of his neck stood up and he felt the same queer feeling he had experienced on Guadalcanal one night when he and a Japanese soldier had stood four feet apart, each unable to see the other in the inky jungle blackness. Steve stood up straight and slowly rotated his head toward the wall of the arroyo. He shifted his left foot slightly and looked behind him. The wall was obscured by a thick group of saltbush that seemed to grow right from the surface of the sandstone. Near the base of the bush he saw an irregular shaped shadow that seemed to move almost imperceptively as Steve stared at it. There was a shape in the shadow that Steve's mind was struggling to connect with a larger whole, much like the shape of an ear might be all that a hunter sees of a deer through the forest foliage. Steve fell back upon his hunting experience and looked away for a few seconds and then let his gaze fall naturally back across the area. This time he saw something else that took him quickly back to the war torn jungle. Few people ever have to obtain the knowledge of what it looks like when a gun is being pointed at you. If it is from any distance, the first time you see it, it registers as someone who has contorted their body into a strange position as the mind struggles to catalog what it sees. From where Steve now stood, there was part of a human nose and a small black circle. The small black circle was the barrel of a pistol. Steve made a conscious effort to speak with the least amount of facial movement as possible.

"Jack."

"Jack, its' Steve. I am here to help you."

Steve waited for several seconds before rotating his eyes back to the spot. The black circle disappeared just as his gaze fell upon it. Steve knelt quickly and parted the lower branches of the thick bush. Jack's head was slumped over the large pistol. Steve felt the thick neck for a pulse, and then stepped out into the middle of the arroyo. A shrill whistle brought Leroy moving at double-time back toward Steve.

It took both men the better part of ten minutes to move the unconscious man from his hiding place to the relatively flat ground of the arroyo. Steve pulled a large first aid kit from his backpack as Leroy evaluated Jack's condition.

"Bullet wound, left side, clean through, only moderate bleeding. Bullet wound upper right chest, no exit wound, heavy bleeding. The rest seem to be contusions and dehydration." Steve stripped several lengths of leather cord off the pack back and kneeled down.

"Let's get the bleeding stopped before we decide what comes next."

Steve worked on the larger wound where the blood flow was the greatest, while Leroy patched up the two holes farther down on Jack's left side. When they were done, Steve made a tent over Jack's head, by using the pack frame and the pack sacks. Jack was still unconscious but his pulse was steady. Steve looked back up the wash in the direction they had just come.

"We're only about a mile and a quarter in. That Jeep can get at least halfway here. You go back and bring it as far as you can up this arroyo. Let some air out of the tires if you have to, though you might be able to make it all the way on the harder rocky parts near the edge. I will carry him toward you, we'll meet in the middle. How far away is the nearest hospital?" Leroy nodded.

"Once we get back to the highway, it is only twenty minutes away in that direction." He gestured in the opposite direction from his house and the gas station. Steve pointed to the pack.

"Take that and the first aid supplies with you, we may need them again. I don't think me carrying him is going to do his wounds any good. I need you to get him over my back so I can get him in a fireman's carry." Both men lifted Jack to his feet and Steve stooped over as Leroy positioned Jacks' body across Steve's shoulders. Leroy then quickly wrapped several of the empty rucksacks tightly around the wounds to slow the inevitable loss of blood from the jostling.

"You got him?" Leroy grabbed up the backpack and the first aid supplies.

"Yeah. He's heavier than I thought. Last time I did this I was twenty-three and there was a whole company of Japs on my heels, but it was also a lot warmer." Leroy tapped Steve on the shoulder as he turned and jogged off up the arroyo.

"Hang in there, I'll be back as soon as I can." Steve steadied himself and felt for the balance point as he took his first tentative steps, placing his boots in as many of Leroy's footsteps as he could. The fact that Jack was unconscious was an advantage in that he was unlikely to make any sudden moves which could throw Steve off balance. Steve also stuck to the soft sandy middle in case he would have to lower Jack back to the ground. If Steve was sure that the Jeep would make it all the way, he would have left Leroy with the stricken man and gone himself. A hundred yards might make the difference in Jack Cathay living or dying and Steve wanted to give him every chance. A half hour later, he had gone 250 yards and was leaning up against the steep edge of the arroyo with Jack's legs gently pressing against the sandstone. It took him several minutes to catch his breath and he wished he had taken more than three sips from Leroy's canteen. His water was in the backpack with the medical supplies and would have to wait until he met up with Leroy and the Jeep. His ears strained to hear the sound of an engine, but all there was in the lonesome arroyo was the sound of the light breeze through the saltbush.

It was thirty minutes later that Steve felt his body beginning to shut down. Though he had felt this many times in the Marine Corps, the older he got the less he could put it out of his mind and continue on. It was taking more and more of his strength just to keep Jack's weight from pushing him down into the soft sand. He began the drill he had taught himself on the long midnight hikes in the pouring rain at Camp Lejeune. With each step he burrowed deeper into himself, leaving the oppressive weight, his numb legs and his enormous thirst on the outside of who he was and severing the connection to the pain.

He didn't know how long he had been moving forward in his stupor when something made him slow down and stop. Before he could summon the strength to lift his head, the grille of the Jeep was within an arms-length and Leroy was gently sliding Jack's inert body off of Steve's back and leaning him up against the hood of the Jeep. With the burden suddenly gone, Steve was able to help Leroy lift Jack and slide him carefully along the vinyl of the back-seat, before he collapsed in the sand and leaned up against the back tire. He didn't know how long he sat there before Leroy began pouring water from his canteen over his head. The water revived him enough to regain his feet with Leroy's help. Together they reapplied the bandages as best they could. As Leroy maneuvered the Jeep in a four point turn in the narrow arroyo, Steve took long sips of water. By the time they reached the highway forty-five minutes later, Steve was feeling better. They stopped and checked on Jack who had moaned several times as the Jeep crawled and shook over a large field of rocks. His vital signs were still relatively stable but he had lost a significant amount of additional blood.

An hour later, Steve and Leroy sat in a waiting room that was just outside the emergency room in the small rural hospital. There were three empty soda cans beside Steve's feet. Leroy paced back and forth in the confined space.

Steve had dozed off when the doctor appeared from behind a curtain. Leroy shook Steve awake. The doctor looked down at Steve.

"Are you Mr. Cathay's next of kin?" Steve shook his head slowly and as he gazed into the questioning eyes of the doctor, he realized that Jack had no family that Steve was even remotely aware of. The closest to that description was Little Moe. Large hot tears streamed down Steve's cheeks as he realized that strangers would have to tell

Jack that his best friend was gone. Steve wiped the tears away as the doctor and Leroy conferred. By the time that Steve stiffly rose to his feet, the doctor was leaving the room. He looked at Leroy.

"He's going to make it. He is still unconscious after the surgery to remove the bullet and he may be that way for awhile, but he's tough and should pull through OK. I think you should stay the night at my place, you look pretty bushed." Steve nodded.

"I am, but I have to get back to Las Vegas. Thanks for the offer, but I'll be OK."

Leroy handed Steve the car keys as they walked out into the late afternoon sun.

"Well, I have to say that was a damn sight more interesting than a basketball game." Steve smiled weakly.

"Jack and I are eternally grateful you were able to make it." They both laughed lightly as they walked to where they had left the Jeep just outside the door of the emergency room.

Steve climbed carefully into the driver's seat and they started back toward the arroyos and Leroy's home and beyond that to Las Vegas.

January 18

I t was two am when Steve drove down the Las Vegas strip in the middle of a small traffic jam as the shifts changed at the major hotels. He was too weary to park his car and walk to the hotel. When he reached the long curving driveway of the Desert Inn, he pulled up to the front doors and took a ticket from the parking valet.

"Don't park it very far away, I'm coming right back." Steve walked beside the still busy casino and pressed the button on the farthest right elevator. Once inside he pushed number nine. He knew that the ninth floor held Tommy's suite and after six o'clock unless you were staying in one of the other suites on that floor and had the special key, the elevator would only take you as far as the eighth. He walked down the long hall of the eighth floor until he came to a stairwell that housed a short flight of stairs. At the top of the stairs was a small phone box. Steve picked up the red phone and pressed the buzzer. After a few seconds a voice came on the line.

"Hello?"

"Hello, who is this?"

"It's Leo, what do you want?"

"This is Steve Cannon, I want to get something to Tommy."

"He don't want to be disturbed"

"I don't want you to disturb him, just give him something in the morning when you see him." There was some muffled talking on the other end and then the door to Steve's right buzzed loudly. Steve quickly opened it and entered the corridor but stayed just inside the door as he saw Leo and a security guard heading toward him. Leo was not happy.

"What you got?" Steve held out the napkin that Tommy had handed him on the golf course. Leo looked at the small square of paper in his hand.

"This is it? What am I supposed to do with this?"

"Like I said, give it to Tommy." Leo snorted and passed the napkin over his shoulder to the security guard.

"You give it to him, and you stay here until he does, in case there is any funny business going on." He pointed at Steve. Steve shrugged and leaned back against the door.

Tommy Carmino pulled the silk sash tightly around his robe as he opened the inner door of his suite to the security guard.

"What do you want? It's after two o'clock in the morning for chrissakes." The guard didn't answer but held out the napkin. Tommy took it and scowled as he shut the door. He turned on the hallway light and unfolded it.

'Sedona County General Hospital, Room 212. You are welcome.'

*

The Tropicana was the last hotel on the strip as you left Las Vegas heading to LA, if you didn't count the Hacienda, which most people didn't. "Haci-Hicksville', or 'Hayseed Heaven' as it was sometimes derisively referred to, was a little misplaced piece of Fremont street with its' massively large back parking lots crammed with campers sporting mostly Midwest license plates. Steve had a soft spot for the property as he had learned to play golf on the short nine hole course behind it from a kindly neighbor when he was a child. He glanced down toward the low pink stucco buildings as he turned into the long driveway of the Tropicana and cruised past the lush greenery. The Tropicana was the one hotel on the strip which spent a lot of money on trying to achieve the image of a tropical resort. The grounds were crowded with palm trees and other exotic plants and flowers from the pacific. That many of them were totally unsuited to life in the desert only meant they had to be replaced by more of the same year after year. Steve parked near the tennis court and walked the fifty yards to the back of the hotel. There was an employee entrance that he knew about, that lead past the main kitchen and down a long hallway to the lobby. Steve stood at the far end of the lobby for several minutes and watched the front desk as they went about their work. When he had seen enough, he took a hundred dollar bill from his pocket and approached the main desk just as one of the younger clerks became free. He slid his hand forward on the cool marble with just enough of the green bill peeking out in front of his fingers to be noticed. The clerk smiled at Steve.

"Good afternoon, Sir, how can I help you?"

"My name is Steve Cannon, and I need you to do me a favor."

"Certainly, sir, I would be glad to help you, are you a guest at the hotel?" Steve shook his head.

"No, but I am meeting later with one of your guests who will be checking in shortly. The problem is, I have only talked to him on the phone and I have no idea what he looks like. What I need you to do is to give me the high sign as he is checking in. I will be over there in the coffee shop." Steve turned slightly and pointed to some empty tables that could be seen through the large plate glass window. The clerk leaned forward to look and then furrowed his brow.

"I am sorry sir. I don't think I am permitted to do that." Steve smiled.

"I understand, it is just that I want to get off on the right foot with this meeting and all, and it would make things a lot smoother if I could come right up to him and greet him, you know what I mean?" Steve straightened up and withdrew his hand leaving the bill behind. The clerk hesitated, then quickly slid the money off the counter top and into his pocket. He moved over to a large set of cardboard flip cards.

"What name did you say that reservation is under, sir?" Steve leaned back over the counter.

"Sutherland, Herbert Sutherland." The clerk nodded several seconds later.

"Yes, here it is." He smiled at Steve as Steve turned and walked across the lobby and through the doors of the coffee shop.

An hour and a half later, he had eaten dinner, drank two cups of coffee, smoked several cigarettes, and read the latest editions of both local papers, when he looked over and saw the clerk staring at him intently. The clerk nodded toward another clerk who was helping someone check in. Steve walked to the front of the coffee shop to get a better look.

The man the clerk indicated was about five foot six inches tall and was wearing an expensive black pinstripe silk suit. He was bald except for thick black hair above his ears on both sides of his head. A bell hop stood behind him with a large satchel that was also expensive. Steve sauntered a little closer and stood in the middle of the lobby pretending to be intently studying something in the folded newspaper he held in his hand. From where he stood, he could only hear small snatches of conversation, but it was clear that Mr. Sutherland was only staying two nights.

Steve walked to the far side of the lobby and sat down on a leather couch near the front doors. He watched as Sutherland gave the bellhop his thick winter coat and a twenty dollar tip, before walking into the casino. Steve followed.

Steve watched as the man played several hands of blackjack, losing four out of five hands and a hundred dollars in quick order. Steve wasn't close enough to see the cards that were dealt, but he could tell that Mr. Sutherland was not used to being in casinos. The noise and the constant movement seemed to distract him, and Steve was not surprised to see him heading for the elevators after losing another hundred dollars on two hands. Steve looked at his watch as he headed to the bar. He ordered a scotch and nursed it for the next twenty minutes.

Room 2064 was at the end of a short hallway and was one of three smaller suites that occupied that end of the floor. Normally reserved for dedicated gamblers, Steve imagined that Sutherland was charged quite a bit to stay in one, based upon his play. He listened at the door before knocking. The door immediately opened. Sutherland was in his shirtsleeves and had a look of surprise on his face.

"I thought it was room service, who are you?" Steve stepped forward across the threshold as he spoke.

"My name is Steve Cannon, Mr. Sutherland, and I am here to ask you a few questions." He stared directly into Sutherland's dark eyes.

"What? Who are you? Questions about what?" Sutherland made the mistake of backing up as he spoke, Steve took two quick steps into the room and closed the door behind him.

"Sit down Mr. Sutherland." Steve pointed to the white couches arrayed along the floor to ceiling windows. Unfortunately for the view, the room looked out over mostly desert and housing tracts butted up against the university. A few lights were scattered up the sides of the far mountains. Sutherland hesitated.

"I really need to know…." Steve cut him off.

"Sit down and I will tell you what you need to know." Sutherland shook his head and turned to comply.

When they were seated across from one another, Steve pulled out his notebook and looked at the man who was staring back at him.

"I am investigating the death of Desmond Rooney and I have some questions I need the answers to. Suppose we start by you telling me what you do for a living." Steve sat with his pencil poised above the notebook.

"I am an entertainment lawyer." Steve frowned.

"Never heard the term before, what exactly does that entail?

"I review contracts for personal representation, recording

contracts, anything where the deal is complicated enough that all concerned need their rights protected." Steve smiled coldly.

"Who was protecting Desmond's rights?"

"I don't understand…Mr…"

"Cannon, Mr. Sutherland, and it won't work to play coy." Steve took a folded piece of paper from his jacket pocket and laid it on the table between them. He sat back in the white cushions and pointed to it.

"You see, I've worked it out, Mr. Sutherland. It is all down on that piece of paper there, which you will sign before I leave. The only thing left to decide is whether you are just a useful idiot or the grand architect of this sordid scheme."

"I.. I.. don't.."

"Shut up and answer my questions, Mr. Sutherland." Steve leaned forward and his face was flushed around angry eyes. Sutherland put his hands up and sat back on the couch. Steve leaned forward even closer, his eyes boring into Sutherlands'.

"Whose idea was it to bring out a four record retrospective of Desmond Rooney's work?" Sutherland gulped.

"It was Desmond's idea. I heard he felt he never got his due as a composer."

"You are right, Mr. Sutherland, but that was four years ago. Curious, isn't it, that now that Desmond is dead, that busy people are taking two days to fly here to do deals?" Sutherland stared at Steve and then looked down at the paper, but said nothing.

"I'll tell you why, Mr. Sutherland. Because someone who is connected to Sandeman Publishing dangled a lucrative record deal in front of Desmond to get him to sign over the publishing rights to the rest of his compositions. When Desmond thought better of it, or didn't like his cut, he was murdered. Isn't that that the way you see it, Mr. Sutherland?"

"No, no, it isn't like that at all. I am just here to get a signature on some contracts and fly back to LA, that's all. Once I deliver the papers, the work starts on the album, that is all I know." Steve smirked.

"Then you will read and sign this paper. It won't protect you if in fact you are part of this scheme, but it might buy you some leniency. If, on the other hand, you are just a messenger boy as you claim, it won't matter one way or the other. Sign it." Steve unfolded the sheet and handed it to Sutherland. He watched as Sutherland read the document. Small beads of sweat formed on his shiny pate as he did so. He looked up at Steve when he was done.

"How.. how do you know some of these things?" Sutherland shook his head and looked down at the document.

"Because, Mr. Sutherland, that is my job. I ask questions, I get answers. I add two and two together until I get four, and I keep on doing it until I get twelve or sixteen or as far as I have to go to get to the bottom of it." Steve pulled a fountain pen from his inside pocket.

"Now sign!" Sutherland took the paper and signed his name.

"There is one name here, I don't know... I don't know if that makes a diff..." Steve took the paper back and folded it into his pocket.

"But you do know the other name don't you Mr. Sutherland?" Sutherland lowered his head slightly and nodded. Steve stood up and looked down at the shaken man.

"This is how it is going to go from here. You are going to stay in your room tonight and not leave. You are not to speak to anyone except hotel staff and no outside calls. Be ready by eight o'clock tomorrow morning, I will pick you up and we are going to pay a visit to the Assistant District Attorney. Do you understand?" Sutherland nodded.

"What am I going to tell the record company?" Steve moved toward the door and grasped the door knob before turning back to the room.

"I'll tell you this, Mr. Sutherland. In my opinion you are just a well dressed buzzard circling a kill, but if you follow my orders and are cooperative, against my better judgement you may still go back to LA with a signed contract. Remember, no outside calls." Steve pulled the door shut behind him and walked to the elevator.

From the lobby downstairs Steve selected a phone near the elevators so he could watch anyone coming and going to the rooms. His first call was to Jim Larsen.

"Jim, this is Steve Cannon, do you have a few minutes for something important?"

"Sure, Steve what have you got?"

"I think I have enough evidence to wrap up the case on Desmond Rooney."

"That is good news, did McCord finally confess?"

"No, but my guess he is he will by noon tomorrow if all goes well."

"How can I help?"

"Be in your office tomorrow by eight-thirty. I am bringing a collaborative witness along with his signed statement. If you concur, I'd like to accompany Detective Polhaus when he makes an arrest." Steve waited while there was a pause on the other end.

"An arrest? You mean someone other than the two we already have in custody?"

"Yes, Jim, I will explain when I see you tomorrow."

"I'm looking forward to it. Perhaps Head Detective Samuels should see this." Jim chuckled at his joke. Steve smiled weakly into the phone.

"I'll see you tomorrow, Jim, goodnight."

January 18

SUTHERLAND WAS DRESSED and pacing back and forth when Steve knocked on the door at ten to eight. The remains of dinner still lay in the silver trays outside the door of the suite. As

Steve entered the room, Sutherland retreated to the glass windows and resumed his pacing.

"Look, it's time to go, we have the DA waiting downtown." Steve looked quizzically at the white complexion and sweaty brow of the man before him. Sutherland stopped pacing and looked across the couches at Steve.

"I've been thinking. I need a lawyer, I need some protection in this deal. How do I know that someone isn't going to kill me like they did Desmond?" Steve folded his arms.

"Well, for one thing I can't think of a safer place than the inside of a DA's office. If you want a lawyer, Attorney Larsen will get you the best one you can afford. As to murder, well, Mr. Sutherland, that is all over in this case. The guy who stabbed Desmond Rooney is sitting in jail and even if he wasn't, he wouldn't come near you unless he was paid. And with your help, in a few hours, there will be nobody with a motive to pay him. Let's go."

Steve walked to the windows and grasping Sutherland's elbow, gently but firmly, steered him out of the room and down the hallway to the elevators.

Steve paced the hallway outside of the DA's office as the attorney reviewed the document Steve had provided and interviewed Sutherland himself. The man had quieted down a few minutes after he had met Larsen and had agreed that he did not need an attorney after all. Steve was looking at the far end of the hallway for an ashtray when Jim Larsen came out of his office. The District Attorney held the statement in his hand as he walked toward Steve.

"This is a pretty amazing document, Steve. Mr. Sutherland has confirmed the specifics and even the timeline. I daresay, I saw the evidence and I would not have guessed at this." Steve forced a small smile.

"Well, all that is fine, but the job is not done. I would like to accompany Detective Polhaus on the arrest, if possible." Larsen nodded.

"Of course, the sooner the better. Mr. Sutherland is happy to stay with me until your task is accomplished." Steve nodded and turned toward the marble steps. As he reached for the handrail, he turned back to the attorney.

"Thanks for your support, Jim." Larsen smiled and waved the statement in reply.

Tam was reading the morning paper over coffee when Steve knocked lightly on the door, walked in and sat down. Tam bent down one side of the paper and considered the private eye in front of him.

"What are you so chipper about this morning? I figured you would still be in Arizona, what'd you find?" Tam turned back to the paper. Steve sat back and propped his feet up on the corner of the detectives' desk and folded his hands across his belly.

"Jack." For a few seconds there was no movement behind the paper, then Tam's face appeared as he dropped the pages onto his desk.

"Jack? What? You found Jack?" Steve smiled and nodded. Tam sat up in his chair.

"How on God's green earth did you do that? Is he OK?"

"No, but he will live. He's in a hospital outside Sedona."

"What happened, did he say?" Steve shook his head.

"No, and I didn't have time to ask. I had to get back here and tie up the Desmond Rooney case. I just got the OK from Larsen to accompany you to make the arrest, so grab your coat and let's go." Tam stood up and took a hurried sip of his coffee.

"Go where?" Steve held the door open.

"I'll give you the directions on the way. I think a black and white is the way to go." Tam pushed by him and started down the hallway.

"I'll go out the back and grab one. I will meet you out front."

As they drove toward North Las Vegas, Steve filled Tam in on the details of Jack Cathays' rescue. Steve called out directions every few minutes and when they turned off Lamb Boulevard, Tam slowed down.

"This isn't the way to Sammy Sanderson's house." Steve looked over at the detective and then out the window.

"No, it's not. Keep driving."

A few blocks later, Steve indicated that Tam should pull over on the quiet street.

"Who lives here?" Steve got out of the car and pointed at the Victorian house across the street.

"Stan Gilman." Tam stood with the patrol car door open.

"Stan Gilman? How do you figure that?" Steve shrugged.

"Everything seemed to point away from him, but the trouble was, there was nothing that pointed to anyone else, so I figured everything might be set up to point away from him for a reason. I started working that angle and here we are." Steve led Tam across the street and onto the wide porch. Steve rang the doorbell and stepped behind Tam. Tam looked over his shoulder at Steve.

"So, I am here solely as a functionary, is that it?" Steve snickered.

"Well, I don't have the authority to arrest him myself, do I?" Tam shook his head as the door opened and Stan Gilman stood blinking at the two men on his doorstep. Tam took a step forward backing Gilman into the hallway.

"Are you Stan Gilman?" Gilman looked up at the red faced cop and then at Steve.

"What is this? Who do you think…." Tam cut him off.

"Stan Gilman, I am arresting you for the murder of Desmond Rooney. Turn around and place your hands together behind your back." Stan started to protest, but Tam moved quickly and forcibly turned him by the shoulders pinning him against a nearby staircase.

He snapped the cuffs and turned Gilman toward the door. Gilman scowled at Steve as Tam pushed him out onto the porch.

"Is this your doing?" Steve gazed evenly at the suspect as he disappeared out the door.

The ride to the station was interrupted as Tam had to stop the car and caution the boisterous man to calm down. Steve continued on to Tams' office while the detective booked Gilman for first degree murder. After calling Jim Larsen, Steve waited in the office for the two men to arrive. While he waited, he called Bernie.

"Steve, how you doing?" Steve could hear the clatter of the breakfast service behind his old friend.

"I am doing very well, and so will you be when I tell you the news. Stan Gilman was just arrested for Desmond's murder." He heard an inhalation of surprise on the other end.

"Steve, I don't believe it, Gilman had Desmond killed?" Steve nodded into the phone, just as DA Larsen entered the office.

"We are right in the middle of things here, Bernie, I will keep you posted." Steve hung up the phone and turned to the attorney.

"Well, the easy part is over." Jim chuckled as he sat down. He held the file that contained the statements of McCord and Shirley as well as the one signed by Sutherland. Steve looked at the file and then at his watch.

"How is Sutherland?"

"Once I heard that Gilman was in custody, I let him get comfortable in my outer office and use the phone. When I left, he was talking to some record company in Los Angeles." They both looked up as Tam walked through the door and stood in the center of the room.

"Well ladies, what's your pleasure?" They both looked at Steve.

"If you're asking me, I say we get Gilman a lawyer, let him sit for a while and pull in McCord and work him over with the story." Tam crossed his arms and looked at the floor.

"Sounds good, but Gilman already has a lawyer, he's on his way." Larsen looked up at Tam.

"Already?" Tam nodded and looked over at Steve. Steve looked in Tam's eyes and shook his head.

"Tam, you're kidding me, right?" Larsen looked from one to the other. Steve looked at the DA and sighed.

"Clifford Jones." Tam nodded in agreement. Jim Larsen sat down in one of the chairs in front of the desk.

"Well, that is even more reason to go armed with everything we got when we question Gilman." The other two men nodded but said nothing. After a few seconds, Steve spoke up.

"Let's get going. How soon can you get McCord's lawyer over here?" Tam was about to speak when Jim spoke up.

"Let me make that call, Detective, I have a felling it might speed things up. They have been antsy to make a deal, so I will grease that wheel." The three men nodded at each other, then dispersed. Tam went down to get the interrogation rooms ready and Steve walked out to the lobby and sat on the long marble bench facing the door. He lit up a cigarette and played the day's events over in his mind.

He was still sitting there twenty minutes later when Clifford Jones pushed his way through the revolving glass door instead of the normal one right next to it. Halfway through, he spotted Steve and with a small smile on his face, slowed his pace, changed directions and walked over to the private eye. He put one foot up on the end of the bench and placed his briefcase on the floor.

"Well, Mr. Cannon, you are up and at 'em bright and early this morning. Second time we have met in this week. Our orbits seem to be in alignment these days." Steve looked away for a second, took a short drag on his cigarette and looked back up at the attorney.

"I wouldn't get too excited, Clifford, it is really a pretty small town, that's all." Clifford nodded.

"You are right about that. Yes, you sure are. I don't think I ever told you that your father had the strong hope that you would go to law school. Always said you were the smart one in the family."

"Well, I don't think he would be too disappointed if he were still alive."

Steve looked across the wide lobby as Tam stuck his head out of an opposite door and looked around. Seeing Clifford talking to Steve, he casually looked around once more and disappeared back inside the booking rooms. Clifford noticed him and straightened up.

"Well, Mr. Cannon, duty calls." Steve waited until Clifford had walked a few feet away.

"See you again, real soon, Mr. Jones." Clifford turned halfway around and smiled with a small wave.

Harris McCord sat slumped in his chair alongside his attorney as the Assistant District Attorney filed into the small interrogation room with Steve and Tam close behind. Tam had made sure that there were three chairs on their side of the table. Once they were all seated, Tam wasted no time.

"Guess who we have right in the cell next to yours? Stan Gilman. And do you know the story he is willing to tell anyone that might listen?" Harris squirmed in his seat and looked away from Tam.

"He is going to say that it was your idea to kill Desmond Rooney and he only went along with it, because he was afraid of what you might do to him if he didn't agree. What do you say to that, Mr. McCord?" Tam leaned back in the chair and looked from Harris to his lawyer and back again. Harris looked wide-eyed at his attorney, Mr. Hildebrand.

'You said…." Mr. Hildebrand grabbed his client's arm.

"Shut up Harris. Now." He looked at Jim Larsen.

"At this point, Mr. District Attorney, I would like to confer with my client and then after that, might I have five minutes of your time?" Jim rose from the table.

"Of course, Mr. Hildebrand, let us get out of your way so you can proceed." Jim moved his head toward the door as Tam and Steve rose from the table as well.

"I'll be right outside, when you are ready." Jim followed Tam and Steve into the hall. Tam spoke first.

"You were right, Jim, Harris and his lawyer are pretty well primed." Jim leaned against the wall, folded his arms and nodded.

"The difference between life and twenty-five years with the possibility of parole is a pretty strong motivator for Harris." Steve interjected.

"Well now we have the scenario where Hildebrand and Clifford Jones are in business together and will be locked in a game of musical chairs where one is definitely going to lose." Jim nodded and thought for a second.

"I am not going to offer Harris a deal, only a friendly word to the court on sentencing. His prior convictions may well sway the judge to give him life anyway. That way we can put both of these murderers away forever. Harris' testimony is key, so if push comes to shove, I may have to cut a deal, but I don't think so. We will have to see how it goes." The door opened and Mr. Hildebrand motioned for Jim Larsen to join him back in the interrogation cell. Tam turned to Steve,

"Let me go down and see how Clifford and Stan are doing. If they are ready, I will put them in that room there." Tam pointed across the hall to a second interrogation room.

"Wait for me in my office. I will come and get you when we are ready." Steve nodded his head and walked back out through the lobby to Tam's office.

Steve had only been waiting fifteen minutes when both Tam and Jim Larsen entered the small office together and sat down. Jim handed Steve a single spaced paragraph that had McCord's signature at the bottom. Steve read it quickly and handed it back to Jim.

"Well that is everything we need, I hope you didn't have to give the store away to get it." Jim shook his head, folded the statement double and put it in the pocket of his jacket.

"Just a recommendation to the court for consideration in exchange for cooperation, standard stuff." He looked over at Tam.

"Is Mr. Jones ready?"

"Yeah, they are both in the room, let's go." The three men filed out, crossed the lobby and opened the door of the larger interrogation room. A small smile moved briefly across the lips of Clifford Jones when he saw Steve step into the room. Once again, there were enough chairs for everyone to sit. In addition, the table was bigger and there was not a cramped feeling that was so prevalent in the other room. Jim Larsen handed Clifford the signed statement by Harris McCord as he sat down. Clifford read it over carefully and set it down in the middle of the table. He looked up at Jim.

"I am familiar with the file on this case because as you know, Mr. Hildebrand is representing the unfortunate and rather misguided Mr. Harris. I see this whole charade as a conspiratorial effort on the part of your office, Mr. Larsen, to make my client a fall guy for some random murder that occurred between drug users. A conclusion, I believe, that is subscribed to by your own Head Homicide Detective, Mr. Samuels. My office is working as we speak to get these charges against my client dismissed. We will be before Judge Briare this afternoon. Why don't we forestall all that unpleasantness and embarrassment and release Mr. Gilman right now. I have spoken to my client and he is prepared to drop the matter of his false arrest." Clifford stopped talking and stared at Larsen. Jim cleared his throat and smiled across the table at his adversary.

"Well, in that case Mr. Jones, I would keep your clerks on standby because Mr. Gilman isn't going anywhere for a long while. We have Harris's statement which you have just read, that asserts Mr. Gilman approached him and solicited him to kill Desmond Rooney for ten thousand dollars half of which he paid on the spot." Clifford held up his hand.

"Mr. Harris is hardly a fount of honesty, Mr. Larsen, and I am sure that twelve jurors will agree. And while we are at it, I object to the presence of Mr. Cannon. He is just a private citizen and has no reason to be here." Jim smiled benignly.

"Well as to your second point, if you had read the file as you claim, then you would be aware that Steve is working on this one case under the aegis of my office. He has developed most of the information the case is based upon and deserves to be present as much as either of us. So now, if we are done arguing about the shape of the table, Mr. Jones, perhaps we can get on with our job.

Unless of course, you have that court order already in your pocket." Without waiting for a reply, Jim turned to Tam. Tam opened his file and looked across at Stan Gilman.

"We have a signed statement from a Mr. Herbert Sutherland that you approached him fourteen months ago with a proposal for a four record retrospective of Desmond Rooney's compositions. At that time, you represented yourself as the owner of the compositions through the Sandeman Publishing company you had recently purchased from the people that Sammy Sanderson had sold it to previously. Mr. Sutherland pitched your proposal to Birdland records who gave the project the green light. A few months later, a review by Mr. Sutherland revealed only two thirds of the publishing rights of Mr. Rooney's compositions were actually owned by Sandeman Publishing, and when he contacted Mr. Rooney directly, he discovered that he disputed your ownership of almost all the compositions that had been selected by the record company for inclusion in the project. Mr. Sutherland was prepared to recommend Birdland Records shelve the project. You convinced Mr. Sutherland that if he gave you some time, you could prevail upon Mr. Rooney to give his blessings to the project. When that didn't happen and Desmond threatened to open negotiations with the record company himself, you contracted to have him killed after you had presented Mr. Sutherland with a document assigning all the rights to all of Desmond Rooney's compositions over to you, using a signature that you yourself, forged. Mr. Sutherland arrived in Las Vegas yesterday to get your signature on the contracts. We have compared Mr. Rooney's signature on the contract you presented to several provided by his widow and they are not a match. We will soon have an expert compare your writing to that which appears on the contract. Anything to say to that, Mr. Gilman?" Stan Gilman, who had been staring down at the table, now looked up coldly at Tam.

"I got nothing to say, that is what I have a lawyer for." Steve snorted.

"Well let me tell you what I think, Gilman. I think that when

Desmond rebuffed you, you saw a golden opportunity. Not only would you get all the publishing royalties but his untimely death would increase the demand for the records many fold. I have been looking for a motive in this murder almost from the moment I first heard about it. It took quite a bit of digging, but I finally found what I was looking for. One thing kept bothering me and it was something that Sandy Sanderson said. Almost apropos of nothing, he claimed that you stole other people's music. Desmond Rooney was the biggest star that ever played in any of your orchestras, so when I started hearing his original compositions and realized how many there were, it rang a bell. The other bell rang when I reviewed the notes I took on our very brief meeting a few days after Desmond's murder. You stated that your meeting with Desmond the week before was to inquire about setting him up with recording dates in LA, a gig he already had and which you would know being in the same business and living there. So, I had to ask myself: How could the main reason for meeting with Desmond not involve the fact that you owned the publishing company that held the rights to so many of Desmond's songs?" Steve stopped and looked down at the table for a few seconds before clearing his throat.

"I can't sit in this room with you much longer, it turns my stomach. I have to go tell a good friend of Desmond and Desmond's wife this whole sordid story." Steve stood up and looked down at Jim.

"I will leave it to you now, Mr. Larsen." Jim nodded as Steve clapped Tam on the shoulder and walked out of the room. He walked back through the plaza and up the wide marble stairs to Jim Larsen's office. When he entered the outer office he saw Herbert Sutherland sitting behind one of the desks writing notes on a big yellow pad. Sutherland looked up and his eyes narrowed as Steve entered the office. Steve pulled a chair across the wooden floor and sat down in front of the man. Herbert Sutherland put his pen down and looked quizzically at Steve.

When Steve walked into Foxy's deli at one o'clock in the afternoon, he spotted Bernie and Rowena sitting together at a table well away from the other patrons. Bernie saw him over Rowena's shoulder and stood up.

"Hi ya, Steve. I called Rowena just after you called me and she just got here." Steve stood at the table and looked down at Rowena's small featured brown face.

"Thank you for coming on such short notice, Rowena." He looked at Bernie and suddenly felt very weary. "Do you think we can sit in the backroom, Bernie? I need to discuss some things with the two of you."

"Sure, Steve, I'll have Walter bring our lunch in there." Steve helped Rowena with her chair and followed the two of them across the restaurant and into the back room. Steve waited until they were all seated before he began to relate the morning's events. Afterwards, he left them alone and went back into the deli to talk with Walter. He followed Walter back into the room ten minutes later, Walter carrying the lunches on a large silver tray.

Steve waited for a few minutes as everyone quietly ate their lunch. He pulled a sheaf of papers from the inner pocket of his sport coat and laid it on the table. Bernie stopped eating and leaned over to look at the small pile in front of him.

"Steve, what is this?" Steve tapped the top sheet lightly with his finger.

"This is the record contract for the four album retrospective of Desmond's work." He looked over at Rowena and waited until her large brown eyes met his.

"All of the rights to Desmond's songs now belong to you, Rowena. I have spoken with Mr. Sutherland and he is confident that if you agree, the deal can go through with just your signature. I want you to think it over and discuss it with Bernie. He can look over the contracts and advise you about how to proceed. I think that whatever you decide, Desmond's legacy is in good hands." Just as he finished speaking, one of the waiters opened the door and pointed at Steve.

"There is someone out here asking for you, Mr. Cannon." Steve nodded and looked back at Bernie and Rowena.

"I will leave you two now, but I will be in touch." Bernie and Rowena both stood as Steve rose from the table. He hugged Rowena and smiled across at Bernie. Rowena held his hand for a few seconds longer as he began to move away from the table. He stopped and looked down at her.

"Thank you, Steve for all you have done for me and for all you have done for Desmond. Not many people believed in him anymore or valued his contribution. If people remember Desmond, it will be because you cared enough to help him when he could no longer help himself." Steve squeezed her hand, bent down and kissed her lightly on the cheek.

"Goodbye, Bernie, I will talk with you soon."

Steve walked through the door that led to the main room. Standing in the middle of the floor was Clifford Jones. Clifford smiled as Steve walked toward him. Steve stopped five feet from the lawyer, put his hands in his front pockets and waited.

"Tommy said I could find you here most of the time, and as usual, Tommy was right." Clifford laughed, but cut it short when he saw that Steve was not smiling.

"Anyway, I just wanted to stop by and tell you no hard feelings, right? You won this one. After you left, I advised Stan to write out a full confession, which he did. So we can all rest easy, right?" Steve didn't answer but continued to stare at the lawyer. Clifford ignored the lack of response and pulled three sheets of paper out of his briefcase and held them out to Steve. When Steve remained where he was, Clifford laid them on the edge of a table next to him.

"Just as I promised. Affix your John Hancock to the bottom there, turn them in at the D.I. and you are a member. Easy as that. I am due in court in half an hour, so I am going to go." He wheeled and headed for the door, stopping to wave as he stepped onto the sidewalk. Steve picked up the papers as he heard Walter come up behind him.

"Everything OK, Steve?" Steve turned around and smiled at the waiter who was carrying a large tray with the remains of several lunches.

"All that going into the garbage, Walter?" Walter nodded.

"Well, throw these in as well." He dropped the papers on the top of the tray, smiled again at Walter and walked out the door.

The sun was just starting to peek through the gray clouds as Steve drove east on East Sahara Boulevard. He turned south onto Boulder highway and accelerated. As he passed the Showboat Hotel he wondered how late visiting hours were at the hospital in Sedona.

Epilogue

BILLY ECKSTINE STEPPED to the microphone on the show-room stage at the Frontier Hotel. Steve sat with Remy and Bernie as they waited for the two am show to begin. They had seen the two earlier shows and decided to stay for the last one. Buck Monari had just left their table after visiting with them and sharing a drink before returning to the bandstand. Now as the blue lights dimmed, Mr. B smiled and looked over the sparse crowd.

"Thank you all for coming out tonight, and thank you to those still here for staying. Our trumpet player extraordinaire, Mr. Buck Monari, would like to play a little something for you. It is entitled: 'We Will All Remember Desmond'." Billy turned back and nodded to the band as they began to gently play the first five bars of the song. Buck stepped up to the front microphone, raised his trumpet to his lips, closed his eyes and sent the smooth notes out into the dimly lit showroom. As the music flowed over him, Steve looked across the table as the light from the candles filled the faces of Remy and Bernie with a golden glow.